Lovelace, Maud and Delos

Gentlemen from England

GENTLEMEN *from* ENGLAND

GENTLEMEN *from* ENGLAND

MAUD AND DELOS LOVELACE

With a New Introduction by

SARAH P. RUBINSTEIN

MINNESOTA HISTORICAL SOCIETY PRESS
St. Paul

♾ The paper used in this publication meets the minimum requirements of the American National Standard for Information Sciences— Permanence for Printed Library Materials, ANSI Z39.48—1984.

MINNESOTA HISTORICAL SOCIETY PRESS, St. Paul 55102

First published 1937 by Macmillan Company, New York
Copyright 1937 by Maud Hart Lovelace and Delos Lovelace
New material copyright 1993 by the Minnesota Historical Society

International Standard Book Number 0-87351-287-1
Manufactured in the United States of America

10 9 8 7 6 5 4 3 2 1

Library of Congress Cataloging-in-Publication Data
Lovelace, Maud Hart, 1892–
    Gentlemen from England / Maud and Delos Lovelace ; with a new introduction by Sarah P. Rubinstein.
        p.   cm. — (Borealis books)
    ISBN 0-87351-287-1 (paper)
    1. British Americans—Minnesota—Fairmont Region—History—19th century—Fiction. I. Lovelace, Delos Wheeler, 1894–1967. II. Title.
PS3523.08356G46   1993
813'.52—dc20   93-9412

10/25/94   F,c   12.95

INTRODUCTION TO THE
REPRINT EDITION

SOMETIMES events pass from history into legend. So it was with the gentlemen from England who arrived in Martin County, Minnesota, in 1873. Tales about the exploits of these young men of the English gentry, or wealthy landowning class, captured the imagination of their American neighbors and were passed down to later generations of people in the region. Maud Hart Lovelace's mother, who grew up in adjoining Faribault County, "told us fine stories of the red-coated fox hunters galloping over the prairie and also loitering around Winnebago City for they particularly liked the tavern there," Maud recalled. Her husband, Delos, who also loved the stories, suggested that he and Maud collaborate on a novel about these unique settlers.[1]

In *Gentlemen from England,* a story about high-living immigrants to the fictional town of Rainbow in Crockett County, Maud Hart and Delos Lovelace painted a vivid portrait of the dreams and disappointments of the English colony at Fairmont in Martin County. First published in 1937, the book was the second novel written together by the Lovelaces. Maud had already drawn on Minnesota's history for two novels, *Black An-*

The author wishes to thank Barbara Carter for her special help in bringing this book back into print.
1. Jo Ann Ray, "Maud Hart Lovelace and Mankato," in *Women of Minnesota: Selected Biographical Essays,* ed. Barbara Stuhler and Gretchen Kreuter (St. Paul: Minnesota Historical Society Press, 1977), 169.

gels (1926) and *Early Candlelight* (1929), and wife and husband had collaborated on *One Stayed at Welcome* (1934). Maud then turned to children's stories and wrote the popular Betsy-Tacy books, while Delos continued his work as a journalist.[2]

This novel about the Fairmont colony is solidly based on historical events. The English who arrived in Minnesota in the late nineteenth century were part of a great wave of European immigrants flooding the United States during that period. As with most new arrivals, their reasons for leaving their Old World homes were chiefly economic. Great Britain was in the midst of an agricultural depression that forced many laborers to look for work in the cities and, when that opportunity failed, to venture overseas. Members of the upper and middle classes joined the tide. Younger sons who could not inherit the family estate had three traditional career choices—the army, the church, or government service. Richard Chalmers, the novel's hero, considers, but rejects, all three options. Being an officer in the army was increasingly expensive, positions in the church were scarce, and a reform sponsored by Prime Minister William E. Gladstone in 1870 required that applicants for government jobs pass competitive examinations. The sons of the gentry, having a classical education, were ill prepared to compete with merchants' sons for these jobs. And some parents—like the novel's James Halliday, a Shropshire merchant with eleven children—moved their entire brood abroad in the hopes

2. For biographical information on Maud Hart Lovelace (1892–1980) and Delos W. Lovelace (1894–1967), see Ray, "Maud Hart Lovelace," 155–72; Carmen Nelson Richards, ed., *Minnesota Writers: A Collection of Autobiographical Stories by Minnesota Prose Writers* (Minneapolis: T. S. Denison & Co., Inc., 1961), 205–12; Rhoda R. Gilman, "Introduction to the Reprint Edition," in Maud Hart Lovelace, *Early Candlelight* (St. Paul: Minnesota Historical Society Press, Borealis Books, 1992).

of finding better opportunities for all of their sons and daughters.[3]

Emigrants from England generally were from a broader range of classes than were those from other countries. On the surface the English seemed to have few problems fitting into American society. They faced no language barrier, were familiar with much of the governmental and judicial system, and shared some traditions. Nevertheless, the English had a feeling of separateness. Those from the upper classes found Americans to be uncomfortably democratic, with little respect for the niceties of social distinction; they did not observe holidays like Boxing Day, and they never made teatime part of their late afternoon routine. Richard Chalmers encounters a republican-spirited Yankee during his first morning in Minnesota in the person of a train companion who exclaims that an Englishman "can't help it because he was born a vassal to some king or queen" (p. 17–18). Being neighbors over a period of years only made the English and the Americans more aware of their differences. The English persisted in drinking toasts to the queen, judged others by their clothes and manners, and even flew the Union Jack.

The English had already begun to settle in Minnesota before 1850, when eighty-two were listed in the territorial census.[4] In the peak year of 1890, census takers counted 21,515 Minnesotans who had been born in Great Britain. Most of these im-

3. Here and below, see Sarah P. Rubinstein, "The British: English, Scots, Welsh, and British Canadians," in *They Chose Minnesota: A Survey of the State's Ethnic Groups,* ed. June D. Holmquist (St. Paul: Minnesota Historical Society Press, 1981), 111–12. See also Larry A. McFarlane, "The Fairmont Colony in Martin County, Minnesota, in the 1870s," *Kansas History* 12 (Fall 1989): 166–74.
4. Patricia C. Harpole and Mary D. Nagle, eds., *Minnesota Territorial Census, 1850* (St. Paul: Minnesota Historical Society, 1972).

migrants arrived singly or in family groups, but there were three attempts to establish English colonies. All had their roots in the powerful and expanding railroad system. The federal government gave the railroads land along their rights-of-way, which they in turn sold to settlers who would become customers for the railroads' services. From a railroad's point of view, colonies made excellent sense. A colony that had unity of aims and purposes would have a better chance of survival.

The Northern Pacific Railway Company fostered two English colonies in northwestern Minnesota in the early 1870s — Furness in Wadena County and New Yeovil in Clay County. Both failed because they were made up chiefly of laborers who had little agricultural experience. The group that settled at Fairmont beginning in 1873 was no more successful than the other two, but its members were different. In offering his land-selling scheme, promoter Henry F. Shearman (Adam B. Crockett in the novel) of the Southern Minnesota Railroad Company focused on the upper classes. He gave English fathers a solution to the dilemma of what to do with younger sons — buy them land in Minnesota, he urged, where they could make their own fortunes.[5]

Martin County is rolling, open country along Minnesota's border with Iowa. Its chief geographic feature is a series of three north-south chains of lakes, with the county seat of Fairmont located on the middle chain. Most farmers selected land on the prairie, but the English preferred to live near the lakes. They bought land next to each other along the middle chain of lakes and built large houses near the lakeshores. In 1880, 219 English people lived in Martin County, which had a total population of 5,249. Most of their neighbors were Americans who

5. Rubinstein, "The British," 111, 119–21; Martin County Heritage Book Committee, *Martin County, Minnesota, History* (Dallas: Taylor Pub. Co., 1988), 104; McFarlane, "Fairmont Colony," 167.

had moved into the area from the East, although there were sizable numbers of Germans (178) and Scandinavians (234) as well.[6]

Whatever their background, when farmers moved into the county they quickly set to work breaking the prairie sod and planting a crop. Most plowed a few acres where they sowed wheat, corn, and oats. The English, however, hired others to break the sod—fifty to one hundred teams at a time—and brought hundreds of acres under cultivation. Other settlers, wrote the Lovelaces, "deserted their own humble breakings to make the easier profits available on the Englishmen's bean fields" (p. 44–45). For the English planted beans, acres and acres of beans that they intended to sell as a cash crop.[7]

Regardless of the crop that the farmers planted, all were devastated by the grasshoppers that plagued the entire Great Plains between 1873 and 1877. On June 18, 1873, the insects descended on the unripe fields of Martin County and ate every bit of green leaf or sprout. Chalmers is so shocked by the result that he reaches for a biblical description: "The land is as the garden of Eden before them, and behind them a desolate wilderness" (p. 67). Farmers tried replanting, but an unseasonably early frost killed the plants before they were ripe enough to harvest. Martin County farmers lost eleven thousand acres of wheat in 1874 and a thousand in 1875, when a quarter of the families received money from the state to help them survive. Other families simply left: there were fewer families in the county in 1875 than there had been in 1870. Martin County was not alone. Between 1873 and 1877 twenty-eight other counties suffered from grasshopper damage, and upwards of

6. Martin County Heritage Book Committee, *Martin County,* 18.
7. Martin County Heritage Book Committee, *Martin County,* 105. The beans were pea (navy) beans; McFarlane, "Fairmont Colony," 167.

16 percent of crops were lost statewide. The extent of the disaster was so great that Governor John S. Pillsbury called for a day of prayer on April 26, 1877, to invoke heavenly assistance in ridding the state of hoppers.[8]

The fact that the English and the grasshoppers arrived at about the same time created a certain mythic aura around these unusual immigrants. The other farmers readily acknowledged that they might not have made it through the plague years if the English had not been there with their supply of cash from home. (" 'They're certainly saving our bacon,' Americans far and near admitted" [p. 68].) After the first grasshopper invasion, the English wrote to their families and asked for money to replant. By hiring people in the county to help them on their land, the English farmers cushioned the impact of the disaster for their neighbors. The next year, in the face of further substantial crop losses, more money arrived from abroad and more residents were able to save their own farms by hiring out to the English.[9]

Although in this book Chalmers and his friends refer to their group as a colony, the term was never actually used by the English in Martin County; it was a name that outsiders gave them because they all seemed to have so much in common. The first to arrive were single, young men from the wealthy classes. They were educated, and some had university degrees. Others had been in the army or navy. A couple were even members of the aristocracy. They had little experience in agriculture or

8. Annette Atkins, *Harvest of Grief: Grasshopper Plagues and Public Assistance in Minnesota, 1873–78* (St. Paul: Minnesota Historical Society Press, 1984), 13–15, 22, 56, 80, 33, 26–27; Martin County Heritage Book Committee, *Martin County,* 104–5.
9. Here and four paragraphs below, see Martin County Heritage Book Committee, *Martin County,* 85, 104–6, 111, 125–26; Rubinstein, "The British," 119.

business, and few of them deigned to get involved in the dirty, day-to-day chores of running a farm.

In their leisure time the English gentlemen maintained the customs that they had known in their homeland. Soon the other residents of the county learned of the Englishmen's passion for hunting. Newspapers carried advertisements requesting that anyone who sighted a fox or wolf let the huntsmen know of its whereabouts. In the novel Cecil Hook "advertised faithfully in the *Gazette:* 'Information as to the whereabouts of foxes will be thankfully received by Cecil Hook, M.F.H.' " (p. 136; the initials stand for "Master of Foxhounds"). The young men rode their horses across the countryside and adjacent farms in pursuit of the elusive fox. If a live prey was lacking, the hunters and pack of hounds followed a drag (a bundle of scented rags) that had been pulled over a rough trail. Americans and immigrants from other European countries had never seen anything like this red-coated troop of hunters.

Within a couple of years the emigration pattern from England shifted, bringing more families than single men to Martin County. Although hunting and hunt balls remained important, other matters needed attention. In 1876 these members of the Church of England established St. Martin's Episcopal Church, a congregation of the related American denomination, in Fairmont. When the Minnesota legislature passed a law in 1879 allowing for a portion of local taxes to be used for a library, the English responded the following year by organizing a lending library, the second in the state. They also founded a bank and a farmers' cooperative cheese factory, and they ran stores, restaurants, and hotels. But the colony dwindled by the 1880s. Some of the young men returned to England, and others moved on to seek their fortunes elsewhere in the United States; a few who had not had their fill of adventure went to Australia. The acres that had been planted in beans were soon devoted to grain crops or dairy farms. But several of the families stayed, operating businesses in town and intermarrying with the other settlers.

Despite their small numbers, the English had an enduring impact upon life in Martin County. Their conspicuous lifestyle, coupled with their many contributions to the county's farms and businesses, made them unique in the region's history. It is this legendary aspect of the colony that Maud Hart and Delos Lovelace captured in *Gentlemen from England.* Through diligent research into county histories and newspapers, as well as interviews with longtime residents, they uncovered a wealth of material about the colony. They also gained a sense of the glamorous lives that the English people lived. True collaborators, they split up the tasks involved in writing the book: Maud researched and Delos plotted; she wrote the romantic parts and he wrote the male exploits, such as the hunt for "Three Toes," the solitary wolf that killed up to forty sheep in a single night. Besides interviewing descendants of the English immigrants still living in the county, Maud toured the area. "I went through one of their old mansions and the bachelor's hunting lodge which had doors so tall that, if the whim struck them, the young men could ride their horses inside."[10]

One Martin County historian concluded that the English "brought drama and color to the hard grimy business of establishing a foothold on the frontier."[11] *Gentlemen from England* tells how they did it. It also presents an accurate picture of rural life in the 1870s—the clash of cultures, the devastation of the grasshopper plagues, the sense of relief that the town would survive because the railroad had finally reached it.

10. Ray, "Maud Hart Lovelace," 169–70.
11. Martin County Heritage Book Committee, *Martin County,* 104.

Introduction XV

"What a curious page they had written in the history of their time and place!" These words from the novel take the final measure of the colonists' exploits. Horseman Harry Earle adds his own judgment: "By God! We played and paid high. . . . Our dollars got nothing much for ourselves. But what else fed the Americans through the grasshopper plagues, and what else paid for the good houses and barns, and for breaking up the virgin prairie?" (p. 347). This fictional summary mirrors the real story of English immigration that unfolded more than a hundred years ago in southwestern Minnesota.

SARAH P. RUBINSTEIN

Editor, Borealis Books
Minnesota Historical Society Press

The authors wish to state that all the characters in "Gentlemen from England" are entirely imaginary.

BOOK ONE

CHAPTER ONE

At La Crosse Richard became aware that the three who had traveled with him since Chicago were bound for his own destination.

"By Jove!" he ejaculated after the illuminated moment. "I saw that chap coming out of Crockett's office. He must be going to Rainbow, too. The lot of them must be."

Another man might have made the connection more quickly, but Richard thought slowly; he was slow in all that he did. The movements of his burly young body were easy, his speech was deliberate, his smile hung fire. A smile broke now slowly over his ruddy face.

"He looked different then. He was dressed differently," he thought.

Here on the gas-lit wind-swept platform of the frontier railroad station, the man was wrapped in an Inverness cape and wore a soft hat pulled down to his nose. The women with him were muffled in shawls, but Richard had observed them on the train. The elder of the two was unmistakably a maid. She was short, squat, swarthy, with heavy gold rings in her ears. The younger one was beautiful after a dark aloof fashion. She carried an aura indefinably foreign; the man, however, was English.

"Army," Richard decided, noting the set of the shoulders, and remembered that he had decided "army"—although even then the man was out of uniform and wearing a bowler hat and topcoat—when they had passed in the doorway of Crockett's office.

They were half a world away now from that garish room in Fenchurch Street, half a world away from the brightly colored map of Minnesota unrolled on a table with Crockett booming above it. Richard's thoughts slipped from the map to his mother's tears at Euston, to flying English countryside, to a tiny rocking cabin, to New York with its giant signs suspended by wire above tumultuous streets, to the luxurious silver palace cars, to the mushroom city of Chicago.

He had come at last to the Mississippi, which bisected this strange continent. The journey was almost ended, and Richard acknowledged his relief. He was not a man for junketing; he was a man for staying at home among familiar and beloved things. Reaching now the last stage of his migration, he was suffused with warm pleasure.

Great Goodlands was half a world away, to be sure, but his own Little Goodlands was waiting just ahead. Out in that icy dark lay Minnesota; and within Minnesota, Crockett County, where English gentlemen were making homes for themselves—truly English homes with lawns, gardens, stables, about the pleasant village of Rainbow. Crockett had described the settlement to his father and himself.

Pacing the platform which was scoured by the bitter wind, Richard went over in his mind the interview with Crockett.

"I saw your announcement, sir, in the *Field*." So his father had begun. The senior Chalmers had removed his top hat courteously, but his voice had held unconscious arrogance in addressing the American.

Crockett, however, had soon won them both. He was a portly handsome man with blatant Americanisms removed from his dress and speech. Only his enthusiasm had betrayed his origin in the newer country. Such fervor, such glowing zeal as he displayed were not native to Fenchurch Street.

"Minn-esota!" He had given the word the thrilling quality of an "Open Sesame"! Yes, he was offering Minnesota lands; that was his great privilege.

He had unrolled a map upon his table. Seizing a pointer with a large well-tended hand, he bounded the commonwealth.

"An area, gentlemen, almost as great as that of France. To the north, the dominions of the British crown; to the south, the plains of Iowa; to the west, wild Dahkotah; to the east, the point of Lake Superior, the river St. Croix, and the noble Mississippi!"

Only a few years had elapsed, he had said, since the Indians were forced from these borders; yet here (the pointer stabbed) at the Falls of St. Anthony were the twin cities of St. Paul and Minneapolis, twin centers of culture with fine churches and schools, metropolitan shops and elegant mansions. Although the destructive Civil War which had halted all progress throughout the nation was less than a decade behind them, railroads now intersected the state, and following their tracks went prosperous towns, neat villages, and well-fenced productive farms.

The climate was admittedly the most healthful in the world; the land, the most fertile in the temperate zone.

He directed their attention to the high plateau in the central and southern portion of the state. He asked them to note especially the southern tier of counties. It was here, he explained, in Crockett County that English gentlemen were buying.

The railroad had not yet penetrated it; the rails ran only so far as Sisseton City. ("See?" The pointer stabbed again. "Sisseton City.") Therefore for a few years—perhaps for a few months only—lands to the west of that point could be bought for a song.

Crockett's eyes—they were small but bright and engaging —had gleamed as he described Crockett County. His broad pink face grew moist with ardor. His voice choked, and he put down his pointer.

It was fair as a park, he had said; a high delightful table-land, a rolling prairie which in spring and summer was carpeted with flowers. Three chains of lakes intersected it from north to south; it held a hundred lakes in all, dimpled beauties, girdled with trees. Crockett County, he had said, was as beautiful as Cumberland, as fertile as Kent.

"And probably as cold as Greenland," Richard growled now, but not in an ill humor. He stamped his numb feet and looked about for the trainman, who had bidden him wait, saying that the horses would be ready in two jerks.

There was no bridge over the Mississippi at this point. The travelers were to cross on the ice in an open sleigh, although it was not yet dawn and the cold was savage. Devilish hard on the women, Richard thought, and stole another look at the beautiful one.

She was almost shapeless in her multitude of shawls. Head down, motionless, she breasted the wind. The maid had sought shelter in a crevice of the boxes. The man strode back and forth, his great cape belling out behind him.

No trainman appeared, and Richard too resumed his pacing. As he dropped his chin into his greatcoat, memory recaptured again the warmth of Crockett's office, the genial persuasiveness of Crockett's voice.

"And land for sale, gentlemen, at five pounds an acre! Think of it! Only five pounds an acre! Your son, sir, may acquire for a paltry eight hundred pounds the estate of a squire in England and devote himself leisurely, pleasantly, to the culture of beans."

"Beans?" the Squire of Great Goodlands had inquired. "Just why, sir, do you propose beans?"

That was another story, Mr. Crockett had implied. He offered cigars. Armchairs were pulled to a circle.

Beans, he explained, puffing confidentially, grew on virgin soil which had been merely turned over. Moreover, they needed no cultivation. This fact was not generally appreciated, and he begged them not to pass it on. There was a fortune in the information for them and for himself.

Virgin prairie, as a rule, was the very devil. The earth was matted with tough fibrous roots, hard even to plough, but gruelingly hard to harrow, to pulverize, to make ready for crop. With beans no such labor was necessary. One turned over the sod, plopped in the beans, and went about one's business. One paid no further attention to the plants until it was time to harvest them.

"I'm shipping out a carload of the finest beans from Brockport, New York. At present, as you may know, that's the bean center of the world. I say 'at present' advisedly, for it can't compete with Rainbow, Crockett County, Minnesota, after the Britishers get started. Eh, my boy? You'll supply Her Majesty's Navy single-handed—if your father decides to send you out."

"Rainbow is the village?" Squire Chalmers had inquired.

"We propose to have a school and an English church there presently."

"And meanwhile this—Sisseton City—is a sizable place?"

Mr. Crockett's lids blinked rapidly.

"For the frontier, yes. A good bright young—city."

"Then what, may I ask, are the drawbacks to the country? No country is a paradise."

Crockett had laughed.

Pausing in his lonely walk along the station platform, staring into a void filled only with night and cold, Richard was glad to remember how heartily Crockett had laughed. He had put his fat cigar on the table, leaned back in his chair, and rubbed his hands together so delightedly that Richard and his father had been constrained to smile, too.

"Right you are, sir. Even Minnesota has its drawbacks. I may mention one in particular."

"And that?"

"The confounded birds, sir."

"The birds?"

"Wild ducks, geese, swans, pigeons, grouse—they fly in positive myriads. I told your son he need pay no further attention to his beans after they were planted; but that's not exactly true. He'll have to be out with a gun to keep the birds away. I'm afraid that annoys you—eh, my boy?"

Richard had laughed, a slow appreciative chuckle, glancing at his father who laughed too.

"My son," the Squire had observed, "will not consider that entirely a disadvantage." Then they had laughed together heartily, with the pleasure of simple men at a simple joke, and Crockett whacked Richard's knee and they laughed afresh.

"But perhaps," Crockett suggested, wiping the dew from his eyes, "perhaps you'll want to fish while your beans are growing? Pike, pickerel, bass—they leap out of our lakes and streams. Why not buy an estate on a lake?" he went on, rising quickly and shaking out a chart. "Which one will you choose? Bird Lake? Lake Crystal? How about Flower Lake here?"

Mr. Chalmers had bought on Bird Lake. Richard had liked the sound of it.

He would have preferred to remain at Great Goodlands. As he waited in the slowly penetrating dawn, which was also, he realized, the dawn of his adventure, and eyed the three as yet strange and unapproachable persons who were to be his neighbors, he admitted that he would have preferred that staying to any going.

But Great Goodlands would go to Edwin. His brother was not a farmer. It had been Richard, always, who rode about with the Squire collecting rents, superintending repairs, breeding a mare, buying a milch cow. His father had, indeed, a special fondness for Richard, who was very like him except that the years had given the senior Chalmers a measurable shrewdness. But the law of primogeniture takes no account of such preferences. And even if there had not been Edwin, there was Albert; Richard was a third son.

Supremely content at Great Goodlands, Richard had always been uneasy when his future was discussed. His father had first considered the army, but he had decided against it. It was not only that commissions were expensive, he explained to Richard. Maintaining one's self in the army was expensive, too; there was no end to the expense.

"I don't think I'd like the army anyway, sir." Richard had been unable to conceal his relief.

He had been equally pleased when his father rejected the overcrowded navy.

They had looked into the civil service, but that was plainly not the place for him. Competitive examinations had been made compulsory, and Richard would have had no chance against the sharp ambitious sons of drapers.

The living at near-by Bramley was in the Squire's gift. It was obvious, however, that Richard had no inclination for the church.

Gentleman farming, so called, was the only remaining

occupation on the list of occupations suitable for gentlemen when Crockett's advertisement had flashed, like a message from heaven, on the troubled father's view.

"It's going a long way from home, Dick; but if what Mr. Crockett says is true, you can earn enough money to bring you back to England a rich man in seven years."

"In seven years," interposed his mother tearfully, "he'll have a wife and children there and think there's no place in the world but Little Goodlands."

His unseen property was already Little Goodlands to them all. His sisters, excited and proud, had bestowed the appellation. The house, of course, was yet to be erected, but the Squire had given Richard money enough not only to plant but also to build a house and start the stables.

His father had been generous. Richard reflected on that now with a glow of appreciation and affection. He paused in his glacial walk before a pile of bags and boxes, of gun cases and crated saddles. Why, his stuff made a mountain!

However, if his luggage made a mountain, that of his fellow travelers made an entire mountain range. This was not surprising, of course, women's dresses being what they were. But how in time did the American trainman propose to get it all across the river?

The other Englishman, Richard observed, had halted a pace or two away. He was making up his mind to speak, no doubt. Perhaps he too had remembered Crockett's office, or perhaps he had merely perceived that the younger man was English. Before he spoke, however, a red lantern swam through the gloom.

"Sleigh's ready, gents. You'll be over the river and rolling on to Rainbow in no time. Never mind your baggage. That's checked straight through to Sisseton City."

"This American system of checking. It's marvelous, isn't it?" said the Englishman in Richard's ear.

Richard turned and looked into eyes which were brilliantly blue even in the gaslight. He met a smile as brilliant as the eyes.

"It is, certainly," he agreed. "I haven't seen my boxes before since New York."

"Nor I. Are you also joining the English colony at Rainbow?"

"I am, sir."

"Bannister's my name."

"I am Richard Chalmers."

They shook hands.

"I shall be happy to present you to my wife before we take off," Bannister said.

The young woman did not turn her head until her husband spoke.

"Lady Meta. This is Mr. Chalmers. Mr. Chalmers is also bound for Rainbow."

"How do you do?" asked Lady Meta. She enunciated each word slowly, in a somber, covered tone. The accent *was* foreign, Richard decided. And how his sisters would crow because she was titled! He mustn't forget to tell them when he wrote.

Having spoken, Lady Meta turned away again, whether from shyness or from arrogance Richard could not be sure. Her face was smothered in veils which concealed her expression.

There was room for them all in the sleigh. The maid sat with the driver. The other three shared a seat and were glad of the warmth of companioning bodies under the buffalo robes. The Lady Meta's veils grew stiff with frozen breath.

She lowered her face into her shawls and sat rigidly in silence.

The sleigh ran smoothly out upon the frozen river, its jingle of bells bizarrely merry. Little by little a gray light had come and Richard could see that their track had been cleared through a heavy mat of snow. The way was impeded by islands, mere snowy mounds through which protruded dark growths of brush and stunted trees. The sleigh glided lightly around the borders of these, and at last the travelers gained an open view.

The great valley spread out before them—a pale white map of a ghostly world. The river and its sheltering hills were all one chalky hue, except that on the hills naked forests made black blurs against the enveloping snow. It was a landscape vast, pallid, and empty—empty except for the biting cold and the jingling of tiny bells—the emptier, it seemed, for a group of little houses huddled on the western shore.

As the sleigh drew near this shore, the height and majesty of the hills grew more apparent. They had almost the stature of mountains, Richard thought—with rocky summits, evidently, for no trees sprang from the heights. They seemed to lean out over the ice-bound river and the small sleeping huts. A station house showed, and a waiting unlighted train, and the thin morning gleam of a lantern.

"I suppose that's Minnesota," Bannister remarked.

Lady Meta raised her head. She looked about her at the wide white waste and up at the overhanging hills.

"Gr-r-reetings to you, Minn-e-so-ta," she said in a bitter voice.

CHAPTER TWO

Rɪᴅ of his greatcoat, seated uncomfortably on a low-backed wooden bench in the shabby railway coach, Richard Chalmers was shown by the early morning light to be a personable young man. Flaxen hair curled closely to his cleanly chiseled head. His eyes were a candid blue. He had a rich high color— the blood ran crimson in his lips—and his teeth were white, giving charm to his slow smile. His body was strong rather than graceful, but it was well proportioned. He had wide shoulders, a broad chest, flat thighs, long legs. London tailors had done well by him, and on the long journey from England men had looked at him with envy and women with pleasure.

In the main he was unaware that he had aroused either emotion. His fancy seldom roamed out of those fields in which his major interests lay. He liked to ride, to hunt, and (after the leisurely fashion of an English country gentleman) to farm. Having these pursuits, he seldom looked for any others.

Ordinarily his manner was assured; it could hardly be otherwise. But his was a modest likable assurance. He thought himself good enough and was heartily admiring of others. He enjoyed in his friends the quick tongue and ready wit which he knew he did not possess. Men almost invariably liked him. He was not yet twenty-two, and a trifle shy with women. He had barely glanced toward Lady Meta since entering the train.

She was seated in full view. American railway carriages were not cut into compartments after the English fashion. Nor were they called "carriages," Richard reminded himself, but "cars," always "cars." This dingy coach was styled "The Ladies' Car"—why, he could not imagine. Certainly it offered no degree of luxury to ladies or gentlemen either.

The small windows were dirty; so was the bare unpainted wooden floor although the attending brakeman swept it briskly with a broom at intervals. The seats had cushions of red cotton plush, but when one reversed them (in search of a clean surface) one discovered burlap bottoms. Richard's end of the car was distinguished by a water tank having a faucet and a tin cup attached to a chain. The Bannisters' end offered a wood-burning stove which glowed and shook with heat. The two women were seated near the stove, but Lady Meta did not unloose her shawls until the train had climbed out of the valley.

This took some time, for the ascent was long and steep to the plateau which Crockett had described.

Since leaving Grand Crossing the train had climbed steadily and with increasing effort. The low moaning whistle never paused as the pygmy locomotive and four small wooden cars wound up and around the precipitous slopes which rose from the Mississippi. They were wild white slopes, bare of habitation, hemming in deep valleys and sharp rock-walled ravines. Frozen streams lay in their depths, spanned by bridges so frail that they seemed to have been tossed up out of jackstraws. The engine traversed them at a snail's pace with that anxious whistle ever sounding. The English all felt easier when they gained the sunny uplands and the whistling ceased and the train gained speed.

Bannister at that point strolled down to Richard.

"There's a smoking car ahead. What do you say to a cigar?"

Richard got out his case and followed.

Bannister was shorter than himself but sturdily built with wide square shoulders giving an impression of tremendous strength. He had heavy black hair with a surprising lock of white in it. This—Richard discovered when they had seated themselves and begun to talk—fell continually into his eyes, and he as continually pushed it away with a strong white hand having an onyx ring upon it. His brilliant blue eyes sparkled as he talked; he smiled frequently, showing square white teeth beneath well brushed mustaches. He was an animated, entertaining talker. Richard listened with admiring attention.

Bannister spoke in lavish praise of the new land, which spread out white and glistening beneath a radiant sky. Both men agreed upon the clarity and pureness of the air.

"It sickens me to remember how I've waded about in London fog!" Bannister exclaimed.

The farms were fenced; the buildings were respectably sized. The towns were small, but the first few were seated picturesquely in a river valley which the train followed for a time. The timber, at first abundant, grew scarcer as they proceeded. Soon it was confined to the banks of the stream. Richard suggested that the settlers must need more fuel than they could find within easy reach.

"But let the railroads bring it in, my lad! Let them bring in lumber, and coal too, and carry away our beans!"

Crockett had confided the secret of the beans to Bannister also, it seemed. The older man was full of elaborate plans. He produced sheets of paper, closely inscribed with figures, which he spread out for Richard's bewildered gaze. He would employ so many men and teams at so much per day He would plant so many beans to the square foot and harvest so many per acre. They would sell at such and such a price, netting such and such a profit. Like Crockett he saw clearly that a fortune could be made in seven years.

He did not, however, propose to return with it to England. "I'm through with England," he said. Momentarily his mobile face darkened. "I don't care if I never go back; don't expect to, in fact." Then he leaned forward, smiling, thumping Richard's knee. "I propose to become an American, my lad. In me you behold a prospective Jonathan. I'm going to farm, make money, run for office—you know, don't you, that they *run* for office? They don't *stand*, as we do."

"They run for everything," said Richard, pleased with his joke. "I never saw such a rushing, pushing, crowding people—"

"Here's one running for a train," Bannister put in, peering out the window.

A tall figure was indeed loping across the prairie. The train was slowing down, screeching, and whistling, and presently the brakeman put his head in at the door of the smoking car to bawl:

"Elbow Room! Elbow Room!"

"There's elbow room, certainly," said Bannister, much amused, for the most attentive survey of the landscape failed to disclose the town. Not a station house, not a rooftop of any sort marred the rolling plains of snow. Elbow Room might some day rival the capitals of the world, but for the time being its thoroughfares and architecture existed only in the whimsical mind of the pioneer who had bestowed its spacious name.

The unborn metropolis yielded a passenger, however. The

tall runner jumped aboard. And with a whistled warning to the crows the train pursued its way.

The newcomer strolled through the smoking car and into the adjoining Ladies' Car with the air of a guest at a soirée seeking to discover who was present. Failing, obviously, to find friends, he returned to the smoking car and paused beside Bannister and Richard. He was as thin as he was tall, with a narrow, sharp, but not unpleasing face. Although his nankeen trousers were shabby and he wore a knitted red comforter in place of a greatcoat, he had an easy confident manner. Eyeing the two Englishmen with frank curiosity, he unwound the comforter and pulled off his close-fitting cap. "English, aren't you?" he asked.

Richard and Bannister admitted that they were.

"Bound for Rainbow?"

They acknowledged it.

The American lowered his rangy body into the seat beside Richard. He pulled out a plug of tobacco and took a generous bite.

"There's been plenty of talk," he remarked, "about Crockett selling railroad lands to you English. Some folks say he's bringing foreigners in too fast. But *I* say"—he paused, and gazed at them benevolently—"*I* say that an Englishman is just as good as anybody else." The Britishers looked sincerely startled. "Just as good as anybody else," the American repeated with great firmness. "So long as he behaves himself," he added cautiously.

Leaning back in the seat, he folded his long legs and arms. Frayed cuffs protruded from his coat sleeves, but they did not impair the grandeur of his manner.

"Don't condemn a man because he's English! That's what I always say. He can't help it because he was born a vassal to some king or queen. He can't help it because he first saw light in that effete old land. If he has the good sense to come over here, roll up his shirt sleeves, and become a republican, why—good luck to him, say I!"

The Britishers were astounded into silence.

Their companion leaned forward, and the metal spittoon rang under the impact of his contribution. He looked up to study them with a bright friendly gaze. After a long but quite unembarrassed pause he continued:

"I've got only one thing against you."

Bannister found his voice at last.

"And may I ask, sir, what that is?"

"It's your attitude in the late war, sir." The American looked sharply from one to the other. "You sided in with those low-lived slave dealers and Democrats. Yes, you did; you can't deny it."

Bannister's eyes sparkled.

"I believe, sir, that Her Majesty's government maintained a strict neutrality."

"Neutrality, hell!"

"But I, personally, sir, made no pretense at being neutral. I personally, sir"—Bannister spoke slowly with angry emphasis—"was heart and soul with the Confederacy."

"Eh? What?" The Yankee stiffened. "What's that you're saying?"

Richard with a grin assisted Bannister.

"And I too, sir, sympathized with the southern cause."

The American fixed them with a sharp belligerent gaze. He unbuttoned his shabby coat and displayed a worn badge.

"See that?" he demanded.

They agreed that they did.

"Well, *I* personally went down South and whipped enough damned slave dealers and Democrats to save the Union."

"Interesting!" Bannister retorted.

"And my great-grandfather personally whipped enough of you British to make the Union in the first place."

Bannister jumped furiously to his feet. Richard, slower to anger, rose more slowly. Both men were completely disarmed, however, by the good nature with which their companion waved them back into their seats.

"Now, now," he said in the tone of one soothing unreasonable children. "Keep your shirts on, both of you. We'll let bygones be bygones." He buttoned his coat over the badge. "No worse than anybody else!" he repeated tolerantly. "And no better! That's what I always say. There's room for you here, so long as you've left your highfalutin lord and lady notions behind you. You'll find good land in Crockett County if you've got elbow grease enough to turn it over. I'll see you there now and again. I've got a farm near Rainbow. Whipp is the name, Captain Bob Whipp." The bewildered Englishmen found themselves shaking a hard but hearty hand.

The train was slackening speed once more and whistling. Captain Whipp jumped to his feet.

"Spring Valley, folks. Ten minutes to eat, and you've got to step lively."

He suited his action to the word, snatching his cap and comforter and striding down the aisle. At the door he turned.

"Those womenfolks in the car ahead belong to you?"

"In a sense," Bannister replied.

"Well, get 'em off! Get 'em off! This is their last chance to eat until Sisseton City." To make sure of his own ration he leaped from the still moving train and legged it toward the station.

Bannister and Richard regarded each other. Richard was the first to burst into laughter.

A wildly clanging gong on the station platform repeated Captain Whipp's summons to food. Leaving Bannister in conference with his wife, Richard joined the line of travelers streaming toward the station. The small platform was crowded; the town, in the winter sunshine, had a brisk and lively air. A well loaded freight car being shunted up the track recalled Bannister's cheerful vision of freight rolling into the country and beans rolling out.

At the steaming lunch counter, beef stew, bread and butter, coffee, and great hunks of pie vanished with unaccountable rapidity down American throats. Richard had only seasoned his stew when Bannister joined him. His wife would not leave the train, he said in a low voice. He would take back some sandwiches.

"Better get Opal to wrapping them up then," a voice shouted. They looked around to see Captain Whipp bolting his pie. "Hey, Opal! Some sandwiches here! What do they like, folks? Ham on rye?"

Bannister agreed; and, reminded of the need for haste, the Englishmen applied themselves to stew.

"Grab your pie! Grab your pie!" their friend and mentor called when the cry of "All aboard!" sounded.

Gripping segments of pie and the fat sandwiches Opal had prepared, they joined the travelers racing toward the train.

Both men were amused, and they pushed, laughing, into the Ladies' Car. Richard, however, observed Lady Meta with a sense of guilt. Cold sandwiches, he realized tardily, were poor fare for a lady who had been up and traveling since dawn.

As they halted beside her, they heard a stir behind them. Captain Bob Whipp approached, laden with a steaming teapot, a jug of milk, two thick cups and a pair of spoons. His manner for the first time was diffident.

"I just thought it was too bad for the ladies to eat cold grub," he apologized. "Opal says the conductor can return these things on the run back."

Lady Meta turned, and Richard for the first time saw her clearly. She was younger than her husband; not older, certainly, than twenty-four or -five. Her figure was exquisite in a black dress which sheathed her bosom and was piled in flounces on her narrow hips. Her skin was pond-lily white, and flawless. Her hair, drawn up from small fine ears, fell in black buoyant ringlets on her neck. Her eyes were arresting, large and dark, under brows which slanted upward above a small straight nose. They were like black soaring wings, those brows. They were expressive—they might be gay or sad or scornful. They were scornful now until she saw the steaming teapot. Then she began unexpectedly to cry.

Bannister was savagely annoyed.

"Hush, Meta! . . . That's very good of you, sir. . . . Hush, I tell you. Don't be childish."

"Just turn that woodbox up on end!" Captain Whipp commanded.

Richard hastily complied, and the American deposited his burden. He set out the cups, poured the tea.

"Milk and sugar, ma'am?" he questioned gently.

"Milk," said Lady Meta. She wiped her eyes and threw her husband a glance compounded of anger and defiance.

Before she took the tea, she put out her hand to the tall Yankee. Her dark eyes, still bright with tears, smiled up from beneath their winged brows.

"It is good to find such kindness in America, sir," she said in her lovely somber voice.

"Well, we know how to treat our women over here," Captain Whipp replied. He bestowed a cutting look upon Bannister as he retreated.

Richard retreated also.

"Don't you belong to them?" Whipp asked, pausing beside Richard's seat.

"No," said Richard.

"That other lady isn't yours?"

"I believe," said Richard, "that she is Lady Meta's maid."

"*Lady* Meta? *Lady* Meta?" Captain Whipp stole a cautious incredulous look behind him. "You mean she's got a title?"

Richard nodded.

The American stole another look. His face glowed with an amazed, an almost alarmed delight. His staunch republicanism melted in that glow.

"Well, wait till they hear that in Rainbow!" he cried, and hit Richard's shoulder a resounding clap.

CHAPTER THREE

FENCES, as the train rolled on, grew more and more infrequent. At first a full half of the land had been confined; then perhaps a fourth of it, and now almost none. It flowed as freely and as boundlessly as all pastures did in the world's beginning.

Timber was growing scarcer, too. Occasionally, near a settler's cabin, a planted grove made a purple rectangular blur against the universal whiteness. But the groves came less often, for the number of cabins was diminishing. There were longer and longer intervals between these habitations, which seemed as the miles slipped by to become progressively smaller, so that at last they were mere cots, huddled with their humble sheds, woodpiles, and strawstacks under smothering blankets of snow.

The all but empty prairie made Richard think of the ocean. One long wave breasted another, and another, in blank monotony. At midday the waves were white and rolled to a blue horizon; by mid-afternoon they were ashen and met an ashen sky. Evening brought no glow to the west, twilight fell abruptly; and then the wastes of prairie were indeed like wastes of ocean, cold, comfortless, and empty.

Richard, looking out from the smoking-car window, felt a growing uneasiness. This was not the land in which he had imagined Little Goodlands. They passed lakes, to be sure, but lakes which were mere unfriendly sheets of ice, so thickly covered with snow that they could be distinguished from the surrounding prairie only by their flatness. It was not on the shore of such a lake that he had pictured his home.

He was glad when Bannister joined him. Lady Meta's husband, his good humor quite restored, was readily reassuring.

"The country certainly seems extremely wild. But with Sisseton City ahead, it must improve soon. No doubt the frontier is the home of extremes."

Richard interrupted Captain Whipp, who was deep in a card game.

"Are we getting near Sisseton City?"

"About an hour out."

Shortly they were informed by the guard—the conductor, the Americans called him—that Sisseton City would be the next stop. Still there were no indications that they were approaching a city.

However, the passing scene was growing increasingly dim. It was blurred not only by nightfall but also by falling snow. A white mist of snow had appeared in the air and was thickening rapidly. The brakeman lighted the kerosene oil lamps which sat in side brackets along the car.

"We *are* coming into a town," Richard announced at last. "It's no more than a village, though."

There were indeed a few scattered lights forward on the prairie. The rude illuminations of whale oil and tallow shone through the windows of small snow-banked houses. The train was indubitably running more slowly, whistling through the curdled clouds of snow.

Richard and Bannister did not move, but they felt a stir around them. Across the aisle a man was shouldering into a buffalo skin coat. Whipp was pulling on his cap and winding his bright comforter; one of his opponents at cards was jovially paying his losses; another was picking up bags.

"End of the line, folks!" The brakeman put in his head with a perfunctory shout.

Bannister jumped to his feet and seized Whipp by the sleeve.

"Your pardon, sir, but do we not continue on this line to Sisseton City?"

Whipp's companions laughed, and Whipp smiled indulgently. "Why, this *is* Sisseton City," he said.

Bannister, before Richard's eye, paled to the color of unwashed wool. Neither Englishman spoke, but the American perceived that they were disappointed to some degree in the local metropolis.

"Jumping Jupiter!" he said with anxious kindness. "This is a fine little place. Maybe it don't look like much, at nightfall, in a snowstorm, but it's a real thrifty little town. Lumber mill, gristmill, stores, a tavern! Si Joslin will keep you in the Farmers' Home as snug as bugs in a rug and put you on the stage for Rainbow in the morning."

Still Bannister did not speak. Richard said slowly: "Well, thank you, Captain Whipp. I'm sure we'll like it after we get used to it."

He was in all honesty more bewildered than dismayed. He tried to say to Bannister that things would look better in the morning, that they always did. But the words came hard, and so he got out of the train in silence; and he found himself waiting on the platform with Bannister and the two women just as he had waited at La Crosse. The air was filled with small sharp flakes; Lady Meta's shawls were already white with them. She looked wonderingly about at the small boxlike station, at the bobbing lanterns, but she did not speak. None of them spoke.

"Si!" Captain Whipp was hailing a small bearded man who, holding a whip like a staff, stood beside his horses' heads. "Here are some English folks. Look out for them, will you? Give them the best in the house. They're a long way from home." He lowered his voice to something more than a whisper. The lady was a real sure-enough lady—a duchess or something. Then he shook hands with the four forlorn immigrants.

"I'll be seeing you soon, folks, and Si will treat you right."

"Sure, I will." The tavern keeper shifted his whip to his left hand, and he too shook hands vigorously with them all. "How'd you get along on the briny? Did the cars treat you good? Well, here's a real Minnesota snowstorm for a welcome."

He held a lantern for their ascent into his conveyance, the box of a lumber wagon set on runners, and spread the buffalo robes with kindly energy. The sled ran smoothly along a narrow street. Bells rang out. Richard began to feel better in spite of the flakes of snow sifting down his neck.

He was again momentarily shocked when they arrived at the Farmers' Home. It was a small cottage with a narrow porch half full of drifted snow. But beyond a tiny storm-shed, the door opened upon comfort—a stove glowing through isinglass windows, a carpet, patent rockers, chromos, a stuffed fish above a door. The ceiling was so low that Richard's head almost grazed it; the room was obviously parlor as well as office, and through the doorway beyond the fish the dining room showed equally stuffy and small. But this did not seem to lessen the snug charm of the place; it was like a firelit cave.

A woman in a cap with streamers, stout and reassuringly tidy, bustled from behind a desk to greet them.

"English folks! My! My! Well, here's somebody will be plenty glad to see you."

Two young men playing chess beside the stove jumped to their feet at her words.

Richard knew at once that they were English. So manifestly, so unmistakably English did they look—in this remote frontier tavern—that he thought he knew their counterparts in his own county, yet later he could not say whom one resembled or whom the other called to mind. Both wore rough shirts and corduroy breeches, stuffed into high boots; both were immaculately shaved. One was compactly large and florid with lightish hair and whiskers, his eyes squeezed shut in a smile which seemed to be his habitual expression. The other was small, lean, wiry, with a wind-bitten face. He reminded Richard of a hardy restless dog.

His opening words were surprising.

"By Gad, Bannister!"

He thrust out his hand, but with a nervous twist seemed to withdraw it. Then he shook himself, more doglike than ever, and completed the greeting. As Bannister gripped his hand, he turned to his companion.

"Trevenen, old boy, this is Kit Bannister—Captain Bannister of the Thirteenth Dragoons."

"Retired," said Bannister, clipping the words. He tossed the snowy lock out of his face and continued in a rush. "Hook, I am happy to present you to my wife. Lady Meta, Mr. Cecil Hook, Mr. Trevenen. And this is Mr. Chalmers, Mr. Trevenen, Mr. Hook."

Lady Meta said her slow, "How do you do?" Hook and Trevenen bowed to her, shook hands with Richard. They regarded the lady, Richard saw, with discreet but lively interest. The snowflakes were melting on her veil, but she did not lift it. She said to Bannister:

"May I have my dinner, do you think, served in my room?"

She spoke in a low tone, but the Joslins were as adept as Captain Whipp at overhearing.

"Certainly, ma'am." "I'll bring it up myself." "You ladies must both be dead beat."

Lady Meta bowed briefly at the threshold.

Relieved of feminine presence, the room broke into uproar. Hook and Trevenen led the way through a low door behind the stove, Trevenen taking Richard's arm as though they were friends of long standing. The barroom was even more cavelike than the office, but it too had its glowing stove, and Trevenen sang out jubilantly for drinks—the best to be had for gentlemen from England! Richard laughed. His uneasiness had vanished completely, and he was sorry to see that Bannister looked even yellower than he had looked on the train. He searched his mind for a heartening remark; finding none, he tried instead to draw out Trevenen.

"How do you find things at Rainbow? Much as they were represented?"

"Good God, no!" said Trevenen. He and Hook burst out laughing. "The thing is an absolute sell."

"What do you mean?" Bannister asked.

"These lands we bought. What did you pay for yours? Five pounds?" Richard and Bannister nodded. "Well, so did we, and they're railroad lands, for sale to every Tom, Dick, and Harry for a pound."

Richard's fears returned with the force of a blow.

"Just the same," said Hook, "the place is deuced jolly. Half the men in town are down in northern Iowa deer-hunting. That sounds like a bit of all right."

"And Crockett told the truth about the birds, damn him," Trevenen put in. "According to what we hear, there never was anything to equal the shooting here in August. Prairie chicken, and every bit as good as grouse."

Had they seen their land yet, Richard wanted to know. No, Hook said, it had been too snowy to hunt it out.

"The country is buried in snow. It's been the devil of a winter—so the natives say. We've only been here a fortnight. In January there was a blizzard, as they call it: a storm of snow and wind which killed a hundred people over the state. And fuel ran short. The farmers lately have been burning their corn."

Treveren predicted that the snow would be gone in another week or so. Then, he said, they could all ride out together to look at their lands.

"Hook and I have adjoining farms and we're going to build a house together. We're not going in for farming so much as for sport."

They seemed to be carefree young men, cheerfully unconcerned at Crockett's deceptions.

The drinks arrived, and the exiles drank to the Queen, to Minnesota, to Rainbow, even to Crockett. Richard began to feel light-headed. His companions, he perceived, were better drinking men than himself. But it was impossible to withstand the hospitable urgings of Trevenen and Hook.

They bade Joslin bring the dinner to the barroom.

"Put up a table for us here, my good man."

Richard saw Joslin's eyes snap at the sight of the gold pieces Trevenen jingled. The American hurried to wait on them. Nothing was too good for them; nothing was too good for the English. No talk here of "vassals" or of "attitudes in the late war."

By nine they were warming to their talk—feats of horsemanship, exploits with gun and rod; by ten they were roaring out songs. At eleven Joslin gave each one a candlestick with a short candle in it, and shortly they were bumping their way up the narrow stairs and weaving along a frigid upper hall.

Trevenen whispered to Richard. "Here's a—tip, my lad. Don't—put out your boots. The blighters—think you're throwing them away. I lost a pair—before I found it out."

Boots, Richard admonished himself sternly. Don't put them out. Mustn't forget! Boots! To make sure that he didn't forget, he left them on. He crept, boots and all, into an icy bed. The sputtering candle showed frost as thick as moss on the pane. The shadows shivered on the tentlike walls. Richard pulled the blankets around his flaxen head and burrowed into his pillows. "The blighters don't get my boots," he thought with hazy satisfaction as the candle guttered out.

CHAPTER FOUR

THEY did not go to Rainbow the next day, nor the next. The snow-swathed prairies were cold and uninviting; the Farmers' Home, although unaired and small, was warm and friendly. If the food was monotonous—boiled potatoes with codfish gravy, the stock dish—the supply of liquor was unfailing. The Englishmen kept dull the edge of their dismay with Mr. Joslin's potations.

In the tiny barroom, a card table stood by the fire. Joslin, scuttling about at endless pains to make them comfortable, declared that if many English gentlemen were coming out to Minnesota, and if they were of like wealth and generosity to these four, he would buy the billiard table for which they were clamoring. "I'll build on a room to put it in," he declared.

Meanwhile the card table stood empty.

Richard was the first to suggest a round of whist or euchre. He was slow at cards and usually lost money when he played, but he gained pleasure from the diversion. His suggestion brought a flush to Hook's face; Trevenen's eyes squeezed shut in his unfailing smile, but he tapped the table and said nothing; Bannister tossed the white lock from his forehead and smiled about the circle with brilliant challenging eyes.

"I am not averse to a game if the stakes are low."

Hook suggested a drink.

Later Trevenen got Richard alone.

"You only met him at La Crosse? Then you don't know. Cashiered out of the army for cheating at cards, Hook says."

Nevertheless, so great was their boredom, in the end they played.

Even as they were driven to cards, Lady Meta was driven to the parlor. She had made clear at first that she meant to keep to her room; her first meals were served to her there. But the mean tent-roofed chambers were meagerly heated through holes cut in the floor; the windows were thick with frost, and when this was scraped off the outlook was only of snow drearily falling or of roofs, fences, woodpiles, scrap heaps drowned in white billows. Toward evening one day she descended to the parlor and seated herself beside the stove.

She did not unbend, however. When she responded at all to Mrs. Joslin's kindly overtures it was but curtly. She treated the Englishmen with distant courtesy.

"She hasn't so damned much to be proud of," Trevenen complained when his smiling overtures were unequivocally checked.

Richard thought that that was the basis of her hostility. It was because she could not be proud of her husband that she could not make friends. He had seen the look on her face when she discovered them playing at cards.

Bannister had sat facing the open parlor door. He played always with a black cigar clenched between his teeth, his eyes shining with blue fire. Lady Meta's eyes had darkened when she saw him, and her expressive winged brows had drawn distressfully together. Then she met Richard's gaze which was quickly withdrawn in great embarrassment, and she must have gained quick mastery of herself, for her voice came easily:

"Captain Bannister!"

When he joined her, she asked his arm back to their room. He was absent a long time, and returned looking disgruntled. He plunged into the game with undiminished zest, however, and high-handedly ignored Richard's reluctance to enter subsequent games. Lady Meta treated the four more distantly than ever.

But in spite of herself she added a touch of graciousness to life at the Farmers' Home. Unwillingly she made a pleasant picture as she sat beside the radiant stove, bent over her skeins of wool. The dark ringlets flowed about her shoulders. The shadow of lashes on her smooth white cheeks was like the shadow of bare trees on newly fallen snow. Her voice when she addressed the maid was gentle: the two conversed in German; once they laughed together over some mistake in the woolwork, and Lady Meta's face in laughter was so young, so defenseless that Richard felt it sad. He wished he had grace and skill enough to make himself her friend.

If she felt his good will, she made no acknowledgment of it. The burly young man with shining flaxen hair and ruddy cheeks, the wiry nervous Hook, the smiling Trevenen seemed alike distasteful to her.

One evening Canada geese passed over. The men ran out of doors bareheaded and looked up at the great V, compact and austere in the opalescent sky. The birds were flying too high for shooting, but Joslin assured his guests that sometimes they flew just above the housetops. Moreover, shortly they would stop by armies to feed and nest in Minnesota lakes.

"And ducks too, thicker than snowflakes. Canvasbacks, ringnecks, redheads, shovelers—a mallard and his wife in every pothole."

The Englishmen set to work oiling their pieces.

Next morning they awoke to the drip of melting snow and looked out to find the twigs of trees and bushes frosted. They inquired about stages and were annoyed to learn that Mr. Beatty's stage for Rainbow had already left; it left early, about seven. They would leave tomorrow at seven then, they told the grieving Joslin, and began eagerly to pack.

Captain Bannister decided that he would not take his lady to Rainbow until he had looked up rooms. So only the four men with their rifles and a fraction of their baggage boarded Beatty's open democrat wagon next morning at seven. Beatty had this day replaced runners with wheels, and he looked apprehensively at the slushy drifts, at the patches of soggy brown grass, at the roads which were rippling sheets of melted snow. His passengers, however, looked up at the rich blue sky full of clouds and smelled the south wind and smiled. It was as though a curtain had been lifted revealing a new world.

Over their glasses, during the snow-bound days, they had often sworn to look up Crockett's man, Jackson, and give him hell. They had been fleeced; at least they had paid five times too much for their land; and Sisseton City was not a second London, while Rainbow, according to Joslin, was hardly a village. But now that they were on their way, they found their resolution weakened.

Unconsciously they had been affected by the prevailing optimism. Whipp believed, Joslin believed, everyone in Sisseton City believed that the land in Crockett County could not be excelled. It was worth whatever one paid for it, and no doubt there *was* a fortune in beans. They had been affected, too, by the flattery which enwrapped them. Nothing was too good for the gentlemen from England (whose gold was flung like feed before hens). Moreover, the geese were back, and the ducks—a flying wedge of canvasbacks had al-

ready been sighted. The mood of the four was hardly dangerous as they inquired about Jackson.

"You'll find him at Anglo-American Acres; that's Crockett's place, a few miles south of Rainbow. I can't take you
there, but I'll put you down at the tavern in Rainbow and
you can get a team."

Beatty could answer any question. He was a short thick
man with flaming hair and whiskers and a flaming face in
which the bulbous nose was the most fiery detail. He was not
averse to a nip when the bottle went round, and the oftener
that happened the more informative he grew and the more
adept with his reins. But in spite of his skill and the bottle
and the four stout horses, the twenty miles to Rainbow used
up half a day. There were mails to be delivered, and the
road was bad.

"Tarnation bad!" said Mr. Beatty. "I've pasted the third
commandment inside my hat, but it's just as well we have
no ladies present."

His passengers at first could see no road at all. It seemed
to them that the route was dependent upon Mr. Beatty's
fancy. He followed a winding trail across the rolling prairie,
keeping to the high land and skirting the ravines and sloughs.
At last, however, the way became roughly clear. They were
traveling west, and far to their left a thin line of brush outlined a little stream whose course ran parallel to theirs.

"Chanyaska Creek," said Mr. Beatty. "Runs into the Sisseton. Mighty pretty too."

The smoke from cabins could be seen in all directions.
Near every cabin a planted grove rose in stubborn defiance
of Nature. They made Richard think of Captain Bob Whipp,
those courageous planted groves.

As they traveled into Crockett County, Mr. Beatty explained its formation. It was laid out in townships, he said.

These, in turn, were divided into sections of one square mile each, and these, into quarter-sections of one hundred and sixty acres, the units the Englishmen had purchased. Two sections in each township were reserved to support a free school. Crockett had told them that in England, and it had not impressed them. Here, in sight of the far-flung tiny cabins, it seemed significant.

"These American farmers are deuced ambitious for their children," commented Hook.

Children in all varieties of patchwork garments welcomed Mr. Beatty at every cabin post office. With the boundless plain to turn in, he managed nevertheless to scrape his wagon wheels perilously against the fence posts, curling his long whip with noisy cries over his horses' backs. Some of the cabins were rude taverns also. Travelers were allowed to sleep on the floor, and at twenty-five cents a head were served bountiful meals. A keg of corrosive homemade whiskey was usually available to all.

Mr. Beatty never failed to take advantage of the last-named offering. Richard's companions indulged also, but Richard dodged the stuff; he had had an enduring lesson that first night in Sisseton City. He was glad when at last they turned due south on the road which led to Rainbow.

Here they met one of the chains of lakes which Crockett's maps had shown. This too ran south, and all along the last stage of their journey they could see at their right the bare timber outlining the lakes and now and again the ice which was softening in patches.

"Crockett told the truth here," Richard remarked. "There are certainly lakes in Crockett County."

"Lakes!" said Mr. Beatty. "Lakes! Why, we have lakes thicker'n mosquitoes."

The Englishmen, rocking along with the noon sun on their heads, felt a mounting excitement.

This dropped, however, when they rounded a slough full of cat-tails, climbed a little hill, and found themselves in Rainbow. Certainly the village was not much. You could hear your own voice from one end of it to the other. It consisted of a group of small frame stores, houses, and barns, all set on the steep bank of a lake. Surprisingly, the houses did not even face the lake. Mean and dingy as they were, surrounded by their woodpiles and strawstacks and manure heaps, they preferred to regard one another—and this despite the fact that the lake was the loveliest Richard had seen in the county. Lake Rainbow was large, and it was edged with a heavy growth of trees. Not willows alone but maples, elms, and oaks crowded to its frozen brim.

As Beatty's wagon splashed down the single street, spraying slush upon the staring townsfolk, Richard frowned down at his folded arms. Had Crockett lied, or was he himself to blame for modeling his imagined village upon the only villages he had known? He had thought Rainbow would be pretty, with neat hedges and cottages, built about a square, perhaps. He hardly knew how to face his disappointment.

The tavern was built of logs. It stood in a grove of burr oaks at the ultimate end of the street. Beyond it a spring stream flung itself into the lake, and beyond that was woodland.

A line of nags was tied to a hitching post outside the door, and a small crowd of Americans watched the four Englishmen as they silently alighted.

Within, the party was met by a hugely fat American, who overflowed his loose untidy clothes. An abundant growth of whiskers did not conceal the worry on his face. Plainly he was troubled by the necessity of serving such unusual guests. His small and spare but equally worried wife stood just behind him, and later half a dozen children appeared.

"Good afternoon, folks," said the fat man. "Glad to have you with us. My name's Oarlock, and this is my missus."

Hook called out at once for drinks, but there were no drinks to be had. Rainbow, Oarlock explained, was a temperance town.

"Well, I'll be dashed!" said Trevenen. Even Bannister, an ardent supporter of American institutions, did not know how to defend this one: a temperance town!

"Gad, if we have to bring in horses and dogs we can bring in liquor too!" said Hook savagely.

"And the stage goes every day to Sisseton City," urged Mr. Beatty, a jocular elbow in Hook's ribs.

They parted with Mr. Beatty after dinner and, having secured four sorry riding horses, set out for Anglo-American Acres.

Again they rode south, and still they followed the lakes. These were connected by slender streams, all closely shrouded in timber. The country was so pretty that their spirits lifted again. Without undue difficulty, in spite of the slushy trail, they found Mr. Crockett's estate.

It was a well-fenced prosperous property. The house was a long one-story building, curiously resembling an army barracks. There were decent stables and outbuildings, all freshly painted a shining white. At one end of the house rose the Stars and Stripes; at the other, the Union Jack. That brought the four Britishers to a startled emotional halt. They did not look at one another for a moment. Softened by the sight of their flag and encouraged by the civilized neatness of the farm, they turned in at the gate.

Jackson came running out to meet them.

"I guess you're the English gentlemen Mr. Crockett wrote me about. I expected you here before this. Come right in. Ole will take your horses."

He ushered them into a long room, which ran almost the length of the house. It looked bare, yet clean and comfortable. Round rugs woven of bright-colored rags peppered the floor; small wooden rockers were scattered about, and there were a drop-leaf table with four attendant chairs, and a chest or two. A Bible lay on a table between two candlesticks; a tall clock ticked loudly on a shelf. Although the Englishmen did not know it, the room suggested New England, where Crockett had been born. They knew only that it did not look like Crockett, the genial, worldly, and suave.

Jackson was a small man with a small pale face. He had small overlapping front teeth which he wetted nervously with his tongue. When engaged in conversation, he looked up with quick darting glances, then away, and even behind him, as though searching for something. The habit was furtive. But he was so hospitable, in a meek way, bringing out chairs and a decanter, unobtrusively making his visitors comfortable, that they did not find it easy to mention their grievances. Trevenen, however, blurted them out at last.

Jackson was surprised, worried, grieved, but—most of all—bewildered.

"I don't understand these matters, gentlemen. I don't know a thing about Mr. Crockett's business. But I do know that you can trust Mr. Crockett. If there are any misunderstandings, he will iron them all out when he arrives. Mr. Crockett would not do a questionable thing. I never knew him to, and I have known him twenty years. He is the soul, gentlemen, of generosity and honor."

He rambled on, looking down and behind him as though searching for a mouse, citing proofs of Mr. Crockett's generosity. Mr. Crockett had furnished gunpowder for Rainbow's Fourth of July celebration; he had sent a barrel of apples to the community's Christmas party; he had taken in a poor immigrant family (Ole's folks; they had seen Ole), and employed them on his estate. Jackson ran on and on, mumbling dull tales of Mr. Crockett's benefactions, until the four young men, who had not been very angry to begin with and were eager now to see their lands, interrupted with assurances of faith in Mr. Crockett, whereupon Jackson dropped the subject hastily, jumped to his feet, and began relieved preparations.

Messrs. Hook and Trevenen had bought adjoining farms, he recollected. Those farms were back toward Rainbow. He had errands in town, so he would ride with them and direct them. The other two gentlemen must ride farther to the south and west. Ole could accompany them; Ole knew the boundaries. Their farms were on the same lake too. Bird Lake, it was called.

Richard was not wholly happy over this news. Gay and charming as Bannister was, Hook and Trevenen would have been preferable as neighbors. "Cashiered out of the army for cheating at cards!" Those words rang in one's ears, somehow. He did not like being isolated on a distant lake in such company. He had a fleeting thought of Lady Meta, isolated in such company for life, and his pity for her took on a personal edge. If he felt subtly tarnished just because he and Bannister had farms on the same lake, how must she feel?

"That's fine, my boy!" Bannister's arm clapped about his shoulders. "We'll know how to pass the evenings, eh?"

"Of course we shall!" Richard shook off his secret distaste. He was a fool to be so delicate. Any man was entitled to one mistake, and certainly Bannister had been right enough at cards in Sisseton City.

Hook and Trevenen led the way outside and mounted their horses.

"Good luck!" Hook cried.

"Here's hoping!" Trevenen added with a laugh.

Ole, lank and blond on a sorrel nag, splashed ahead of Richard and the Captain. The trail was so narrow that they had to ride single file, and Bannister could only shout his jubilant anticipations; Richard need not reply at all. For perhaps an hour, they progressed so. Then, near a cabin-post-office-tavern such as they had visited in the morning, they struck off across open country. At last they rounded a rise of ground and came within view of Bird Lake.

Seen from this height, the wings which gave the lake its name were easily discernible. They joined at the northern end, one running directly south, the other to the southwest. The three horsemen stood at the junction of the wings looking down on the portion which ran south. This wing had strong high banks. It appeared to be deep, and Richard was sure that in summer its water would be clear and fresh. The other wing was little more than a slough. Brown reeds and cat-tails were held in the frozen slush, and the land adjoining it was plainly swampy.

Richard had studied the map Crockett had given him, and he knew where his land lay. To his relief he saw that his lake frontage was at the southern end of the good wing. He had a high bank full of trees, and beyond that his acres stretched out over prairie. Bannister was looking bewildered, and Ole was peering toward the southwest. He waved an arm now toward the swampy wing.

"Dat ban Bannister," he said.

Richard knew why Jackson had gone with Trevenen and Hook. It would not be easy to tell a gentleman come all the way from England that land for which he had paid five times the market price was swamp land. With all his heart Richard was sorry for Bannister. No one in their group had taken such an interest in the bean-growing project as Bannister had; no one had so simmered with plans and extravagant hopes.

Bannister sat erect on his horse and stared across at his swamp. The western sky was glowing with sunset, and the melted patches in the slough ran red.

"Let's ride over," Richard suggested. "It can't all be swamp. You must have acres of good land behind."

"No doubt," said Bannister. "But Exile Hall is going to stand by the lake. It is going to stand with its feet in that slough." He laughed at the prospect.

He whirled toward Richard, and his brilliant eyes gleamed as they gleamed when he played at cards.

"Lady Meta will be at home there to all her friends," he said. "The bullfrogs can play for her receptions."

"The fellow isn't right," Richard thought to himself. He felt the cold wash of contempt.

"See here," he said. "You're upset. Come on, let's ride over and have a look."

"Go look at your own land, lad. I'll meet you at the tavern for the ride back."

He wheeled his horse and cantered off.

Again Richard followed Ole in silence. The boy halted at last, and Richard too reined in his horse. Ole was pointing, explaining in his broken English. Gradually his meaning came clear. Richard's land ran from the lake to a distant grove on the south and from a distant grove on the east to some point in the west marked by an invisible stake. There was no natural object on the plain to mark it by.

Richard tried to listen, but he felt unspeakably forlorn. He was fortunate in his land, he knew. It was level, arable. It had timber and water. But where was he to begin, in making a home? How was he to turn this almost treeless prairie into a Little Goodlands? If only he could talk to his father!

The sun was low now, and a chill was creeping from the frozen lake. Crows were cawing and flying above his land.

At home at this hour they would be having tea. His father would tramp in, ruddy with cold; his sisters, his brothers, his mother would meet by the library fire. The great silver tray would be placed before his mother, with the silver pot upon it and the plates full of slices and slices of thin buttered bread. The dogs would come in and stretch out close to the grate. Edith would slide down to play with them and be sent to wash her hands. . . .

The empty plain like a riderless horse rode off to meet the evening sky.

CHAPTER FIVE

AMAZEMENT, like the torrential streams of that spring's thawing, overflowed the countryside as the magnitude of the Englishmen's plans became apparent. Whenever two Americans met—on the road, in the Log House, in Judson Oates's general store in Rainbow—they exchanged incredible bits which their own eyes had seen. Women in sunbonnets walked miles to view the astounding operations; covered wagons, jogging westward, halted to marvel. Even the game birds, winging their way to the north, seemed to pause an extra moment over the Britishers' bean fields.

These presented a spectacle which might have been especially fashioned for the high-flying ducks and geese, the armies of passenger pigeons. Pedestrian man could never view more than a fraction of it, the little scene exposed from whatever lowly point of vantage his feet were able to gain. From the air it could have been seen in panoramic richness, the whole extravagant outpouring of toiling horses and men, laboring in unprecedented numbers under the bright spring sky.

Not least among the amazing aspects of the spectacle was the fact that no Englishmen were found among the toilers. The laboring host was exclusively American. The Englishmen paid the hire—and a handsome hire, too. The alluring rates were set forth in the *Crockett County Gazette*. Reading them, native settlers from far and near deserted their own

44

humble breakings to make the easier profits available on the Englishmen's bean fields.

"A couple of seasons like this," said Judson Oates, "and a lot of us can retire and live off our interest." He added with his tight sour smile: "What's more, we'll have some of these Englishmen working for us, unless they've got a well of money you can't pump dry."

The rates of hire were that extraordinary.

For breaking virgin land . . . . $3.00 an acre
For cross ploughing 2.00
For rolling 30
For harrowing 1.30
For planting 1.50

With good animals pulling his plough, a man could make upwards of seven dollars a day. He could do this for days on end, because the Englishmen were not satisfied to break only twenty or thirty acres the first year, as the frontier practice was. Astride their newly bought horses they rode the boundaries of their newly bought lands and ordered the whole turned over. Bannister went farther. Not content with the arable portion of his own quarter-section, he rented additional acres.

"You mean you want it all ploughed up?"

"Every foot of it."

"Mister, you're going to have plenty of beans!"

They planted, of course, only beans. Everyone, it appeared, had shared Crockett's secret—one Barrowcliff, rumored to be the nephew of an archbishop, genial Harry Earle from the East Indian service, the three handsome Neville brothers, and the other British who poured in during April joined Richard, Bannister, Trevenen, and Hook in planting beans. Jackson, actively proving Crockett's faith in his own scheme, planted beans too, as lavishly as did the British—beans, beans, beans, up and down the undulating acres.

The seed for this unprecedented planting came out of a box car which stood on a siding at Sisseton City, a whole box car full of beans shipped in from Brockport, that bean center of the world which Crockett so confidently predicted Rainbow would shortly rival.

Early and late, while the gratified Englishmen trotted their horses happily about the countryside and watched the bourgeoning of their fortunes, ploughs rolled the virgin grass under. Up turned the black, rich, mealy earth. After the ploughs had done their part, the sweating planters came in pairs. One carried an axe; one, a bag of seed. The axeman hacked a succession of holes in the tough fibrous furrows. The bagman dropped in the seed and with a quick drag of the foot covered it with earth. Hack! Hack! Hack! Drop and drag! They labored from dawn to dusk.

"Sixteen acres this week. That should be twenty-four dollars. Here you are, my man."

The clipped speech of the English, that frequent casual "my man" was a trifle irritating to the Americans. But gold was balm even to proud sons of liberty; and the pay was cash down and no waiting, not only for ploughing and planting but for everything the Englishmen required—horses, fence posts, hay, road making, house building . . .

They followed American procedure and put in their crops before they erected their buildings. And even when the beans were planted they were in small hurry to erect their homes. Transient myriads of geese, ducks, and swans still rested in Minnesota marshes; the prairies were alive with cranes in great flocks (the Englishmen delighted to watch their clumsy courting dances).

The Englishmen were comfortable at the Log House, and

when that was filled they overflowed to the houses of the town—to the Tompkinses and the Oateses, the Warrens, the Eatons, and the Smiths. The townsfolk took their children into their own beds in order to find beds for the English, the tall, genial, free-spending young men who wished tea for breakfast and brought tin tubs with their luggage.

There were still no women with the immigrants except Lady Meta and her maid. Several of the newcomers were married, but they proposed to bring out their families the following spring. All except the Bannisters planned to return to England in the autumn and spend the winter there.

Bannister had installed his lady at the Log House. One end of the loft was curtained off for her, and it boasted a soap-box dressing table and a chair as well as a bed. Rainbow called this the Bridal Chamber, but not in Lady Meta's hearing.

Despite her lack of privacy she maintained her aloofness. She managed to hold herself away from colonists and townspeople alike. The natives of Rainbow were intensely curious about the titled lady, but only one of them saw her at close range.

This was the Oarlocks' aunt, a tiny person with white side curls, who lived at the Log House upon a vague arrangement which permitted the Oarlocks to call upon her for occasional services.

The Oarlocks were proud of Aunt Kibbie. She was a person of distinction in Rainbow. Aunt Kibbie had read her New Testament one hundred and thirty-two times, the Old Testament sixty-five times. She preferred the former, she said, because it was less upsetting.

She had bird-bright eyes which tried to make up with their sharpness for the dullness of her ears. She was very hard of hearing, and labored under the gentle delusion that everyone else was hard of hearing, too, as a result of which Richard overheard one of her colloquies with Bannister's lady.

"Really!" Lady Meta was saying, the foreign roll to her *r* more pronounced than usual, as she tried with affectionate gravity to conceal amused delight. "Tell me more, dear Aunt Kibbie."

"Well," said Aunt Kibbie, consulting a little black book. "There are three million, five hundred eighty-six thousand, four hundred eighty-seven letters in the Bible."

"Not so!"

"And seven hundred eighty-eight thousand, seven hundred sixty-seven words."

"Impossible!"

"Sixty-six books, one thousand, one hundred eighty-nine chapters and thirty-one thousand, one hundred two verses," recited Aunt Kibbie.

"Can that be true?"

"It is," said Aunt Kibbie, "a fact." She closed her little black book, took off her spectacles, folded them and laid them atop. Then she peered brightly into Lady Meta's face.

"Would you believe," she asked, her voice indignant, "that the word 'girl' is put down just once in the Good Book although 'flea' is there twice and 'dog' forty times?"

"Herr Gott!" said Lady Meta. "We must speak to the Pope."

It was as well, Richard thought, in view of Aunt Kibbie's rampant Methodism that Lady Meta did not lift her voice for that remark. He saw her pat the old lady's shoulder with a smile so tender and indulgent that he could scarcely believe he was watching the frigid Lady Meta.

To everyone but Aunt Kibbie, however, she continued inaccessible. She took her morning tea behind the curtain, and on every pleasant day she and her maid quitted the tavern early, laden with blankets, pillows, and sketch books, and did not return until dusk. They did not go through the village; they crossed the little bridge and vanished into the woods about the lake.

Richard was much surprised, therefore, to encounter her one day on Main Street. He had returned early from his fields to hear that there was mail from England, and without remounting his horse hurried out to Oates's store which served also as post office. Mail came every day; Mr. Beatty brought it by the stage; but not every day was there mail from across the Atlantic with home letters and copies of the *Sketch* and *Graphic* and the *Illustrated London News*.

It had rained that morning. New-washed, the spring world was enchanting. Wild plum flashed white in the woods along the lakeside, and beyond the newly budded trees the lake gleamed brightly blue. Lilacs overhung the fences of the village; their great purple clumps suffused the air with sweetness. Orioles swung and whistled in the trees while women made their gardens and gossiped above the piles of burning leaves.

Above and about one were glories enough to make one forgive what lay beneath—the rich, black, sticky mud. The town had no sidewalks, and Richard blessed his stout boots as he tramped the eighth of a mile which lay between the Log House and Oates's store. When he glimpsed Lady Meta afoot his first thought was that Bannister should have gotten her a horse. No wonder she was standing stock-still in dismay! Then he perceived that she was not only standing still; she was rooted in deep black mud.

Richard hurried up to her.

"I say! I'm frightfully sorry. Won't you let me help you?"

Her lifted face was both embarrassed and amused. The

uptilted brows were embarrassed, but the surprising soft red mouth was smiling. She wore a small gray hat with a cluster of violets placed where the straw dipped just over her eyes, and a gray poplin walking dress with a second bunch of violets at her throat. There were gray gloves on her hands and gray boots on the slender feet so firmly fixed in the mud.

"Isn't it absurd?" she said ruefully, and added in explanation. "You see, there is mail from home. And the day was so pleasant—I thought I would not send Hanni—"

Richard bent to the ground and cleared the mud from her feet. Then he swept his arm beneath her swelling panniers and lifted her from the ground. The odor of violets poured into his face as he carried her easily, feeling a proper masculine pleasure in his strength.

It was easier to carry her than it was to decide what to say when he put her to the ground before Oates's store. She now appeared to be more amused than embarrassed.

"You are strong!" she said, her brown eyes shining. "That is what makes you men the way you are—domineering, arrogant; it is simply the fact of your being so strong. If I were that strong, I could be the same."

Richard blushed. What, he wondered, was the answer to that remark? She slipped her hand lightly into his arm.

"You too are looking for letters, are you not? Shall we go in?"

In the doorway they encountered a familiar figure—tall, thin, rangy. Lady Meta recognized him ahead of Richard.

"Captain Whipp!" she cried. She put out her slim, gray-gloved hand. "You should have been the one to rescue me instead of Mr. Chalmers," she went on radiantly, and extended her muddy boot in explanation.

"I wish I had been, ma'am," said Captain Whipp. "I'll

give myself the honor of cleaning those boots, if you'll permit."

"Damn these Americans!" thought Richard, amused and chagrined, as Whipp lifted Lady Meta to a cracker-box and, producing a jackknife, began to scrape away at the slender boots.

"You said you would come to see us, but you never did," she reproached him.

"I've been busy with my planting, ma'am."

"I hoped you might show up to work in the bean fields," said Richard.

"Not me. I'm interested in my own fields." Bob Whipp drew a layer of mud from Lady Meta's undersoles and looked up to explain. "It's all right in the short run to let your own farm go and work for the British. But I'm thinking of the long run. I've got the best eighty acres in Crockett County, and I want to see them broken and in crop."

"Are you putting in beans?" Richard asked.

"Beans, hell! I'm putting in wheat and corn and potatoes. And what's more," Whipp added with his ready belligerence, "I'm putting them in myself. The way you English play straw boss gives me a pain."

He cleaned the jackknife and returned it to his pocket, pulled out a red bandana handkerchief and proceeded to polish the gray boots briskly.

"Watch out," he said, peering up at Richard, "that you don't throw away your money and your lands after them."

"What do you mean?" asked Richard.

Whipp nodded toward the interior of the store.

"Yonder's the best little mortgage taker in Crockett County. He's going to have a lot of fun foreclosing some year when it forgets to rain."

"You mean Oates?"

"That's just who I mean. He's a skunk. My apologies, ma'am."

Richard and Lady Meta looked curiously into the store, where Mr. Oates, unconscious of being thus adversely described, was affably conversing with a customer. He looked less like a skunk than like a mole, Richard thought. He had a snout-shaped face above a short thick body. And his hair, eyebrows, and whiskers were abundant although they were brownish red instead of velvet black.

"You know what he did," Whipp demanded, "while I was down South fighting the slave dealers and democrats?"

"What did he do?" Lady Meta asked in the same indulgent tone she had used to Aunt Kibbie.

"He paid some boy to do his fighting and went as a surveyor on government lands, bought the best, and started a pile that's been growing ever since."

"Has he a wife?" asked Lady Meta.

"He's buried three. Money with them all. The third one wasn't cold when he took the one he's got now." Bob Whipp paused and then said, "I buried my wife, and I'll give her due honor before I take another." His tone was sober and neither of his companions answered.

"Did you know I had a fourteen-year-old girl?" he asked them, brightening. "Pretty as a new dime, too. What say you ride out to see us some day?"

"That would be charming," said Lady Meta, smiling.

"Jolly," Richard agreed.

"Head west along the Pennell road. You'll know my farm, because I've got three trees. Three cottonwoods. The Three Sisters, I call them."

He stood up, pocketing his handkerchief. Lady Meta's boots were as clean as they had been when she left the Log House.

"I sure am glad to see you, ma'am," he said.

"And I am glad to see you." Once again she put her hand in his. She looked into his face with a smile. "Thank you very much, Captain Whipp."

Whipp shook hands with Richard, picked up his bundle of groceries, and loped off to the hitching post.

"I really love him," Lady Meta said.

Judson Oates blinked when Richard and Lady Meta came together up to the post-office window.

"Mr. Chalmers, isn't it? And I suppose this is Mrs. Chalmers?"

"This is Lady Meta Bannister," Richard said.

"Humph!" said Oates as he sorted out their letters. It was plain that he considered their association questionable. But Richard had purchases to make, and the storekeeper was cautiously civil.

Lady Meta was engaged with her letters. When Richard returned to her, she showed them to him with a smile. They bore stamps unfamiliar to Richard.

"You have been in Munich?" she asked.

"Once. On a holiday to the Tyrol."

"My mother was a Bavarian, and I lived in Munich as a child. We too went in summer to the mountains." She looked away with a softened dreaming face.

"If you will wait here, Lady Meta, I'll fetch a horse for you."

"Thank you. I should hate to spoil Captain Whipp's clean boots." She smiled with complete friendliness as he departed.

Her good will for her fellows had been too long denied, Richard thought, as he tramped homeward. That was why it had blossomed now, so suddenly, into this friendliness and gayety. He was borne out in his opinion after he returned with horses and they were returning to the Log House together.

"Oh," she said impulsively, "it is so good to have a friend!"

Richard felt guilty. He was truly sorry for her. He knew that she needed a friend in the colony, but he was aware also that he did not think of her as a friend. To him she was a woman, beautiful, spirited, and charming, with the perfume of violets in her dress and a gleaming red-lipped smile.

He turned silently to look at her.

She was regarding him anxiously, and when he saw the wistful look in her eyes, the tremulous appeal on her lips, the tension of her figure, and the foreign aspect of the letters she was clutching, he surrendered to compassion.

"Have you heard that we are going to be neighbors?" he asked.

"I am glad," said Lady Meta.

CHAPTER SIX

"DICK," said Bannister, "what do you make of these grass-hopper stories?"

Richard smiled. It was the day his bean fields first showed green; overnight, across all his rolling acres, a verdant haze had spread. Along row after row, when you looked closely, pale sprouts and tender leafage were pushing through the black crumbling earth. Looking upon this generous promise of rich harvest, Richard could not yield to grasshopper stories even a measure of alarm.

In the first place they were really less than stories; they were hardly more than rumors. They dealt with a vast raven-ous army of insects which had come out of nowhere into the west and was moving westward, eating every growing thing and leaving desolation in its wake. The rumors had been persistent, and they had been coming for almost a month now. Taken at their face value they meant that another plague of locusts had descended upon the land. But who-ever had heard of such a visitation outside the pages of the Bible? Whoever had witnessed one in life?

"Grasshopper stories!" Richard laughed. He had been walking his horse along the western boundary of his land when Bannister came trotting up, and now he halted. "That's just what I think they are, grasshopper stories! Bob Whipp stories might be another name for them." Pleased with his joke, he amplified it. "Bob claims that everything in Minnesota is bigger and better than you can find anywhere else. Wouldn't it be just like him to claim that the grasshoppers are bigger and worse?"

"But these aren't Minnesota grasshoppers," Bannister pointed out. The excitement which always showed so quickly in his electric-blue eyes lighted his face. "They come from some place out west. And today I heard that they had reached the western border of the state."

"But they haven't reached Crockett County," Richard said confidently.

No, Bannister admitted.

"And they never will," Richard predicted. "We'll hear stories of all the damage they do to the north of us and to the south of us, but we'll never see any done here."

"Probably they'll get their bellies full before they reach here," said Bannister, falling in with Richard's mood.

Richard took off his wide-brimmed hat and passed the palms of his hands across his closely clipped, tightly curling flaxen hair. He turned his head to survey his greening acres, and a smile spread slowly over his face.

"Kit," he said. "They just won't care for beans!"

Bannister's report was the first which brought the grasshoppers into Minnesota, but it was not to be the last. From then on, wherever one went in Rainbow, conversation centered about the locusts' progress. The rumors multiplied, and some of them were undeniably sobering. But they were also so confused, so fantastic, so extravagant that the more level-headed men continued to disbelieve them.

How could one believe, for example, that the creatures rode the wind as men ride trains of cars? According to accounts from the west, they would ride ten miles eastward upon a favoring breeze, drop down upon a green area, eat it bare, and then when the wind was right rise and fly on. But only when the wind was right! They adhered to one direction as though following a railroad schedule. That was absurd on the face of it. Equally impossible to credit were the statements about the damage they inflicted. They ate the very leaves off the trees, it was said; they stripped the countryside bare of every shred of living green. Billions, trillions of insects, so reasonable men averred, could not cause the devastation ascribed to these "hoppers."

Merely to look at his broad green fields gave Richard reassurance. Enough grasshoppers did not live to eat bare such an acreage. And that the whole countryside—his own fields and those of Bannister, Barrowcliff and the rest—could be eaten bare was not to be believed. No! Some greater Whipp out west had talked, and his tall tales had grown taller as they journeyed, in the way tall tales do. . . .

The tale lingered about Rainbow, but the optimists continued to scoff while the green haze on the beanfields deepened, the pale sprouts grew stronger and darker, the seed leaves fell into the furrows and the true leaves sought the sun. The bean crop was early and fine. So too were the Americans' crops of wheat, oats, barley, corn, potatoes. Farmers everywhere told one another that the yield would certainly set a record, unless those hoppers . . .

On an evening in the second week of June, Richard and Trevenen rocked in a boat in front of the Log House. In the bottom of the boat, at Richard's feet, a catch of pickerel and bass grew higher with the passing twilight. The sun had set in a glow of liquid gold which still ran in the waters along the western shore. Gulls and swallows soared above the lake, yielding their bodies to the air in calm delight.

Richard had just dropped another bass to thresh on the

pile at his feet, when Hook cried loudly from the dock. He called again, but neither Richard nor Trevenen could understand him.

"We'll go in," Trevenen said. "We wouldn't know what to do with more fish than we've caught already."

They drew in their anchor and rowed easily, the drops of water falling from their slowly moving oars in beads of silver.

"The grasshoppers have reached Crockett County!" Hook cried as they approached.

For the first time Richard felt a sizable alarm.

"The beggars have stopped out Pennell way," Hook went on. "They're eating the township out of house and home."

"The deuce you say!" Trevenen shouted back.

Pennell township, thought Richard with foreboding! That was getting close to home.

He was puzzled in the midst of his anxiety by Hook's interest in the situation. Hook was not an enthusiastic farmer; he had shown all along a marked indifference to the beans. Why should he be so worried now about hoppers? It developed at once that worry did not lie behind Hook's interest.

"Some of the Americans are riding over tomorrow to see them," he explained cheerfully as his compatriots disembarked. "I think it would be good sport to do the same. We could take our guns and bring back some game after we'd looked at the beastly pests."

Richard laughed, and whatever alarm he had felt died with his laughter.

The next morning they were up and off in the gray mists of dawn. The same four who had come into Rainbow together cantered through the sleeping town. For some miles they retraced the same route, moving northward along the chain of lakes. Then they met the road which ran east to Sisseton City, west to the frontier.

They took the westward turn and soon left the lakes behind them. Their trail wound through a sea of waving grass as high as their horses' bellies. This was woven with an unfamiliar red and yellow bloom, with daisies and the fragrant prairie rose. Wild strawberries grew in such abundance that the men swung off their horses now and then to fill their caps with spicy helpings. Game was equally abundant. The great cranes were gone, but the big sickle-billed curlews moved majestically in search of food; and from all over the prairie sounded the upland plover's mellow cry. Prairie chicken ran everywhere, but it was illegal to shoot them at this season.

"Thought it was a snipe," said Bannister, winking as he brought one down.

"Damn it, Kit! Stick in your glass! You've enough game now to supply the Log House for a week."

Bannister shouted with laughter at Hook's savage tone, but he respected the nesting grouse for the rest of the journey.

Now and then the Englishmen passed the home of a settler; often a mere dugout, covered with sod. But nowhere across the acres of billowing grass, under the bright sky full of wind-tossed fleecy clouds, was there any hint or trace of ravaging locusts.

"Where is this confounded army we've been hearing about?" Bannister asked at last. "If it was the proper sort of an army, we'd be seeing the advance guard now. They'll run into trouble if they try to invade enemy country without sending out reconnoitering parties."

This brought casual laughter from the others, and the four rode on building up the conceit of an invading hopper host going through all the tactical operations practiced by armies of men. It had come to be well on toward noon when Richard cried out suddenly:

"By Jove! The Three Sisters."

"Where?" demanded Trevenen, the ladies' man.

"Whipp's place," Richard explained. "He told me that three trees marked his farm, and there they are."

Three tall cottonwood trees stood out against the sky. The men put their horses to a trot, and in a short time the bulk of Whipp's house rose against the horizon. Then his fields took character in the midst of the rippling grass.

These were small in comparison with the broad acreage which the Englishmen had planted, but they were flourishing and admirably tended. The wheat and oats made clean green lines against the earth. The corn was not yet high enough for hilling, but Whipp was busy with a hoe among his potatoes.

Richard shouted. The American straightened, leaned briefly upon his hoe to inspect the arriving party, and then came toward them at an exuberant lope.

"If it ain't the Johnny Bulls! Climb down and give your nags a rest. Come on into the house and make yourselves to home."

As they alighted he pretended a heavy regret.

"Wish I could offer you something better than coffee to drink. But I don't touch the other stuff. Bridey's ma hated it, and I got clean out of the habit."

"Who is Bridey?" Trevenen asked, pronouncing the name as Whipp did, as though it were a diminutive for "bride."

"Bridey's my daughter, and I sure wish she was home. She climbed on to her pony not an hour ago and rode off to her ma's cousin Lonabelle. Lona's man's got a place five, six miles south."

He led the way to his buildings, which were somewhat more substantial than most of those they had noticed on the prairie. They were built of logs with the popular shake roof of the region, reinforced on roof and walls with stout chunks of prairie sod. The barnyard was observably neat, flanked by a thriving kitchen garden. Petunias and nasturtiums in a small bed by the house promised less well.

"Pindling," said Bob Whipp regretfully, "although Bridey wrestles with 'em like a preacher with a lost soul."

The kitchen into which they entered served also as dining room and parlor. Stones had been pounded into the ground to make a floor, and much of the furniture was hand-hewn out of logs. The room was clean and well ordered, lighted by two glass windows. A tin cup in the center of the well scrubbed table bore a bouquet of prairie roses.

"Bridey takes after her ma," Whipp said. "She's a tidy housekeeper." The pride in his voice yielded for a moment to humility. "Her ma used to say she wanted just three things—a real floor, glass windows, and an elevated oven stove. She didn't have a one of them. But Bridey's got the windows and the stove, and come harvest she'll have the floor. You can bet your beans on that!"

It was plain even to the unschooled Englishmen that other details of the house had been arranged with an eye to Bridey's convenience. Beside the stove was a towering pile of wood; the water pail was full; and all along the walls were pegs for hanging gear and utensils out of the way.

Richard recalled Whipp's scornful words to Bannister. "We know how to treat our women." The statement was true, he thought, at least of Americans like Whipp. Englishmen would have to learn from such Americans, if they were going to bring their women into this wild country—and hold them.

He thought of Lady Meta and tried for a fleeting moment to picture her life in Exile Hall. It was next to impossible to hire women servants, hereabouts. She would, of course, have her Hanni's assistance, but Hanni was a lady's maid and had no other skill. The thought of Lady Meta, her hands always gleaming with jewels, making bread or tending chickens was too fantastic to hold him. He returned to Whipp's kitchen.

Whipp was making the coffee as handily as any woman. And while it came to a boil he sliced bread and set out butter with a plate of cold fried plover and a bowl of wild strawberry sauce.

"If I do say so myself," he commented, "Bridey's bread's first-rate. So's her butter. And if you can find another fourteen-year-old girl who can fry birds any tastier than that, just show her to me. That's all I ask: Just show her to me."

While they ate the Englishmen told their errand. Whipp's mouth tightened in real concern.

"I figured to ride west myself today. Guess I'll saddle up and go along."

"You aren't worried about the hoppers, are you, Captain?" Richard asked.

"I don't waste time worrying," Whipp replied. "But this wind we've got today is the kind they ride on."

"If you believe those fantastic stories," Trevenen put in.

"I've talked with a man from Pennell township," Whipp answered grimly. He emptied his cup and returned it to the table with a bang. "But it takes more than a mess of hoppers to scare me," he added, rising.

"And it takes more than a mess of hoppers to scare the British," Bannister put in, clapping Whipp's shoulder. "Come along, old chap."

Emerging from the house, they blinked at the blazing brightness of the prairie. In spite of his two glass windows, Bob Whipp's kitchen was dim. The sun was a little beyond its meridian, still high in a brilliant sky. The prairie grass still swayed in the wind. Richard thought it looked like dancers curtsying.

Bob Whipp licked his finger and held it upward.

"Still blowing out of the west," he said.

"Does that mean they're coming, Captain?" Bannister asked excitedly.

"Let 'em come," said Whipp, "and let 'em ride over. Let 'em ride clean over."

All five men strained their gaze toward the west. The prairie air was clear, transparent. Except for the usual haze where blue met green, there was no blur which might indicate approaching hoppers. Nevertheless, as they saddled their horses and swung into the saddle, all felt an increasing tension.

Richard was affected by Whipp's words. "Let 'em ride over! Let 'em ride clean over!" The American believed in the hoppers, he expected them, he was willing them to pass him by.

Conscious of the emotion of their riders and refreshed by food and water, the horses cantered briskly out to the trail. There, checked by a cry from Bannister, all of them halted. In the brief space which had served to bring the party out of the barnyard, the look of the horizon had changed. A cloud had appeared, a new shining cloud. It lifted out of the blue as far to the left and to the right as the eye could reach.

Hook was the first to speak.

"If that cloud means hoppers, it means a hell of a lot of them," he said.

"We'll find out in two jerks. Come on," said Whipp. He went forward at a gallop. The Englishmen followed.

The cloud thickened. It could not lengthen because already it reached from north to south, as far as the riders could see, but it thickened. Slowly, very slowly, it moved up from the horizon as though it were a curtain being drawn up to cover a window that was the whole sky.

The men remained incredulously silent while their horses ran for a mile or more over the prairie. Then Bannister called attention to a change in the phenomenon.

"Look!" he shouted and pulled his horse up short. His outflung arm pointed to a shadow which spread over the earth to match the dark curtain rising into the sky. "They blot out the sun!" he cried.

"A man can't tell a thing from this distance," Whipp said deep in his throat, and urged his horse forward again.

After another mile, all drew in their horses. It was useless to go farther. From this point a man could tell everything. "God almighty!" Whipp whispered.

The cloud of locusts moved upon them riding the wind from the west. The host was so close now that the five men could make out the single swarms which combined in countless numbers to form the cloud. But of the cloud's depth and width they could tell nothing. Its dimensions seemed to their horrified gaze to be the dimensions of the sky. The host flew quite high and, as it approached, Richard thought of a snowstorm bathed in light.

By now the insects were almost overhead. The shadow that they cast darkened the prairie no more than a furlong in advance of the horses' hoofs. The horses took fright. The advancing shadow, the tossing cloud, were more than they could understand. They flung their heads up and pawed, and Bannister's animal wheeled and bolted.

The others followed gladly but at a slower gait. It was not necessary to race. The pursuing cloud came only at the speed of the wind and that was not fast. It did not so much advance as drift. Looking back, Richard could see how eddying currents of air made whirlpools which caught one swarm—perhaps, a hundred swarms—and sent them swirling at right angles to the army's true line of advance. Sometimes the air currents brushed a vast mass of the grasshoppers right or left as a hand might brush through heaped-up leaves. It was then that the magnitude of the host became apparent. When he first saw such a movement Richard expected the blue sky to be revealed. Instead, fresh myriads of grasshoppers poured into the space which the wind had briefly cleared. Not for an instant was he able to see the sky.

From time to time small detachments broke away from the high-flying army and dropped down. Always, however, before they reached earth the wind lifted them back to the mother host.

"If the wind holds they might pass entirely over our country," Trevenen shouted above the whir of wings.

Richard tried to measure the wind. Wasn't it dying? Was it as strong as it had been when they all set out from Whipp's farm? He whipped his memory until his head whirled, trying to recall how the wind had felt. He believed that it was weaker now.

"The wind is stronger!" cried Whipp.

Looking aside at the American, Richard perceived that they had retreated to Whipp's farm. The sod-roofed house and barn were just behind them. To the right ran the tidy kitchen garden, and behind stretched those small carefully tended fields of corn, wheat, oats, potatoes . . . All about rose the tall prairie grass.

When Richard's eye fell on that he knew whether the wind was stronger or weaker. At noon the grass had swayed and bowed like a ballroom full of ladies, curtseying. Now it only quivered like water stirred by a breeze.

The shadow of the grasshopper army reached the western boundary of Whipp's land and drifted on. The humming beat of the countless wings grew louder.

"Look out!" Bannister cried, and as he turned his horse in quick retreat he spat in loathing.

The grasshoppers dropped to earth on the fading wind. Richard turned his horse too and so did Trevenen and Hook. With no difficulty they kept in the clear. Safe in the open, they watched the horde descend, as they might have stood in the sunshine and watched a prairie rainstorm beat down before their eyes.

Whipp had held fast. He had beat his horse into trembling submission and now he sat upon the animal in the midst of the grasshoppers. They covered his land, his crops, his house. They covered him. They were on his hat, on his shoulders. They crawled up and down his legs, and across his boots thrust deep into their stirrups. They were on his left hand which held his horse relentlessly in its tracks. But his right hand was clear. His right hand, balled into a fist, pounded the crawling host. As methodically as a pestle strikes down into a mortar, it struck and struck and struck.

CHAPTER SEVEN

"The land is as the garden of Eden before them, and behind them a desolate wilderness."

Richard remembered his father reading the words.

Each morning at Great Goodlands, the family and servants gathered for prayers. In addition to the Lord's Prayer and other supplications, the Squire read always a chapter from the Bible. He was an uninspired reader—his son recalled with a smile that hurrying voice; but Holy Writ, Richard had discovered, survived even a matter-of-fact rendition. Odd verses had a way of leaping into one's mind, months after, miles away from the time and place they were uttered. It was so with the writings of the Prophet Joel. Richard had heard them as a carefree boy, avoiding his mother's alarmed gaze, aiming paper pellets at Hankins' outraged dome. He heard them again in homesick discouraged exile, surveying his ruined crops in Crockett County, Minnesota.

The locusts had descended upon the Rainbow countryside just as they had upon Whipp's farm. Their hunger was furious and incredible. Their jaws were wide open for food before their wings brought them to earth, and almost nothing green escaped them. Within twenty-four hours there was not a beanstalk left. Grain fields and gardens were razed; trees were stripped of their leaves. Men stood by helpless and watched the destruction of their hopes, the loss of weeks of toil.

There followed the unbearable invasion of the insects into every private place. They crawled along one's clothes, into one's pockets; they were loathsomely underfoot even in one's house. They tainted water; they spoiled food—sometimes in ways so unexpected that they would have been ridiculous if food had not become so scarce. Hens ate the creatures, and eggs were too rank for any palate. The offending hens could not be eaten in revenge, for their flesh too held the strange repulsive flavor.

In some places the army remained only for a day or two; in others, it ravaged for weeks. From all, it departed in an identical manner. When the wind came suitably from the west, the insects rose. They formed a great cloud which mounted higher and higher. It hung suspended for a moment, shimmering in the sun, seeming to survey and reckon the ruin it had wrought. Then it swept eastward and vanished.

And then Crockett County found new cause to be thankful for its Englishmen.

"They're certainly saving our bacon," Americans far and near admitted, as the racial determination of the immigrants made itself felt in an activity which offered help to all. Even Whipp, who had been so resolved to keep his independence, accepted the solution offered.

"Hell!" he said. "If they want to hire the whole county, I won't hold out and spoil their record."

He took the wages offered by the indomitable squires and sons of squires, and so did all the other natives whose humble crops had been eaten down to the roots. In other counties afflicted by the locusts, men were returning east by regiments to earn money for next winter's supplies, for next spring's seeds, even for present necessities. It was not so in Crockett County; the English gave work to all.

For the English planted again. Over their hundreds and hundreds of acres, they ploughed and planted again. And having replanted they began to build, continuing their demand for labor. Carpenters, masons, plasterers, painters, bricklayers were needed. Supplies of all kinds poured into Rainbow, and clerks and teamsters were required.

Hook and Trevenen began to build the Eyrie. More importantly, they built the Eyrie's stables. The house was comfortable, after a bare masculine fashion, but the stables were the marvel of the county. Their imported stallion, Thunder, their blooded mares were housed in quarters worthy of their ancestry. Barrowcliff constructed a simple country mansion. Bannister reared a towered and turreted home. Richard at last, doubtfully, put up Little Goodlands, but his house was not a success.

Up to the time of his coming to America, Richard had never known a sense of inadequacy or failure. This feeling had been born in him when he first saw his land. He had found himself almost incapable of looking at that bare plain and saying: "Here my house will stand. There I will put my stables. That way my fences shall run."

With the planting of the beans he had regained a measure of confidence. He was a good farmer, and he knew it. The hoppers had found no cleaner fields than his. But after his crop was gone, discouragement settled upon him again. The second planting brought him no joy. It was time to build his house, and he had no heart to begin, nor any plan.

In England he had sometimes taken charge of repairs on tenant farms. He had always enjoyed the work and done it well. But in England he traded where his father and grandfather had traded before him, with honest trustworthy folk. He had not needed to haggle or bargain. Oates cheated him at every turn.

He would not have minded so much if the results had pleased him. But the results appalled him. Staring at his house on the day the painters left it, when it stood ready for the furniture already en route from Mankato, he wondered how he had been inveigled into building so hideous a thing.

He should have asked advice, perhaps, from Hook or Barrowcliff. He was by far the youngest member of the colony. But for that very reason he strove to be independent. He knew what kind of house he wanted; he thought he had described it to the American carpenters. But they had built him what they thought he ought to have.

His house did not even face the water. Americans did not build their homes to face scenic beauties, it seemed; they preferred to look out upon the road. Bannister had built Exile Hall with its feet, as he had promised, in the marsh. Barrowcliff's house on the bank of Flower Lake was charmingly placed. The Eyrie was perched on a high knoll which commanded both Pass and Flower lakes. But Little Goodlands faced the road and the prairie, and burr oaks hid even from its kitchen windows any glimpse of Bird Lake's shining waters.

It was a small frame boxlike house. Set into its right forecorner was a narrow comfortless porch. From the porch one door led forward into the kitchen; another, at the side, admitted to a tiny parlor. Behind the parlor lay an equally tiny bedroom which opened also into the kitchen. There was only a loft above. Three low-ceiled minnikin stuffy rooms for Richard who liked lofty ceilings and wide spaces above all else in any dwelling!

The structure was painted a flat yellow. It had no shutters. There were, of course, no vines or flowers to mitigate its bareness. Perhaps, thought Richard, flowers would help. But even as he tried to comfort himself by envisioning gardens like his mother's, he knew that nothing would help so hideous a house.

It was hideous, and it had been expensive. It represented trickery and fraud. He wished he could set fire to it and clear the landscape of it.

"If the Governor hadn't been so damned decent, I would, by God!"

All he could do, however, was to mount his horse and ride away. For weeks he continued to live at the Log House. But the memory of Little Goodlands weighed upon him, sapping his confidence.

The summer was hot. Day after day, the thermometer soared above a hundred. A stifling wind from the southwest blew over the hopper-ravaged fields. Often at evening the sky was torn by lightning; thunder split the air in deafening claps, and water poured down in torrents. But next day the heat was unrelieved.

The air teemed with mosquitoes. Men slept with netting tacked about their beds; they rode or walked abroad with netting wound about their heads. They kept small fires burning on the windward side of their houses—smudges, the Americans called them.

The English passed the time with hunting and fishing. They gathered at the Eyrie for trap shooting and hurdle jumping. Richard and Bannister, Hook and Trevenen, Harry Earle and Alfred Neville—Slabs, his comrades called him— ran a hurdle race to help the Americans celebrate the Fourth Day of July.

Richard was a magnificent horseman. The plaudits of the Americans, the admiration of his fellow-British as he took the hurdles at this rural festival, eased his sore heart. So too did Lady Meta's graceful praise.

"I could do better on my own horse." He towered above her, embarrassed and delighted.

"This one is not your own?"

"No. Hook loaned her to me. My American nag is all right for riding, but she doesn't know how to jump."

"You have not brought your horses over?"

"I hope to bring a hunter next spring."

He wiped his hot face, and his drenched head on which flaxen hair curled. Lady Meta, cool in white organza under a wide-brimmed hat, smiled at him.

July gave way to August, and the English forgot the heat and the mosquitoes. They forgot their second crop of beans which was now in snowy flower. Richard forgot Little Goodlands, his chagrin and self-distrust. For the chicken season was upon them.

The British soon learned to call it the chicken season. It was the great hunting season of the year, when the pinnated grouse or true prairie chicken and his cousin, the sharp-tailed grouse, were surrendered by law to the mercy of the hunters. Sportsmen poured into Rainbow from St. Paul and Minneapolis, from the more distant cities of St. Louis and Chicago. They brought dogs as well as guns, but many of the dogs changed owners shortly. The British were willing to pay fabulous prices for the animals, and the Americans could not hold out. Richard bought a pair of black and tan Gordon setters, Nellie and Shot. He grew fond of them both, for the affection in their deep soft eyes assuaged an ache in his heart. Bannister, in addition to his bird dogs, had secured a liver-colored hound, an ugly-tempered brute which he christened Fang. The animal was no good in the field, but its master would not hunt without it.

"Fang is a watchdog," Bannister explained. "A man needs a watchdog in this country, and Fang is perfect. He obeys me at a word, and I take him around to keep him in the habit."

Certainly the beast was obedient. It yielded a savage submission which delighted Bannister.

Alone and in pairs, the hunters ranged forth each morning, returning with such quantities of birds that the pile of feathered corpses outside the Log House resembled a winter woodpile.

"Fifty-eight today." "Sixty-five, for me." "I had hard luck; only bagged forty."

Sometimes a group of sportsmen rode out together in open two-seated wagons and separated into pairs only when they reached the prairies. On one such occasion, Lady Meta was included in the party.

She looked pale, Richard thought, and the hand which she put into his clung with a secret unexpected pleading.

"I am glad you are coming," she said.

"I've been surprised," said Richard, "that you haven't joined us before. Don't you enjoy shooting?"

"It terrifies me," she answered.

"Then why are you coming today, ma'am?"

Before she could answer, Bannister turned toward them. She stiffened and dropped cool lids over her eyes. Bannister swung a careless arm about her.

"Don't you think I was wise to make her come, Dick? It's lonely business sitting at home all day."

"It is a pleasure to have her," Richard answered.

"Ride with us, won't you? There's room for you and one other behind, with all your dogs and the baskets. Lady Meta and I will take Fang and the guns."

"Oh, no!" The cry seemed to come against her will.

"Perhaps," suggested Richard. "Lady Meta would prefer the baskets."

She flashed bright hostile eyes upon her husband.

"I should," she said.

"Of course, my dear." His tone was injured. "But I wish you would learn to like Fang just a little." He rubbed the head of the hound, who crouched at his feet.

Richard pondered the conversation as he arranged the baskets and assisted Lady Meta into her place. It was absurd to think that Kit would make her come against her will. Kit was a fool, and his standards were questionable; but he was the soul of good nature. Nevertheless it was clear that she did not like coming.

During the ride she unbent a trifle. Richard and Trevenen sat behind, Richard holding Fang quiet at his feet; and Lady Meta turned her small head frequently. She wore a wide shade hat which charmingly framed her face and ringlets, and a thin dress of blue and white striped stuff.

"Devilish pretty," Trevenen murmured to Richard. But his bold eyes failed to shift the direction of Lady Meta's backward glances. They went first to Richard always, and for Trevenen there was only an indifferent unintended overflow.

Hook, Harry Earle, and the senior Neville brothers rode in a wagon just behind. The day was fine, not too warm, with an invigorating breeze across the prairies. Meadow larks whistled above the bending grass. The red lilies, the daisies, and the Queen Anne's lace of summer were mingled with autumn's goldenrod and asters. The trail led out of the grasshopper district; fields of golden stubble soon patched the green carpet of grass. There were few fences, and the wagons rolled freely from native grass to stubble, skirting standing corn and newly ploughed lands.

This was the country which prairie chicken loved, mixed farm and prairie country. The wagons were halted in a bit of shade near a stream, and Bannister ordered Fang to watch them. The heavy morose dog sprawled out beneath a wagon box, instantly obedient. The men scattered, releasing their dogs. Richard and Bannister lingered to spread a rug for Lady Meta, who brought out pillows and a novel. Then they followed, and Nellie was soon on a point.

The two men enjoyed good sport for several hours. At first Richard's thoughts stayed with Lady Meta. But soon he forgot her in the exciting routine of the sport. The dogs pointed, and the men advanced. Birds rose with a whir and guns cracked in the waiting air. A bird was cut down or a bird escaped, sometimes in a drift of feathers. Bannister was full of excited exclamations, but Richard spoke only to the dogs. "Steady, Shot!" "Fetch, Nellie!" "Seek dead, Shot!" "Come here, Nell, old girl!"

Richard was an excellent shot. The leather thongs set into his belt were soon burdened with birds. He felt that he had taken his quota, but he waited, to watch Bannister. The Captain too was a famous shot. He too had taken a fair quota, but he gave no indication of stopping. His blue eyes blazing, his smile fixed and constant, he loaded, sighted, shot, loaded again.

At last Richard said, "I'm taking my birds back to the wagon."

"I'll come along," Bannister rejoined. "I need more shells."

"You haven't had enough?"

"Lord, no! Not while the birds are still cluttering up the prairies."

Lady Meta rose as they approached, but not to greet them. She turned and walked down to the stream. Richard unburdened himself of his birds before going to join her. Bannister, however, seemed eager to show her the kill.

"I'm glad that you had good sport. But don't show them to me, Kit."

"But see what beauties they are, and how many I've got."

"More than enough, I should say."

"What do you mean by that?" he asked angrily.

"You've killed more than we could ever eat or give away."

"Well, I haven't killed all I'm going to kill." He began to throw the birds sullenly on the ground.

She walked away with bent head, and after a moment touched a handkerchief fiercely, reluctantly, to brimming eyes. Then she turned back with forced determination.

"Please, Kit, let us have luncheon now. The others came by a moment ago and said that they would join us presently."

"To hell with them all!" said Bannister. He kicked at the feathered pile on the ground, scattering the poor limp bodies. He strode to the wagon, supplied himself generously with shells, and strode away.

Richard slowly picked up the birds. Bannister had been brutal. Sometimes he thought the fellow was batty—brimming with good humor and vivacity at one moment; at the next, bursting out like a fury. It was incomprehensible, of course, that Lady Meta should object to shooting. But it was even more incomprehensible that a husband should treat such a foible otherwise than tenderly. If he were in Bannister's place, Richard thought, Lady Meta should never put eyes on a dead bird.

She had walked away again. When she returned she was tremulously smiling.

"Husbands and wives are one, are they not, Mr. Chalmers?" Her foreign accent was more perceptible than usual; her tone was light. "Therefore I may apologize for my husband's excessive rudeness. Tell me, do you know how to make coffee?"

They grew gay over his attempt. She gathered small sticks for the fire which he managed skillfully enough; but both of them stared blankly at the mixture of ground coffee and egg-white which the proprietor of the Log House had put into a snub-nosed pot.

"We must send for Captain Whipp! My dar-r-rling Captain Whipp!" cried Lady Meta.

They risked filling the pot with cold brook water and placed it on the fire. The venture was crowned with success. An odor of ineffable deliciousness seeped through the air as they spread a red cloth on the grass and set out sandwiches, hard-boiled eggs, cold broiled prairie chicken, potato salad, pickles, apple pie, a frosted cake.

"If they don't come soon," said Lady Meta. "We will eat it all, every bit."

She was merry now. Richard was pleasantly conscious of her liking for him. He wondered at it, for they had not, he realized, very much in common. He had heard her talking with the Barrowcliffs about London, about plays, the opera, art exhibitions—things which bored him, and which he did not understand. And she frankly abhorred the things which interested him—farming and hunting. Yet he knew that she preferred his company to that of any of the others.

When the meal was set out and the coffee removed from the fire, they sat down together. She fell silent, first giving him a smile which seemed to say:

"With you I may be silent if I choose."

They sat for a long time without speech, enjoying the drowsy warmth of the day. The blue sky was full of eiderdown pillows. The willows bent sleepily to the sleepily bubbling stream. A mourning dove called "Coo-ah-coo" from some remote and peaceful place.

Richard felt her eyes upon him. When he glanced toward her, she laughed softly, lifting her slanting brows.

"Do you know that you are very handsome?"

He smiled sheepishly.

"How nice that you are blond! Wasn't your mother pleased that you were blond?"

"I've heard," he said, "that I was a big red baby. Hideous!"

"I don't believe it!" she cried. "I'm sure that you were white and gold."

"I roared. You may count on that," grinned Richard.

Smiling at him radiantly, she asked, "You are coming to call at Exile Hall?"

"Of course. Are you ready for visitors?"

"The house is ready. And we have three chairs. We are still waiting for most of our furniture to come from Mankato."

"I have no doubt," said Richard, "that the tea table will have arrived by the time you return from England."

Her face darkened. She looked suddenly older—bitter and unhappy.

"We are not going back to England."

Of course not. Richard knew that, and he knew why. Men who quit the army for the reason that put Bannister into mufti were content to stay away from home. Richard could have bitten out his tongue.

She rose to her feet, put the pot back on the fire.

"I wonder why the others do not come," she said, strolling away as though to look for them.

Richard rose too.

"Ass, stupid idiot!" he muttered under his breath.

CHAPTER EIGHT

Frost took the second crop of beans on the seventeenth night of September.

There had been promise of a bountiful harvest. Captain Bannister had estimated his profits with that unbounded gusto which marked his optimistic moods and had confided his prospects to the editor of the *Gazette*.

"An average hill in my beanfields consists of five stalks, upon each of which hangs an average of eighty-three pods containing an average of five beans each. One may easily compute the gratifying total of four hundred and fifteen beans to a stalk and two thousand, seventy-five beans to a hill." The editor published the letter under the caption, "Congratulations, Friend Bannister!"

He might have added an admonition not to count beans before they were picked, but he withheld it. Like most of his neighbors, he was charmed with the free-spending English gentry. Affection for them swelled to delirious heights after the early frost.

Their response to that disaster was admirable. Discouragement, it seemed, was not in them. They proclaimed that of course they would return in the spring, and of course they would plant beans. It took more than hoppers or a beastly frost to make Englishmen change their minds. They packed for England, sketching plans for their return. And they did not hasten their departure. The Indian summer weather was deliciously soft and balmy. Once again the punctual blue-winged teal led a procession of ducks and geese across Minnesota skies. Great flocks of cranes were back on the prairies (magnified by the clear air, they looked like flocks of sheep). Mr. Richard Chalmers announced in the *Gazette* that he would pay liberally for a pair of live cranes in good condition.

Captain Whipp brought them to him. Richard was at Little Goodlands, packing his bags in the mean bedroom off the kitchen, when he heard the creak of wheels and looked out to see Bob Whipp aloft on a spring wagon. The tall American jumped to the ground and carefully lifted a box out of the wagon. Two long necks poked through slats from the box. Shouldering this burden, Whipp loped toward the kitchen door.

"Gosh knows why you want 'em, but here they be!" he shouted, as Richard ran to meet him.

"I want them to take to England as a present to my father. Whipp, old man, they're beauties!" Richard cried.

"A mammy and a pappy!" Whipp said proudly. He put the box to the ground, and the two long necks, topped by bare red heads, waved like tall grotesque plants with red blossoms.

"How the deuce did you get them?" Richard asked.

"Snared 'em in a cornfield."

"Well, I'm delighted. I hope they'll dance their minuet for the Governor next spring." Richard drew out his purse and selected a bank note. "I can't tell you how grateful I am," he began. But Whipp shoved the bank note back into the purse and the purse into Richard's pocket.

"None of that!" he said belligerently. "This here's a present. You know—what you get on Christmas. Didn't you ever get one before?"

"But I placed an advertisement—" Richard protested.

"I know. I was glad to be tipped off. The fact is," Whipp went on, "we all owe a plenty to you English. What with the hoppers eating our crops, and the frost taking what the hoppers forgot, and a mess of prairie fires cleaning out our hay, and Judson Oates standing ready and willing to write chattel mortgages, it's a good thing we had you Johnny Bulls around."

Richard flushed with pleasure and shook Whipp's hand.

"You'll stay to dinner," he said. But he was relieved when Whipp refused.

He did not enjoy guests since the Martins had come. Jackson had sent him the Martins—the man as a farmer, the woman as a housekeeper. Martin was competent enough; but he was a sullen mopish fellow, and his wife was lazy and a slattern. She grew more slovenly as she found her young employer too diffident to reprimand her.

They all ate at a table together—that was the western custom; Richard had known he must expect it. But he had not foreseen how distasteful it would be. He had not anticipated Martin smelling so generously of sweat, knifing his food, nor Mrs. Martin rising laboriously to serve them, preceding every useful motion with the futile one of tucking in her hair. Her face was almost pretty, for her rich high color had survived ten years of marriage. But her hair was incurably wispy; two front teeth were missing; and her breasts drooped to the roll of fat which pressed down upon her apron strings. She emerged from the kitchen now, exclaiming over the cranes.

"By the way," said Whipp, addressing Richard, "I brought out an invitation to you from the Eyrie."

"That's jolly," Richard replied.

"They want you to come in for some high jinks. They're celebrating going away, I guess. They asked me, but I said no. There's too much"—he tipped an imaginary bottle— "going on for me."

Richard laughed.

"When do they want me?"

"Whenever you can come. There's to be hunting tomorrow and a big feed tomorrow night."

"And next day we leave for England," Richard said. His words were matter-of-fact, but they set up a vibration within him. Could it be that he was to see home again? Could it be that Mr. Beatty's lumbering stage could initiate a journey which would end in the comfort, the beauty, the lost dearness of Great Goodlands?

Whipp glanced at Mrs. Martin. As she did not withdraw, he said casually, "I hear that the Bannisters aren't going."

"I believe not," Richard said.

"Won't the lady find it pretty lonesome here?"

"I'm afraid she will."

Tucking back her hair, Mrs. Martin burst into the talk. "Maybe by the end of a Minnesota winter, she won't hold herself so high and mighty."

"Why not?" Whipp boomed. "She *is* high and mighty." His vehemence reduced the woman to silence.

He seized Richard's arm and walked him toward the wagon. "I'll ride over to see her now and again," he said.

Lady Meta, Richard was aware, had a friend in Captain Whipp. And Captain Whipp, he knew, was equally aware that Lady Meta had a friend in Richard.

"I hope you will," Richard said. "I'd hate to spend a winter—"

"—snowed in with that guy," Whipp supplied, jumping to his seat.

Richard returned to his packing buoyed up by the thought of the party at the Eyrie. Life at Little Goodlands was unspeakably dull. It was lived for the most part in the kitchen, for the parlor was held sacred to company.—Mrs. Martin was horrified if either man set foot within it. And Richard could not withdraw to his bedroom, except for sleeping, without offending both his housemates.

He hoped that the morrow would be fair, and scanned the skies. Some days before, the enchanted weather had ended. A series of rains had washed out autumn's brightness, had dimmed and drenched the world. The sky today was heavy with clouds, and towards evening it began to rain. It rained all night, and when Richard set out on his ride it was still relentlessly raining. But there would be good cheer at the Eyrie even if the hunt must be abandoned. He said a cheerful goodbye to Mrs. Martin; Martin was bringing the baggage to tomorrow morning's stage. He set off in a downpour, guiding his horse carefully along the sodden trail.

From a rise of ground above Bird Lake, Exile Hall could ordinarily be seen. (From the house at Little Goodlands, only its tower was visible.) Today, however, the gray fall of rain blotted out the view. The Bannisters might be at the Eyrie; in any case, Richard had bidden them farewell. He had called, as Lady Meta had asked him to, but a few days since.

Kit in a radiant humor had shown him over the house, a strange house to be found on the Minnesota prairies! It was built of dark brick in a heavily Gothic style with high pointed windows and a frontal tower into which the entrance hall was set. It was this tower which Richard could see from his home. He had glimpsed beneath its roof a puzzling bit of color. It proved to be ruby-colored glass in the window of a third-floor oratory. (Who prayed, Richard wondered, in this lofty place of orisons—Kit or Lady Meta, or Hanni with the gold rings in her ears?)

The house with its deep stairwell, its high shadowy rooms, was gloomy, almost eerie. The floor had no carpets—Kit was expecting some, he said, to be sent from the Orient. The furniture was massive and dark.

Lady Meta had done her best with the drawing room. A fire had been burning in an open grate. (How the devil, Richard thought, had he been persuaded to stoves?) English and German journals and many books were flung about. A piano had stood open.

She had played, at Richard's request. She was an accomplished pianist, he found, and Richard was fond of music. But even more than her music he had liked the look of her seated at the piano, her dark head bent, the firelight sparkling on her slim jewel-laden hands.

She was still in his thoughts when he entered the avenue of newly transplanted beech trees which led up a hillside to the Eyrie. Before he had half traversed the drive, he was sure he would not find her at the house. Sounds of revelry issuing therefrom indicated a purely masculine assemblage.

It was a masculine looking place, this abode of Hook and Trevenen, set boldly on an eminence overlooking the two lakes which today were tumbling vats of gray beyond blowing, dripping trees. The avenues of beeches had been set out with precision; so had the pines which surrounded the house in a geometric design. The stables and kennels were large and neat. The house was large and plain—but not too plain.

"We ordered just a bit of trimming. Didn't want the blooming place to look like a barracks," Hook had said, indicating the fretwork underneath the gables and the ridgepole which bore a gilded ball.

The driveway ended at a porte-cochère where Richard now dismounted. An American farm hand turned stable boy came out to take his horse. He did not trot, as a stable boy would have done in England. He took his time, pointedly independent.

The entrance door, on which the paint was barely dry, had already been scratched by hounds. It was an astounding door —a good ten feet high.

"What do you mean to do? Ride the horses in?" Richard had asked on his first visit.

"A jolly good idea!" Trevenen had replied. "But only on special occasions, old chap. Don't try it until you've killed a buffalo at least."

The entrance hall, to which Richard admitted himself, was spacious and lofty. The floor boards were wide; the walls had been plastered and tinted icy blue. Stairs went up from this hall, and it contained also a rack for billiard cues and guns. Here were on display the heads of various animals killed by the masters of the house.

A door at the right admitted to the dining room. The scullery lay beyond, and the meat room beyond that, bristling with nails as long as fingers for game to hang upon. A door at the left of the hall admitted to the drawing room. The billiard room lay forward. All these rooms and the chambers above were high and wide and tinted the same icy blue. All the doors were nine feet high.

The house was furnished plainly but with comfort. It was clean; a woman came daily from the town to cook and scrub. Hook and Trevenen planned next year to bring out a housekeeper from England.

"She used to be my nanny. She's a Tartar," Trevenen would say, shouting with laughter.

It was as well, Richard thought now, that she had not yet arrived. Smoke and the smell of liquor were heavy in the house. Six hounds were sleeping in the drawing room. Bannister's head was pillowed upon Fang; but his brilliant eyes were open, fixed on the ceiling, and he was roaring out a song. Two of the handsome Neville brothers were playing at cards, quarreling bitterly as they always did. Hook and Barrowcliff were dispensing drinks. Barrowcliff looked sheepish; the spirit of his uncle, the archbishop, always hung upon him a bit at such affairs. Trevenen and Harry Earle were engaged in a battle of billiards. Richard joined their audience, and after the game ended, took a cue himself. But he did not fail to notice that Bannister was growing very drunk.

"The ass has been here drinking for two days," Hook said.

"What about his wife?"

"She has that maid with her, you know. He doesn't seem to be worried."

But Richard worried, as the rain hammered at the windows. He opened an outer door. Rivulets grown to muddy rivers rushed frantically toward the lakes, wind twisted the dripping trees, and the scudding clouds were so thick and dark that the light on the world was that of evening although the time was early afternoon.

Bannister had roused from his rest against Fang to make a drunken progress through the room, throwing the white lock out of his eyes as he struggled to stand upright, singing his song, less and less intelligibly, to impatient gamblers, billiard players, diners. It was useless to try to talk to him, Richard could see. Presently the Captain returned to Fang and fell into a heavy sleep.

Richard found Trevenen.

"I'm going to ride over to Exile Hall. Those two women might need food; they might need firewood; they might be in a devil of a situation."

"You're quite right, old man." Trevenen clapped him approvingly on the shoulder. But his smile was roguish; Richard did not like it. "Don't forget that we're having roast pig here at eight—unless you should find things too bad there; we'd quite understand . . ."

"I'll be back by eight," Richard answered shortly.

He shouldered into his waterproof cape.

The ride to Exile Hall was fantastically arduous. Before he had gone half the way, the rain turned to sleet and snow. The road, bad at best, glazed under his horse's hoofs. Twice the animal fell to his knees, and they progressed at a snail's pace. Water froze on Richard's hair, on his eyelashes. The horse was bearded with rime. A cold wind swirled about them, and Richard bent close to the animal's neck, speaking to him softly:

"All right, old fellow. We'll soon be there. There's a hot mash waiting for you, my lad, when this journey is ended."

The ground was already white, branches were white, roofs were white. The lakes tossed up waves—Kit Bannister's white lock, reproduced a thousand times, impatiently flying.

Richard passed Anglo-American Acres, took the cross-country trail, met the fork where two paths diverged—south to Little Goodlands or west and south to Exile Hall. His horse held stubbornly toward home, but Richard swung him to the right. He gained Exile Hall at last.

It stood dark and unfriendly in a world sheeted with white. Richard knocked at the door; the sound reverberated as though through an empty house. But shortly a candle flickered, and Lady Meta pulled open the door. She was wrapped in a shawl and looked pale and anxious.

"It's you. I'm so glad. You have come from Kit?" she asked.

"Yes, I have. He's all right, ma'am."

"Come in, do."

"I'll take my horse to the stable, if I may."

When he returned to the house, she was standing in the

center of the great bare drawing room. It was filled with a light bright glow.

"Warm yourself quickly," she said in a strained voice. "It's only paper."

Richard looked about. The foreign journals which had given the room its only cheerful touch were gone. Anger against Bannister exploded within him.

"I'll find something to make that a real fire," he said, and bolted out the door.

In the barn he hurriedly broke up some loose lumber. He ran back to the house, and soon the fire had a steadier flame. Lady Meta put off her shawl. She wore a pansy-colored sacque belted over black silk petticoats.

Her dark eyes were large and troubled. It was difficult for Richard to meet their gaze as he said what he had to say.

"Kit's not quite himself. He's been celebrating a bit too long. But he asked me to ride over to make sure you were all right—"

Her lips curled in a faint incredulous smile.

"You need firewood. What about food?"

"We have enough food."

"Well, you'll soon have enough firewood." He was glad of an excuse to leave her. He was glad too of the necessity for violent action. Seasoned wood sawed into stove lengths but still as big around as a half hogshead was piled against the barn. Richard caught up an axe and soon had a pile of properly small pieces at his feet. When he carried an armload into the kitchen he observed that Hanni was not there.

"She's not well," Lady Meta explained. "She has a bad cold, and this morning she insisted upon going out into the rain to look for wood. I made her go to bed. She is very precious to me . . ." Her voice trembled into silence.

After a moment she went on gayly. "However, Mr. Chal-

mers, I can cook. Perhaps you remember—the chicken shooting—how we made coffee. Won't you stay to supper with
me? Don't refuse. I've been so lonely—"

"I can't stay," Richard said. "They're expecting me back."

"Of course. I am sorry. It is a party, I know—"

"That's not the reason—" He broke off and flushed. Lady
Meta flushed too.

"And again of cour-r-rse," she said. The foreign tones
came out in her voice. She walked violently across the room.
"Herr Gott, you English!" she said.

Presently she paused in front of him.

"But I shall give you a cup of tea, at least. I insist upon
it. Even if, as a consequence, they say you are my lover."

She laughed, and Richard laughed with her, although he
was shocked at her words.

She made the tea awkwardly. When he saw how undexter-
ous she was at this small household task, he hoped that her
Hanni would soon be well. He drank the tea uneasily.

"When do you think Kit will be home?" she asked.

"By tomorrow, certainly. But just in case he should be delayed—I'm sending a message to Bob Whipp—"

"Thank you," she said stiffly.

Her position, he was aware, was intolerably humiliating.

He put his cup on the table, and they walked to the window together. The storm had subsided; the twilight world
was wintry white.

"Just think," she said, looking out. "It is only October.
Does winter—in this land—come so early?"

"Every trace of this snow will be gone by tomorrow,"
Richard answered. "You will have weeks of fine weather
yet."

"But this makes one feel the winter," she said in a low
voice.

He put on his cape, and she caught up her shawl, following him to the door.

"You are going to see England," she said.

"Yes," he answered.

"Look at London for me. Will you?"

"I live in the country, you know. But I'll go up to London."

"For my sake?"

"For your sake."

"And tell me about it in the spring."

He opened the door—the dusk smelled freshly of snow—and she put out her ringed hand, holding her head high. But when Richard looked into her eyes, he saw that they were full of tears.

She tried to ignore them. "Goodbye. You have been very kind—" And suddenly she was sobbing in his arms. Richard held her painfully. He kissed her soft cheek.

He knew that she clung to him not as a woman who loved, but as a woman who was terrified and lonely. Yet the pressure of her body, the silkiness of her cheek, caused him to tremble.

"I hate to leave you," he said.

"I hate—to have you go."

"Can't I look up your people in England, tell them how things are?"

"No, no. They didn't want me to marry Kit."

She pulled herself away and brushed the tears from her eyes.

"I am all right now. Forgive me. *Auf Wiedersehen.*"

When he returned on his horse, she still stood in the doorway, holding her shawl about her. Richard lifted his hand, and she smiled; but she did not speak again.

A good thing, thought Richard, striking his horse, that he

was going. He would be wise, he knew, never to return. But could he bear not to see her again? And even if he could bring himself to such a resolution, could he possibly ask permission to abandon the Minnesota enterprise? What could he tell his father that would justify such a request?

That the English had paid more than the market price for their land? But it was worth all they had paid and more. That the locusts had eaten their crop? But the locusts would not come again. The land was fertile, the locusts were gone, the colony—as Crockett had promised—was made up of gentry. He could hardly tell his father that he was afraid to trust himself with another man's wife.

Halfway down the drive he turned his head. Lady Meta still stood in the doorway, motionless, wrapped in her shawl. He remembered that she had stood so, as still as an enchanted figure, on the station platform at La Crosse.

BOOK TWO

CHAPTER ONE

WHEN Richard swung off the train at Sisseton City on an evening late in the following April, he was surprised and moved by his response to the now familiar prairie world.

He had not known that he loved the prairie sky, that vast ethereal arch, complete, uninterrupted, compensating by the variety of its shifting clouds and changing colors for the monotony of the land beneath. He had not known he loved it, but he knew when he saw it now, flushed with evening, bending majestically above the little town, satisfying to the soul and eye.

He had not known that he had come to love the prairie, but certainly affection swelled in him as he rejoined it, the great spring-awakened plain, smelling of dewy evening, which lay about the town.

The planted groves, rising to the east, the low timber following the stream to the west, were as familiar to him as the face of Si Joslin whom he espied waiting on the platform. Si had not changed; nothing, it seemed, had changed. (Richard's look—had he known it—had changed, between this April and the last one.)

Almost imperceptibly the brightness of his youth had dimmed. He was not yet twenty-three. His hair was as crisply gold as ever, his color as youthfully high. But his blue eyes were less eager. Faint lines hardened the expression of his mouth. He had come last year and left defeated. Would he leave this year, defeated? Would he, indeed, leave at all?

His face lightened in his slow smile as he shook hands with Si. It was good to be back, he said, surprised to find that he meant it. Then he hurried to the baggage car to assist in unloading Kentish Beauty. His father had made him a present of the mare—she was out of Squire Chalmers' own prize Beauty by Brigadier, the finest stallion in Kent. The Squire had kept her for Richard since her birth; she was now almost four years old.

She was a beautiful animal, high-necked, small-footed, with a shining brown coat marked with white. She whinnied at sight of Richard, and he fondled her nose.

"No more baggage cars for you!" he told her. "You go the rest of the way with me on your back."

When he had saddled her, he led her out proudly. She was as unlike the solid farm horses gathered at the station as Richard himself in his London clothes was unlike the farmers in overalls who welcomed him with shouts or laconic salutes.

"You're coming to me for the night?" Joslin asked. But Richard shook his head. He found himself anxious to be on his way.

"Beauty needs exercise," he said. "I'll get started now if you'll ask Beatty to bring my traps tomorrow."

"I've added a wing to the hotel and put in that billiard table."

"Good!" Richard cried. "Does that mean that more English have come?"

"*More* English! *More* English! Have you any left in London?" Si roared at his joke. "There's been a regular procession since March. And not just bachelors! Lord, you should see the Hallidays. You may, at that," he added.

"They made such a late start. You'll likely catch 'em on the road."

"And who are the Hallidays?" Richard asked.

"An English family. Thirteen strong, counting the pa and ma. Plenty of young ladies amongst 'em too," said Joslin with a waggish shake of the head. "Ought to make wives for some of you young bucks."

Richard laughed and mounted to Kentish Beauty's back.

As he cantered into the west, following as of old the distant line of timber which marked Chanyaska Creek, he realized that Joslin's pleasantry had stirred the thought of Lady Meta. It was a thought which he seemed always to be trying to suppress. He was deeply disturbed by his preoccupation with Bannister's wife. More than any other factor, it had caused him to dread the return to Minnesota. He detested his house, to be sure, but if he got a good harvest he would build another. He would, in any case, send the Martins packing. With Kentish Beauty, Nellie, and Shot, he had the beginning of a home. It would be pleasant to shoot and fish with Trevenen and Hook, to see Bob Whipp again. But there was no gainsaying that his feeling for Lady Meta threatened trouble.

He was definitely aroused by her. He had struggled to transform what he felt for her into friendship—he thought he was succeeding—but he was not helped by his conviction that she shared his emotion.

Richard was the son of a happy united home. He had no wish to become entangled with another man's wife. He had an urgent wish not to become so entangled, and resolved again for the thousandth time to avoid the Bannisters. Upon that resolution he quickened Kentish Beauty's pace.

The sun was lower now; the towering heavens were gloriously painted with blood-red and tawny rivers, with flame-tipped purple peaks, with calm lakes of aquamarine. Meadow larks tossed globes of song over the sweet-smelling prairie. Now and then Richard passed a farmer ploughing, stealing the last burnished daylight hour.

He had left Chanyaska Creek and was well past the southerly turn when he heard far ahead the sound of singing. Peering into the gathering dusk, he saw what appeared to be almost a cavalcade. A three-seated lumber wagon was attended by three horsemen—one riding on either side and one behind. The horsemen, he could see as he drew near, were young men; tall, fair-headed, all of them. But there must be girls in the wagon, for the song held the chime of lighter voices. They were singing a round; it took Richard back to England, to his school days:

> *"Come to dinner, come to dinner,*
> *There's the bell, there's the bell,*
> *Bacon and potatoes, bacon and potatoes,*
> *Ding dong bell, ding dong bell."*

With a burst of laughter, they began again at the beginning:

> *"Come to dinner, come to dinner,*
> *There's the bell . . ."*

Kentish Beauty trotted alongside the hindmost horseman.

"Hello," said the boy, eyeing Kentish Beauty with swift admiration.

"Hello," said Richard, smiling. "Are you the Hallidays?"

"Right."

"I'm Richard Chalmers."

"And you're English too. How jolly!" said the boy. "Come on and meet Father." He led the way to the lumber wagon. The song died down in an excited buzz of conversation.

The daughters of the house with one or two younger boys occupied the back seats of the wagon. Richard saw a blur of tall girls with chignons; small girls with flowing hair; small boys in sailor suits; dogs; a bird cage.

The father and mother sat on the forward seat, the father holding the reins. He was a tall bearded man, made taller by a towering silk hat, and Richard was to learn that he rarely relaxed from that aloof dignity which so successfully shields a father against too-great familiarity from his children. But the shrewd eyes above graying whiskers had the light of humor in them. Mrs. Halliday was likewise tall. (No wonder, thought Richard, that the three young horsemen were six feet high.) She was a tall woman who would always be slender, though clearly she did not much concern herself with the fashionable apparel which her figure would have justified. Her mantle, her wide bonnet were suitable but not modish. Her hair, like her husband's, was somewhat gray. Her eyes were youthful and unclouded, her mouth tender. There were lines in her face, but her skin was fresh as a rose.

Both parents shook hands cordially with Richard. Then the mother spread a half amused, half admiring gaze over her brood.

"It's a long task for me to introduce the children. But it goes quickly when they do it for themselves."

The young horsemen, as from frequent practice, ranged alongside one another, facing the new acquaintance. The boys in the wagon sprang to their feet. The girls stirred zestfully and turned toward Richard their bright merry faces. Richard, from experience gained in a home where such performances were rehearsed with gusto, perceived that the Hallidays were about to present for his amusement, and also their own, a gay bit of family ritual. He waited.

The tallest horseman squared his shoulders.

"Jim," he cried, and thumped his chest.

Like bass bells in a chime the other sons continued the play.

"Reg," said the second horseman.

"Charley," called the lad who had acted as Richard's guide.

"Gerald," came the first voice from the wagon.

"Albert," said a child with solemn care.

Then it was the daughters' turn, although they modestly refrained from thumping their breasts. Instead each pointed an identifying finger at a spot about midway between throat dimple and solar plexus. "Dora." "Catherine." "Elizabeth." "Geraldine." "Margaret." "Victoria."

Richard made a bow which tried to acknowledge all the introductions at once. Then eleven out of the eleven young Hallidays began to talk.

"Is there good hunting here?" "Is that an American horse?" "Is Rainbow pretty?" "Do you like Minnesota?"

Richard seized that question.

"You'll like it better after you get to know it than you will at first," he said.

A girl answered in a clear voice: "Oh, we're sure we'll like it. It's in the stars."

The flood of questions poured on.

"Are there many English here?" "Do you have balls?" "Have you found it to be true that the soil is good for beans?"

Richard tried at first to answer, but he gave up the attempt and laughed instead. While he dealt with one question, ten more showered about him.

Mr. Halliday asked him what part of England he came from. When Richard told him, Mrs. Halliday found that she knew some one in his village: Miss Gibbs, the vicar's sister.

Miss Gibbs was little and persistent and shrill. She made Richard think of a cricket. He had often dodged her in the churchyard after Sunday morning services. But it was a delight to find some one in America who knew her.

"You don't say, ma'am! Miss Gibbs!" He blushed with pleasure.

The Hallidays were from Shropshire, they said, though of late years Mr. Halliday had been a merchant in Leeds. He hoped, he said, to open a shop in Rainbow. Richard hoped that he would, and chuckled as he anticipated Judson Oates's chagrin.

Little by little the color in the sky had faded. Even along the horizon no trace of pink remained. Stars appeared, mere pin pricks in the vasty sky. Frogs began to clamor in the sloughs.

They had made a late start, Charley remarked to Richard. And a broken axle had delayed them on the road. But it did not matter, for the trail was plain and they knew where they were going; Jackson had engaged lodgings for them with a family of the town. They would live in lodgings, he added, while they built a house on their land.

"I hope to God it's good land," Richard thought fervently. He asked where it was located.

"Near the village, I believe. On Flower Lake."

"That should be good," said Richard, reassured.

He had slowed his pace to the pace of the cavalcade. Its comradeship, its friendliness surged about him, carried him on. He felt that he marched with a conquering army.

The night deepened, and stars in uncounted millions powdered the heavens. The Hallidays started to sing again, in parts. They were plainly adept at part singing. Richard liked to sing too, and presently he joined the basses. The prairie rang to "All Among the Barley," "England, Beloved England," "The March of the Men of Harlech." The younger children snuggled into the older daughters' laps. They fell asleep to the roll of the wagon, the beat of hooves, the sound of singing.

Lights twinkling far ahead took even Richard by surprise. There was an eddy of excitement as the party entered Rainbow. Richard guided them to the house where their arrival was expected. He lifted out of the wagon one soft drowsy lump.

"You'll come to see us?" "You'll come to see us often?" All of them were cordial, none more so than the calm-faced mother. Busy as she was with the task of unpacking her brood, she paused to take Richard's hand.

Richard was warmed through and through. He waited until an American woman came out of the house with a lighted lamp, then he swung to Kentish Beauty's back and rode off, whistling.

He slept soundly in the loft of the Log House and was on his way to Little Goodlands early. The sun was strong. The lakes which he followed on his southerly course winked in innumerable golden ripples. Birds flew across his pathway bearing clay and wisps of grass in their beaks. Beneath the bare trees delicate spring flowers pushed through the mat of last year's leaves.

It would be pleasant, Richard thought, to begin the spring's business, to rake and burn, to plough and plant. The ploughs must already be busy on his land, for he had written Martin to engage men and begin. When he reached his own fields, he found that they were indeed humming with activity. Ploughs, horses, and men were making his broad acres ready for the planting.

Martin sighted him and came to the roadside. His greeting was cheerful enough. At once, however, he blurted out sorry news.

"Has anyone told you that the hopper eggs are hatching?"

"You mean—they didn't winter-kill?"

Richard was aghast. It was known that the locusts had laid eggs before departing, but no one had dreamed that these could survive the icy sword of a Minnesota winter.

Martin nodded glumly. "That warm day last week, they started popping."

Richard jumped from his horse and ran into the fields. The earth was alive with the tiny grotesque offspring of last summer's visitors. He strove to conceal the sickness of heart which the sight of them created.

"Smallish, aren't they?" he asked.

"Husky, though."

"Not husky enough, I fancy, to stand the cold weather we have here in May."

"On cold nights," said Martin, "they sleep all in a heap and keep each other warm."

"Well, some night will come along so jolly cold that they'll never wake up."

"I hope you're right. You think we'd better go ahead and plant, then?"

"By all means." Richard kept his casual tone. But a bleak despondency settled down upon him as he cantered away.

Hoppers! Was the whole fantastic cycle to begin again? And if so, what was the sensible course to pursue? Frowning with anxiety he turned in at the gate of his barnyard. Nellie and Shot rushed upon him in ecstatic welcome. But his ugly little house gave him no welcome. The dirt about the kitchen door almost approached squalor. Mrs. Martin was barefooted when she came to greet him, tucking wisps behind her ears.

"Why, Dick! We didn't expect you quite so soon or we'd have had things cleaned up around here."

Richard unsaddled Kentish Beauty, but before going out to his fields, he called the dogs and ran down the steep path which led to the lake. Here his rowboat was tied to a crude pier. The spot had served before as a place of refuge for him. He liked the sound of lapping water, the view of distant shores and wooded islands.

"I wish I'd cut away some of these trees and built my house on this bank." The failure to do so seemed the worst of all his infernal stupidities.

He untied the boat with urgent fingers. He would, by God! He would throw off this depression of spirits! It went beyond the discouragement caused by hopper eggs. It was what he had struggled with all last year—a blank despair.

He had felt no touch of it in England. An atmosphere of security, of fond approval had enveloped him as soon as he entered his father's door. He had been his own self there, peaceful, confident, and happy. But the enemy had not been conquered; it had only been waiting for him here at Little Goodlands. He seized the oars; the dogs, clumsy and eager, crowded into the boat.

Before he had pushed off, however, he heard voices on the bank.

"He was here a minute ago. He went down to the pier. I'll call him."

"No, no. I will find him. You may take the horse if you will."

The answering voice, low and musically somber, belonged to Lady Meta. Richard looked up to see her descending the path.

She wore a black riding dress, and a small round black hat, tied with a black scarf which floated out behind. She was thinner, he saw. Her face seemed all luminous black eyes. But a flashing brightness transformed her when she caught sight of him. She waved; he jumped to his feet; their hands met over the stern.

"Don't get out. I'll get in— May I? Will you put out those dogs?"

The dogs went out with hurt indignant yelps. A worldly faint perfume came into the boat with Lady Meta.

Their hands continued to clasp as she sank to a seat. He sat down opposite her. Her smile died, and she looked gravely into his face.

"You do not seem glad to be back."

"No. I'm not glad to be back." He had been last night, he thought, as the words fell from his lips, but all that buoyancy, that expectancy had passed.

"Of course not." She did not seem to resent his honest answer.

After a pause, Richard asked, "How was your winter?"

Her face twisted, and she turned it away.

"I don't know where to begin. Have you heard? . . . My Hanni died."

"Hanni? Oh, Lady Meta!"

"Yes. She was ill when you left. She never got better."

Tears sprang to her eyes, and she unclasped her hand to take out a handkerchief and dry them. Then she put the hand back into Richard's.

"My poor Hanni!" she said in a pitying voice. "And so— I was alone with Kit. Richard, it is not only that he drinks. Sometimes I think—he is not right. Otherwise he would not do the things he does . . ."

Her dark head swept down to her knees.

"God in heaven! What a winter!" he heard her sobbing softly.

She lifted her head at last. "*Ach*, it is over!" she said. "It is over, and the spring is here. Come, we will not even talk of it."

She dried her eyes again, put regardful fingers to her hair. This time she did not return her hand to his. She clasped her hands about her knees and dropped her gaze upon them. The boat, stirred by a breeze, which sent the water scudding in bright waves, rocked to their silence.

"There should be some happiness in life. Is it not so?"

Richard did not answer. The waves carried their drifting boat free of the pier.

She looked up at him, and he saw himself mirrored in her eyes; not in their dark pupils alone, but in an expression . . . It appraised and approved his strength, his shining youth. A smile slipped over her face.

"So!" she said, in tender challenge. "You are not glad to be back!"

Gone, vanished like the wave just broken on the shore, was Richard's thousandth resolve.

"You can make me glad!"

"I will, Richard," she whispered.

"You can make me glad, glad, glad . . ." he heard himself repeating.

A picture formed and floated before his eyes. The cavalcade of Hallidays, astride their horses, crowded in their wagon. Almost as it formed, it faded. But one face persisted after all the others had dimmed, the face of the girl who had said, "It's in the stars." He saw it for an instant as though it were a miniature, the sort that a man cherishes and carries next his heart. Wings of light brown hair, tanned cheeks touched with rose, wide expectant eyes . . . Then that too disappeared.

Lady Meta's eyes held him closer than her hands had

done. They were dreaming, full of promise. The perfume which he breathed did not come from the spring-awakened world but from her soft body, swaying toward him with the rocking of the boat. Her voice, low and laughing, broke through mazy clouds of rapture.

"Richard! Not here! Richard! There are too many Martins about."

The boat, of the wind's volition, had floated some yards from shore—a few shining yards from the steep tree-crowded bank, a mile, perhaps, towards the nearest island, a clump of yellowing willows. Richard shook himself sharply; his hands set upon the oars. Lady Meta, as he rowed, filled his view.

CHAPTER TWO

THERE was some truth, Richard discovered, in Si Joslin's report of regiments of English marching into Crockett County. The immigrants now made a sizable colony around the lakes of Rainbow. There were the Lovells, just such a prosperous, middle-class family as the Hallidays. There were the Scatchetts, the Burne-Smiths and the Throops. Unmarried recruits had come, faintly aghast at the scarcity of women in the new land and inclined to envy those who, alone the year before, were this year sustained by brides, or wives with full-fledged families.

The colony was, on the whole, genteel. "Tolerably genteel," Lady Throop always phrased it, in the letters she sent off interminably to London. (Letter writing was Lady Throop's major exercise, although a woman so large, so tightly corseted, and so short of breath might advisedly have taken to something more strenuous.) Both the army and the navy had contributed retired officers to reinforce Captain Bannister. These, incidentally, acknowledged their changed environment by accepting the Captain with no more than a glance at his record. They were humanly curious enough to want to make sure that he was the same fellow, but having found out that he was, they let the matter rest. The church was embodied in several sons of clergymen as well as in Barrowcliff, the archbishop's nephew. Graduates of Oxford and of Cambridge now walked the streets of Rainbow (and had to repeat their requests in Judson Oates's store before their broad *a*'s and clipped *r*'s became intelligible).

Lady Meta was no longer, of course, the only person of rank. To be sure, Sir Mortimer Throop had democratically waived his title. He announced that in America he was plain Mortimer Gerald Cyril Henry De Quincey Throop, Esquire. But Lady Throop did not at any time relinquish her appellation, and her breath grew short and plainly audible with resentment when anyone ignored it.

Richard had acted true to race when he decided so spontaneously to plant in spite of the menace of the locusts. All the English planted. Moreover, with true British tenacity they planted beans. Over an incredible number of acres, nothing but the humble legume. No corn, no grain—they but grudgingly gave space to kitchen gardens. They wanted more and still more of the beans in which Crockett had inspired their faith. Beans and only beans, they felt, would make (or repair) their fortunes and take them back to England, rich men, in seven years.

The fame of the Britishers' beanfields spread that season far beyond the confines of the county. Marveling sightseers from all sections of the state came to inspect them. Editors all over the state described them with extravagant admiration— and did not fail to note what Crockett County had noted so amazedly the year before, that the English did not personally either plough or plant. The older Halliday boys might have been found coatless in the fields, but they were exceptions and served only to make the general rule more striking. The main body of the Englishmen watched the work from horseback (or went fishing if the day were fine).

The *Crockett County Gazette* serialized the story of the bean fields in its items of personal intelligence:

"Wanted by Mr. Halliday: Eight teams for ploughing."

"Captain Bannister requires six additional teams."

"Bids solicited for 2000 hardwood fence posts. Messrs. Trevenen and Hook."

In the *Gazette* the English were always "noble sons of Albion." The journal was full of references to "true British pluck" and "British pertinacity and courage." These multiplied as the season progressed. It was just that they should do so; for the virtues they extolled were indeed exemplified by Rainbow's English colony that summer.

The young locusts did not die. By the time the beans showed green, they were able to nibble off that green, and they lost no time in doing so. Stonily, stubbornly, the British planted again. The young hoppers gained wings and took their flight. The beans showed green a second time and hope, like a cool breeze from the sea, swept the unhappy prairie country.

"Shoo, grasshoppers, don't bodder us!" sang Bob Whipp, who was working in Richard's fields since the locusts had taken his own spring planting. But the hoppers did not hear or heed his injunction.

Toward the end of July a new army appeared out of the west. Riding the wind, full-grown and hungry, the host descended upon Crockett County's beanfields and wiped off the crop as cleanly as fire would have done.

"Here's to next year!" said the colonists, some in one way and some in another.

The more temerarious gathered in that new wing of the Farmers' Home of which Joslin was so proud. They ringed the imported billiard table and raised their glasses high.

"A plague on the locusts great and small, and all their sons and daughters!"

"I say, drink to Crockett!" Trevenen shouted.

"Crockett!" Captain Bannister cried bitterly, and sent his untouched glass crashing through a window.

The others could meet this calamity light-heartedly, he thought. They did not have his broken dream of a regenerating security. He stared at them defiantly with brilliant, blazing eyes. Richard Chalmers, his face sober, turned his eyes away.

The Hallidays, the Lovells, and the other solid families took the disaster in their stride. Turning away from their ravaged fields, they planned ventures into business. Halliday carried out his intention of opening a shop. Oates's store, although Oates would not admit it, no longer filled the needs of the rapidly growing town. Lovell, who had come well heeled, organized a bank. Barrowcliff was still weighing opportunities. He leaned toward a lumbering mill, but there was so little lumber . . .

The family men proceeded also to organize a church. Wardens and vestrymen were elected; contracts were let for the erection of a building. Meanwhile, services were held in the hall above Oates's store. It seemed strange not to pray for the Queen.

She was toasted often enough in the English Club which Captain Bannister promoted. The organization was called a club; much was made of the fact that in the clubrooms home journals were available. But everyone knew that liquor was also available, that nominating the place a club was merely a means evading the restrictions imposed by a temperance town. The Americans winked at the evasion; they were understandably indulgent to their "noble sons of Albion."

There was hurdle racing at the Eyrie. There was cricket—likewise at the Eyrie. The Americans gathered in numbers to watch that singular game. There was boat racing on all the lakes, for the English had imported racing shells as well as sailboats; Richard, Harry Earle, Trevenen, and Hook comprised the winning team. Trevenen and Hook had sent to Virginia for foxhounds. There would be organized hunts in the autumn. In the autumn too there would certainly be balls. The handsome houses springing up around the lakes cried out for balls.

The English for the most part did not scatter to the prairies. If Crockett had sold them land there, they abandoned it, and bought new land from the Americans, impoverished by locusts and all too eager to sell. They built on the wooded lake shores, close to one another and close to the village. Few of them required town houses. The Throops, of course, had a house in Rainbow as well as Pinewood on Crystal Lake. But the former was hardly a necessity.

The Hallidays were building on Flower Lake. Their park would slope down to its waters. Green Lawn, they had already named their home after the sward they saw now in the mind's eye only. It was a fine spacious house. All summer long the building of it had kept Rainbow agog. In Rainbow it was never called a house. It was invariably "the Halliday mansion."

The *Crockett County Gazette* reported on it faithfully. It was three stories high; it boasted eighteen rooms; a seven-hundred-dollar veranda would surround it. Visitors were forbidden to enter the structure except during work hours; but while the workmen sawed and pounded, the inquisitive trooped through.

The family was scattered. The senior Halliday had found that accommodations in Rainbow were excessively rude. He and his older sons were still in lodgings in the town, but Mrs. Halliday, her daughters, and the younger children were summering in Mankato.

An incident of which Mr. Halliday was unaware took place there.

Dora Halliday swept into the room she occupied with her sister in Mrs. Higgins' Select Boarding House, bearing a handful of letters.

"Cathy! Cathy! Mail from home! And you and I have a round robin letter from Mill Cottage." (That was the school they had attended together in England.)

She paused in surprise, for the usually responsive Cathy did not answer. There was no leap to light feet, no widening of shining hazel eyes, no rush of words—none of the transport which Cathy often manifested towards pleasures far less thrilling than mail from home. There was only a hasty ineffectual attempt to conceal the litter of papers, books, and pencils with which her table was spread.

"You don't need to put your things away because *I* come into the room," Dora said indignantly.

She was the oldest sister, although the smallest of the three who had attained their teens. She was dark where the others were blonde, or close to blonde, gently dignified. Cathy adored her and grew penitent at once at the reproach.

"I was working on a chart," she said, a little breathlessly.

"But I know all about your astrology, darling. I think it's wonderful. Didn't you see Vic's measles in the stars, and Charley's broken arm, and our coming to America? I wouldn't tell Father for the world. Whose chart is it? May I know?"

Cathy's soft color deepened.

"If you like. It's Richard Chalmers'."

"Richard Chalmers? You mean the young man who guided us into Rainbow?"

"Yes."

"He was very good-looking," Dora said reflectively.

Cathy did not answer. She sat looking down at a sheet of scented paper on which the heavens were charted.

"Have you seen him since that night?" Dora asked.

Cathy shook her head.

"Then how did you come to know his birth date?"

"Before we came away—I gave Gerry my telescope—to find it out."

"Your telescope? Your *telescope?*" Dora was incredulous. The telescope, as all the family knew, was Cathy's dearest possession.

"He'll loan it to me sometimes," Cathy said, speaking now in her usual eager rush. "And he earned it. It wasn't so easy for him to find out—all I needed to know—without letting anyone suspect."

"That day he went fishing! The day he was *supposed* to go fishing."

Cathy nodded.

"The young rascal!" Dora breathed. Then, as the romantic significance of Cathy's revelation struck home, she blushed as furiously as though the revelation had been her own.

"Cathy!" she cried. "You're not—you don't really mean that you're in—"

Cathy rose abruptly. Her flowered morning dress with its tightly buttoned bodice, its skirt demurely bouffant and gravely long, added maturity to a straight slender figure. She was not so much pretty as radiant; radiance lay in her light movements, in her eager speech, but especially in her eyes. Between wings of light brown hair, above tanned cheeks touched with rose, Cathy's eyes looked out on life with a glowing expectancy.

"Dora," she said, "you might as well know. I am in love with that young man."

"Cathy!"

"It's true," she answered. She walked quickly across the room to her sister's side.

"Dora," she said, "do you consider me frivolous?"

"No-o-o," reflected Dora. "No, I don't. You like to dance, you like fun, and pretty clothes. But Mother depends upon you, ever so much. No! Of course, you're not frivolous."

"And I've never been in love before."

"Not that I know of."

"Come now, you'd know. Have I ever cut out pictures of the Prince of Wales or Mr. Irving, kept hair in a locket, or sent valentines, like Bess? Have I now?"

Dora shook her head.

"And have I ever been soft about the young men Jim and Charley are always bringing about?"

"No," said Dora, laughing. "Plenty of them have been soft about you."

"Well, they needn't be," said Cathy. "For I'm in love with Richard Chalmers. I intend to marry him, too."

Dora put her hands to her ears.

"Cathy!"

"I know," said Cathy. "It sounds bold. But don't worry. I won't let him see. We're meant for each other, Dora. Look at our charts." She fled back to the littered table and found two sheets of scented paper on each of which the heavens were charted in a wheel-like figure. "I am Aries-born, he is a Sagittarian; and with the conjunction of my Jupiter to his Moon in the seventh house, there should be great happiness." She halted to frown. "But I can't understand this delay unless it is a temporary affliction of Saturn."

"Cathy," said Dora, "forgive me. But are you sure, darling, it's not just that he's so very handsome?"

Cathy swept the papers into a drawer and closed it with a

click. She turned upon her sister, her eyes glowing, her cheeks flushed.

"He happens to be handsome," she said. "I can't help that. I can't even say that I would have fallen in love with him if he had been as ugly as sin, for—he's not as ugly as sin. He's just as he is, and I love him."

Dora took her sister's hot cheeks between her hands and kissed her on the forehead.

"I shan't say anything more," she said. And then she asked promptly, "But what do you expect to *do* about it?"

Cathy looked troubled.

"Why do I have to do anything?" she asked. "I will, of course, if I have to. But why shouldn't *he* do something? Other men do."

"Of course. I dare say he will," Dora said comfortingly.

Cathy's face took on again the expression of mystic abstraction that it always wore when she studied the science of the stars. She pulled open the drawer, took out once more the sheets of scented paper.

"Perhaps he won't," she murmured. "He is coming into a very bad aspect—his Venus is frightfully afflicted by Uranus."

She slipped again into her chair, picked up her pencil. Dora, with an awed glance, tiptoed out of the room.

CHAPTER THREE

THE Rainbow Hunt was inaugurated on a Saturday early in October. The meet was called for eleven o'clock; it was not yet midday when the tardiest horseman cantered up the avenue of beeches leading to the Eyrie to join the expectant cavalry milling on the lawn. Yet when one surveyed the world from that lofty place where Hook and Trevenen had built their house, it seemed to be the hour of sunset. The sky, to be sure, was a noonday blue. The sun was properly high in the heavens, striking through the scattered clouds impartially in all directions. But certainly a sunset was apparent in the mad confusion of colors which autumn had spilled upon the world. It ran over the prairies in a mingling of purple, red, and orange. It swam in the lake where trees of lemon-yellow, of copper-pink, of ruddy brown were reflected in the water. Golden clouds lay on distant fields where planted groves had been rooted yesterday.

"Capital day for scent," remarked one rider after another, which being interpreted out of British reticence meant that the world was a glory of color, that the air tasted like iced wine, that it was well to be alive, to be in Minnesota, to be in pursuit—shortly, so one hoped—of a fox.

The foxhounds had come only the preceding Wednesday from Virginia, and few members of the English colony were missing from the company assembled at the Eyrie. Not all of those present would follow the hunt; but they would at least watch its departure, they would lunch at the Eyrie and return in the evening for the Hunt Ball. No colonist would have been willingly absent upon this day of days, even had he been obliged to come astride a mule.

No mules were present, and only a few too stalwart horses hinted of the plough. There was a good proportion of finely bred hunters, long-necked, lean animals, quivering in anticipation of the run. Red coats gleamed here and there, worn with white breeches and high patent leather boots. Hook, the Master of the Hounds, was thus attired, and Trevenen who was serving as whipper-in. The ladies were in sweeping habits of black or dark blue cloth, with high-perched round small hats.

The ladies expected and received but small attention. The hounds were the cynosure of eyes. Most of the men had found time since Wednesday to pay their respects to the pack, but it was one thing to see twelve couple of trained hounds in their kennels and another to watch them led out, ready for work. Now their heads and tails were erect. Whips were needed to curb their bristling eagerness. They did not yet move with the machinelike precision which Trevenen desired, for they were bewildered by their strange surroundings and the inexpert urgings of American farm hands transformed into grooms. But Trevenen, beautifully mounted on Solo, an excited smile graven on his face, was everywhere at once, and the hounds were a credit to him, and to Hook, and to the Rainbow Hunt.

"They lack some of the points one would expect in a Leicestershire pack, but they're a good even lot," Sir Mortimer Throop—finding his hunter alongside Kentish Beauty—remarked affably to Richard.

"They'll give us fine sport, certainly," Richard agreed.

Harry Earle, erect on a gaunt impatient gelding, joined in.

"It's the best trained pack in the States. You'll have to cross the Atlantic to find one better."

"Have you gents had some of this?" A freckle-faced boy proffered a tray laden with small glasses. "Mr. Hook said I wasn't to miss anybody."

The three horsemen accepted their glasses and inspected a whitish liquid curiously.

"It's made out of currants," the boy volunteered. "Soaked in whiskey. There's ginger in it too. Mr. Hook made it himself, and he said, 'Any lad who drinks a glass of this will never funk a fence!'"

Harry Earle burst out laughing.

"By Jove! Jumping powder!"

"Success to fox hunting!" said Sir Mortimer, lifting his glass, and the three men, laughing, drank the toast.

Even before the fiery liquor found his veins, Richard was aware that he was happy, happier than he had been for months. He held a light rein on Kentish Beauty, who was dancing with impatience, and looked out across the animated field. He sighted Lady Meta's graceful figure. She was wearing the black habit she had worn the day she sought him out at Little Goodlands. She was very lovely, and she had been kind to him; but she had not made him happy.

He was not, he had told himself a little contemptuously more than once over the summer, he was not a man of the world. He was a man, where he had been a boy last year, but he was not a man of the world. No passage of time could transform him into such a casual hedonist as—Trevenen, say, who took his pleasures where he found them, untroubled and serene.

Richard had been constantly troubled by his relationship with Meta. His self-condemnation was not accompanied by any condemnation of her. He had no censure for her who had been graciousness and beauty to him, who had wiped out sometimes for a few hours his homesickness, his self-mistrust, the memory of his empty fields and dreary house. Bannister's cruelty had justified her, and she loved Richard quite as much as her light code demanded.

But Richard did not love her as much as his code demanded. That, he sometimes thought, was at the root of his guilt. He was straightforward by nature. But a liaison would not have given him this shame and self-aversion if he had been truly, faithfully in love. He well knew that he was not in love at all.

She was not his kind of woman. He had known that all along. She was civilized according to Continental standards— that was her way of pointing the difference between them.

"You English with your love of horses and hounds, your passion for hunting—you are barbarians, really."

She had said it in affection, laughingly, but she had meant it.

Well, perhaps she was right, Richard conceded now. Certainly, as the hounds were thrown off and the hunters cantered out to their work, he felt an uprush of primitive joy.

After a quarter of an hour's exploration, a hound gave tongue. The scent was good, and shortly the pack was off in full chase, the field of mounted hunters galloping after. The bay of the hounds, the cry of tallyho were music to Richard's ears. He was exhilarated by the smooth rise of Kentish Beauty's body as she took the first snake fence.

That first fence, into Judson Oates's pasture, was not formidable. All the hunters achieved it safely. The second one stood in a slough.

"Neville has taken a cropper!" Bannister shouted.

Richard looked back to see the handsome Yorkshireman picking himself out of the mud.

Most of the women, he noticed, had turned back. The diminished line of riders proceeded with augmented zest. The pace sharpened.

On through the slough, scattering blackbirds! Up and down hill! Over another snake fence and across a field. An American farmer, busy at fall ploughing, waved an enthusiastic arm. The fox led them for some miles around the border of a lake. Timber there made it hard going. Then he struck open prairie, and the pursuit changed to a glorious breath-taking gallop.

It became clear now that the hounds had lost the fox, but the loss did not seem catastrophic. He would afford them a run another day. Who, Hook shouted, was hungry enough to eat? Everyone was, it appeared. The hounds were whipped off, and the hunters turned back toward the Eyrie.

One woman had stayed with the hunt—a tall girl in a blue riding suit, with lively light brown hair which floated in the wind. Richard saw that she was a Halliday girl, the one he had liked. Meeting his eye, she waved her hunting crop. He smiled and saluted in return. But he did not ride over to her side. Instead, for the ride back to the Eyrie, he joined the group which was rallying Percy Neville.

The meal was set out on side tables around which hungry hunters were crowding. There were rounds of beef and ham, boiled chickens, cold game pies; there were vegetables in silver dishes having hot-water wells underneath; there were grapes and apples in autumnal piles, pots of tea and coffee. It was all presented with full benefit of gleaming napery and shining silver service, for Miss Tabby Joy now presided at the Eyrie.

Miss Joy had undertaken the American adventure. Sometimes Hook and Trevenen wished she had not found the necessary courage. But Miss Joy quailed at nothing. (Her employers quailed only at her.) Tall, thin, with a red false front and the stiffest of caps, collar and cuffs aggressively snowy on a dress of scratchy black rep, a black silk apron and a bunch of keys which rattled like a summons to doom, Miss Joy ruled the Eyrie with the firm hand it required. Drinking, she permitted; gambling, she permitted; hounds and oaths and fighting, she permitted. Men will be men, she was wont to remark icily when called upon to defend her sufferance of these things. But dirt she did not permit. Hook and Trevenen wiped their feet. And meals at the Eyrie were not only served on time; they were eaten when they were served.

"Dash it all, we might as well be married, if we're going to be racing home like scared boys at meal time." Thus Hook and Trevenen were wont to complain.

Nevertheless, in spite of such rebellious murmurings, the masters of the Eyrie were proud of Tabby Joy, especially upon occasions such as this.

Nothing flustered Miss Joy; nothing tired her; nothing daunted her. They wished to have ten house guests? Very well. Luncheon for sixty or seventy-five? Very well. A ball the same night. with a sit-down supper at midnight? Very well.

"If we had a royal command that Her Majesty the Queen was coming, Joy would only say, 'How many covers, Mr. Hook?' "

Certainly, she was proving their boasts today, Richard thought as he joined the crowd jostling shoulders in the dining room. The table seemed freshly set, although many of the company had already eaten and gone. Meta had left with Lady Throop: the Bannisters were quartered for the night at Pinewood. Most of the English families who lived on outlying estates had been invited to houses nearer to the Eyrie for the duration of the festivities. Richard himself was staying at the Eyrie with Earle, the Neville brothers, and other favored cronies of the masters of the house.

He had just entered the dining room when Cathy Halliday came up to him. It was no wonder, Richard thought, that he had remembered her over the others. She was like a fresh wind, or—or—like a young fruit tree in full bloom. Her wide eyes were shining with the happy expectancy he had noted in them before. She spoke in an eager rush.

"Do you mind if I tell you? I think you ride frightfully well. My brothers are good riders, Charley especially, but they can't hold a candle to you."

Richard smiled. "It seemed to me," he said, "that all morning I was trying to keep up with you, and doing a poor job of it, Miss—"

"Cathy. I'm one of the three grown-up ones."

"Oh, you are, are you?" he returned, much amused.

"One of the three grown-up girls, I mean. Some of our brothers are older. But there are just three of us girls in our teens. Dora is nineteen, I'm seventeen, and Bess is fifteen. And do you know what we've done?" Richard shook his head. "Each one of us has taken a small child to tend. Dora's taken Vickie. Bess has taken Albert. And I have Maggie. Only I have Charley, too, and he's more care to me than Maggie."

"The one who rides so well?"

"Yes. He needs ever so much looking after."

"For example," Richard urged.

"Well—I let him in my window when he stays out after ten," said Cathy, and they both laughed.

"Father winds the clock at ten," she explained.

"I know. So does mine."

"Have you sisters?"

"Dozens!"

"Which one let you in the window?"

His own laugh sounding in his ears reminded Richard of home. He was startled to realize that he had not heard it often in America. It was hearty enough now. One had to laugh with this girl.

She turned toward a table. Clearly she assumed that they were lunching together.

But they were not.

Richard had anticipated such an encounter as this and had early determined how to deal with it. He would not divide his allegiance. So long as he was linked to Meta, however secretly, he was resolved to stand clear of any other tie. Casual friendships he was prepared for; but this, he realized, already promised more than that. He was drawn to this girl. He had never forgotten their one meeting, and the sight of her now stirred him afresh. He forced himself to speak positively.

"I hope you will excuse me, Miss Cathy. Hook is waiting for me. But do let me carve you some of this chicken before I go."

Cathy said nothing, and he carved the chicken in a sorry silence. Her gaze upon him was thoughtful, troubled. When he gave her the plate she spoke with a humility born of innumerable debates with frank brothers.

"Have I talked too much? Perhaps you don't like girls who talk."

"Oh, but I do!" Richard cried. He was dismayed. In none of his anticipatory resolves had he considered that the party of the second part might be disturbed by his attitude. "I do," he repeated. "I talk so poorly myself. When you talk you help me enormously."

"Do I?" Cathy asked. "Really?" Her sigh was tremulous with content.

Richard grew panicky. There must be no circumlocution, no delay.

"Goodbye," he said abruptly.

"Goodbye," said Cathy. Her voice was soft. She smiled. Two Nevilles, one Barrowcliff, Trevenen, and Harry Earle were waiting, Richard saw, for his place.

"Goodbye," he said again.

"Goodbye," said Cathy.

Richard made his way out to the stables. He had had no lunch; he did not want any.

There was nothing to do for Kentish Beauty. She had been excellently cared for; she had been watered and brushed, and now she was snorting with hearty pleasure over the last grains of oats in her feed box. Richard stroked her, lingered for a moment with his arm over her back.

He struck out into the Eyrie's woods, scuffling the red and yellow leaves. Once he paused, scowling, to kick at the stump of a tree. He walked faster and faster; squirrels and chipmunks raced out of his path. But, however fast his pace, he could not outstrip one thought. It pursued him to pierce him sweetly, not once but again and again.

"She likes me," Richard thought.

CHAPTER FOUR

"I'll stay away from her tonight," Richard resolved, peering between two lighted lamps into the mirror where his reflected image with anxious eyes and heedful fingers struggled with the loops and ends of his tie.

It was a white tie, for the ball was to be a most formal occasion. Hook and Trevenen had spared no expense in introducing the Rainbow Hunt; they were—in their own phrase—doing the thing up brown. The ball was to be as elegant as Miss Tabby Joy and a riotously welcomed remittance from England could make it. And Miss Tabby Joy could work wonders, as all of Rainbow knew, while the remittance from England was exceptionally large because of the locust plague, reported with calculated detail in the last several letters home.

An orchestra had come from Mankato. The musicians were being fed now and would be installed in the entrance hall under the stairs. Chambers in impeccable order awaited the ladies, their shawls and velvet cloaks. The drawing room and the dining room had both been cleared for dancing. Supper would be served in the billiard room at midnight. Champagne was already cooling in great tubs; oyster patties were rumored.

Richard missed his sisters more acutely than he had yet missed them since coming to America. He was unaccustomed to going to a party without having first undergone their reassuring scrutiny. Their cries of approval, their embarrassing praise of his blondness against the dark broadcloth of his long-tailed coat, their commendation of his tie, his pearl studs, his gloves bolstered his courage, strengthened him against the uncertainty he always felt when he heard the tuning of fiddles. He revolved before the dim recesses of his mirror. Harry Earle, with whom he shared a room, was absorbed in his own tie. He was intent, withdrawn. If his coat sat well enough to help along a conquest, what did he care how Richard's coat sat, or whether it sat at all?

"I could use some of Hook's jumping powder. What about you?" Richard said.

"I, too," responded Earle, springing out of reverie. "Gad, I'd rather take a fence than dance the schottische any day! By the way, isn't that Miss Cathy Halliday a charmer?"

"See you later," muttered Richard, and left the room abruptly.

A lamp had been lighted beneath the porte-cochère. Richard stepped out into the autumn night. He was met by the faint chill with which October quickens appreciation of its beauty. The smoke from distant burning prairies assailed his nostrils with its nostalgic smell. Clouds were moving lightly across a deep blue sky. In the east their fleecy masses were burnished by the rising moon. It was still concealed, but Richard knew it would be full tonight. He felt its hidden glory.

He strolled past the lighted kitchen. A confusion of savory odors emerged. Within, Miss Tabby Joy, a general in a stiff white cap, marshaled her raw recruits.

He walked to the lake, listened to its whispering, watched the dark waves which so soon would be painted with a lavish silver brush. He felt uneasy, reluctant to return to the house. But the roll of carriages was continuous now. Carriage lights sparkled like fireflies on the drive. He let himself in at last through the nine-foot door which admitted to the billiard room.

Ladies had possessed themselves of the Eyrie. They made free with it, overran it with the calculated ruthlessness which their sex is wont to show when admitted by sufferance to a masculine domain. The smell of tobacco and whiskey had yielded to the fragrance of perfume. Feathers tossed against the ice-blue walls. Long trains trailed gently over the wide floor boards which hitherto had known only the thumping assault of oversized boots.

The flag of the invaders was white and red, for white and red costumes were *de rigueur* tonight. But never before had white and red been combined in such variety. Snowy tarlatans and gauzes were set off by red sashes. Rosettes of red ribbon lifted white overdresses into impudent posterior puffs. Lady Meta wore gleaming ivory satin, with a necklace and bracelets of garnets and a coronet of garnets on her curls. Her roving dark eyes were bright. This was her world, or at least an acceptable counterfeit. She smiled at Richard as he bowed over her hand.

They spoke with each other but briefly. By agreement he was never conspicuous among her cavaliers. He asked her to save him a dance. Then he slipped unobtrusively into the background of males.

The piano was sounding an urgent "A" which the fiddles were anxiously trying to achieve, when there was a stir at the drawing-room door and Cathy Halliday came in.

Richard thought again of a wind, of blossoms showering down.

Other people than Richard, when Cathy Halliday entered a room, found their minds turning in the same instant to a bright confusion of lovely things, to memories which had—as a matter of fact—very little to do with Cathy. Like Richard they thought of flowers, or of dancing beams of light, or of larks singing. Now, mind you, Cathy did not sing like a lark. She was a joyous singer, but all of her sisters had more melodious voices. She was not flowerlike either, nor did her fine strong body resemble light. But there was within her so deep a well of happiness that her presence almost never failed to make other people happy, with the result that when they saw her they were inspired to remember those other sights and sounds which had also made them happy. Cathy did not tonight blow into the room; she did not fling herself into the room. She moved with that propriety and grace which her mother had instilled, and which a two-foot train required. But she made Richard think of the wind, which he loved, of a fresh spring wind entering.

As she paused in the doorway, there seemed to be a special bit of her fragrance, her beauty, and her charm for every person in the company. For at least an instant each one present felt himself to be the particular and special object of her attention and interest. So felt Richard (and indeed her eyes sought him out at once), but so also felt Harry Earle and Mrs. Lovell and Slabs Neville. Lady Meta said to Trevenen:

"Who is that charming girl? Won't you bring her over?"

Before he was able to do so, however, piano, violins, cello, and bass viol agreed upon a note. They swept into the stately music of the opening quadrille. Trevenen offered his arm to Lady Meta. Hook led out Lady Throop. The members of the company took their places—Richard found himself facing a bouncing Lovell girl.

When the quadrille ended, Richard escaped to the billiard room. There, because he was resolved to avoid another encounter with Cathy, he marooned himself while the program of waltzes, polkas, schottisches, and galops, interspersed with old-fashioned English square dances, ran its tuneful course. At first he found some good opponents for billiards. He and Hook had an excellent game. But as the evening advanced, as the musicians warmed to their work and the dancers— drugged by music and the familiar warmth and scent—forgot Minnesota and remembered only England, the billiard room emptied. At last Richard's exile was shared only by old Major Scatchett who had the gout and could not dance and was therefore devoting himself wholeheartedly to getting drunk. He became at last so garrulous that Richard stepped warily into the hall and straight into the path of Cathy Halliday.

She did not seem displeased.

"Aren't you going to ask me to dance?" she asked.

Richard murmured acquiescence.

"Now?" she pursued.

Now, he agreed.

The orchestra went into a waltz.

All of his life Richard was to remember that waltz. "Tales from the Vienna Woods," it was called; he knew its name, for his sisters had played it on the piano back in England. As Richard put his arm about Cathy, a Neville dashed up.

"See here, Miss Cathy! I've been looking for you everywhere. Isn't this my dance? Dick, you'll have to give her up."

Give her up? Richard felt the pressure of her slim straight body against his encircling arm. Their feet were already moving to the languorous measures of Johann Strauss's waltz. Give her up, at this enchanted moment? Give her up, now that his arms held her, when he could feel her heart beating softly against his own?

"I'm so sorry, Mr. Neville. But I promised this dance to Mr. Chalmers."

They moved away silently in waltz time.

"Tales from the Vienna Woods." As it unwound its silken evolutions, Richard's sullenness fell away, his confusion fell away. He felt only a pervading peace. Past and future ceased to exist. There was nothing but this moment, this flawless moment, this pure untroubled bliss. There was nothing but this eternity of waltzing with Cathy in his arms.

He liked to dance, especially to waltz, and Cathy moved like embodied music. Her head was slightly bent; her face wore the grave poetic expression it wore when she studied the zodiac. Then, as now, she dwelt on another sphere. Higher and higher she rose on the ascending spirals of the waltz. When she sank, it was to Richard's arms. On and on they danced, through the dulcet mutations of the music, silent and united.

It was partly because both of them were richly good to look at, partly because they danced with such harmony and grace, but it was also because their inner stillness penetrated the crowd that more and more of the dancers joined the on-lookers and more and more of the onlookers looked at Richard and Cathy.

Mrs. Halliday found herself thinking, "Cathy is very young to marry."

Mr. Halliday found himself thinking, "Well, I've nothing against the young man."

Sally Lovell found herself thinking, "It must be wonderful to be in love."

Hook found himself thinking of a girl in Dorset.

Old Major Scatchett, bleary-eyed at the doorway, found himself thinking confusedly of his youth.

Trevenen found himself thinking, "I always had the idea—for all they were so damned discreet—that there was something between Dick and Bannister's wife." And he glanced curiously at Lady Meta, who was dancing with Barrowcliff.

Lady Meta found herself thinking, "After all, I can't permit that." She would not, she resolved, subject her pride to such a blow as the loss of this lover would occasion.

Richard and Cathy, unaware of the maze of thoughts, moved surely through the mazes of the waltz.

When the dance ended, Richard did not gallantly clap his hands. He stood like a man awakening from a dream. Cathy, rose-cheeked, looked up at him and smiled. They walked as though by prearrangement through the drawing room and down the hall where the door had been opened to admit the cool night air, and out into the night.

The full moon, now unobscured by clouds, poured a lush white radiance over the world. The stars hung low, as they often do on the prairie.

Cathy drew her breath. She snatched a topic literally from the air.

"The Pleiades are back in the sky. Have you noticed? Or don't you know the stars?"

"Only Venus and the Big Bear."

"That's a pity. It's rather fun to find our familiar home stars over here in Minnesota."

"Are you homesick?"

"Oh, no! Not at all. Still it's pleasant to run upon a bit of England."

"I can imagine that."

"Can you? Then you must surely come to see us. Our house is a bit of England—a pretty noisy and rampageous bit, sometimes." She paused, then went on in a headlong rush. "We want you especially because—you see—you were our first friend here." Richard did not answer. Cathy added with slashing directness, "You *are* coming, aren't you?"

Richard also was direct by nature. He hated to lie. So he kept silent.

"Aren't you?" Cathy asked again.

When for a second time he did not answer, fear like a trickle of icy water ran down Cathy's spine. She turned and looked into his face.

"I shouldn't have lied," she said. "We don't want you because you were our first friend here. I—I want you."

Still Richard did not answer.

Trevenen swung through the doorway. By the light from the lamp still burning in the porte-cochère, his face bore the gratified expression of a stage supernumerary unexpectedly entrusted with a part. He made straight for Cathy.

"Miss Cathy, I've come with a royal command. Lady Meta Bannister thinks you waltz so beautifully—she wishes to meet you."

"Oh," said Cathy, "how kind of her! I'll be there presently."

"You had best go now," said Richard. He could not embroider the release with polite phrases. And having spoken it, he dared not linger. He knew she was quite capable of refusing to accept his departure. He left her to Trevenen and walked rapidly away toward a lake heartbreakingly overlaid with silver.

Cathy accepted Trevenen's arm.

Lying in her bed that night, after the lamp had been blown out, Cathy spoke to Dora.

"Dora, isn't Lady Meta Bannister Captain Bannister's wife?"

"Yes, dear. Isn't she lovely?" Dora, still excited by the ball, was eager for conversation.

"Oh, she's good-looking enough."

"Good-looking! She's a beauty. And why she wanted to come out here in the wilderness! She, an earl's daughter—"

Cathy interrupted. "Well, do earls' daughters have more husbands than other people? Are they allowed more, I mean?"

"Whatever are you talking about! You know they aren't."

Cathy was rudely silent. Dora at last sent a question over the bridge of dark. "What are you thinking of, Cathy dear? Tell me, please."

Cathy answered shortly, "Of the way she looked at me."

"Of the way she *looked* at you?"

"Yes—and of Richard's chart."

"Of Mr. Chalmers' chart? But what has Lady Meta to do with that?"

"It is *my* opinion," said Cathy savagely, "that *she* is the disrupting force. You remember I told you his Venus was afflicted—"

"Cathy, Cathy! Do you know what you are saying? Why, she's a married woman."

"I wish she'd remember it," Cathy replied.

Dora was silent, genuinely shocked.

Cathy felt the rebuke implicit in her sister's silence, but she was not contrite. She sat up, with a jerk of two neat braids tied with ribbons at the ends. Her arms in long white sleeves, ruffled at the wrist, clasped themselves fiercely about her knees. Dora could see her plainly in the light from a wasted moon pouring in silver opulence through the window.

CHAPTER FIVE

THE Americans of Crockett County found their gentlemen from England continually surprising but never more so than this autumn after the fox hunts were established.

"The damn fools!" one farmer after another would exclaim in a kind of admiring contempt as the cavalcade of hunters swept by. "The everlasting damn fools!"

Red-coated, white-breeched, booted and spurred, mounted on big horses with banged tails, the British galloped furiously, at risk of life and limb, in pursuit, seemingly, of twenty-four baying hound dogs, ugly brutes with flapping ears, who, in turn, raced in pursuit of—of all animals—a fox.

The Americans hunted for two simple practical reasons— for food and for skins. But this mad hunting of the British was purely for pleasure. It had to be so, with twenty or thirty grown men and a handful of ladies concentrating all their energies and hours of their time upon one trivial and useless fox. The pastime was doubly profitless, for they hunted at prodigious expense. The horses were pampered animals, worthless on a plough. The hounds, as all of Rainbow knew, had been obtained from Virginia at the cost of a small fortune.

There were other expenses incidental to the sport. In the heat of the chase the riders sometimes churned through cultivated fields. Their lunatic jumping over barriers in their path led to broken gates and fences. They paid for what they destroyed promptly, without argument. Sometimes, in fact, they overpaid.

Now and then, a Yankee would refuse their money.

"I've had my pay. You put on a good show. It's as good as a circus, any day."

When they encountered such a genial soul, the English would whip out their flasks. There were drinks all around— to the farmer, to fox hunting! For one reason or another, almost all the Yankees were glad to see the English tearing through their lands.

The only trouble with the performance was that there weren't enough foxes. Mr. Hook advertised faithfully in the *Gazette:*

"Information as to the whereabouts of foxes will be thankfully received by Cecil Hook, M.F.H."

But even if no fox could be found, the English rode to hounds. A wolf was an exciting substitute; and, lacking either fox or wolf, a rider in advance of the rest dragged a bag of aniseed over the ground. The hounds followed that scent, and the English rode after at a breakneck pace. That, to the Americans, was the ultimate folly.

"The everlasting damn fools!"

Bridey Whipp had heard much talk of the fox hunters, but she had never seen them. She wasn't one to go far from home. Sometimes she climbed on her pony and rode over to Lonabelle's. That was usually after her father had scolded her because she didn't see enough young folks.

When he did that she looked at him with a sidewise, half shy, half teasing glance that reminded him of her mother in their courting days.

"Don't you worry about me not meeting young folks," she would tell him. "If ever I find a 'young folks' that I think I can't do without, I'll know how to meet him."

So the argument would end in joking and in her going to Lonabelle's. But it wasn't going to Lonabelle's that Bob had meant when the argument started. It was going in to Rainbow to dances, or out to strawberry festivals and ice-cream socials, places where she could get herself a beau.

Not that Bob was seriously disturbed about her chances of getting a beau. She was exactly like her mother, and he had no difficulty remembering the pother her mother had thrown him in at will. He urged her to a more forward course than seemed natural to her only from a reluctant sense of obligation. Her mother, if she had lived, probably would have had a clearer sense of timing, would have known whether it was now wise to push the girl a little or whether it was right to hold off. But Bob knew only that a woman needed a husband—a husband meant children and a home of her own—and that husbands weren't found by sitting at home. Most young girls liked parties, the boisterous heated gatherings where mates were found, but Bridey didn't seem to.

"I like staying at home with you," she always insisted, putting her soft young arms about his neck. And her voice was so pleadingly sincere that Bob always yielded—or compromised on Lonabelle.

He found the situation the more puzzling because Bridey was pretty. "They don't come any prettier," he was wont to assert in perplexity to the cow as he milked or to the tips of his horses' ears as he drove into Rainbow. She looked, he sometimes thought, not unlike Ginger, the little tortoise-shell cat who was his only rival in her affections. Her soft curls, held back by a comb from her small earnest face, were just the reddish tint of Ginger's fur; so were her soft eyes; so were the tiny freckles sprinkled sparingly on her fair fine skin. She was tiny of feet, of hands, of waist, but she was a worker. She could accomplish as much in a day as a woman grown. Bob could never give over boasting of her—of what good jams and jellies she made, of how her butter and her cheese were the best in the county, of how she knitted his socks and comforters and made her own clothes . . .

She was wearing an apron of her own fashioning, a new pink and yellow apron, the day she made the acquaintance of a fox hunter.

Lonabelle had given her the remnants of cloth. They were hardly more than scraps. Anyone but Bridey, Lonabelle had said, would have put them into a quilt. Bridey had utilized the pink scrap for a bib and skirt. A ruffle of yellow outlined the skirt, and yellow provided the belt and pockets and trimming for the bib. It was a treasure of an apron.

Bridey hoped that so much yellow would take the curse off the pink. She should not wear pink, she knew, with her red hair. But she did fancy it so!—and she never wore the apron out of the dooryard. Even a red-haired girl, she thought, might risk a pink apron (well flounced with yellow) when she was all alone in her kitchen baking bread.

The last batch of loaves, tinted a delectable golden brown, had been drawn from the elevated oven of the stove. She had buttered the crust, enjoying the rich smell. Her father would like a slice, or half a dozen, with some fresh apple butter when he returned from Rainbow where he had gone to sell the calf. She was surveying her work with pride, her back to the door, when a wild yowl caused her to fling about.

Ginger rushed in like a miniature wild cat. Behind her, in pursuit, came a great hound. Bridey had a horrified vision of flapping ears, crimson tongue, gleaming slavering jaws . . . She leaped for Ginger. But she was too late.

Bridey screamed. The sky beyond the door was blotted out by a horse, then a blur of red and white swept into the room which was whirling about her head like a waved flag. She leaned against the wall, and through the slowly clearing haze saw a very young man strike the hound and pull it out of the room, saw him pick up Ginger's mangled lifeless form. He went out of doors, and when he returned his hands were empty. Bridey began to sob.

"I'm so frightfully sorry," he said.

Still Bridey sobbed, uncontrollably. She turned her head to the wall, and her soft curls clung to her cheeks.

"Is there anything at all that I can do?"

"Oh, go away! Please, go away."

She did not look around to see whether he had gone; but evidently he had stayed, for after her sobs were exhausted he spoke again.

"I say!" he said. "I feel terribly. Please tell me there is something I can do."

Bridey looked around then, her breath still quivering, and dried her eyes and cheeks with a yellow ruffle of apron. Although the man was so tall—all the English were giants, so her father said—he was not much older than herself. He had a round smooth face and brown tousled hair, and there were actually tears standing in his eyes.

Those tears touched Bridey's tender heart.

"I'm all right now," she said.

"But isn't there something I could do? When we injure chickens or cattle, we pay for them, but I suppose—"

"Oh, no, no!" she cried as his hand went to his pocket.

"I was afraid that wouldn't help. But I wish I could do something."

"You—you can help me bury Ginger," said Bridey.

"Thank you, ma'am." His sober humble tone paid tribute to her gentleness.

He found her father's shovel and went out to the cotton-wood trees, where he started digging furiously. Bridey rummaged in her bureau drawer, pausing just once to bury her face in a pile of petticoats. She found a box with a picture of Niagara Falls on the cover, which she had saved since the Christmas before last when a pair of shoes had come in it. She took this out to the boy.

Her huntsman went into the woodshed and returned with the colored box, tightly closed. Bridey, aloft on the seat of a wagon which her father had been greasing in the yard, looked determinedly away. She stared at the dull November prairies, stretching to a mackerel sky, while Ginger was buried under a cottonwood tree.

The young man joined her presently. He hopped up to the wagon seat beside her. They sat in silence.

"My father calls those trees the Three Sisters," Bridey volunteered at last, nodding toward the cottonwoods.

"Who is your father?"

"Bob Whipp."

"Why, I've often heard of Captain Bob Whipp."

"He's my father. I'm Bridey Whipp."

"I'm Charley Halliday."

The big iron-gray horse tethered to a near-by post looked inquiringly at his master, seated inexplicably in a wagon with empty shafts. His master sat on beside the girl. Her tears were dry now, but there were stains on her soft cheeks. Her little face was sad.

"I'm afraid," she said, "that you'll never catch the others."

"I don't care."

"I have to go in anyhow. I'm cold."

"I'm sorry." He .was contrite. "Of course, there's no warmth at all in that little pink apron—"

Apron! Remembering the apron, Bridey blushed. The stranger had seen her—a red-haired girl—wearing a pink apron! Color poured up from her throat.

He was charmed and mystified by the sunrise in her cheeks.

"Did I say anything wrong?"

"Oh, no! Only—I wouldn't have you think—"

"Wouldn't have me think what?"

"That I don't know better—than to wear pink. Me, with my red hair."

He laughed. He could hardly stop laughing. He laughed until she was offended—almost. He pulled off his red coat.

"Well, let's see how you look in this."

"No, I won't."

"Yes, you will."

She was tinier than ever, she was enchanting, almost lost in its folds.

"How old are you, anyway?" he asked.

"Fifteen."

He said that he would be twenty in January. Three members of his family, he said, had their birthdays in that month. They always celebrated together on the day nearest to the birthday of them all.

She watched him curiously as he talked, and when he paused she said: "Why do Englishmen talk the way they do?"

"How do they talk?"

"Funny."

"Funny! Well, I like that. We don't talk half as funny as you Americans do."

She laughed, showing teeth like grains of milk-white corn. She tossed the ginger-colored curls.

"You do so."

The iron-colored horse whinnied, unregarded.

Bridey clambered down at last, and the red coat returned to its owner. When he said goodbye, he took her hand; it was so small that he took the second one.

"It takes two to make a handful," he said.

Again the color rushed into her cheeks. It was fun, he had discovered, to bring about that sunrise.

"Have you forgiven me, Miss Bridey?"

"Yes."

"May I ride out to see you sometimes?"

"I don't see why you shouldn't."

She turned her head away, but his laughing gaze pursued it.

"Well, do you see why I *should?* Do you want me to?"

"Not if you don't want to."

"Well, but if I *do* want to?"

Fencing and parrying, old as time! But the ancient game made the huntsman's heart beat like the hooves of horses in the chase. It caused the color to flow and ebb in Bridey's cheeks. Ginger, her darling, not an hour buried, already forgotten! A fox, an hour ago, the most thrilling quarry in the world, forgotten too!

"If you really want me to come, you'll give me a kiss," he said.

"Oh, I couldn't! I *wouldn't.*" Bridey, her hands pinioned, twisted until her flushed cheeks were hidden by her curls.

But Charley found a cheek and kissed it. Bridey pulled herself free and rushed for the house. He watched her pink and yellow apron flutter inside the door, which closed softly behind her, before he untied his chafing and indignant horse and swung himself in elation to the saddle.

CHAPTER SIX

IT WAS a winter of snows.

The first fall came in November, and after that until spring no three days passed without a replenishment of fresh white snow upon the cushion of snow which padded the world. Sometimes the flakes were large and clinging, like bits of torn wet paper. Sometimes they were hard, like tiny bullets. Sometimes they swirled crazily. Sometimes they fell in straight unending lines which seemed to be pulled from the skies in ropes by tireless invisible hands. It was snow, snow, snow, from November until May.

Richard had never known such prodigality of snow. At first he thought it beautiful. When the sun came out in a brilliant sky, the glittering white-sheathed landscape looked like a scene from a pantomime or a picture from a Christmas story. He contrasted the winter favorably with the gray damp winters of England. He liked the fierce but invigorating cold.

At first, too, he enjoyed the sports of the season. Most of the colonists became enthusiastic skaters. The Americans had scraped clean of snow a stretch of ice upon Lake Rainbow, and this was one of the few common meeting grounds of Americans and English. The English followed an American lead again in organizing sleighing parties. Richard did not go to these, lest he meet Cathy. He bought a cutter, however, hung Kentish Beauty with bells and frequently made the run to Sisseton City for a day of billiards and the comfort of Si

Joslin's place. The Farmers' Home was now expanded almost beyond recognition. Two wings had been added, each higher and larger than the original house. A veranda encircled the building, and a picket fence hemmed in the grounds. Many Englishmen spent the entire winter there.

Fewer of them had returned to England that autumn— almost none of the family men. Trevenen and Hook lingered until after New Year's Day, and their presence added considerably to the gayety of the holidays. They were responsible for the horse races held on the ice of Lake Rainbow. They offered purses . . . mile heats for the three-minute class, half-mile heats for the green class, and a free-for-all race which provoked much hilarity. But after the advent of the new year, the masters of the Eyrie departed; the appetite for winter's pleasures was first satisfied, then satiated. The English in their innocence began to think of spring. Winter, however, had just begun.

Richard came to loathe the very sight of blowing snow. Incarceration at Little Goodlands grew harder and harder to bear. No attempt was made to heat the parlor or the bedrooms; communal life was lived in the unaired kitchen, which was filled with the voices of the Martins raised in constant acrimonious dispute. Certainly Martin had cause for resentment against his wife. She was a slovenly housekeeper, and her cooking, over the months, had gone from bad to worse. But Richard felt with some justice that what he, her employer, was willing to endure in silence her husband might pass over for the sake of peace. Martin, however, seemed glad to have an object on which to vent his ill humor.

He was at all times a bad-tempered man, but in summer work provided an outlet for his irascibility. In winter, when he was confined to the house, almost idle, his choler swelled and swelled until it seemed to fill the rooms. He treated his

employer civilly, but Richard suspected that only his presence saved the woman from physical abuse.

Richard despised himself for keeping the pair on. He had
returned from England determined to discharge them. His
involvement with Meta seemed to have paralyzed his energies; his life hung in abeyance waiting for that to end. Sometimes sitting at a dirty table over ill cooked food, listening to
the wrangling of the Martins, a vision came to him of the
dinner table at Great Goodlands, candle-lit, gracious, and
serene. He would jump from the table, mumbling some excuse, and bolt into his bedroom. There he would rehearse in
a fierce whisper the few words necessary to rid himself of his
housemates. But he did not speak them. The winter moved
on through snow and wind and cold.

Richard smoked; he tried to read; he wrote innumerable
letters which he mailed for the most part in the stove. It was
hard to write letters which did not betray too much discouragement when there was no home news to occupy his pen.
Mail from England came through with great irregularity.
More than once Richard struggled through mountainous
drifts to Rainbow only to discover that there was none at all.
Beatty got from Sisseton City with the local mail—not even
blizzards could daunt Beatty and his horses; but the trains
were less doughty. They weakly permitted themselves to
become embedded in snow.

When the mail was delayed there was small comfort in
Rainbow. Social life was at a standstill. The winter's program
of illness was in full swing—colds, grippe, pneumonia, diph-
theria; smallpox was raging in a near-by town. Richard
dropped in at the deserted club, bought a can of tobacco from
Judson Oates, and then there was nothing for it but the long
trip back.

He would gladly have joined the bachelors wintering at

Joslins'. They passed the time well enough with pool and billiards, liquor and cards. But he would not desert Meta. It was for her sake he had remained in Minnesota.

Maidservants would not stay at Exile Hall. Few hired girls, to use the American term, were available in Crockett County. Girls could be wives; they did not need to be servants; and if they went into service at all, they chose their places with the utmost independence. Exile Hall was gloomy and remote. It was three stories high, and the work was hard. There were tales told about its savage dog, about the captain's drinking and cursing and the lady's weeping in the night.

Meta had found a stout boy of eighteen or so who kept up the fires, washed the dishes, scrubbed the floors. He slept in the barn and had so far escaped a quarrel with Kit. With the boy to help her and Richard to cling to, she struggled through the winter. When Kit was drinking and dangerous, she climbed the stairs to that third-floor oratory which might be seen from Little Goodlands. There she hung out a flag if it were day, a lantern if it were night. She hung them out also when Bannister was gone and Richard might come to her. The arrangement was not satisfactory. Minnesota snowstorms permitted no reliance upon such simple signals. So Richard accustomed himself to riding over to Exile Hall for carefully casual visits. He forced himself to conquer the embarrassment he felt in Kit's presence and he sat over endless games of chess with the Captain, who was sometimes surly and as often completely charming.

Richard hated these visits. The thought of Cathy, which he succeeded fairly well in banishing at other times and places, came irresistibly upon him in the drawing room at Exile Hall. To the three secluded there Cathy made always an invisible fourth. Wide-eyed, smiling, sitting erect as young ladies from Mill Cottage are trained to sit, she looked on while Richard drank wine with the Captain, while he was checked or checkmated with jubilant shouts by the husband he was deceiving. The more bitterly Richard hated himself, the more vivid became the hallucination of her presence.

She and Richard had barely met since the night of the Hunt Ball. He had attended no more parties, and on the hunting field and skating pond he had kept at a distance from her.

"Damn it, I only saw her that one day," he would protest aloud, ploughing homeward through the snowy dark after a visit to Exile Hall. "I wouldn't have believed it if anyone had told me, that I could fall in love like that."

There was no doubt about his being in love. To meet one of her brothers on the street in Rainbow, to glimpse distantly from the Rainbow road the rooftop of her home, caused his heart to drop. He woke sometimes to the faint imagined strains of "Tales from the Vienna Woods." For weeks after the Hunt Ball he had felt caged and desperate. Now he was bruised and sore, like one who has flung himself vainly against bars.

He was helpless to take any step in her direction. It was Meta's privilege, he felt, to break off their relationship. When she did so—if she ever did, and if Cathy were not already bespoken by one of the many bachelors of Rainbow . . . When Richard contemplated those conditions, he had always the cold comfort of remembering that in the beginning she had liked him. No decorous young lady could have shown more plainly than she did that she liked him.

Brooding upon this, he came into his own kitchen after an evening of chess at Exile Hall. Martin, unshaven, slumped beside the stove. Mrs. Martin was setting bread. There was a trenchant silence in the room.

The two dogs lay as usual near the stove, and they rose

at Richard's entrance. But they did not burst upon him with welcoming barks; Nellie came toward him whining.

"Why, Nell, old girl, what's the matter?" Richard stooped to pet her, and as his hand touched her side she whimpered.

"She got caught in the door," Mrs. Martin volunteered. Martin did not look up.

Richard sat down and took the dog between his knees. She stood trembling while he felt her gently over. He discovered no broken ribs, but she whimpered again when he touched one spot on her side.

"Has she been sick?" Richard asked.

"All over my clean floor," Mrs. Martin answered.

Martin got up abruptly. Nellie, between Richard's knees, emitted a low growl. Martin did not speak, nor did Richard, but both knew that Richard knew that Nellie had not been caught in the door. She had been savagely kicked.

Ordinarily the two dogs slept in the kitchen. Tonight Richard spread a blanket for Nellie beside his bed. Shot in tenor yowls pleaded to share the blanket, and he was permitted to do so. The dogs soon fell asleep, but Richard did not. He lay in bed burning with fury. That surly unshaved brute had kicked Nellie, Nellie who was not second even to Kentish Beauty in her master's affections. Lying awake, long after Martin's snores penetrated from above, Richard punished himself with the remembrance that he had once seen Kentish Beauty shy away from Martin. Had she been ill treated in small ways which Martin thought Richard would not discover? Or perhaps—most painful thought of all—Martin had not feared discovery but had counted upon that lethargy which had permitted his wife to make a sty of the house and himself to indulge in moods of unforgivable moroseness.

Next morning after breakfast Richard said shortly:

"I've decided to let you go, Martin. I'll pay you for the full month but I want you to leave today."

"What the hell!" said Martin. "It's that dog, I suppose."

"We won't go into that."

"I suppose," said Martin, "you know that good help's hard to find." Richard did not answer. Martin raised his voice. "And being a God-damned Britisher, of course, you can't lift your hand to a pitchfork."

Richard got to his feet. But Mrs. Martin with some two-edged words checked his advance.

"Don't argue with him, Tim. I'm sick of this hole anyhow. Nothing to do here but look to see whether there's a flag hanging out at Bannisters!"

Richard was thrown into confusion by the threat. Or was it a threat? Perhaps, he told himself, she meant simply what she said. Perhaps she had not made the damning observation that the appearance of the flag was followed always by his immediate departure. In any case further quarreling with the Martins was unwise.

"I'll drive you in to Rainbow this morning. Get your packing done," he said to end dispute.

The silent drive was broken by a stop at Anglo-American Acres. There Richard left the Martins in the sleigh while he went into the house and talked with Jackson. He explained that he was letting the Martins go.

"I can't find any other help and get back by tonight. Can you spare Ole to look after my stock today and tomorrow?"

"Of course, Mr. Chalmers. Yes, indeed."

Jackson wetted his front teeth nervously, looking about and behind him, after his stealthy habit. It would be hard to spare Ole, he said, but he would do so. Mr. Crockett had told him always at any cost to oblige his Englishmen.

"Thanks," Richard said, and started away. But Jackson detained him.

"Oh, Mr. Chalmers!" he said. "Could you use an English lad on your farm this spring?"

"What lad?" Richard asked.

"No particular one. Mr. Crockett is sending out a lot of them, and I am placing them with farmers hereabouts."

"What wages will they get?" Richard inquired.

"No wages at all, Mr. Chalmers. That's the beauty of it." A smile overspread Jackson's pallid face, and he laid a confidential hand on Richard's arm. "It's an exceptional opportunity. But I know Mr. Crockett wouldn't want me to pass you up. You get the services of a hired man absolutely free—beyond the cost of his keep."

Hurried as he was, Richard paused to puzzle this out.

"But the young Englishman," he said. "What does he get out of it?"

"He learns farming," Jackson explained triumphantly. "Mr. Crockett puts it so nicely." He pulled a brightly colored brochure from his pocket. " 'For a mere hundred pounds . . .' No, that's not the place. Here it is. 'I will locate your son in a home of comfort and refinement where under ideal conditions he can learn the art of American farming.' "

"I see. I pay my servants," Richard answered shortly.

Back in the sleigh he boiled at this new scheme of Crockett's. The plan came clear enough. The lads involved were undoubtedly gentlemen's sons—about as accustomed to hard work as were lilies of the field. Their fathers had paid Crockett liberally for placing them where—they believed—the lads could observe only. As a matter of fact, of course, they would be doing work worth good wages—for nothing.

Well, nothing could be done now to prevent it. Within another month, the young colonists would be on the ocean.

And meanwhile, Richard told himself, he had enough to worry about.

He worried, as the sleigh slipped along the familiar road to Rainbow, about Meta.

Always before, when going to Sisseton City, he had apprised her of his intention. He had never left Little Goodlands without making sure that things were going well at Exile Hall. But today there had been no chance to do so. She would hardly have wanted him to stop after what Mrs. Martin had said. He felt reasonably sure, moreover, that it was safe for him to make the trip. Last evening, playing at chess, Kit had been in good humor.

He would give up any idea of finding a cook. Finding a cook would take time—cooks were scarcer than diamonds. He would try only to pick up a man to do the chores, and the two of them would manage until spring. Making these decisions, Richard felt braced and strengthened. Throwing out the Martins seemed to be taking a step toward Cathy. He left the resentful couple at the Log House, overpaid them but got no thanks for it, and in cheerful spirits proceeded to Sisseton City.

The day was overcast. With fur cap and gloves, greatcoat and buffalo robe, he was snugly warm. The snow was well packed, and the sleighing excellent; Kentish Beauty's bells made a continuous optimistic chime along the flat pale miles.

When he entered the Farmers' Home, Joslin called a genial, "Hi!" and shook hands with hearty pleasure.

"I'll be here for the night," Richard told him. "Will you have my horse bedded and fed?"

"She'll get tre .ent I wouldn't better if the Queen asked me," Joslin promised.

From the far side of the imported billiard table, Harry Earle racked his cue and came forward exuberantly.

"It's the hermit!" he shouted.

The three Nevilles clattered in from the bar, and from their rooms upstairs came half a dozen young bachelor colonists who found these winter quarters preferable to frozen farms.

"This calls for a spree," Earle declared.

"Just a little one," Richard agreed. He refused to begin even that until he had completed the mission which had brought him to town. But Joslin was as ready with promises about a hired man as he had been about Kentish Beauty.

"Come morning," he said, "I'll have you a dandy hand. What's your choice? Fat, thin, long, short?"

"If he'll wash his neck and half the dishes, and keep his boots out of my dog's ribs, I don't care what he looks like," Richard replied.

"The boot business is easy," Joslin said. "But the neck washing'll be harder. Will every Saturday night do?"

It was good to be at Joslin's, whether playing billiards at which he won or cards at which he lost or merely joining in the yarn-spinning and drinking. He was careful about that last. Most of the others, he noted, were drinking far too much. A warning bell rang in Richard's head. As the night wore on he drank only when he could not avoid his friends' importunities, but he grew downright skillful at this. More than half the time he escaped the irrepressible Neville brothers with their repetitious, urgent, "Here! Try a sample of this."

The Neville brothers with their samples were staging a rather heavy-handed imitation of the commercial travelers who now stopped in numbers at the Farmers' Home. The Englishmen found the commercial travelers—"drummers," as they were more often called—entertaining. Coming as they did from strange towns and cities, into which after a short visit they disappeared, and from which after an interval they emerged again, the drummers were a link with that great world from which the Englishmen felt themselves so sharply exiled. The news of the day on these traveled lips took on a fresh significance. It was one thing to read in the newspapers the newest twist to the Beecher-Tilton quarrel, the latest clue to the Charley Ross kidnaping, but it was quite another to hear the same reports related by some one who had got them virtually at first hand in—St. Paul, St. Louis, or La Crosse. The drummers in their turn were fascinated by the colonists, whose foreign idiosyncrasies they described with telling effect in towns to the east and south.

Among the drummers who drew their wooden armchairs to the barroom stove that evening, was one whom Richard especially marked. He was short and round and as vivacious as the checks and stripes which figured so prominently in his modish coat and trousers. He was so excessively vivacious that Richard at first thought him of French or Italian extraction; but it turned out that his name was Johnny Devlin. The famous spirit, Katie King, had just been exposed as a fraud. Johnny Devlin had seen ghosts which were not frauds; he had seen them all up and down the line. He described them to the spellbound Englishmen far into the night, his brogue becoming richer with the increasing horror of his stories.

The Farmers' Home had charms. It was difficult, next morning, for Richard to break away. But Si had found his man.

"Joe Gimbel, Mr. Chalmers."

Short and wiry, Joe Gimbel squared away before his new employer, in an attitude evenly balanced between utter self-confidence and bluntest independence.

"If you don't like me, you're hard to suit," his darting brown eyes seemed to say. "But if you don't, a lot I'll worry."

Richard suggested that they all go back to the stable and meet Kentish Beauty. She looked Joe over, then lipped his coat sleeve amiably.

"I think he'll do very well," Richard told Joslin. "And I'd be glad to keep him on for the spring work."

There was one difficulty. Joe was not willing to leave at once. He said he had business, but the stubborn set of his shoulders suggested that he meant to prove his independence by not snapping too hungrily at a job.

"I'll be with you come morning," he promised. "I'll catch me a ride into Rainbow this afternoon, and you'll see me bright and early tomorrow. I'll make it, General, if I have to crawl."

Partly in appreciation of that flattering "General," Richard suggested an easier mode of travel.

"When you reach Rainbow," he suggested, "stop at the Log House. I'll arrange with Oarlock for a horse to bring you the rest of the way."

This plan was agreed upon, and Joe brought Kentish Beauty out at a trot, the sleigh-bells jingling so heartily that one of the Nevilles popped a drowsy head through an upper window.

"How the devil do you expect me to get my beauty sleep, Dick?"

Richard waved his hand as he urged Kentish Beauty to a trot.

He meant to call at Exile Hall that night. He had, he reckoned, ample time. However, there was snow in the air, aimless drifting flakes which might yet thicken and bring delay. So he made haste while haste was possible.

At the point where the road turned south toward Rainbow he encountered a delay which he had not anticipated.

A black blot on the snowy landscape ahead turned out to

be an overturned sleigh. Urging Kentish Beauty toward it, he discovered Johnny Devlin's hired livery, and the exasperated, snow-covered figure struggling to salvage sample case and personal effects was the animated little Irishman, not so carefree now.

"Damned crowbait!" Johnny growled, and jerked his head toward the adjacent prairie.

A furlong off, his rawboned horse pawed the snow in an optimistic quest for the remains of last year's grass.

"Runner hit a rock, and the crazy plug acted as if we'd exploded a bomb."

It took them an hour to fish the last of Devlin's goods from the snow, to catch the horse, and to discover that the harness was wrecked beyond immediate use. They piled everything into Richard's sleigh and tied the rawboned horse on behind.

"I guess we need a drink," Johnny said. He fetched a flask from a hip pocket. "Have a long one," he urged. "It doesn't cost me anything. I sell it."

"But Rainbow," Richard answered, "is a temperance town."

"Oh, well!" said Johnny, and winked.

The wink reminded Richard that, after all, temperance towns may have clubs. Johnny emphasized the fact.

"I guess I won't have to sell water in that place of Bannister's," he surmised cheerfully. He continued with a note of admiration. "Some of you Englishmen certainly know how to down the stuff. And I'll tell you what. Rainbow's going to vote pretty soon on licensing. If it votes 'Yes,' I'll be doing plenty of business there. What's more, some smart young fellow can make a lot of money in a saloon."

"I dare say," Richard said.

In Rainbow, Devlin would have had him to dine, but Rich-

ard now was late. He ate hurriedly, delaying only while
Kentish Beauty finished her oats and hay. Then, having arranged for Joe's horse, he pushed on.

The snow was thickening, as he had feared it might. The
flakes were sharp and fine, and they fell in a veil which concealed the road so that he had to travel somewhat more
slowly. It made the going harder for Kentish Beauty too.
Darkness came on before he passed Anglo-American Acres.
At Little Goodlands, Ole had everything in order, but he
was anxious to start home before the waxing storm made that
impossible. He got off at once.

Richard saw that he would need a fresh horse for the ride
to Exile Hall. He stabled Kentish Beauty and fed her, working quickly now, for his thoughts began to run somewhat
apprehensively before him to the great bare drawing room
at Exile Hall where he and Kit had played at chess. That had
been only night before last. But time would not have passed
so quickly or so pleasantly there. He flung a saddle over a
fresh horse, his holiday mood dropping from him.

CHAPTER SEVEN

WHEN Richard and Bannister went out to the barn where Kentish Beauty was stabled, Lady Meta dragged her armchair across the bare floor of the drawing room to the window which looked away toward Little Goodlands. The drawing room was dim, unlighted except by the candles about the chess table, and in every corner shadows hung thick. Out of doors, however, the full moon spread a mauve radiance over the snowy prairie. Leaning forward, Lady Meta tried to fix in her memory the eerie sheen which the transforming light from the night sky cast across the level, white-blanketed land.

Kentish Beauty trotted out from behind the concealing bulk of Exile Hall. She footed vigorously to loosen muscles grown stiff during the long wait in the cold stable, and as she moved into the distance her shadow grew into a vast gloom which threatened to overwhelm the whole landscape.

Some of that gloom seemed to flow into the room and over Lady Meta as the door opened and Bannister returned. He stopped at sight of his wife in her changed place, then went wordlessly to his own chair beside the chess table.

"Did you and Richard make any plans for tomorrow?" Lady Meta asked.

She hoped they had, although she asked not so much to know as to rekindle if possible the amiable mood which the games had fostered.

"No," Bannister replied sullenly. "I suggested a hunt, but he said he was engaged."

"I am sorry," Lady Meta said.

Bannister snapped his fingers to rouse Fang from the opposite side of the fireplace. The dog stood up and looked expectantly toward the rack beside the kitchen door on which hung Bannister's firearms, pistols and guns, all loaded for instant use.

"I wish your being sorry could help," he told her.

He picked up a chessman.

"Here, Fang!" he said sharply. "Fetch!"

He tossed the piece into a far corner of the room and the hound leaped in snarling pursuit, his claws rasping over the floor as he slid to a halt and snapped up his quarry. This was a game that Bannister had devised for the hours of his worst boredom, a time-killer to be taken like a drug when his mind was too inert to cope with the empty endless nights. It was a game that began with all the white and black pieces in their proper places on the chessboard. It progressed as white and black pieces were tossed alternately for Fang to fetch. It ended when the two colors had been reversed in their positions. Then it started again. It could go on, it had gone on, over and over, for hours.

Lady Meta hated the childish game. Sooner or later the monotonous clatter of the tossed pieces, the sliding claws of the dog, began to rasp her nerves until she had to choke down hysteria. She feared it, too, because always the meaningless performance created in Bannister a self-contempt which bred his harshest mood.

Loneliness filled her being, her heart, her spirit. She was emptied of every other emotion. She sat in emptiness, vast and stark. Behind her the walls of the drawing room seemed to expand into infinity. The bare floor stretched away even beyond the limits of her imagination, and still on this vast plane the game went on.

"Fetch!" Her husband's voice, bored, scornful of himself and all the world, rose out of the immense emptiness as regularly as dripping water. "Fetch!"

The small clatter of the tossed pieces followed, then Fang's terrifying snarl and the drawn-out intolerable sound of his claws tearing at the planking.

She wanted to cry, "Stop!" but before the evenings of winter were a month old she had learned the uselessness of any plea. Instead, while she still controlled the hysteria which strained her throat, she stood up and walked to the stairway.

Fang watched her, and it occurred to her that if Bannister had pointed in her direction and said "Fetch!" the dog would have been snarling at her throat as he now went at the ivory chessmen.

"Good night, Kit," she said.

"Fetch!" Bannister ordered, and tossed another piece.

"I am going up to my room, Kit."

"Why not? Fetch, Fang!"

Upstairs and in her own room the loneliness receded and her throat eased. She had, she reflected, at least this to be thankful for, that this was her own room. How shocked the good Englishwomen of the colony would be if they should learn that she and her husband occupied separate rooms! The conjugal double bed was as sacred to them as their wedding rings. But it seemed to Lady Meta that life would be scarcely endurable except for these four walls within which she might retreat. Bannister still insisted upon his right to enter. But he exercised the right less and less. It was more than a month since the sound of the lifting latch had warned her to summon that submission which helped to preserve a semblance of amity in Exile Hall.

She undressed, dropped her jewels into the case which she always—to Kit's annoyance—left carelessly about, and reached for the long flannel nightgown that she disliked but that the bitter cold made imperative. Beneath the thick blankets on her bed, she lay looking out into the moonlight. She slept.

The door opened. Resting on her side with her face to the door, Lady Meta awakened but did not move. From behind lowered eyelids she saw Bannister enter. She knew that she ought to acknowledge his arrival. She tried to open her eyes and pretend a smile, but she could not. Her body grew hard and unyielding.

When he came beside the bed and bent down she found a fair ground for rebellion. Sober he was bearable, but in liquor he was, she sometimes believed, more beast than his dog. She lay motionless, trying to make him believe she was asleep, but when his hand moved toward her she could not check her wincing shoulder.

He shook her roughly.

"I knew you were awake," he cried.

She opened her eyes and looked up at him; but her gaze was expressionless, and she made her body continue hard and disobedient beneath his touch. He started to shake her again. He had had experience with blank submission and resigned indifference and had come prepared for these, but he was disconcerted by rebellion. He withdrew his hand uncertainly and shrugged.

"Go back to sleep," he said. "I'll leave." He laughed again. "Only a proper husbandly solicitude brought me in the first place. I was afraid that you might not have enough blankets."

Long after the door had closed behind him, Lady Meta's body continued rigid and impervious. She knew that later he would find some way to punish her, but she had, she comforted herself, gained a permanent profit from the night. He would come to her even less often hereafter. Her body grew pliant again with the thought, and she slept, but only in snatches. An incessant clamor from the drawing room would have broken her rest even if her own mental tumult, inspired by the encounter with Kit, had abated.

The noise downstairs divided into loud distinguishable voices. Lady Meta sat up in her bed. Sharp, clear light was pouring through the window. While she had drowsed, the dawn had passed. One voice, then, would belong to their only servant, the boy who would have come in from his bed in the hayloft to begin his chores.

The voices were quarrelsome. Bannister was furiously angry, and the boy was defending himself resentfully.

"I left plenty of wood! But you can't expect it to last if you hang out till daylight licking that bottle."

What Bannister replied, Lady Meta could not make out; but the boy's next retort made it plain that he had reacted as she would have expected him to react to such defiance from a servant.

"Like hell you'll do any whipping! Where do you think you are, mister?"

Bannister's reply again was muffled, but again the boy's retort made the progress of the quarrel clear.

"Keep that whip down! I won't—"

Fang snarled, and then Bannister's shout came harsh and plain.

"Get him, Fang!"

"Keep that dog off!"

"Take him, Fang!"

"Keep that dog off!"

"Take him, Fang!"

Lady Meta sprang from bed. As she reached her door,

another door crashed below. She realized in breathless relief that the boy had escaped. She rushed to a window.

Brandishing a club, the boy was backing swiftly toward the stable. Fang circled just out of the club's reach, his snarl breaking with frustrated anger. Just below the window, Bannister shook a riding crop as he urged the dog to attack.

"Take him, Fang! Take him!"

The boy got to the stable, paused at the wide doorway a watchful instant, then leaped within and slid the door shut. Bannister started forward. Fang poked a baffled nose down to the crack along the sill and growled.

The door had hardly closed when it flew open again. The boy stood in the opening once more. He had remained inside just long enough to loose one of the haltered riding horses from its stall. The horse stood beside him now and in his hand he held the halter strap.

"Damn you!" Bannister shouted. "Stop him, Fang."

But there was no stopping him. He whirled onto the bare back, his booted heels thwacking the round flanks, and the animal shot toward the open prairie.

"I'll jail you for this!" Bannister shouted.

The boy waved a derisive hand.

Fang raced in pursuit, but the snow, halfway up to his belly, tangled his feet.

"I'll jail you!" Bannister repeated.

His face was drained white as he ordered the laboring dog back from the hopeless chase.

In the face of that anger Lady Meta dressed slowly. She took the precaution to climb to the oratory to hang out the flag. Reassured by the thought that Richard would see it, she descended to the drawing room. Bannister now leaned against the fireplace. His always brilliant eyes were glowing. He greeted her with an ironical gallantry which she recognized at once—it sprang up always at a certain stage of drunkenness.

"I have just done you a considerable favor, my dear."

"How thoughtful you are!" she answered in kind.

"I have just thrown our solitary servant off the place."

"And that helps me—how?"

"Isn't it obvious? It leaves you only Fang and myself to prepare breakfast for."

"Of course," cried Lady Meta pleasantly. "How stupid of me not to have seen at once! And has Fang given his order?"

"The usual porridge. No meat, mind you! Meat only every other day."

"And for yourself?" she repeated.

"Suppose I were to ask what any husband has a right to ask."

"We are discussing breakfast."

He walked over to a decanter which stood in the center of the chessboard, whose pieces were strewn about the room.

"If you will fill this," he said, "I'll have all I require."

The whiskey supply was kept in a barrel in the cellar. Her heart beat thickly as she descended with a candle into that tomblike place. She filled the decanter there and brought it back.

"And a glass?" he inquired, with the air of one who is being reasonable to the last degree.

She brought a fresh glass, filled it and gave it to him.

"Perhaps"—he extended the glass—"you will join me?"

"It is scarcely," she answered regretfully, "my kind of a breakfast."

He bowed agreement, and she walked out into the kitchen.

Although she could not see, she could feel his gaze following her, and she knew that he was growing tired of their byplay, was falling back into the furious mood she had seen when she stood in the window watching the boy's flight.

There was some porridge left after she had fed Fang, and she heated this. The porridge was ample, with a cup of tea. She made the tea strong, black almost, and lingered over its bitter potency.

"So you prefer not to sit with me."

Bannister came out of the drawing room, his glass and his decanter in hand. She measured the decanter's contents in alarm. She had never known him, she thought, to take so much in such a little time.

"Won't even sit with me!"

He seized the teacup on its way to her lips. The hot tea spilled into her lap. He stood over her.

"Now," she told herself, "it is coming." And she braced herself for blows. They did not follow, however. He looked down at her for a space; then his sullen expression lightened. He laughed.

"Splendid," he cried, approving his own inspiration. "I know what to do with you. Last night you wouldn't sleep with me. This morning you won't even eat your porridge and drink your tea in the same room with me. You like to be alone, do you? Right! I'll see that you have your fill of being alone."

He jerked her to her feet, jostled her back into the drawing room, and flung her into the chair he had occupied, between the fireplace and the chess table.

"Fang!" he called. "Here!"

The liver-colored dog trotted into the room, his chin hairs still white from the milk in his porridge bowl.

"Watch her, Fang!" Bannister ordered. "Watch."

Fang looked doubtfully at his master.

"Watch her!" Bannister ordered. "If she moves from that chair—take her!"

Fang reared on his hind legs and barked.

"If she moves," Bannister repeated.

The dog understood. Five feet in front of Lady Meta, he laid his head on his big paws. His upper lip drew back in a soundless warning.

"Kit!" Lady Meta gasped incredulously.

"It is what you want, my dear," he told her in a flat voice. "You can be alone to your heart's content. I'm going in to the Club. If some one comes along, you may get your liberty—I mean companionship—before I return. But we happen not to live on a main traveled highway, so I doubt that anyone will come."

"Kit, you can't do this."

He shrugged into his greatcoat, took his gloves from the mantel over the fireplace, and shook back the white lock before ramming on his cap.

"Not even Dick will come," he went on. "He was here last night, and today he is engaged. I can virtually guarantee you the pleasure of complete solitude until I come back."

"Kit," she pleaded, "you can't leave me this way. The fire will go out. I haven't enough on to keep from freezing."

He took the stairs three at a time, and was back at once with the blankets from her bed. He dropped them beside her chair.

"These kept you warm last night," he said.

"Wait, Kit! Wait!" she begged. "Beat me. I'll let you. I'll never tell. But don't leave me alone with that dog."

He chose a rifle from the rack, hesitated over a pistol, decided against it, and drew on his gloves.

"Watch her, Fang!" he commanded. "Mind! If she leaves that chair, pin her down!"

The door closed behind him.

"Kit!" cried Lady Meta, and started to her feet. The dog snarled. She dropped back into her chair.

She heard Bannister whistle on his way to the stable. She waited in unbelief. He must be playing with her. He had to come back. Not even his mad hatred could agree to such cruelty as this. She waited, holding her breath for the slightest sound that would foretell his return. Faintly, through the closed doors, she heard a horse trot. Through the window she spied Bannister riding away.

The road did not take him past Little Goodlands. But she had hung out the flag. Richard would see it, if only it did not snow. She looked anxiously at the bit of sky revealed by the window. It hung over the pallid world like a gray pall. But there were as yet no flakes in it, none of the faint drifting specks which knew so well how to multiply, how to thicken, until they shrouded any view in turbid white.

Fang whimpered from the post to which he had returned. Crouching there, he threw brief uneasy glances after his departing master. But when Lady Meta stirred, his muscles tightened and his gaze returned to her again.

On the hearth the fire burned bright and strong. The backlog, however, was more than half consumed. For all that she sat so close to the fire, Lady Meta found that the arm of her chair was chill to her hand. A cold draft moved along the floor about her feet. Around the four sides of the window pane, a heavy rim of frost stood witness to the bitterness of the past night.

The frost rim, Lady Meta discovered, was a reliable though imperfect thermometer. It could not indicate how much colder the room grew from hour to hour, but it spread toward the center to prove that the cold increased.

"He must mean to come back shortly," she thought at noon.

Fang made no move when she reached out and drew the blankets thickly around herself.

"He cannot mean to keep me here all night," she thought when twilight darkened the room. She remembered suddenly that Richard, if he had not already seen the flag, could now no longer see it.

She threw off the blankets and straightened her legs. The dog roused. Anger gave her courage. She stood up stubbornly. Fang leaped. From his crouching posture he flung himself heavily against her. His teeth set into her dress. His bulk drove her back. She screamed. He drew off, snarling.

The blankets were scattered but he permitted her to reach out and gather them. By degrees she barricaded her body against the bitter air. The effort grew into an elaborate scheme to seal herself in from the cold. The scheme was all the more engrossing because it had to be carried out in almost total darkness. The moon was full, she knew, but it must be obscured by clouds; only the faintest light came through the frosted window. The scheme failed at a thousand points. The cold worked in here, in there, and each break in the defense could be remedied only by the most careful, the most minute adjustments of the blankets. She forgot, in all those adjustments, even to be hungry. She did know, however, that she was unutterably weary, and a moment came when she realized that she was about to drowse off.

When she awakened, she was sure that she had fainted, as well as slept. Her body was numb with cold. Her arms were without feeling, and at first she could not move them. She knew now that she was hungry, and that she was parched with thirst. The room was lighter, much lighter. Morning, she told herself doubtfully, must have come. She looked at the clock and was dully amazed. Not only the night had passed and morning come. It was close to noon. She had been in her prison chair for more than twenty-four hours. Richard had not come, and now she abandoned hope of him. The air was full of small menacing flakes.

Fang lay as he had lain before he faded into the darkness of the night before. His flesh hung loosely on his flanks. He was cold, too; but his eyes had opened at her first stirring, and as she straightened he raised his upper lip fiercely.

She began to plan desperately. Perhaps she might throw the blankets over him and manage to escape into the kitchen. Or push the chess table over to distract his attention. Perhaps she could make friends with him. Perhaps she could find a club and hold him off as the boy had done. She looked around. The room was bare of any wood. Then she saw the rack of weapons, the pistols. If she grew quiet, if she sat without a sound and utterly motionless, the cold-weary dog would nap. Bit by bit she could move her chair nearer to that rack.

She grew quiet, she sat without a sound, almost without breathing. The dog napped. She braced her feet against the floor and pushed. Fang came alert, but she had moved her chair a fraction of the distance toward the pistol. She had done it once and she could do it again!

She grew warm with the struggle. Each quick fierce thrust made her blood race; but terrifying as the movements were, she dreaded them less than the tense suspended moments in which her pulse beat feverishly while she waited for the dog's eyes to droop, his head to sink between his outstretched paws.

She was halfway to her goal when Fang grew puzzled. He was aware that something was wrong, and yet there his charge continued, in her chair as his master had ordered. He prowled uneasily, but finally he went back to his familiar spot and lay down again.

It was, literally, a task of hours to reach that pistol. Lady Meta despaired of ever crossing the floor, but little by little she made her gains. Toward the end she improved enormously upon the old business of pushing. She waited until Fang had surely drowsed. Then, as stealthily as though she had been robbing the house, she half raised herself from her chair. Standing so, she seized the chair arms and lifted the chair. Then she swung sideways. Once she gained half a foot.

When she was at last actually beneath the gun rack she rested. She would need all the little strength that she had. The dog would surely be on her before she could stand up, turn, and take the necessary step to the rack. She must block him off with a blanket for as long as she needed to reach the pistol.

Hands flexed and ready, she stood up. Fang leaped, but the cold had tightened his muscles and he was slow, so that she got the blanket in his way. It spoiled his pounce. He dropped, whining his rage, and as he fell she flung the blanket over him, like a net. While he worried free she got the pistol.

Armed, she backed away toward the door. Fang leaped again. There was no blanket this time to stop him as he drove straight at her throat. She twisted frantically. His jaws locked upon her shoulder. And as she staggered, his body lying against hers, she thrust the muzzle of the pistol under a foreleg and pulled the trigger.

She fell. "He will be at my throat next," she thought. "I have nothing to stop him now." She checked a scream, half uttered. "I must be quiet," she thought. "If I am quiet, if I lie as though I were dead, he may let me be." She lay as though she were dead and waited for the dog's puzzled withdrawal. A warm moisture soaked through her dress to her breast, but Fang's weight did not shift. As realization comes slowly, upon awakening, she realized that his hold had loosened. He was dead.

She twisted free of his slack carcass and stood up. With the knowledge that he was dead she pitied him.

"You poor thing," she said. "You poor thing. You couldn't help yourself any more than I. You only watched as you were told."

She began to sob, slow, muted, tearless sobs. She had escaped her terror, but she was still afraid. Her fear now was of the house and the death in it. She could not remain another hour, another minute.

Pain recalled her hurt shoulder. She was thankful to find that she could move it. The flesh was torn, and her own blood flowed down to join the blood of the dog upon her breast, but Fang's teeth, stopped by the thick cloth of her dress, had not gone deep. She started for the kitchen, the walls of her throat seeming to crumple with thirst. The water in the pail was frozen over, and she had to break the ice with a heavy stick. She drank slowly, warming each swallow in her mouth before she let it trickle down. When she had slaked her thirst, she found her coat, her heavy boots. With dragging movements, she put them on.

Out of doors, the snow was coming down in earnest. The skies at last were ready to empty themselves of that great burden which had pressed down during the day and the night and day of her imprisonment. Darkness would follow soon.

She was not sure that she had strength to climb to a horse's back, but she must do it somehow. Somehow she must get to Little Goodlands. She held her hand to her shoulder and walked unsteadily toward the stable.

CHAPTER EIGHT

W HERE the trail wound out of the swamp and began to climb on Richard's land, Lady Meta's horse whinnied excitedly in recognition of one of its kind. Lady Meta lifted her head. She could see no more than she had been able to see in the gloomy recesses of the swamp, only snowflakes churning madly in a monstrous immensity of dark. But almost at once Richard appeared beside her.

Without a word she gave herself up to the inexpressible solace of his presence. Relief flowed over her in great waves, like sobs, as she felt herself lifted in his strong compassionate arms, placed before him on his saddle, carried forward at an urgent pace with her tired head resting at last in profound security upon his breast. She saw dimly the ghostly mounds of white which were his outbuildings, his stables; she caught an Elysian gleam of light. She was not aware that she was swooning; she knew only that as Richard bore her over the threshold of his house she sank beyond exhaustion, into the peace of utter oblivion.

When she awoke a fire was crackling close to her ears. She listened for a time without opening her eyes. Then she lifted her lids—just sufficiently to take in the stove, which glowed red along every seam and appeared to be vibrating with heat.

She closed her eyes and rested. Repose lapped her on every side. When she lifted the lids again, she raised them higher and saw that she was in bed in Richard's kitchen. He had evidently brought his bed from the adjoining bedroom and had set it up here close to the stove. She was bundled in some flannel garment not her own, but it was snug and she was happy. She moved, and her sore shoulder pained her. Pain, she resolved, should not intrude upon this deep content, and she lay rigid.

But that rigidity recalled the night—how long ago!—when she had lain rigid beneath her husband's touch. It brought back the morning after that night, and the long chain of horror began to unwind. She opened her eyes, wide this time, and surveyed the kitchen, which was very dim although night did not seem to have come. Richard was sitting on a chair beside her bed.

"Go back to sleep," he said, as though she had spoken. "Don't try to talk."

She eased herself among the pillows and closed her eyes again.

When she awoke a second time, Richard was lifting a steaming kettle from the stove. Before she spoke she took him in with her bright eyes. The tall rugged form, the flaxen hair, the sober face—how very sober he looked! Even more so than usual, and he was almost always grave. That, she thought, was because he had not loved her. She had held him, but he had not loved her.

She moved, and the shoulder twinged, and a small cry escaped her. Richard turned at once. Pity flowed over his face, and he put down the kettle and came to stand beside her bed. He tucked the blankets closer about her shoulders.

"Don't try to talk," he said as he had said before. "After a while I want you to tell me all about it. But now, just rest."

"I am rested," she said. "I should like some tea."

"I was just making some."

While he filled the cup, she let her eyes wander slowly

about the room. That dim light! It was pale yellow like lamplight, and yet the lamps were not lighted. She realized at last that daylight was seeping into the room through an obscuring curtain of snow. Above the drifts, which surmounted the window ledges, that curtain of falling snow waved and twisted in the wind. Wind, of course! The roaring noise she had heard did not all come from the stove. A torrent of wind was roaring about the little house.

How good to be here, warm and safe, with Richard!

He brought the tea, and after it had cooled a little she lay against his arm, and drank. When the cup was empty, she relaxed again among her pillows. After a time she asked:

"This storm? . . . How long?"

"It was last night that I found you. It is morning now, eleven o'clock. The blizzard is the worst one of the winter." He went on presently. "I ran a clothesline out to the stable last night, or I never could have found my way to feed the animals. It's a trick I got from Martin—"

He checked himself somewhat abruptly. The name "Martin" repeated itself in Lady Meta's mind. Cautiously, not to renew the shooting pain in her shoulder, she turned her head to seek the Martins. They were certainly not in the room.

"The Martins. Where are they?"

"I let them go, Meta—the morning after I played chess with Kit. I went to Sisseton City that day to find other help. That was the reason I didn't see your signal—if you put one out."

She was silent, pondering this. It came to her at last that if the Martins were gone, she had passed a night alone with Richard. That was why he had checked his speech; he had been afraid that the knowledge would trouble her. But somehow it seemed unimportant. For his words had sent her thoughts back to her hanging of the flag. She had come downstairs—and filled Kit's decanter—and cooked breakfast for Fang—and then . . .

"He left me alone," she said. "With Fang . . ."

Richard's face was racked with pity.

"I know. I dressed your shoulder."

"He said, 'Take her, Fang! If she moves from that chair—' "

"Meta! Meta!"

"I shot him," she ended in a whisper, tears beginning at last to run down her cheeks. "I shot him. Poor Fang!"

He found her hands.

"Don't talk about it. Rest and sleep."

But she wanted to talk, and finding a hollow in the pillows which gave comfort to her shoulder, she related the story of her day and night of horror.

He listened without interruption. When she had finished, he said:

"He must be going mad!"

"He loves to torture—people and animals."

"He will never torture you again, Meta. I'm going to take you away."

It was pleasant to hear that, even though it was not true. And it was not true, for she would not let it be true. But all that must wait. She could talk no more now. She was content to sleep again.

When she woke, a new yellow light had come. This was true lamplight, she perceived. She had been wakened by the door opening to admit Richard. A fierce sweep of snow-laden wind came in with him. He pressed his body hard against the door to close it.

He had been out to feed the stock, he said, unwinding his muffler. She had slept for hours, and now she must have some soup. He had made it himself, and she must show her approval by drinking a great deal . . .

She saw that he was purposely keeping his tone light, and she was grateful.

As she sipped the soup, she heard a scratching on the bedroom door.

"What is that?" she asked.

"Shot and Nellie." His tone was embarrassed, and she comprehended that he had put his dogs away fearing that the sight of them would wound her.

"Oh, let them come in to the fire, poor dears." They trotted gladly out from the cold room, and she stretched a hand to Nellie. She was rewarded by the look in Richard's face.

The soup strengthened her. She swallowed some toast. Richard talked determinedly about the storm. She was grateful to him again, for his talk kept her from her thoughts, although there was little he could tell her about blizzards. She had had enough experience of this American phenomenon. He continued to chat as he ate his own supper, and finally she grew drowsy. Through the night she slept by snatches. Richard kept up the fires and napped in his chair, the dogs at his feet.

But he was alert to her slightest stir or sound. Lady Meta marveled at how tenderly he nursed her. All his loneliness, all his gratitude to her, all his deep pity found expression in the gentleness with which he tended her through the storm-filled night.

He was good, she thought. Truly good. He deserved what she was now resolved to give him, what her period of horror had strengthened her to give him, his release.

In spite of the sadness inspired by the thought of a parting, she felt content. When she woke in the night to hear the wind howling, the thump of the dogs' tails, or Richard's breathing, she thought with a deep calm:

"After all, something is accomplished. It wasn't all for nothing. Nothing ever is."

By morning the wind had abated, and Lady Meta was truly convalescent. She sat up in bed, her arms in the turned-back sleeves of Richard's dressing gown, and drank coffee and ate eggs and toast. Richard talked more freely of what she had undergone.

"I was worried by this wound," he said, as he dressed her shoulder. "I knew there was a storm coming and that I could not get you to a doctor. If the wound had been critical, I should not have known what to do. But for all you were so ill, you did not have a fever. Or at least, only a slight one. I knew that was a favorable sign. And now, see! The marks are healing splendidly."

But Lady Meta stroked his hand and would not look.

"Now that you are better," he went on, "I want to repeat what I said last night. I won't let you go through anything like this again. I don't know just how I can break away from Rainbow. I am still dependent on my father, as you know. But I'll do it somehow. I'm resolved to take you away."

Still Lady Meta only stroked his hand. At last she said: "A little later we will talk of all this. Now I want to talk about myself. I want you to understand my situation more fully."

And while the wind died, and the dogs slept, and the fire rumbled, she talked, filling in the gaps in his knowledge of her life's story.

She told him of her father's ardent marriage, before coming into the title, to a young Bavarian countess, her mother. The marriage had not been approved by her father's family.

The earldom was impoverished, and he had been expected to marry money; the Gräfin was as indigent as he.

Meta had spent her childhood with her mother, who had continued in Bavaria while her husband passed more and more of his time with his people in England. Then her mother had died, and the embarrassing evidence of an unfortunate union had been put away in a Swiss school. Shortly the young widower, just come into the title, had married again, more suitably. The second marriage had brought forth a son, and the son had succeeded to the earldom at eighteen when his father, Meta's father, had died.

Meta, a little less than twenty-one then, had been summoned. She had gone by way of Italy, stopping there to visit some of her mother's people. On the ship which took her to England, she had met Kit Bannister returning from India.

They had fallen madly in love. Reaching England, she had not waited to acquaint herself with her half-brother, before yielding to Kit's entreaties and marrying him. Within a few months, the charges against him had come out.

Her brother had been furious. There had been no ties of affection between them to help him in finding forgiveness. He had given Kit money to buy his American farm and then had packed them off. There would be a check, he said, twice yearly. Beyond that he cared to have nothing to do with the Bannisters.

"But he must have something to do with me now." Lady Meta rose on her pillow. For the moment her lovely face looked less lovely than resolute.

"What I shall do," she went on, "is write to my brother. I shall bring all my powers to bear to persuade him to let me come home. And, Richard"—she paused—"there must be no scandal here. My record must be good.

"That is one reason," she added after a pause, "why I am

going to break off our— What shall I call it? Whatever its name, Richard, we must end it."

She looked softly into his face to see the effect of her words. She was sure—she felt a deep conviction—that he did not love her. If she were mistaken, she might just possibly accept that gallant offer of his.

"Break off!" he repeated.

From the way he said it, although he tried to make his voice strong with protest, she knew that they could never go away together.

"It is quite necessary," she said, "as you can see."

He sat as though revolving in his mind all that she had told him.

"We'll do whatever you think best," he said at last. "But I'm ready, Meta, to throw up everything here and take you away."

"I know you are, but I won't have it. You see," she said, leaning out to touch him gently, "you don't really love me.

"Don't think you have failed me, Richard. This is not a reproach. If I felt bitter once, because I could not make you love me, that bitterness was washed away by my terror— during those hours with Fang. I was not aware that I was thinking while I sat there; yet somewhere in my mind thought must have been going on—for as soon as I awoke here in your cabin, one thing was clear in my mind: 'Richard must be free.' "

"It is because I did not come," Richard muttered. "But, Meta, I would have come. I went to Sisseton City, because— I could not wait to get the Martins out. And things had seemed all right with you the night before—"

"Of course," said Meta. "And you came in time. Why, Richard, I owe my life to you."

As he was still silent, his face strained with emotion, she leaned out again to touch his cheek with her hand.

"You have been my true friend," she said, "and I want to keep you for my friend."

Richard took the hand and kissed it.

"And the first thing I ask of you is," she continued, "to leave me. Oh, not now, this moment, but in our lives, I mean. You can help me most that way. It is very necessary, Richard, that there be no gossip about us. There has been none as yet, I feel sure. I want you to start at once going about. Go out to parties; go to call on that pretty girl you waltzed with."

Richard got to his feet blindly.

"Promise me, Richard."

"If you ask me to, I will promise."

"And you must feel as free as air. You *are* as free as air, this moment, Richard."

Richard did not answer. He walked to the window, then went hastily to the door.

"Meta," he said, in a changed tone, "the storm is over."

She lifted herself in her bed and looked out. The wind had indeed relapsed into silence. The fields of snow lay undisturbed beneath a lemon-colored sunset.

"It seems unbelievable," she said, "that it could have ended so abruptly."

"We were talking," he replied, "and did not notice."

"We must decide at once," she said, "just what explanation we will offer for my presence here. Some one will be coming. Kit may come."

"I'll cook you some supper," he said. "And then we will plan."

Before closing the door, he inhaled a great draught of air. Was it, Meta wondered, more than a physical draught? Was he tasting also the sweet air of freedom?

He added wood to the fire and put the kettle to boil. Meta watched his vigorous movements. She felt sad but cleansed and relieved; she knew he felt the same. She lay back on her pillow.

At that moment of peace there came a battering at the door.

"Kit?" Meta whispered, starting up. "Do you think it is Kit?"

But it was not Kit. It was Joe Gimbel, the reliable hired hand from Sisseton City, twenty-four hours late.

"I came on from Rainbow as soon as the blow began to let up," he announced cheerfully, as Richard opened the door. "Ain't another son-of-a-gun got out of town ahead of me, and only one came with—"

He stopped at the unexpected sight of a woman, a beautiful woman abed in his bachelor employer's kitchen.

"Come in to the fire," Richard said.

Joe stamped his cold feet and, pulling off his heavy mittens, held his cold hands with gusty satisfaction close to the hot stove. Cautiously he continued to stare at Lady Meta, lying with her cloud of black hair foaming over the blankets.

"This is the wife of Captain Bannister whose land lies next to mine," Richard said. "The Captain was away, and she had an accident."

"Captain!" exclaimed Joe. "An army-looking fellow? Say, I'll bet he was the one that came out with me from Rainbow. I left him down the road a piece. Said he was going home."

Richard answered that it was very likely. He added that Joe might take a look at the stock. He was anxious to get the fellow out of the way before Kit arrived.

Joe went out, after stealing a last ebullient look toward the bed, and Lady Meta said quickly.

"Kit will be here any moment."

"Let him come. There is no need to lie to Kit."

"What you said to the man was perfect."

"It was the truth."

Polite knuckles begged admittance at the door; or rather, they warned of an arrival. For Joe Gimbel did not wait to have the door opened. He came in hastily.

"Say," he said casually as he closed the door. "That Captain fellow is coming. Right behind me."

Outside, a voice cried, "Whoa!"

The door burst open. Bannister rushed in.

"Dick!" he cried. "Meta is gone. Do you—" He stopped and stared as Joe had stared at the bed's occupant. The fear in his brilliant eyes changed to anger, an anger all the greater for the strength of the fear it had displaced.

"Well, by God!" he drawled. "We certainly have made ourselves comfortable!"

He shook his head and smiled rebukingly, as one of wide experience might correct a pair of innocents.

"But wouldn't it have been more discreet to put yourselves up at Exile Hall?" he asked.

"Steady, Kit!" Richard said. "Meta came here wounded by that mad dog of yours."

"A good story!" Bannister conceded. "But it hardly goes far enough. Oughtn't you to add something about flags— signal flags?"

Richard said nothing. Meta paled.

"A couple named Martin," Bannister replied, "told me quite a bit about flags."

"Lady Meta had to have some means of protecting herself when you got crazy-drunk," said Richard.

"A Bayard," Bannister murmured. "Pure and without reproach."

"I saved Meta's life!" Richard shouted. "Will you try to get that through your stupid head?"

"Stupid, am I?" Bannister said. Anger broke through his calm, and he shook his head, tossing the white lock. "But not as stupid as you thought!" he cried in a choked voice. "Not stupid enough to be your cuckold!"

He drove his fist abruptly. Richard took the blow and struck back. Bannister staggered back to the wall, gathered himself there, and charged. He got in another blow, but now Richard was ready. Angry and ashamed, but more angry than ashamed, he struck as hard as he knew how. Bannister fell and lay motionless.

Joe gave a prolonged whistle.

"General," he said, "you certainly can hit."

Richard brushed his arm across his face. He looked toward Meta. She was looking whitely from her husband to Joe Gimbel.

"Joe," said Richard, "saddle a horse and ride into Rainbow for a doctor."

"Sure," said Joe.

"On your way, stop at Anglo-American Acres and ask Mrs. Jackson to come over. Tell her she's needed here to nurse Captain Bannister's wife."

"Sure," repeated Joe.

"Just that," said Richard. "Don't say anything else."

"No, General. Sure, General," said Joe, as he retreated.

CHAPTER NINE

THREE base-burner stoves carried the burden of heating the eighteen-room Halliday mansion. They were strategically arranged. One stood in the wide, truly English entrance hall; a second, in the sitting room which flanked the great hall at the left and front; a third, in the dining room, which lay at the right and rear. Thus the three stoves bisected the house neatly at an angle. The drawing room at the right and front, and the library at the left and rear, had fireplaces, and a range roared in the kitchen.

"Next year," said Mr. Halliday, who had not quite foreseen how cold Minnesota winters might be, "the upper hall shall have a stove."

Meanwhile the adventuring Hallidays thought it no hardship to discover in the morning sheet edges stiff with congealed breath and water frozen in their pitchers.

It was the matter of stoves, no doubt, which had settled early in the winter the choice of a room for family gatherings. The sitting room was always cozily warm. From fall until spring a fire burned red behind the isinglass windows of its stove, and the horses' heads in the polished nickel trimming flung their wild manes in a warm glow. To the sitting room the brothers and sisters repaired after supper for those sessions of reading and knitting which filled the winter evenings. Stockings, heavy gray woolen stockings, occupied the fingers of the girls. The male Hallidays, except for the father, wore knickerbockers or breeches. Many long stockings were required, proper work for sisterly fingers. Mrs. Halliday herself knitted her husband's socks and would not yield them even to Dora, whose work was exceptionally fine.

While the mother and sisters knitted, the brothers took turns in reading aloud. The Waverley novels had been knitted that winter into Halliday footgear. This evening "The Talisman" was coming to its glorious conclusion, which made more surprising the fact that Cathy's mind was engaged with a request, which she planned to make of her father. She gave not a thought to the parting of the Saladin and Richard, and only mechanical attention to the heel she was turning. How and when her father should be approached were the problems which engaged her.

Of course, Charley was reading—that might have accounted for her wandering attention. Charley was an abominable reader. His stumbling was acutely distasteful to Reg, who loved books and loved to read, and would have been content always to fill the role of reader. But Mrs. Halliday believed that the poor readers needed practice, so no one's turn was skipped, and poor Reg fidgeted now until his mother gave him a mildly reprimanding look. Gerald, one of the twins, was roasting apples at the back of the stove. As each one reached the proper stage of rosy softness, he slipped it silently to its owner. Meanwhile Charley stumbled on, Reg scowled, and Cathy, in her thoughts, anxiously pursued the arguments she should use to her father.

She knew it would seem absurd at first mention—a ball, just now; the weather had been so violently bad. But if she could put her case properly that very fact of bad weather could be advanced as a reason why the ball should be given. The morale of the colonists was getting low. This last blizzard, coming so unexpectedly when it was almost spring, enduring for two days, had dealt the final blow, and now that the air had cleared and the temperature was rising, it was the exact felicitous moment for a ball.

Moreover the fact that winter was (probably) over, that spring was (one hoped) here at last, cried for a celebration. That very morning Cathy, shoveling snow with Gerald and Gerry, had seen a flock of small gray birds. The American hired man had called them juncos, and had said that the gathering of the juncos was a certain sign of spring . . .

Cathy lost her thread of reasoning. Her heart leaped these stumbling arguments to the real reason why there must be a ball. She must see Richard, she must . . .

What kind of winter had he had? How had he fared through the endless snow and cold? It was unbearable not to know. She had not sought him out after the Hunt Ball. She had said enough then (too much, Dora would have thought), and she had resolved to accept the delay which she believed was in their destiny. But now—his chart showed that he was approaching a crisis. Perhaps he needed her. Perhaps she could help him. Or perhaps, she admitted to herself, flinging down the stockings and jumping to her feet, it was merely that she had reached the point where she could no longer endure not seeing him.

Fortunately at that moment the novel came to an end. In the burst of talk which greeted its finale, Cathy walked to the window and pushed the draperies aside. Snow, ghostly in the starlight, drifted over the porch. It panoplied the once green lawn which gave the house its name, and swathed the frozen lake which began where the lawn ended. The line which led toward Richard's home (Cathy had traced it on a map) led directly through the bole of a snow-laden oak. How often her fancy had pierced that bole, had traveled over miles of snow-sheeted land and ice, in an effort to find and picture

Richard! Well, she would see him with her eyes, she resolved. And she turned back to the room.

Dora had folded her knitting and now rose.

"I'll make the tea," she said.

Bess rose too and took her place at the piano.

Their father loved the nightly family singing. He stayed in the library alone throughout the reading, but as Bess's hands found the first preparatory chords the library door always opened and Mr. Halliday in his old brown dressing gown sauntered out as though by chance. Cathy pondered hastily. Could she plead her cause better when the music would have put him into a mellow mood but when, of course, there would be other people around, or alone with him now in the library? She decided on the former course. The others would all want the ball and would add their entreaties to her own. Dora, indeed, had promised to do so.

Cathy hurried to the buttery and brought in the cups. They must be warmed, else the hot tea would crack them.

The Hallidays loved to sing. No family amusement was more cherished than this one of standing up together around the piano and raising their voices lustily in chorus. Cathy, having put the cups to warm, slipped in beside Charley. He threw his arm about her shoulders, and they sang fervently together "Fair Shines the Moon Tonight," "Flow Gently, Sweet Avon," "Annie Laurie." Cathy poured out in song some of her sadness, some of her longing for Richard.

When the rest had tea, the father took whiskey and water. This was the only time that he ever indulged in liquor. Not even wine was served in the house—too many boys about, Mrs. Halliday always explained cheerfully. She managed to give father's whiskey and water a medicinal appearance, but it was plain that he enjoyed his slow sipping of the nocturnal draught. When he had finished now, Cathy slipped to the arm of his chair.

"Father," she said, "are you feeling benevolent?"

"Benevolent?" He glanced up sharply. "Why, yes, my dear, I suppose I feel benevolent. That was very pretty singing."

"Then, sir, I have a favor to ask."

"What is it, Cathy?"

"A very big favor. Are you sure you won't mind?"

"I'm alarmed. What is it, please?"

"I want the Hallidays to give a ball."

Her words were greeted by an approving uproar. Cathy broke through the clamor to plead:

"We've been so shut in. I think it would do us good; and not just us, but all the English people."

"And when would you like to give it?" That was an encouraging question.

"At once! Tomorrow night. The boys could ride out in the morning in every direction inviting everybody."

"What does your mother say about it?"

"What does she always say? 'Ask Father,' 'Whatever your father says, my dear.'" Cathy took her father by his side-whiskers and shook him. "Father, you know very well that you are the one and the only one who has the power to declare, 'There will be a ball at Green Lawn tomorrow night.' Please, Father!"

"Please! Please! Please!" chorused the others.

"I think Cathy's quite right—about the morale of the colony. A ball would do everybody good." That was Dora, keeping her promise. Bless Dora, thought Cathy! Her voice was so serious and so sweet that whatever she said carried weight.

"Very well," said Mr. Halliday. "If your mother approves." He checked the delighted babble which greeted his words. "I have seen and appreciated—although I don't believe I have mentioned it before—that my daughters have worked hard this winter, harder than they have ever worked before, harder than I dreamed they would have to work when we decided to come out to Minnesota."

"We like Minnesota."

"We don't mind it, Father."

Mrs. Halliday smiled at her husband over the bobbing heads. "You'll work hard tomorrow, getting ready in one day to entertain the colony," she said.

"But we can do it! We can do it!" cried Cathy.

"We'll get up at five—at four!" Bess put in.

"We boys can't help, alas and alack!" said Charley, winking at Jim. "We'll be riding around the country delivering invitations. By the way, where *are* the invitations?"

"There's no time to write them!" Bess raised a cry of dismay.

Cathy slid a look to her father.

"I've written them," she said and, running to the secretary drew out a pack of cream-colored notes addressed in purple ink.

Somewhere in the pack was a note like the others, addressed to Mr. Richard Chalmers, Little Goodlands. It was, in fact, the third note from the bottom. Cathy's heart raced as her father took the pack. He opened the topmost note.

"Hum," he said. "I dislike these French phrases." He had to object to something, and so he had selected the "*Répondez s'il vous plaît.*"

"Oh, but, Father!" cried Cathy. "We have to have that." (Otherwise how could she know that Richard was coming?)

"I'm afraid it's necessary this time," said Mrs. Halliday. "We have to know how many to prepare for."

"Well, next time put it into English," said Mr. Halliday gruffly, and went into the hall to wind the clock.

Cathy ran to get the prayer book. Her brothers hastily arranged the sitting room for prayers. She could hear prayers tonight with a thankful heart, Cathy thought, dropping to her knees.

Her father had consented to a ball . . . "Most merciful God, who art of purer eyes than to behold iniquity." She would see Richard . . . "To our prayers, O Lord, we join unfeigned thanks for all Thy mercies." But would she? Could she be sure he would come? She had not seen him at a party of any kind since the Hunt Ball at the Eyrie.

Cathy pressed her hands against her eyes. She prayed eagerly, fervently: "O God! Let him come! Please, please, let him come!"

". . . in whose name we offer up these, our imperfect prayers, Amen."

CHAPTER TEN

Mr. HALLIDAY had spoken truly when he said that his daughters had worked hard that winter. Soon after coming to Minnesota, Mrs. Halliday had realized that competent servants were not to be obtained. In England she had never done more than efficiently manage her household; but with the same calmness and courage which had enabled her, for her children's sake, to agree to her husband's plan of emigration, she had set out to learn the mechanics of housework; and her daughters had learned with her. She hired an American woman to teach them; Mrs. Tompkins had thought at first that the lady was joking; she could not believe that this mother and these daughters knew literally nothing about bread or pastry making. She had been equally surprised by their diligence and their aptness in learning.

"Your ma's got the feeling for bread in her fingers," she confided admiringly to Dora. "Otherwise she couldn't have picked it up so quick."

Mrs. Tompkins came in to do the washing, but she had no time for the ironing of a mountain of shirts, collars, cuffs, petticoats, drawers, aprons, dresses, and linens. This labor was added to the heavy total of labor inevitable in such a household. There were eighteen rooms to be kept clean and in order; a family of thirteen to be fed; younger children to be cared for (Reg and Dora taught them as well, hearing lessons every morning); sewing; mending; darning.

Dora, Cathy, and Bess agreed that their mother had enough to do if she directed operations. Early in the winter they had taken upon themselves the necessary manual labor. They divided it according to an ingenious plan. Each week one was cook, one was housemaid, one was lady.

The cook had charge of the kitchen and pantry; that was the week of grave responsibility. "When is Dora cook again?" Jim would inquire caustically upon discovering that the beef was overdone. Cathy shone at desserts. "No doubt about this being Cathy's week!" her loyal Charley would declare when a fragile Spanish cream, decorated with citron, was borne proudly to the table.

The housemaid had charge of the sweeping and dusting. She made the beds and brought up to the bedrooms every morning three heavy pails of water which were then apportioned to those pitchers in which it nightly froze. The housemaid was also mistress of the lamps; twenty lamps were cleaned and filled each day; on Saturday the chimneys were washed.

The lady had nothing to do, nothing worth mentioning. She merely ordered the sitting room, served at the table, washed, and wiped the dishes, and lent a hand with the beds.

They changed work each Saturday night.

The Halliday girls had certainly not been idle over the winter. Yet not one of them resented the extra toil involved in the hastily improvised Spring Ball. They had been up since long before dawn; it seemed to Cathy to be the middle of the day, although it was only nine o'clock, when Charley sought her out in the kitchen. He was booted and spurred for his ride. His portion of the pack of invitations peeped from his jacket pocket.

Cathy was making trifle. She stood before the kitchen range holding in one hand a spoon at which she was staring speculatively, and in the other a blank book which her mother had brought from England with cherished family recipes written on its pages.

Slices of sponge cake must be soaked in wine; that had been done. These must be placed in a deep glass dish; that had been done. Then a rich boiled custard must be poured over the whole to fill the interstices of cake and permeate the dish with velvet goodness. Tonight, at the last moment, whipped cream would be added. But now there was this matter of custard . . .

According to the book, it should be lifted from the fire at the instant it coated the spoon. Had it coated the spoon, or hadn't it? Just what constituted coating on a spoon? At that horrible moment of indecision, Charley approached her.

"Sis, I want to ask you something."

"What is it, dear?"

"Do you think it might do—do you think it might be jolly —to ask some Americans to the party?"

"Why, Charley, whom would we ask?" Cathy squinted darkly at the spoon. It *was* coated; it had been coated before. No doubt she had let the custard cook too long, and the trifle would be ruined. She was aware, through her confusion, as she hurriedly removed the basin from the stove, that Charley had not answered, and she went on absently:

"They never *are* asked, you know. I don't believe they'd have the proper clothes, or know how to behave. But I'll speak to Mother—"

"Oh, never mind!" She looked up to find Charley's face a deep embarrassed crimson. Before she could speak again, he had bolted.

Cathy emerged sharply from her preoccupation with custard. Had Charley acquired an American friend? It must be a girl, or he wouldn't have blushed. She ran out to the driveway. But she was too late. The boys were cantering down the snowy drive—Jim, Charley, and Reg on horses, Gerry on his pony. Which brother, Cathy wondered, forgetting Charley for a moment, bore the note to Richard?

The thought of Charley returned, as she walked slowly back to the kitchen, over the crunching snow. If only she had minded what he was saying! If only she hadn't been so muddled by that custard. She cherished Charley's confidence and was troubled now by a feeling that she had failed him. But worry was soon lost in work.

There was plenty of work. Those midnight sit-down suppers, without which no ball was complete, were hearty affairs. In addition to the trifle, Cathy was making that Spanish cream for which she was famous, and individual mince pies.

Dora was busy with the chickens. The boys had killed them before they left. Over the boiled chickens, Dora would pour, while it was hot, a white sauce made from giblet gravy, milk, and butter. There would be roasted chickens also.

Her father later would come into the pantry and disjoint the birds. He would even start to slice the breasts. Then the joints would be put back into place against each chicken, the slices of breast would be restored, and the bird tied with white ribbons. Later, at the table, the ribbons could be untied, and carving was a simple matter. Mrs. Halliday always contrived to place good carvers before the chickens and the cold boiled tongues and hams. Her husband was a famous carver. So was Mr. Lovell. And one or two of the younger men (Mr. Hook, if he were only here) might be trusted in a pinch.

It was late afternoon before the four riders (who had met by appointment after their labors in order to make an impressive return) trotted up the darkening drive. They had been instructed to wait at every house while the requested *réponse* was scribbled, and they stamped into the hall, their pockets full of notes, to be gleefully set upon by their sisters. "The Scatchetts can come." "The Barrowcliffs are coming." "The Nevilles and Mr. Earle are riding over from Sisseton City." Informative cries rose on every hand as torn envelopes rattled to the floor. Cathy stood still with the note which had been her booty clutched unopened in her hand. The hand was trembling, and her cheeks were going from red to white, but everyone was too much engaged to notice. She heard Bess cry:

"Oh, dear! The Bannisters can't come! And I did so hope they could. I love to look at Lady Meta."

"What's the matter?" Cathy's mother asked.

"She's ill, and so is the Captain. Isn't that odd?"

"Not at all odd, this weather, I should say."

Cathy heard their voices as though at a distance. She felt, ridiculously, faint. She had never fainted in her life, but now she must faint, or know without delay whether Richard was coming. She opened the note in her hand.

It was written with a blunt black pencil.

"Accept with pleasure.—Richard Chalmers."

"*Accept with pleasure.*" Was it more than an acceptance to a party? Was it an answer to what she had told him, to what she had let him know and feel last autumn at the Hunt Ball?

Cathy ran down the hall, into the deserted kitchen. It was not far enough away. She retreated to the woodshed, and out to the snowy lawn. The sky was dark blue, austere, and cold, behind tall black tree trunks and a filigree of twigs and branches. Cathy laid the note against her burning cheek, she pressed it to her lips.

There was supper to be eaten before one might dress. It was a hurried supper, to be sure, and afterwards the sisters laid the table, so that there would be nothing but coffee and such last-minute things to attend to at midnight. They brought out the fine linen cloths with "J. Halliday" woven into the border, the solid silver which was stored in a chest in their father's dressing room, the Indian Tree china that dwelt in the china pantry, while the dishes used every day were kept in the dining room cupboard. A supper was a supper indeed when Mother let one use these precious cups and plates.

And a ball was a ball indeed when one had programs! Hand-tinted programs with tiny pencils attached! At first it had been assumed that there would be no time to make them. But the pencils were on hand in mother's desk, a gross of wee white pencils on cords with tassels at the end! Mother had brought them from England, thinking that such frivolous trinkets might be hard to procure in the new world.

"Bess is no good at cooking," Cathy had whispered to Dora, "and her water colors are dear. Let's let her out of everything, if she'll make us programs."

Dora had agreed. And as the paints and brushes were set out, Cathy had hung about her sister anxiously.

"Remember! It's a spring ball!"

"Remember that I'm an artist, and you're only a cook," Bess had replied loftily.

She had produced truly charming cards, sprinkled with robins, violets, and buttercups. The dance list, done in a delicate chirography full of shaded loops and spirals, announced a program of twenty dances opening with the quadrille which Mr. and Mrs. Halliday always led off together and ending with the Swedish Dance which brought balls at the Hallidays' to a sometimes riotous conclusion.

There had been no time, of course, to procure an orchestra. Those unfortunate persons who could play the piano were assigned certain dances for which they must provide the music. Cathy was happily unaccomplished at the piano, but

Bess and Dora could play; so could Sally Lovell and Mrs. Barrowcliff; Reg could play divinely—if he would. He consented magnanimously to play the two waltzes. As he went upstairs to dress, Cathy waylaid him.

"Reg, that second waltz, would you play a certain one?"

"If you like. What shall it be?"

" 'Tales from the Vienna Woods.' "

"Right."

Cathy did not merely run; she flew up the stairs on wings of joy.

The younger children had been given permission to stay up until nine. Cathy sang as she brushed Maggie's hair, as she slipped the excited child into a clean frock, tied her sash and the tassels on her boots. Dora and Bess were still busy with Victoria and Albert, so Cathy took time to look in on Gerry whose ears often needed inspection. (Geraldine roomed with Bess; her toilet would have expert supervision.)

Cathy and Dora were in their room at last, seriously at work.

The sisters shared their bed and wash stand, but each had a dressing table, a bare pine table with skirts of dotted muslin gathered over underskirts of colored cambric. The looking glasses were swung up on stands and stood upon the tables. Gravely the two girls put their lamps where the rays would light the mirrors. Swiftly and in silence they went about the business of washing and dressing. They wore the white muslins which their mother considered suitable for parties. Dora's ribbons were blue; Cathy's were yellow; Bess's would be pink. Above the snowy, freshly ironed ruffles of her dress, Cathy's cheeks were scarlet and her eyes like the stars she loved.

Dora had long since been told that Richard was coming.

"Mayn't I loan you something, dear? My cameo? A bracelet?"

"Not a thing," said Cathy. "I don't seem to have sense enough to care how I look. I seem to think he's going to—think I look all right."

"You look lovely. Only—don't shine so, darling, or everyone will know ..."

They laughed in each other's arms, Dora's eyes wet.

"Hurry, girls!" came their mother's voice from below. "A carriage on the drive!"

They ran down to join her.

Mrs. Halliday stood regally beside her husband in the hall, her small lace cap with its trimming of marabou feathers, her purple satin gown, as familiar, as much a matter of course, at a ball, as his white tie, gloves, and tail coat. Dora floated into place beside them. Cathy danced to open the door.

In no time at all the spacious rooms were full of people. Talk and laughter darted through the doorways as nimbly as did Maggie, Victoria, and Albert, who were making the most of their unaccustomed privilege of staying up until nine. They were everywhere at once, bumping, peeping, giggling. They gathered under the stairs to whisper their observations. They looked on round-eyed at the opening quadrille, in which their father and mother, looking awesomely tall, frighteningly inaccessible, moved to the beat of the music.

Cathy was Charley's partner for that opening quadrille. She moved like thistledown in advance and retreat, in slow revolution and curtsy. Richard had not come. But that was no wonder. Little Goodlands was far distant. Several people who lived much nearer at hand had not yet arrived.

When the quadrille ended, Cathy whispered to her mother

that she would put the children to bed. She did so, in dilatory fashion, taking them first to the kitchen for cakes, lingering in the nursery. She went then to her own room to look at her glowing face in the mirror. She wanted Richard to have come without fail by the time she descended.

At last she ran down the stairs, fearing to look in any direction, so sure was she that her eyes would find his face, and that her own face would betray her love. But it was safe to look anywhere at all. He was not there.

A polka and a galop had gone by. They had come to the first waltz. Reg played it, and Cathy danced it with Slabs Neville. But although she heard herself chattering merrily, there was a curious stillness at her heart. What could have happened? Had he had an accident? She saw him thrown from his horse, helpless in the snow. When the dance ended she hurried to her room again, pulled his note from her bosom. Yes, he had said "Accept"; she had not dreamed it. "Accept with pleasure.—Richard Chalmers." She returned the crumpled paper to its tender haven, and went bravely down the stairs.

The clock in the hall struck ten. Every chime was a blow at her heart. Thirty minutes passed, and the half-hour struck. "Oh, Richard! Richard! Where are you?" Slowly the inexorable moments were creeping toward the second waltz, that waltz which she had long ago marked with his initials, that waltz for which Reg had promised to play "Tales from the Vienna Woods."

He *must* come in time for that! Even if he came now, Cathy thought desperately, something would be lost; some freshness of joy, some ecstasy had passed. Never mind! She would be satisfied with what was left if only he would come!

Square dances followed round dances. One pianist gave willing place to another. Men went up to the third-floor quar-

ters of her brothers or out of doors to smoke. Girls ran upstairs to mend torn ruffles or tuck in wilting curls.

The second waltz arrived, Reg took his place at the piano.
The beloved melody curled through the room, seductive,
enchanting, and men scurried to find partners. "Mayn't I
have it, Miss Cathy?" "I'm sorry. It's taken."

Cathy fled to the kitchen. She busied herself there thrust-
ing wood into the stove, changing dampers, grinding coffee,
but the music pursued her, wreathing through the air, winding in the dance like a malicious sprite . . .

The waltz ended simultaneously with a ring at the front
door. Cathy walked out to answer it with a calmness born of
the deepest grief she had ever known. Even if this late comer
should be Richard, she could greet him calmly, she felt.

But it was not Richard. It was Percy Neville, the only other
expected guest who had failed to arrive. His brothers had
marveled at his absence. "We dropped him at the club. He
only stopped for a—er—for a smoke." He had had an abundance to "smoke," Cathy thought, admitting him; his handsome face was flushed, and the liquor, so rich on his breath,
had plainly loosened his tongue.

"Evening, Miss Cathy. I hope you've been an angel and
saved me a waltz. I'm dashed sorry to be so late, but I almost
didn't get here at all."

Mr. Halliday looked into the hall.

"Oh, Percy! Catherine's admitted you—"

"I was just telling Miss Catherine how sorry I was to be
late. There's news in town, sir. Dashed sad news. I'm afraid
we're in for scandal."

The excitement in his voice had reached the drawing room.
Men and women hurried out, and Percy, proud of his tale,
told it before he could be checked.

It was not a story that women should have heard; the girls

did indeed withdraw to the outskirts of the circle. But Percy's voice reached them. Every word came clear to Cathy.

"Dr. Shaw, the American doctor, just returned from Exile Hall. He was treating Bannister for shock and a broken head. Dick Chalmers knocked him down."

"But where? Why?"

"In Chalmers' house. Night before last."

"But what was the reason?"

"Kit found Lady Meta there. He'd been in town drinking for two days, and Lady Meta, it seems, spent the time with Dick—"

"But this is making a mountain out of a molehill," came her mother's calm clear voice. "Mr. Chalmers has a married couple keeping house for him."

"He'd dismissed them, ma'am. Just before. They're in Rainbow now, and they bear out the doctor's story. They say that Dick and Lady Meta used to signal with a flag—"

Mr. Halliday cut in.

"We will not hear any more, Mr. Neville, if you please." His voice was heavy with disapproval. His resentment at Percy for reciting such a tale, in a home in the presence of women, stiffened his anger against Richard. "If Mr. Chalmers should call, you will not receive him," he said audibly to his wife, and offering her his arm he led the way back to the drawing room.

Cathy opened the great front door and closed it behind her. The icy wind tore through her thin dress, but she did not feel it. She lifted an agonized, twisted face to the sky.

The door opened and closed again. Dora came up behind her.

"Darling! Precious! Maybe it's a lie."

Cathy did not answer.

Above the dark mysterious oaks shone her stars and planets. She knew they were piercingly brilliant in the winter sky. But they trembled—they dimmed. Cathy turned blindly for the solace of Dora's arms. She buried her wet face in Dora's bosom.

BOOK THREE

CHAPTER ONE

THE snows of winter slid into Rainbow's lakes and streams. Trains, still ending their run at Sisseton City, began once more to disgorge Englishmen: younger men this spring, mere boys, some of them, and—it immediately developed—differently situated from those who had come before. The new arrivals were not landowners. They did not stride from the train with maps, asking to be shown their estates. They were quietly taken in charge by Mr. Jackson, and after a short lapse of time—three days, a week, a fortnight—they might have been found in residence at the Farmers' Home, or at the Log House, or at the new Balmoral House in Rainbow. The old taverns were quite eclipsed by this imposing hostelry which was three stories high, completely shuttered, girdled thrice by narrow open verandas and fringed along the Main Street side by a row of armchairs. There or elsewhere the season's crop of colonists took up their quarters, and the least adept among them soon learned to drink and gamble as they waited for remittances from home.

What had occurred in the three days, the week or the fortnight in which they were missing from the public view? This had occurred! Jackson had fulfilled Crockett's part of that bargain which Jackson had once explained to Richard. The bargain had been struck in Fenchurch Street. Mr. Crockett had received plump hundred-pound fees, in return for which he had engaged to place these younger sons of superior family, classical education, and habits of pleasant idleness where they might learn "the art of American farming."

Translated into plain frontier speech, this meant that they were parceled out to farmers as unpaid hands. The young men did not grasp the situation at first, although they were taken aback when they saw the houses, the "comforts and refinements" of which had been so loudly praised to their parents. The lands were good and well developed; the barns were often handsome; but the houses ranged from sod shanties and dugouts to small frame structures like the house at Little Goodlands. The hands slept in the loft or in the barn and washed in a tin basin outside the kitchen door.

Bewilderment caused the young colonist to accept the situation for the moment. He had heard tempting tales of the hunting and fishing which Minnesota offered, of the chance to pick up railroad lands for a song. After all, he argued, it would not be so bad to stand around and watch the Americans work; and a knowledge of their ways would certainly be useful when one had to direct one's own men. But the next morning at five he was rudely awakened, given a fork and told to clean out the barn. He endured it for three days, a week, a fortnight. None endured it longer.

Life was not so bad after he put the farm behind him. Rainbow was seething with the excitement of growth.

"Up-and-comingest town in southern Minnesota," its citizens were quick to proclaim.

"Ding dong," cried an American, and the answer, prescribed by custom was, "Toot, toot!" which meant that the railroad could not stay away much longer. By Christmas, at the latest, everyone believed, it would have left Sisseton City behind.

The Balmoral House was not the only new ornament to the town. The Englishmen had their church up. St. Ethelburga's, it was called, after St. Ethelburga's in London. The Americans had their schoolhouse up, a square two-storied building with a belfry; and a number of small freshly painted houses dotted the muddy lanes, which stretched away from the Main Street.

There was half a block of sidewalk on the Main Street. It lay in front of Mr. Lovell's small stone bank and the big brick general store in which Mr. Halliday now successfully competed with Judson Oates across the way. From the second story of these buildings hung the doctor's and attorney's signs. (The dentist came from Mankato once a fortnight.) Humbler one-story buildings made up the rest of the straggling thoroughfare which now concealed the beauties of Lake Rainbow for more than a mile.

On warm spring days all doors stood open, and each small establishment sent into the balmy air the odor of its trade or craft. Bolgers' Drug Store smelled of drugs in spite of the new soda fountain. The Boot and Shoe Emporium and Walker's Harness Shop exuded an aroma of leather. Scorched leather and rubber scented the blacksmith's shop, which—like the livery stable with its sharper effluvium—was a favorite gathering place of social spirits. The feed store sent out a dusty golden smell. The office of the *Gazette* was redolent of ink. Soon the cosmopolitan impression which Main Street offered to the olfactory sense would be complete. Saloons would pour their beery odors over hospitably swinging doors.

Of course, even now, no one was going thirsty. The English Club was still in operation, with Captain Bannister, an increasingly eccentric figure, offering the young colonists tall tales of his Indian service along with tall drinks. But a club could not quite fill the place of a saloon, a real saloon with green baize curtains and sociable brass rail. So thought Rainbow, which had voted licensing at last. And so thought Johnny Devlin, who was in town looking for Richard.

"Chalmers? You won't find him around," the fat host of the Log House declared.

"Why not?" Devlin inquired. "I thought he was a social young buck."

"Oh, he's hiding out. He got mixed up with a woman, and everybody's giving him the cold shoulder nowadays."

Johnny whistled. He slipped his beringed hands into the pockets of his checkered pants and strolled thoughtfully up and down the tavern's common room.

"How can I get a message to him?"

"Jackson's boy Ole is in town for the mail. He'd take a message. They're neighbors. And there's no chance he won't find Dick at home," Oarlock added, eager to reintroduce the scandalous topic.

He had not, however, in his zest for gossip, overstated Richard's case. What he said was virtually true. Richard was, so far as the conventional element among his countrymen was concerned, an outcast. He had indeed exiled himself on his farm. What was more, he was in the hour that Devlin inquired for him experiencing there the bitterest moment he had so far known.

"It's the end of the fight," he was saying to himself, staring down at a patch of rich black earth which was teeming with tiny insects.

Like many of the colonists he had abandoned beans this year. Some had stocked their farms with sheep, to the delight of the great gray wolves that once had trailed herds of buffalo across the Minnesota prairie, and that still appeared now and then although the buffalo had long since drifted westward. Dick had planted wheat, oats and corn along with the Americans, who were making another undaunted bid for success. All had feared a repetition of last year's disaster, and all had fought it, none more doggedly than Richard. He had burned the grass on his meadow lands, and ploughed and harrowed his fields against the grasshopper larvae. But in spite of all his efforts the eggs had hatched, and this morning —a May morning with a sun as warm and velvety as the sun of mid-July—he had found the infant hoppers swarming over his land.

His land had failed him! It was not the loss of crops alone which he saw as he watched the ugly insects, wingless as yet, crawling, jumping, intertwining in a dark mass in the sun. It was the loss of hope, the loss of a way out of the pit into which he had fallen. He had been headed for that pit the glittering winter night when he cantered into Rainbow in response to Cathy's invitation. It was ironical to remember that, for he had believed then that he was beginning life anew.

Meta had broken the bond between them. His mind was at ease about her, for although she had returned to Exile Hall it was under the Jacksons' protection, and she had assured Richard that she would remain there only long enough to make preparations to leave. Richard had not felt happy exactly, riding toward the Hallidays' ball. He was still too close to Meta's misfortunes for that. But he had been full of hope and courage, resolved to take his future into firm hands, and make it worthy of Cathy. Then he had dropped in at the Log House. Aghast at what he heard there, he had gone on to the Club. It had become clear to him then that he would not dance that night with Cathy. The American doctor had returned from Exile Hall, and his story was in everyone's mouth, that damning story which was so damningly upheld by the Martins' innuendos.

When the senior Halliday cut him on the street the following morning, Richard knew that ostracism was decreed.

The bachelors of the hunting set had stood by. "Come out any time," Trevenen had urged after the Eyrie was opened for the season; but Richard had speedily noticed that when women were to be present there was no specific invitation. Hook had finally intemperately admitted as much. "Damn it!" he had cried. "We think it's a rotten shame. But the family men just won't have you, Dick. You're the sort who coaxes married women into rigging up signals with petticoats and lanterns."

For Richard, rather than Meta, had been singled out for judgment. Richard did not resent that. Yet he was aware of a sardonic humor in the situation. Meta, in public opinion, was a victim.

Meta had not tried to induce this view. She had been aided unwittingly at the outset by her illness and enforced seclusion. The former had aroused a degree of pity for her, and the latter had given time for the storm of disapproval to subside —or to focus upon Richard. It was no fault of hers either that her subsequent demeanor had been perfect. Her manner had been completely assured, albeit gentle, as befitted the manner of one who was ill and needed friends.

As soon as it became apparent that none of the English ladies meant to call at Exile Hall, she had been prompt to write to Lady Throop.

Lady Throop, upon receiving the crested note, had found herself unable to resist its invitation. The prospect of a stream of letters, London-bound, retailing the confidences of the Earl of Blackmore's sister, had overcome her scruples, and her husband had approved her going.

"It is natural that she should turn to you," he had said with pompous satisfaction, "the only other lady of rank . . ."

With a delightful sense of intimacy, Lady Throop had ordered out her sleigh and hurried to Exile Hall. Arriving there, in all her corseted magnificence, her breath grew shorter and shorter as she hurried to Lady Meta's room intent on revelations.

There had been no revelations. Lady Meta from the first took the position that there was nothing to be told. She touched with understandable brevity upon the horror she had undergone—the cruel hours with Fang, the appalling ride to Little Goodlands, her collapse there. But she treated it as a matter so well known that it did not need expansion. Expansion, her manner indicated, was for her future plans, not for her past experiences which she wished only to forget.

"Of course," she said, "I am unable to remain at Exile Hall. I have written to my brother. And until I receive his reply I shall stay in the village. I told him that I should ask your advice upon a residence there."

Lady Throop's fingers itched for a pen. "We felt, Sir Mortimer and I, that the Earl of Blackmore was looking to us . . ." She could fairly see the characters leaping to inky life.

She bent over Lady Meta, a pale appealing figure in the great gloomy bed.

"My darling!" she cried. "What residence could you possibly need, when my home is yours!"

Lady Meta had demurred a little, but only, it was plain, to make sure that the invitation was sincere. Lady Throop gave that assurance, her mind meanwhile rushing ahead, putting pen to paper: ". . . have as our guest, the Lady Meta Bannister. Poor thing, she was frightfully mistreated by her husband. No wonder her brother, the Earl of Blackmore, opposed the match."

"I refuse to move one step," Lady Throop declared aloud, "unless you return with me."

Lady Meta had found strength to rise and dress and pack. She had settled herself comfortably at Gray Gables, the

Throop town house, and there, before ever she acknowledged herself no longer an invalid, she received the cards of every matron in the English colony. Eventually she received the matrons themselves, and in a sufficient number of instances, their daughters. When she finally went down into Lady Throop's drawing room, she received the husbands and the sons, and these, having bowed over her hand and taken tea with her, went out into the world convinced that there was in all Rainbow only one scoundrel more of a scoundrel than Christopher Bannister. That super-scoundrel was, of course, Dick Chalmers.

Lady Meta knew that they left her believing that, and she was sorry. She tried to prevent it, expressing gently her obligation to Richard. But her attempts were half-hearted, both because she knew they were dangerous to herself, and because she believed them to be unnecessary. A man could weather a little scandal. This cloud would blow over, and Richard emerge none the worse off. She was impatient with him for accepting even temporary ostracism. He could have escaped it if he had given thought to ways and means. Had not she escaped, and from a danger far greater than his? If you wore an air of guilt, how could you expect that people would not believe you guilty? You invited condemnation.

Certainly Richard was condemned. Every father took the attitude which Cathy's father had taken on the night of the ball. Every wife heard the same words. "If Mr. Chalmers should call, you will not receive him." They all agreed. No mother cared to have her home invaded by a great lusty young man reputedly expert in the arts of seduction.

Richard—at first confused, then sore, then angry—had buried himself at Little Goodlands.

And now this refuge had failed him. Turning away from the patch of land in which the young hoppers were squirming, he went to the stables, saddled Kentish Beauty and without a word to Joe, who watched from the kitchen, galloped out of the barnyard.

He was going at such a breakneck pace, nearing Anglo-American Acres, that he failed to recognize Ole until the lank young Scandinavian called out his name.

Richard halted impatiently then, while Ole delivered his message. A man wished to see Mr. Chalmers at the Log House.

"What did you say his name was?"

"Yan Devlin."

John Devlin! The liquor salesman whose overturned sleigh had delayed him upon a return from Sisseton City!

It had been an unlucky delay, Richard thought, pushing on. Everything might have been different, if he had reached Exile Hall that day before the storm broke. He could have taken Meta to Jackson's . . .

"Might have," "could have"—Richard refused to traffic in "might have" and "could have." But he took a sullen satisfaction in keeping Devlin waiting. Let him cool his heels! He rode through Rainbow without dismounting, out the Pennell road to Bob Whipp's farm.

Bob Whipp loped out, waving a rifle in one hand and a cleaning rod in the other.

"You're just in time," he shouted. "I'm going hunting and you've got to come along." In his high spirits he did not notice Richard's opposite mood.

"We're going after the smartest wolf in seven counties," he said. "A big lone bitch that's been killing sheep and cattle all over the place. We got her mate a year back, but she gives us the slip every time. She never fails to leave her mark, though—the tracks of a right fore-paw that has only three toes."

"I can't go today," Richard said.

Only then did Captain Whipp really look at his visitor.

"Something wrong, Dick?"

"Would you like to farm my land? You and Bridey can have the house to yourselves. I'm clearing out."

Bob pulled a blade of tender grass, and chewed it thoughtfully.

"What's eating you?"

"Nothing. But the filthy hoppers will soon be eating my crop."

"Maybe not. Maybe they'll move on before they get hungry."

"And maybe they won't. Will you farm my land, or won't you? Speak up."

Bob bristled. (Captain Bob Whipp, as he often was heard to remark, wouldn't take anybody's lip.) But then he scrutinized his visitor's face, and he must have seen the trouble in that set and dusty countenance, for he laid a friendly hand upon Kentish Beauty's bridle.

"Get down off that nag and give her a fill of oats. And yourself a fill of Bridey's coffee."

Richard yielded to the affectionate attack. But not even Bob Whipp could persuade him from abandoning Little Goodlands. He would not pass another night there, he said savagely. And after the coffee was drunk and the pipes were lighted, the Captain gave Richard's plan serious consideration.

"If you're bound to give up, I might as well take on your land. I'll do better for you than most; I'm a good farmer, and what's more I'll treat you fair and square, which is more than some folks would do. It would be to my advantage," he conceded. "Your land is first rate, and all of it is broken. Lonabelle's man could manage my farm along with his own."

He looked toward Bridey, who was tying on a sunbonnet

before the kitchen mirror. She was going, she had said, to Lonabelle's.

"How'd you like it, pet?"

"Why, I'd like it, Pa," said Bridey, smiling shyly.

"Dick's house is fixed up handier than this. (What with the pesky hoppers, I've never yet got her that floor.) But of course it's a long way from Lonabelle's . . ."

"I know," Bridey interrupted eagerly, "but—" she paused.

"It's nearer Rainbow," her father supplied.

Even in the midst of his wretchedness, Richard found himself marveling at how Bridey had changed. When he had seen her upon previous visits to Whipp's farm, he had thought her a pretty little thing. But today she was more than pretty. Her cheeks were warm, her eyes were sparkling. What had caused the transformation? Was it that she was growing up?

"Well, if Bridey agrees—and I guess she does—it's a bargain," Bob Whipp said.

"That's fine, Bob." Richard rose.

"We'll scare out them hoppers and get a crop for him, won't we, Bridey?"

"*You* will, Pa."

"And when Dick gets tired of hotel victuals, he can come out for a home-cooked meal. Eh, Bridey?"

"I'm afraid," said Bridey, blushing, "that my cooking wouldn't taste like much after the hotel."

"Well, of all outlandish remarks!" Bob shouted, scooping her into an arm.

But he stopped laughing when he got outside with Richard.

"Dick," he said, "I know as well as you do, that it ain't just hoppers is driving you off your land."

Richard did not answer.

"It's this talk going around."

"You know," Bob went on, as Richard busied himself with

Kentish Beauty, "if you let people talk long enough, they get tired of talking. They just shut up of their own accord."

"Thanks, Bob."

"And what's more, a lot of folks feel like I do, that you had a right to swing on Bannister."

"But then again," Richard answered, "a lot of folks don't." And he waved farewell abruptly and urged Kentish Beauty to a rapid pace over the undulations of the prairie. Meadow larks soared up, singing. Acres of marigolds carpeted the sloughs with lavish gleaming yellow. A farmer was sowing grain. He walked away, under the vivid sky, a basket slung to his shoulder, flinging out seed with wide sweeps of his arms, now left, then right, now left, then right. It was no day for a man to be giving up his land!

At the southerly turn of the road Richard met young Charley Halliday. The lad was acutely embarrassed.

"Good God! I'm not a leper!" Richard thought, as Cathy's brother colored and gulped over a word of greeting. Whatever its cause, Charley's discomfort served a purpose in Richard's career. It helped, when he reached the Log House and Johnny Devlin, to persuade him to the latter's plan.

Rainbow had voted licensing, though by a thin majority. The town would still have been a temperance town except for commercially minded citizens who wished to keep their rich Englishmen content. Johnny wanted an Englishman running one saloon. It would be a center, he declared, for the whole British crowd; it would be a gold mine. Richard protested that he had no funds. No matter, Devlin would back him. He would take a half-interest, and Richard's share could be covered by notes. The profits would easily take care of them, Devlin explained, and he drowned all objections in a flood of glowing prophecies.

The plan fitted into Richard's mood. It fitted in also with certain necessities. For two years his father had been sending him a generous allowance. In two years Richard had not harvested a bean. It was difficult, he knew, for his father on the other side of the Atlantic to comprehend the completeness of the ruin the locusts wrought. But the Squire had continued the allowance without protest and recently, when the letters from his son had betrayed unhappiness, he had suggested that Richard come home. But Richard did not wish to go home. Much as he longed to see England, he could not bear to face his parents, nor his sisters, who had sent him off with such bright hopes, nor his brothers, who were doing so well in their several undertakings. If, however, he could make some money! That would be different. So he fell in with Devlin's plan.

He opened the Kentish Arms, and he knew almost at once that he had made a mistake. Whipp had been right when he said that people got tired of talking. The colony's ban upon him would have been lifted if he had not taken this socially damning plunge.

Meta, when she heard of it, sought him out at the Log House. It was the first time he had seen her since the storm of scandal had broken, and he paid tribute to her imprudent gallantry when she entered the common room, a markedly modish figure in her pull-back dress with a flowery wisp of a bonnet perching on her forehead.

"I am looking for Mr. Chalmers. Oh, there you are, Richard!"

He rescued her at once from a room frozen into staring silence.

Back at her carriage, she launched into pleading. He must abandon this mad plan. He must go about again, mingle with people, not hide himself as though he were guilty and ashamed.

"*Herr Gott!*" she said. "If you are a seducer, what am I? And yet Lady Throop takes me to Guild meeting, and we entertain the colony at tea!"

Richard told her that he would do what he could. He bowed over her hand, and her carriage rolled away. But Richard looked hopelessly after its departing wheels. He did not feel free to break his engagements with Devlin; the matter had gone too far.

He fell deeper into the pit, and from its gloomy isolation he was mocked by the outcome of events. For the locusts departed early, after doing a minimum of damage. The cultivated fields that summer were marvels of fertility and beauty. Richard on the farm could have made an assuaging success, while at running a saloon he was a hopeless failure.

The Englishmen gathered at the Kentish Arms, true. But they left little money there. "Put it on the book, Dick!" Richard put it on the book, and there it was promptly forgotten. The notes which Devlin had so airily assured him would take care of themselves, fell due with alarming frequency, and there was no money to meet them. Moreover, Richard had no industry where this kind of work was concerned. He brought Joe in from the farm to tend bar, and he himself led a life of polished idleness, falling in with every trivial plan. The most serious activity of himself and all his patrons was waiting for mail. It was curious, Richard thought, the way they all waited for mail, as though life in England were the real life, and this one only a dream from which they must awaken soon.

He was pursuing that thought, musing over his ledger, on the night he met Paul Bevan.

CHAPTER TWO

PAUL BEVAN appeared near closing time of a rainy August evening. Richard was alone in the saloon. He liked to sleep late in the mornings now (morning was the damnable time when one could not escape one's self). Joe was a bright and early bird. So Richard let Joe go home as the summer evenings waned, and Joe did not look for his employer to appear much before noon.

Richard kept the ledger—but only half-heartedly, because the notes due and the unpaid accounts were always so deplorably large, moneys taken in so deplorably small—and it was usually with the ledger open in the lamplight that he sat when he was alone. On some nights he made no proper entries at all. He made instead a record of his dreary days.

"Got up late. Had a fit of the blues." "Lost fifty dollars at the Sisseton City track." "Big mail. Letters and papers. All drunk." "Oysters at the Balmoral with Hook. We'll shoot tomorrow if it clears."

Sometimes there were small observations.

"Mother's birthday today." Or, "The Guv writes that he has a new hunter which can outjump Kentish Beauty, but I doubt that." Or, "The breast plumage of a passenger pigeon is iridescent and beautiful enough to adorn C." He put down these and other small thoughts because they were things he wanted to say and there was no one to whom he cared to say them. This night he had written, "Can't make out why I don't get more mail." And after a moment he had scribbled blackly, "Can't make out either why the mail seems so damned important. Get it through your thick head that you live here, *here*. In Minnesota. Not in England." He was frowning over that when a strange young man pushed through the swinging doors.

"Another one of Crockett's young apprentice farmers," Richard surmised, rising. "And a different kind," he added quickly. For the young man had an arresting face, thin and deeply marked, with gray-green eyes and a sweep of heavy black hair thrown dramatically from his forehead. He carried a violin case which he swung to a table, calling out to Richard as he did so:

"Something to drink, my man."

"What will you have?" Richard asked.

"I don't care. Hell! I don't even know. I never drank anything stronger than lemonade in my life."

"Then a glass of wine will do for you," Richard returned.

"The devil it will! I want enough to make me drunk, roaring drunk, drunk enough to forget a certain Mr. Crockett and the art of American farming."

"So that's it," said Richard.

"Yes, my man. That's it."

When Richard brought the wine, the young man was regarding him with interested eyes.

"See here! You're the proprietor—you're Chalmers."

"Right," Richard replied.

"I've heard about you."

"I dare say."

"Crockett bring you out, too?"

"Yes, but with a different game. I came to make a fortune in beans."

The visitor nodded.

He pushed his wine away, almost untouched. It was clear that what he wanted was a chance to unburden himself in talk. Richard listened willingly, for the young man talked well, in an easy, articulate flow.

He was indeed one of Crockett's apprentice farmers— one of the late comers; they were still arriving from England at the rate of one or two a week. In the remote farmhouse to which Jackson had assigned him, he had inquired the night of his arrival about "the facilities for a bath," and thereafter "facilities for a bawth" had been bawled at him by American hired men whenever he came near them. Unlike most of the apprentices, he had not even attempted to perform the duties required of him. From the first he had stood scornfully aloof.

"And therefore I was not embarrassed by the necessity of resigning. My departure was suggested, it was even urged— as I recall—by the toe of the farmer's boot, by a pitchfork, and by a number of heads of cabbage, remarkably well aimed by his otherwise stupid progeny. All because I would not pitch hay, milk cows, and curry horses! And I explained to the blockhead that it was impossible for a violinist to do such things, that to punish the muscles of his arms and hands like that would ruin them forever, for playing."

He leaned toward Richard.

"Perhaps you understand the absolute flexibility and control which a violin demands—demands mercilessly, unceasingly. One kind of strength is required to lift and pull, another kind, to play a Bach fugue."

Richard laughed.

"What I don't understand," he said, "is why your parents sent a violinist out to be a farmer."

"Easily explained," replied Bevan with a shrug. "My stepfather wants me out of the way. He hates me, because I am a violinist like my father, because I am a constant reminder to my mother of my father, because before her second marriage my mother and I roamed Europe together and heard music and studied and played . . . Oh, God, those were lovely days!" Bevan slid his long hands into his black hair.

He jerked suddenly upright and folded his arms. "Oh, not all of us over at the Balmoral come from happy loving homes! There's one half-wit amongst us. Have you seen Aspinwall? He's the son of an admiral, they say. He'll never see England again. Then there's Bruce Bromwell. Hint of illegitimacy there. Reaches up somewhere to royalty. And Jack Redding. You know Jackie. This must be the place where he's drinking himself sodden. He's an orphan, and his uncle wants him out of the way. Isn't he a charming kid? Doesn't he know how to make the greenbacks fly?"

Richard was silent.

After a pause he said: "Can't you take the allowance your people send and study in America? Or start to play before the public if you are ready for that?"

"I'm almost ready," Bevan answered. His face in a sudden glow of pleasure looked younger, less distraught. "I've studied with the masters—Vieuxtemps, Wieniawski. M. Vieuxtemps wept, he *wept* when my stepfather took me out of the Conservatoire at Brussels. Yes, I would not be afraid to begin if I had a little money."

The glow died out of his face.

"But I haven't," he said. "And my stepfather will see to it that I do nothing so pleasant. I might make a success as a concert violinist, and that would bring me back to London. No, he'll send my allowance direct to Jackson, and unless I rot here in Rainbow I shan't see a penny of it. But here's a penny for your wine," he added, throwing down a coin.

"Play something for me instead," Richard suggested. He

glanced up at the clock. "It's closing time. Wait! I'll lock up, and then we won't be disturbed."

While he busied himself with shades and doors, Paul took his violin out of its case. He smiled as he dusted it lovingly, tucked it beneath his chin, and proceeded to put it in tune.

"Like music?" he called out to Richard, over the rattle of rain upon the roof.

"Yes."

Paul's gray-green eyes were shining now. He did not speak again, but when Richard returned and seated himself at a table, he began at once to play.

Richard leaned forward on folded arms. And presently he forgot the strange young man and the story he had told. The violin was sobbing, laughing, dancing, fighting, loving in a life of its own. It spoke from its heart to Richard's heart, and Richard raised his head to listen.

He had come this summer to have a different look. He was handsome still but in a different way. It seemed that his flaxen hair had darkened, but that was because his face had darkened. It was thicker, heavier. His mouth was bitter, and his blue eyes were hard. But listening to Paul Bevan's music, he looked as he had looked when he came to Minnesota. He thought of Cathy, and his eyes softened; his mouth took on a tender curve. Paul Bevan did not know or care. He was not playing for Richard; he was playing for himself.

This was a reunion with his violin, a reunion of passion and delight. His eyes glowed in a pale transfigured face; his mouth lost its frame of cynical lines and became yielding, sensuous, dreamy.

He had begun with some Hungarian dances, playing eagerly, urgently, as though to assert his own fierce need and fiercer joy. Now, warmed and once more sure of mastery over string and bow, he shifted to Paganini. One after another the fiery caprices fell from his fingers, as clean and brilliant as a shower of sparks. Dazzling, yes! But Bevan was insatiable tonight. Something deeper in him needed to speak. The strings gave out the beautiful opening phrase of the Kreutzer Sonata—compelling, arresting as a spoken challenge. He abandoned himself, a leaf in the wind, to the glory of storm which followed. When at last it was over, Bevan paused. There was a moment of silence. Then for the last time he lifted his bow and played Bach's Air for the G String. It stilled and reassured him, this noble contemplative utterance and, when the last full-throated note had died away, he laid aside his instrument.

He and Richard could hear the rain again..

Richard shook himself.

"Thank you," he said. "I can understand how your teacher felt."

"Can you?" Paul asked eagerly.

"I can. I think you play—marvelously."

"Of course, I do."

Paul began to stride up and down the room. The lamplight threw his shadow on the walls, elongated, grotesque, moving in a quivering silence which he broke presently to say:

"I told you my father was a violinist. He was no good, poor devil. But I'm different. I've got an Hungarian grandmother. Nothing like an Hungarian grandmother to make a violinist."

"That's an idea."

Paul stopped his pacing before a brightly colored lithograph, advertising the coming to Sisseton City of Barnum's Great Roman Hippodrome. He stared at this with an il-

lumined face, but it was clear he did not see it. Presently
he burst out:

"I will be a great violinist. By God, I will! And when I
am you can tell that I played here, just for you, in your
saloon."

Richard's laugh was short. But it was impossible to be
offended by Paul. It was too clear that he saw people only
in his own reflected light.

Yet he had seen Richard clearly enough to take a liking
to him.

"Where do you live?" he asked suddenly.

"Over at the Log House."

"Why not the Balmoral?"

"Oh, I stayed at the Log House years ago. Before the
Balmoral was built."

"Well," said Paul. "I'll take my traps out of the Balmoral
and move over with you."

Richard laughed, then he hesitated.

"Bevan," he said. "I'm not a good one for you to take
up with. I'm—not in favor with the good folks of the
colony."

"I know. I told you I remembered your story. You were
mixed up with a woman."

"Well," said Richard. "I had the name of being."

"Oh, don't be British! What the devil do I care? And
what the devil do I care for this ratty little town? Ten years
from now it will only be known because I once lived here.
I haven't met any of the English families, but I despise them.
If I met them, I wager they'd want me to play for their
dances."

"Some of them," said Richard, "are top-hole."

"Well, I sacrifice them. I renounce them. To hell with

them! Love me, love my dog! No, Chalmers, my boy—
what's your first name? Dick? No, Dick, my boy, I quit the
Balmoral tonight and go to the Log House with you. We'll
take a room together. You can swear while I practice double
stops, and I'll doze while you tell me how many ducks you
bagged. Is it a bargain?"

"It's a bargain," answered Richard.

He blew out the lamps, and they unlocked the side door
of the saloon. The rain was over, and the darkness was fresh
and moist. The two young men started down the muddy
street, Bevan swinging the case which held his violin. He
held it in his right hand, and his left hand took Richard's
arm in a firm affectionate grip.

CHAPTER THREE

THIS was the birth of a friendship which, unaccountable as such attachments often are, nevertheless waxed strong and was balm for Richard over the winter which followed.

The Log House was less crowded since the new Balmoral had opened its doors. Richard had a vast ground-floor room in the wing which had been added the previous year. It was sparsely furnished, for he had tossed out most of the horse-hair chairs and sofas and all the heavy draperies. Guns were stacked in a corner; a bottle of whiskey sat with a glass upon a table. Shot and Nellie slept where they pleased, and the place had a doggy smell.

This asylum Richard now shared with Paul along with the routine of his life.

He cannot be said to have shared his burdens; Paul took no interest in Richard's burdens. He had some curiosity about his friend's past but no concern whatever about his future. On one of the few occasions when Richard's troubles impinged upon him, he cried:

"What the devil does it matter that you are buried alive? You're just a damn nice fellow. But for me, Paul Bevan, with my gift, to be stuck away here—that is something to make the gods weep."

The sincerity of his selfishness palliated it. And his fits of despair were infrequent. His usual mood was one of caustic gayety which made him an enlivening companion. Moreover, an unexpected loyalty had caused him voluntarily to share Richard's ostracism. As word of his talent spread through the English group, he received social overtures which he took a racy pleasure in rejecting. He enjoyed repeating to a troubled Richard the pungent terms in which he couched his refusals.

It was, perhaps, small hardship for him to be deprived of the colony's social life. He detested middle-class pleasures.

"God, how I hate to hear a girl in a blue sash sing 'The Gypsy's Warning'!" he said fervently. "What you have helped me to escape, my lad!"

He found a Bohemian atmosphere far more congenial in Richard's haunts—the curtained recess of the saloon, the Balmoral's oyster bar, the gaming tables of the Farmers' Home, and the neighboring race tracks.

Richard did not this year follow the hunt. Ladies followed the hunt. Hook and Trevenen had not said he was unwelcome; they had merely failed to notify him of the opening event; and Richard thereafter had stayed scrupulously clear of the red coats. He tried to satisfy his passion for horses at the race tracks, and he became a familiar figure all over southern Minnesota, handsomely tailored, impeccably laundered, known as a constant drinker and a no less constant gambler. Paul grimaced at the sight of liquor, and nothing would induce him to risk a penny on a horse, but he accompanied Richard cheerfully on all these expeditions. He even kept an account in a small black book of Richard's gains and losses. He preferred, however, to keep his friend at home.

"Come now, stay home tonight. I shall play for you the Bach G-Minor Sonata."

He always said, "I shall play for *you*," but Richard noticed for whom he played. He played facing his mother's portrait, which stood in a velvet frame upon his chest.

It was she who had given Paul the Hungarian grandmother; she had given him also his thick black hair and his glowing eyes. The gaunt outline of his face did not come from her, however. There was about her features a melancholy softness which made Richard think of Meta. Paul was bitterly lonely for her. He talked of her for hours on end.

"She'll slip me some tin if she can. But it won't be easy. The old man counts her jewels every night. He makes her put them all on for dinner."

She received very few of his letters, he confided to Richard. But she knew the reason why and wrote faithfully by every boat. Indeed, although his mother was Paul's only correspondent, he received more letters than Richard received from his large affectionate family.

Richard's ties with his family were weakening. His parents knew nothing of the Kentish Arms, and they were troubled by the brevity and dullness of the letters in which he tried to conceal his present interests.

"You have grown away from us, Richard," his mother wrote.

She asked him several times whether he went to church, and at last Richard resolved to go in order to be able to tell her that he had gone. One mellow October Sunday he went to St. Ethelburga's for morning prayer.

The maple trees, meeting above the path, seemed actually to tinge the air with their radiant golden color. Bright leaves were thick underfoot. Petunias, asters, and cosmos still showed in the gardens, and the picket fences were patterned with crimson vines and purple berries. On such a day last autumn the first hunt had been held. The scent and sheen of the morning brought Cathy sharply to his mind. He was aware that he would see her in the church, and he walked more and more slowly while the bells of St. Ethelburga's rolled and pealed as though making vocal the agitation of his heart.

He arrived late and took a seat in the rear. For some time he knelt and rose and knelt again, in the progress of the service, without looking about. At last, however, the new rector settled to his sermon; he was the Reverend Cyril Cathcart, a young Oxford man who was acting, Richard had heard, as tutor to the youthful Hallidays. While he talked, in a fresh voice which matched his fresh spectacled face, Richard lifted his head.

The choir appeared to be made up of Hallidays. The singers all wore black robes and stiff black hats, and at first Richard could not distinguish one from another; but presently his vision cleared and he saw Cathy. She was looking at him, and as he looked back into her face between the blurred heads of other worshipers, he knew that she had not changed.

When the choir marched out in the recessional, she passed near him. He knew, although he kept his face lowered to his book. He felt her radiance as she passed, and he was sure he heard her singing:

> *"Through the night of doubt and sorrow,*
> *Onward goes the pilgrim band . . ."*

Richard slipped out before the doxology was sung. He had not quite gained the street when he heard footsteps running behind him and turned to see Cathy, still in cap and gown. The wind was blowing her hair about her glowing cheeks.

"Oh—Richard!" she said. It was the first time he had heard her speak his name. He felt himself flushing, as his hand went out slowly to enclose her hand. "Richard!" she said again.

Before he could answer she went on, speaking as she always did, eagerly and swiftly. "I am so glad you came. I am so glad to see you again."

"I am glad to see you," said Richard.

"I've wanted to find a way to tell you—that I am your friend. You have more friends than you think."

"If I have you—" Richard began. He meant to go on to say that, if he had her nothing else mattered. But he was always slow with words, and now he could not bear to squander time in speaking.

He knew that they had a moment only. A louder burst of organ music indicated that the doors of the church had been flung wide. He could feel rather than see the congregation surging from the church. He wanted to spend that moment gazing upon the unforgotten wonder of her face. So he was silent.

He did not loosen his hold of her hand and, like a hungry man set before food, he gazed at the wide, shining eyes, at the tremulous mouth below the burnished wings of hair. Cathy returned his look no less earnestly. Her gaze—he actually felt it—picked out the changes that the months had brought, touched pityingly the harassed marks about his eyes. His own eyes found no reason to show any mood except one of delight. She was, he told himself, flawless. The wind filled her gown, and she seemed to sway tenderly toward him.

He heard steps ruffling the fallen leaves.

"I've made a mess—" he began in a low voice.

"But you can make everything right," Cathy interrupted

quickly, and again the wind on her gown made her seem to drift toward his arms. "It isn't too late."

She was talking against time. Already they were the goal of a dozen conscientious members of the Reverend Cyril's flock. At least a dozen were advancing, a disorganized but determined band bent upon saying the conventional word to the visitor, however suspect, in their midst. The Reverend Cyril himself was fidgeting on the steps, eager for once to cut short the chorused greetings, the studied approval of his sermon, in order to assure the prodigal of his welcome. Richard's protesting glance, though it had been ten times as protesting, could not have stayed the general pious resolution to record a public gesture of magnanimity.

Miss Tabby Joy was the first to reach him, but her loud, forthright greeting was cut short. She was hastily swept away by Lady Throop, who surged close, breathing so audibly that Richard was put in mind of Mr. Beatty's team making hard going of it through a muddy spring road. She advanced with lorgnette uplifted, but she lowered it as she stretched out the other, white-gloved hand.

"Mr. Chalmers!" she exhaled stentoriously, but her tone was gracious. "Sir Mortimer and I were recalling with satisfaction the parable of the lost sheep. I trust that you remember the words of Our Lord: 'Likewise joy shall be in heaven over one sinner that repenteth, more than over ninety and nine just persons, which need no repentance.'"

It was intolerable, and the rearguard moving up in Lady Throop's wake was no less so. Cathy was the first to give way. Her gaze, despairing now, met Richard's for a last instant, then she fled. Richard was glad. He would not have been the first to go, but even for Cathy he could not have stayed.

He, too, fled, and he did not go to church again. But that

look which had passed between him and Cathy as their hands clasped he put away in his heart. He did not often take it out to look at it. It did not give him pleasure; it filled him with sorrow and shame. For some months he did not see Cathy again; nor did he see Meta.

But there was lively talk of the Bannisters in Rainbow. At first this concerned the Captain only. He had continued living at Exile Hall, but most of his days were spent in town. He shunned his old companions and cultivated instead the newcomers to the colony, as well as Americans to whose society he had ever been partial. They listened credulously to the tales which he was increasingly fond of telling. The tales grew increasingly fantastic.

"Damn the fellow! He didn't fight in the Crimea, but according to the stuff he is handing out in Oates's store he took Sebastopol virtually single-handed," Hook told Richard one day with amused irritation.

"At the age of seventeen. He was a drummer boy," Trevenen grinned.

The Americans who hung about Oates's store and the livery stable were not learned in European affairs. They did not embarrassingly check up dates or the military units engaged in battles. They relished the Captain's stories and matched them with stories of their own, sagas of adventure on an earlier and more picturesque frontier.

This yarn spinning had a curious result. Late in the autumn a short work of fiction appeared in an eastern periodical. It was a story of the American West; its locale, in fact, was present-day Rainbow, but it pictured a Rainbow new and startling to English and Americans alike. Indians had been absent from the Minnesota scene since the Sioux massacre more than ten years previous, yet this narrative ran red with blood from tomahawk and scalping knife. Buffaloes too belonged to Minnesota's past, but the hero of this tale, an English ex-army captain, charged a herd of buffaloes with sensational effect. The author, said a footnote to the piece, knows whereof he writes. Captain Christopher Bannister lives on the plains of western Minnesota.

Rainbow chuckled, but good-naturedly. The Yankees passed the magazine from hand to hand. It was fun to see that yarn of old Aunt Abbie's in print. It was fun, too, for the town to have an author. Sisseton City had the railroad, but it did not have an author. A second tale appeared, and Kit began to be something of a figure.

It was a pity that he lay so much of the time in drunken solitude, for when he appeared on the street he was worth seeing. His bearing and dress were boldly military. His shoulders were square; his chest arched; his mustaches bristled. He could not affect a uniform nor sidearms, but his trousers bore martial strips of braid, and he carried a sword cane.

His wife was still the guest of the Throops. She had accompanied them to Pinewood for the summer. Now, with the approach of winter, they were planning to return to Gray Gables, taking her with them.

Lady Meta was secretly resolved not to return to Gray Gables. Over her early tea one crisp autumn morning, she planned ways and means of escape.

Long since, she had received from her half-brother an answer to the letter which recounted her treatment at Kit's hands. She had concealed from her dear friend, Lady Throop, the unbrotherly tone of this communication. She had promptly written again, entreating him to be more kind. His response had been slow in coming, but when it came it made his position dishearteningly clear.

He did not desire her return to England. If she returned she would not continue to receive his support. Moreover, he refused to have her wandering alone about American cities. A wife's place, he stated explicitly, was with her husband. He had written to Captain Bannister. The Captain now understood that further abuse would not be tolerated. He would be amenable, the Earl of Blackmore believed, to any living arrangements Lady Meta might suggest. Lady Meta was to remain in Rainbow. Captain Bannister was to treat her with respect. So long as both of them fulfilled these conditions, they might expect their semiannual remittance.

He had them at his mercy, thought Meta, folding her numb hands about the warm cup. (Fires had not yet been ordered, and even in bed she was cold.) He had them at his mercy, and they were also at each other's mercy, she and Kit. Either one could cut off the other one's support.

Plainly it was a case for compromise, and Lady Meta desired a compromise which would remove her from Pinewood.

Her welcome there was still warm but it would not remain so forever—it could not, in the nature of things. What was more, she was getting heartily bored with the Throops. She was bored with her pompous host, with her gushing hostess, with their eight uninteresting children, with the obligation to be cheerful, with the constant necessity for tact, with not being mistress of the household. With not being able to order a fire! Summer in the spacious country place had not been so bad; but Gray Gables was smaller, more compact. Winter would drive them all to the refuge of the drawing-room grate. Lady Meta's nerves rebelled at the prospect.

She refused to return to Exile Hall. That was out of the question. Two winters there had been enough; she would die rather than undertake a third. There remained then only what Rainbow offered, and that meant the new hotel, the Balmoral.

Shining with white and green paint, ringed with three tiers of verandas, it seemed to the Americans the last word in elegance. To European eyes it appeared humble enough. But to Lady Meta now it was a faultless haven. The more she thought of the lost bliss of independence, the more she yearned for the Balmoral. But how could it be made to look decorous, proper, for a married woman to live alone in a hotel?

She put aside her tea, rose, and began to dress, her lifted winglike brows expressing both the urgency of her problem and her determination to find an answer for it.

Serving herself to kidneys at the family breakfast, Lady Meta began to smile. She tried to restrain the smile, but it glimmered forth in her eyes and danced at the corners of her lips.

Lady Throop, who was suffering from a cold, complained that she was not able to drive into Rainbow to match worsteds.

"Let me do it for you, dear Lady Throop."

It was arranged that the victoria should take Lady Meta to town that afternoon. Fortunately the young folks were having a picnic. Not one asked to accompany her.

Arriving in Rainbow, Lady Meta matched the worsteds, but she did not linger in Halliday's store. She finished the business with despatch and drove to the Log House. She did not alight there. Richard lived at the Log House. She had risked one visit within its doors, but she would not risk a second. She waited without while the coachman took in the message that Lady Meta Bannister wished to speak with Aunt Kibbie.

While she waited for Aunt Kibbie, Lady Meta almost

hugged herself with pride. The thought she had had at breakfast was pure inspiration. She could live anywhere, anywhere, with Aunt Kibbie as her companion. What scandal could live, what gossip could possibly survive the purifying influence of one who had read the New Testament one hundred and thirty-two times, the Old Testament sixty-five?

"No doubt it is sixty-six, by now. All the better!" thought Meta in delight.

Aunt Kibbie emerged smiling. She had not changed at all. She was small and bright-eyed as of old, her snowy hair in sausagelike side curls.

She was so deaf that Lady Meta had to choose between shouting her proposal to all Rainbow and writing it down. The latter course was bad enough, for Aunt Kibbie read with painstaking deliberation. Habitually she dealt only with words which deserved the weightiest consideration.

It was slow going. But when most of the scraps of paper in her purse had been covered, Lady Meta had got over the idea that she wanted Aunt Kibbie to come to her as a companion. She hoped that she had managed tactfully to convey that she would expect some of the service rendered by a maid. If she hadn't, she reflected, she didn't really mind. She would serve herself, and gladly, if Aunt Kibbie would play chaperon.

"Why don't you stay—" Aunt Kibbie began. But she stopped before uttering "here," and for that Lady Meta loved her. Aunt Kibbie had tact, too. She had remembered in time that Richard was at the Log House.

"I'll come and glad to," Aunt Kibbie declared. "Delia can spare me. But I've got to have wages," she added in a small determined shout.

Lady Meta wrote hastily that, of course, she expected to pay a wage.

"Would a dollar and a half a week be too much?" Aunt Kibbie wanted to know. "Of course," she explained, "I'd mend and help out."

Lady Meta laughed at such a quick solution of her problem, and one so well within even her limited income.

"A dollar and a half every Monday morning," she wrote, concluding the agreement.

Inside the Log House some one was playing the violin. There emerged from the open windows of a ground floor room a disarming little tune in the minuet measure, charmingly played. Meta recognized it, the "Deutscher Tanz," by —and she smiled to herself—by that composer who surely had a perfect name. Karl Ditters von Dittersdorf! It was exactly like his music, she thought, quaint and sturdy and gay.

Lady Meta scraped her purse for a last clean bit of paper.

"Is that the violinist who has taken quarters with Mr. Chalmers?" she wrote.

Aunt Kibbie nodded.

"Mr. Bevan. His first name's Paul."

"He plays beautifully," said Lady Meta's pencil.

Aunt Kibbie pocketed the paper. She would show it to Mr. Bevan. He might not care whether Rainbow liked his music, but he certainly would not turn up his nose at praise from Lady Meta. Why, she was almost a princess!

Meta drove away in a glow of satisfaction. That, she rejoiced, was arranged! In warm elation she settled her hat, a hat just the width of its feather which curled down over her brow. But nearing the English Club, to which she had directed the coachman to take her next, she grew taut and anxious. Now she must see Kit and persuade him to her plan. The task was repugnant, and it might be difficult—or, again, it might be ridiculously easy. Kit was unpredictable.

She waited nervously while the coachman went into the Club in search of him.

Kit came out with the sword cane tucked cavalierly under one arm, his hat poised gallantly. It was the first time she had seen him since leaving Exile Hall, and she noted immediately the eccentric details of which she had heard.

He bowed over her hand, then drew once more erect, throwing back his white lock in the familiar gesture.

"Kit," she said. "I want to talk with you alone."

Bannister's brilliant eyes narrowed in sardonic humor.

"Why not suggest to Lady Throop that she invite me out for tea some afternoon?"

"I want to talk where we won't be overheard."

"How about a drive then? Tomorrow?" he proposed.

"Our driving days are past, Kit." She threw so much melancholy into her voice and smile that her husband grew pliable.

"What do you suggest?" he asked.

"Tea. At the Balmoral. Now."

The new hotel was accustomed to Englishmen demanding tea in the afternoon. The service was prompt. And over the fragrant cups, Lady Meta put her case.

"My brother will not continue to support us unless we both remain in Rainbow. I do not feel that I should stay longer with the Throops. I cannot live at Exile Hall; you may have Exile Hall. But out of the money my brother sends I want enough to enable me to live with a companion at the Balmoral."

Bannister flushed.

"I don't need the Earl of Blackmore's money," he said angrily. "I have been successful with my pen. Haven't you heard? And shortly I am to go on a lecture tour."

Meta wished she could believe him. Try as she would, she

could not persuade herself that his writing or his lecturing were important.

"That is splendid," she said. "Then you won't mind making me an allowance?"

"Not an allowance, my dear! Not an allowance!" He raised a reproving finger. "I do not believe that your brother would approve of your having an allowance. But I shall take care of your account at the Balmoral. And naturally you shall have a little for clothes and other expenses."

"And from Exile Hall," she said quickly, "I should like my piano . . ."

"Naturally! Naturally! I will have it sent in at once. And a driving horse. But not your jewels," he added sharply. "The earl would not wish you to keep the jewels here in a public hotel. At least not if he knows, as I do, how careless you are with them."

Meta sighed. She would have liked having her jewels again. She was fond of the quaint necklaces, bracelets, brooches, and tiaras, precious and semiprecious stones in heavy old-fashioned settings, which had been her mother's. She valued too the few, fine jewels which her father had bequeathed to her.

But the care of her jewels was a mania with Kit. He had secreted them about the house at Exile Hall. She had had only her rings during her long stay with the Throops.

She attempted a protest, knowing it would be vain.

"But, Kit, even here, there are balls sometimes."

"In such cases, my dear, communicate with me. And now," he went on briskly, "we will arrange for your rooms. How many shall you need? You want a companion, you say."

"I have arranged," said Lady Meta, "to have Aunt Kibbie Oarlock stay with me as companion."

Captain Bannister burst into a gusty laugh.

"Marvelous!" he cried. "Magnificent! Meta, that is an inspired idea. For you to borrow the cloak of Aunt Kibbie's respectability, the shadow of her virtue—"

Lady Meta regarded him coldly.

They parted amicably, however. She was reasonably well pleased with the interview. To be sure, she detested Kit's supervision of her financial affairs. But, as she had told herself that morning, theirs was a case for compromise.

Her spirits rose as she inspected her rooms. The prospect of being her own mistress filled her with delight, even though she was to be mistress of a limited domain—a tiny drawing room and a larger bedroom, one corner of which would be screened off for Aunt Kibbie.

The drawing room was amusingly ornate. Cheap lace curtains, stiff enough to stand by themselves, fell to the floor before long narrow windows. The bright green carpet was spotted with flowers that looked like multicolor cabbages. There was a tall mirror in a frame of carved black walnut, having a marble shelf at the base. The tables were black walnut too, and the chairs were upholstered.

There was, she saw thankfully, room for her piano.

"My piano will be sent in tomorrow," she told the clerk, smiling, and stepped for a moment out on the narrow balcony from which she could view the miniature world of Rainbow.

Starting back to Pinewood, she asked the coachman to drive slowly. She wanted time to think out a statement of her plans and a farewell which would sacrifice nothing of what she had gained with the Throops.

She found Sir Mortimer and his lady alone; the children had not yet returned from their outing. The overworked servant was taking out the tea things.

"But I'll order some fresh for you."

"No, no, my dear. Don't trouble." She had, indeed, had tea with Kit. But she would have spoken so, Lady Meta reflected, if she had been perishing for tea! How fine it would be to be free of this necessity to respect another's domestic arrangements!

She plunged at once into her subject.

"I have heard from my brother," she said. "He is, as always, generous and kind. But he still doubts the propriety of my returning to London. He feels, quite understandably, that a wife's place is with her husband.

"Naturally," she went on swiftly, "after all that has happened, he does not wish me to live with Captain Bannister. He merely thinks that while my husband stays in Rainbow, I should stay here too. And he agrees with me that I have trespassed long enough on your hospitality and kindness. And so . . ."

Then it came out, the Balmoral, Aunt Kibbie . . .

"Tell me, dear Lady Throop," Lady Meta ended, "what is your opinion of the propriety of this arrangement? And you, Sir Mortimer, may I write my brother that it has your entire approval?"

The suite at the Balmoral was already reserved, and Lady Meta had every intention of occupying it, whatever the Throops' opinion might be, but there was no hint of this in her sweetly pleading gaze.

Sir Mortimer coughed, awaiting a signal from his wife. He knew—it had been discussed between them—that the prolonged presence of a distinguished guest in their modest establishment was difficult. It would, moreover, be still more difficult in the near future, since Lady Throop was to present him with a ninth offspring. He was ready to give Lady Meta's plan whole-hearted endorsement. But he knew that women had their own ways of handling such affairs.

They had, indeed!

"But you know how welcome you are with us!"

"I know you have been more than kind."

"I simply cannot bear to have you go, my dear."

"I shan't be far away. Tell me, please, do you think my plan is suitable?"

Lady Throop paused and tapped her cheek.

"As for that," she said at last, "I shall be guided entirely by Sir Mortimer's opinion. But it seems to me, my sweet, that if you really must leave us—and you know how we hate to have you!—but if you really think best to go, you have made an excellent plan. Your choice of Aunt Kibbie is—"

"Quite so!" said Sir Mortimer. "Lady Throop has put my own thought into words!"

Lady Meta glowed upon them both.

"And you will come to see me often?"

"Of course. Of course we will."

"And I may continue the piano lessons to darling little Cuthbert?"

"How charming, how amiable of you to think of that!"

Lady Throop mentioned tea again. (She was not afraid to approach the overworked maid, now that the family would so soon be reduced by one.)

But Sir Mortimer had a better suggestion.

"Perhaps, my love," he said benignly, "after all she has been through—a glass of sherry?"

Lady Meta sipped the sherry, happier than she had been for days. To be chained in Rainbow was, no doubt, an unenviable lot. But in her own drawing room, however small— with her piano for solitary hours—with dear Aunt Kibbie, so afflicted by deafness, to act as chaperon for such times as she chose to entertain, Lady Meta felt that she could look forward to a winter not devoid of pleasure.

CHAPTER FOUR

THE Hallidays were making ready for Christmas.

Upstairs and downstairs, outdoors and indoors, in secret and in open view, multifarious preparations for a proper celebration of the holiday were going on at Green Lawn.

Bits of sewing were whisked out of sight whenever almost anyone entered almost any room; the racket of mysterious carpentry floated from the woodshed; uproarious rehearsals of charades and pantomimes were in progress on the third floor; and every evening the sitting room echoed to jubilant bursts of Christmas music.

The choir of St. Ethelburga's, as Richard had observed, was composed largely of Hallidays. It was their obligation, therefore, to see that the Christmas service was provided with suitable music. The Reverend Cyril Cathcart was anxious about the music, no doubt; that was the reason he called so often at Green Lawn and looked so approvingly at Dora while she sang.

The church and the house must both be decorated. The Hallidays culled evergreens along the snowy lake front. Branches of red cedar were nailed over the doorways; and the prettiest tree was brought to Green Lawn intact to be decorated with candles after the German fashion which Queen Victoria had introduced at Windsor.

No less a ceremonial than "bringing home Christmas," as this pillaging of the woodlands was called, was the manufac-

ture of the pudding. Before the dark spicy mass went into
its bag, the entire family was called to the kitchen; each
member—down to Vickie—gave the mixture a stir; and there
were dropped into it with an hilarity almost equaling the
hilarity with which they would be withdrawn at Christmas
dinner, a ring for the first to be wed, a button for the one
who would not be wed at all, and a threepenny bit predicting
riches for the finder.

Cathy had always loved Christmas. Ever since she could
remember the smell of evergreen, the music of the Christmas hymns and carols had evoked delight.

> *The moon shines bright*
> *And the stars give light*
> *A little before the day.*

She liked that one best because of the stars, but every one
of the familiar melodies had power to send shivers of joy
along her spine. Every small family observance, every bit
of Christmas ritual was dear to Cathy. She would never allow
a single ceremony to be omitted, and for days preceding the
holiday she went about with a glow on her face and a great
bunch of Christmas greens pinned to her dress.

So it had been in other years, and she tried this year to
enter as usual into the spirit of the season. She succeeded so
well that only her mother and Dora were not deceived. They
knew that Cathy was not happy. Her mother knew in the
way mothers know. And Dora knew for, as much as anyone,
she was in Cathy's confidence, and she tried hard to keep
her interest in Cathy's love story fresh now that her own
love story was being so sweetly told.

For some weeks after the Spring Ball Cathy had not mentioned Richard. That first night she had wept on Dora's

breast, and more than once during the nights which followed Dora had been awakened by Cathy's smothered weeping and had taken her sister into her arms for comfort. But without words, for Dora had soon perceived that this was a matter of which Cathy would not talk.

Cathy could not talk, for she had been wounded to the heart. She was proud with the generous pride of the happy and open-hearted. It was not easy for her to think that another woman had had for lover the man she, Cathy, loved, the man to whom she had not scrupled to reveal her love. Cathy, although stoutly loyal to Richard in public, did not in private doubt that he had been Lady Meta's lover.

This was a sorrow she could not confide. It was one she could only accept and endure. And she did not accept nor endure it without yielding to it something of herself, a bit of her youth, a modicum of her overflowing joy. Life which she loved had done this to her.

Yet she never once doubted that Richard was her love. She could not doubt it, for she knew her own heart. There his name was graven, and there it would be graven till she died. She knew what the stars foretold, and often alone in her room she comforted herself with their mystic symbols. They showed separation and sorrow, yes, but they also showed happiness ahead.

She never questioned her father's decision that Richard should not be admitted; in fact she acknowledged its rightness. It was right that Richard and Lady Meta should be punished. The only wrong thing was that Richard should be punished and Lady Meta be entirely absolved. Mrs. Halliday was not one of those who took her daughters to call on Lady Meta, but Cathy would not have gone even at her mother's suggestion. At balls and teas, at bouts of tennis and archery on green country lawns, wherever she encountered Captain Bannister's wife, she treated her distantly. But for all that, she did not deny the justice of Richard's banishment.

When she heard of the Kentish Arms, however, her heart melted. His punishment had been too hard if it had driven him to this. Richard, her Richard, keeping one of those places which her brothers were not allowed to enter! If he could do this incredible thing, then indeed he needed championship.

But there was no way in which she might champion him. She could not tell him she still loved him; he had never asked for her love. She could not seek him out; it was his privilege to seek her out. Let him seek her out and she would have the courage to ask her father to lift the ban.

He had not sought her out, and Cathy had done two things. She had put her faith in the stars, which foretold that they would one day be united, and she had kept on loving him.

She did not often see him. Richard was not often seen in Rainbow. Green baize curtains masked the interior of the Kentish Arms, and Richard did not lounge in the doorway of his place nor dart out to greet friends. Gambling rooms, race tracks, the places where he spent his days were far from Cathy's orbit.

But Cathy caught more glimpses of Richard than Richard caught of her. She had cultivated a seventh sense which was always seeking him. It picked him out unerringly—on the street, in front of the Balmoral, in Oates's Hall when itinerant entertainers performed there. He seemed in these glimpses like a stranger, older, harder. But she told herself always that he was the same, her Richard, whom she loved.

And once she had seen that Richard. He had been his true self when they spoke and clasped hands in the churchyard. That was a glory day in Cathy's heart. That was the memory she treasured.

"He will come again. Or he will find me somewhere. And while I wait, I will be happy."

Firm in this resolution, she had gone about as usual. Slabs Neville, Harry Earle, the Lovell boys, Hook had found her radiance undimmed. She had fought so hard for happiness that she had almost achieved it; but she was not happy now, getting ready for Christmas.

It seemed strange to be going through these loved observances with such a heavy heart; to be wrapping gifts, stringing cranberries, painting Christmas cards, bantering Jim and Dora about the ring in the pudding—for there was only one ring, and Jim and Sally Lovell were as far gone in love as were Dora and her Cyril—to be taking part in all this merry-making with pain so insistent in her breast.

She had never seen a more beautiful Christmas Eve. The world was already submerged in snow, and yet snow kept on falling, a gray mist in the air, a soft white burden on naked branches, on the porch rails and fences of Green Lawn. It seemed strange to look out at the falling snow and to hear her brothers and sisters practising the carols—

> "*And all the bells of heaven shall ring,*
> *On Christmas Day,*
> *On Christmas Day,*"

and to find herself wishing, for the first time in her life, that Christmas were over.

Where would Richard be tomorrow? He might have been invited to the Eyrie. Yet she doubted that he would go, for he could not in the afternoon accompany Mr. Trevenen and Mr. Hook on their round of Christmas calls. Would he be at Little Goodlands with the Whipps? She suspected rightly that he disliked Little Goodlands. She had a dim saddening conviction that he would spend the day seeking forgetfulness of it in heavy-hearted carousal. It seemed strange to be thinking that, as she watched the falling snow and listened to the carols.

There was another strange sad thing about this Christmas. Charley was unhappy too.

Cathy believed his low spirits were concerned with that American girl whose existence she had first suspected on the day of the Spring Ball. She had become certain since that there was such a person. Again and again throughout the summer and autumn Charley had been locked out. On such occasions, as Cathy had once told Richard, he came in through her window (her window and Dora's, but it was Cathy always who heard the whistled signal). Their father was quite aware of this arrangement. Often, as Charley was stealing up the third-floor stairs, his parent's night-capped head emerged. Once the senior Halliday spoke sharply:

"Young man! You keep late hours!"

But he continued to lock and bolt the door, leaving it to Cathy to admit the culprit.

Cathy had not performed this service without indulging in a little teasing. "How's your Yankee?" she would whisper, following Charley into the upper hall. Charley would laugh, and he did not deny that he had been in American company. He had even told Cathy a little about the girl. She was pretty as a primrose, he said.

It came out that they met at the house of her second cousin. Cathy had not liked the sound of that.

"Charley! Charley! You should call on her at her home."

"But she doesn't want me to. She won't let me, in fact, until—until I've told Father."

"Told Father what?"

"What good friends we are."

"Well, tell Father then."

"Oh, there's no hurry. It's rather fun this way. Besides, I hate to give the guv a shock."

It was true, Cathy had acknowledged to herself, that such an arrangement would give their father a shock. He was hardly aware that Americans existed in relation to his family or himself. But he was fair-minded; he would be the first to admit that there were American families socially equal to the English. There was no excuse for Charley to postpone his revelation.

"You Aquarians!" Cathy ejaculated. And Charley pinched her cheek and laughed. He knew of her researches into the occult science, and Cathy had often reproached him with the faults of his sign. She did so now, huddling her dressing gown about her. He was agreeable, she said, and kind-hearted, and generous, but he should guard against a tendency to vacillate, to procrastinate, to look lightly upon promises—

"I know. I know. What's to eat in the house?"

And so the laughing conversation ended. But there had been little laughter from Charley since winter settled in.

He still rapped Cathy up now and then, but he did not come in the window smiling. He was sober, troubled, anxious. What was more, he would no longer talk of the girl. When Cathy mentioned her in the accustomed bantering tone he acted as though he did not know whom she meant. And yet—Cathy felt sure that the girl was still important to him. She discovered on Christmas Eve that she was right.

Just before tea, she and Charley went out for a last load of cedar boughs. In lifting a freshly cut branch, Cathy scratched her wrist. The blood flowed, and Charley searched his pockets for a clean handkerchief. He brought out by mistake a fine gold chain from which a heart-shaped locket dangled.

He crammed it back in embarrassment, and Cathy cried: "Don't worry. I won't look. I know it's too near Christmas to be curious."

But she thought as they walked homeward through the softly falling snow, through the mauve radiance of twilight, that the locket would not appear with the family Christmas gifts. It was intended for the American girl; she must still be Charley's sweetheart.

Cathy resolved to talk with Charley. Christmas was a good time for straightening out tangles; and Charley was entangled somehow—something was making him unhappy. Moreover, his chart showed disaster ahead. Not being an Aquarian, Cathy spoke impulsively.

"Charley," she said, "don't be angry with me. But I want to talk with you about your American girl."

"What about her?" Charley asked. His tone was almost surly, but it was something, Cathy thought, to have him once more admit the girl's existence.

"You told me last summer that you were meeting her secretly. Are you still doing that?"

"What if I am?"

"Why, Charley, you know better. If she's a nice girl, you ought to call at her home, meet her parents—"

"She *is* a nice girl," Charley interrupted. "She's a fine girl."

"I'm sure she is. Then why don't you treat her with respect?"

"I told you," said Charley, his voice rising in painful tension, "she won't let me. She says her father would want to be sure that my father and mother approve."

"That's quite proper. That makes me like her."

"Well! You know as well as I do that Father and Mother wouldn't approve. Her father is a farmer. And I—I'm serious, Cathy."

Cathy stopped, dropping her cedar boughs, which sent up through the gathering dusk a feathery cloud of snow.

"Charley dear, if you're serious, that is all the more reason why you should talk to Father. You must have courage. You can find it. I could find it if I were in your place. I would talk to Father; I wouldn't be afraid to tell him whom *I* love, if it would do any good—"

She had never mentioned Richard to Charley before. His arm came around her at once.

"I know, Sis. I've known all along how you feel about Dick Chalmers. I think he's a fine chap. I think he's just about the finest."

"Do you, Charley?"

"And he's going to get out of this mess he's in. You wait and see."

"I *am* waiting," said Cathy, in a trembling, almost angry voice. "That's one reason why I want you to talk with Father. Your little Yankee—she's waiting, too."

Cathy had to stop there, to sniff and turn her head. Charley also was unable to speak for a moment. Then he said:

"I'll talk to Father, Sis. First chance I get. Honor bright."

Both of them were glad that the twins at that moment came bursting out the door.

"I say, Cathy, when you give me my beard for the pantomime, make it a good one, will you?"

"Like old Major Scatchett's, Cathy."

"Major Gerald Halliday Scatchett!" And the twins went off into the senseless laughter of the very early teens. Gerry turned a Catherine wheel. Geraldine began to mould a snow-ball, chanting as she did so:

"Merry Christmas, Major Scatchett! Merry Christmas, Major Scatchett! Merry—"

"Children, children, you'll catch your death!" Cathy picked up her cedar boughs and waved them toward the door. There was no chance for further talk with Charley, but she gave his arm an approving squeeze as they went in to tea.

High tea, it was, on Christmas Eve, with crackers and bonbons and iced cakes, and all the children beside themselves with excitement. After tea Reg went to the piano; and there floated through the house the familiar strains of the "Blue-beard March." The whole family trooped to the third floor, to that large room papered with sheets from the *Graphic* and the *Illustrated London News* where dwelt together in reasonable amity Jim and Charley, Gerald and Reg. Their beds had been removed, and a curtain divided the room into two parts; the part nearer to the door was filled with chairs which were plainly labelled "stalls" and "pit." A large card, beautifully lettered by Bess, announced that this was the Crystal Palace, that the Christmas pantomime of Bluebeard was to be performed. And performed it was, with more zest than subtlety, by the five youngest Hallidays, Gerald playing Bluebeard in a beard which far outshone the Major's.

Cathy was companioned through the merriment by the ghost of Richard's loneliness. It stood close beside her also as she waited with her brothers and sisters outside the closed library door;

> "*O Christmas tree,*
> *O Christmas tree . . .*"

sang the Hallidays—contraltos, basses, and tenors falling into line behind Dora's sweet soprano. The sliding doors flew open, and there in quivering radiance stood the illuminated tree. Its aromatic odor multiplied its magic by the number of years of remembrance each Halliday had known. Bygone Christmases in a bright happy chain trooped into the room.

There was no light in the library save candlelight and fire-light. That was enough, however, to reveal the piles of gifts beneath the tree. Each pile was plainly marked with its owner's name, and the younger children fell upon their portions with shouts and squeals.

"Wait your turns, now! Wait your turns!"

This was a reminder of a family ruling that each member should open one gift in turn while the others looked on. It was a ruling made only to be forgotten, as it was forgotten now in a wild confusion of delight.

The gifts were very simple, most of them homemade: blotters and pen-wipers and slippers. The boys had fashioned their father a bookcase, their mother a sewing table. Charley had bought Maggie a doll; Albert, a horse and wagon; Vickie, a Jack-in-the-box. But there was not among all his gifts a heart-shaped locket on a slender chain.

Cathy looked about at the scene of gay disorder. Familiar as it was, she seemed never to have looked at it before. In other years she had been a participant, not an observer of the scene. This year it stood out as though it were a painting in a gallery.

The glow of candlelight! The gala litter of papers! Her father in his shabby dressing gown surveying them all with a benevolent expression! Bess, her big dimples showing, undressing Maggie's doll! Jim swinging Albert to examine the top of the tree! Her mother, misty-eyed!

Cathy found tears stinging her own eyes, and she walked away to the window. She looked out at the slow sweep of the snow.

"Richard, oh, Richard!" her heart cried. "When will I have you beside me here? Next year Jim will have his Sally; Dora, her Cyril. They will be bringing their children soon, to Grandfather Halliday's tree . . ."

"Cathy, shall we make the tea?" It was Dora, slipping a loving arm into Cathy's. They went together out to the frigid kitchen.

According to family custom, the Halliday children wakened their father and mother on Christmas morning with song. They gathered before the door of their parents' bedroom, making quite a creditable choir with the three tall older brothers and Gerald lined up at the back, the four older sisters standing just before them, the children hand in hand in front. They always sang first "Christians Awake" and then "The First Noel," which was their mother's favorite. Cathy could not remember when Christmas Day had not begun so, with her brothers and sisters gathered about her in the winter morning dusk, and that stirring old hymn rising:

> *"Christians, awake! Salute the happy morn*
> *Whereon the Saviour of the world was born,*
> *Rise to adore the mystery of love,*
> *Which hosts of angels chanted from above."*

Beyond the twin windows of the upper hall, the world gleamed ghostly white. Snow at last had ceased to fall. The bare shapes of the trees showed black, the sky was purplish blue, for the sun had not yet risen.

But it was shining when the Hallidays sat down to their holiday breakfast; the family started to church through a world of dazzling brightness. On lawn, lake, and wood, on roofs, pumps, and fences, light masses of fresh new snow caught and reflected the sunshine. A pair of cardinals who were wintering at Green Lawn added a bit of Christmas color.

The Hallidays formed just such a cavalcade as they had formed when Richard saw them first upon the road to Rainbow. Today, however, they were festively attired. The father supplemented his usual high silk hat with Sunday's gold-headed cane. The brothers sported new cravats. The mother wore her (three-year-old) best bonnet, and Vickie a new Rob Roy pelisse. Maggie, except for the shorter skirts which revealed her buttoned boots, showed her older sisters' silhouette—a pancake hat and muff before, skirts draped to a hump behind. They entered St. Ethelburga's churchyard to the happy pealing of bells.

"Merry Christmas, Mrs. Lovell!" "Merry Christmas, Miss Joy!" "Merry Christmas, Major Scatchett!" (The twins doubled up with mysterious mirth at their father's genial greeting to the Major.)

The small church, hung with greens in honor of Our Lord's Nativity, was crowded. The Hallidays, black-robed, sang fervently. The Reverend Cyril was pink-cheeked and earnest, uplifted by his love for Dora and his reverence for the day. The ritual took its grave poetic course.

Cathy looked for Richard, but he did not come.

"I will not keep expecting him. I will not," she declared. She devoted herself like a curate to the responses:

"Lift up your hearts."

"We lift them up unto the Lord."

"Let us give thanks unto our Lord God."

"It is meet and right so to do."

The service was long, since communion was celebrated. At last, however, it was ended and the Hallidays were at home once more, the Reverend Cyril in their midst. And at long last dinner was on the table—roast and boiled turkeys, strange American vegetables, mince pies, the pudding brought in burning with a sprig of holly atop. (Dora blushed as crimson as the holly berries when Vickie got the ring.)

Dessert was placed on the library table: apples and oranges, raisins and figs. Nuts from their own woods were brought out and cracked. By the time the dishes were washed and wiped, callers were dropping in.

Only bachelors came, for Christmas was a family day. But Mr. Hook and Mr. Earle, two Nevilles, more than one of the ex-apprentice farmers rang the Hallidays' bell. They gave expert and unasked advice to the senior Halliday, who always concocted the Christmas punch himself and was busy with it now. Vickie and Albert assisted, rubbing loaf sugar violently upon lemons.

Slabs Neville's gaze was turned to Cathy, but Cathy's was turned to Charley.

"Have you talked to Father yet?" she signaled severely.

Charley through scooped hands replied, "Hold your horses!"

The injunction was just enough, thought Cathy. Certainly there was no chance now for private conversation. The room rang with talk.

This concerned the Bachelors' Ball, a social event of the holiday season. It was to be held at the Balmoral on New Year's Eve. All of the English (with three exceptions) were expected to be present. A few Americans also would attend. Regarding that, Jack Redding had a story to tell. One American bachelor, he said, had heard that the Englishmen wore gloves to evening functions, and he had made a trip to Mankato especially to purchase a pair.

"He showed me what he brought back. The finest pair of black kid gloves I ever laid eyes on, by Gad!"

Hook could not wait for the laughter to subside before he capped this story with another.

"You won't believe it, but I give you my word it's true. You know the Eaton boy. He came to me and asked if I had an extra tail coat; wanted to borrow it, he said."

" 'Man,' said I, 'do you think you could wear my coat?' (I'm on the smallish side, of course, and he is as big as an ox.)

" 'Oh, that doesn't matter, Hook,' said he. 'I'll just carry it on my arm to show 'em I own one.' "

Charley's face turned scarlet. Cathy waited only for the laughter to die down; then she spoke earnestly.

"I think there are many Americans just as well versed in social customs as we are, Mr. Hook."

"Oh, of course, Miss Cathy." "Many of them." "There's Dr. Shaw. He's coming to the ball."

Agreement with her statement was general, but it came too late. The harm had been done. Charley not only had quitted the room. Cathy heard the front door close.

The punch was ready at last. Hot water, a tumblerful of rum, and a tumblerful of brandy had been measured into the bowl.

"Where's Charley?" Mrs. Halliday asked, as the glasses went round. There were eleven in her brood but not one was ever absent without her taking cognizance.

"He's gone out," offered Gerry.

"Gone out?" No member of the family went out on Christmas evening. Even Jim, although engaged to Sally Lovell, stayed by the paternal hearth.

"Oh, he hasn't gone far, my dear." Her husband's tone was reassuring. Cathy heard his casual explanation. "He'll be back presently, I'm sure. He wants to speak with me. Quite particularly, he said."

Mr. Halliday lifted his glass.

"Ladies and gentlemen, the Queen!"

Cathy drank to the Queen with chagrin and disappointment welling in her breast. Charley had, then, mustered his courage. And all for nothing! She knew her Charley. He would not quickly muster it again.

"Ladies and gentlemen, the President of the United States!"

She drank that also in dejection.

Then at last, as twilight was drawing in, they drank "to the health of absent friends." Cathy lifted her glass to that with warming eyes. She drank with a gravely tender expression, Slabs Neville watching her.

"When do we play 'Snapdragon'?" whispered Maggie, bored with this drinking of toasts.

At bedtime Dora told Cathy that she was engaged to marry Cyril. Cathy hugged her and kissed her and whirled her about the room.

"Darling, may I be bridesmaid?"

She seemed so sincerely happy that Dora ventured timidly:

"Cathy, do you still feel sure? About Richard, I mean. Slabs is such a dear—so much in love with you. And you've seen Richard so little. Could you possibly be mistaken?"

Cathy's hands dropped away.

"Could *you* be mistaken," she asked stonily, "about Cyril?"

Dora was too gentle to answer as she might have answered: that her Cyril was a clergyman, while Richard was the proprietor of the notorious Kentish Arms; that her Cyril had spoken to Father and was making plans for their marriage, while Richard made no gesture toward Cathy although the months ran into years. Dora was too gentle to say this. She said instead:

"Forgive me, dear. It's only that—I'm so happy. I want you to be happy, too."

When Dora was asleep, Cathy slipped softly from their bed. She drew her flannel dressing gown about her and tiptoed to the window. It was closed, and the outer window was furry with frost. Cathy opened the inner window and scraped a small corner of the outer one down to the glass.

She could see a wintry moon, some wintry stars—Sirius blazing brightly at the Great Dog's mouth.

"Not another Christmas!" Cathy whispered. "Not another Christmas without him. Please!"

Waiting is a task for the brave, for the resolute, for those who believe in their stars.

CHAPTER FIVE

THE importance of the Bachelors' Ball grew with every hour. Between Christmas Day when it was discussed at the Hallidays' and New Year's Eve when the fiddles were tuned, it had swelled like a rolling snowball into the grand event of the season—of any season, so far as Rainbow was concerned. Nothing like this had been known since two fur traders founded the town.

The bachelors of the colony were doing themselves proud. They were resolved to repay the hospitality of the families in a manner which would leave no doubt of their appreciation. Not only was the orchestra coming from Mankato. Hothouse flowers, cotillion favors, the ices were coming from St. Paul. The dining room of the Balmoral would be cleared for the grand occasion and decorated with Christmas greens and candles.

Two bachelors did not expect to attend. It was not that they had not been invited. No bachelors had been invited; they had, instead, been approached by the committee and bluntly directed to "dig up." Richard and Paul Bevan had not been so approached. And a third subject of the Queen was well aware that he would not be welcome at the ball. Captain Bannister had signified early that he would not be present. He was, he said with the utmost regret, lecturing that evening on the subject of the Crimean War, in Winona, Minnesota.

Bevan took his snubbing as a joke to be enjoyed whole-heartedly.

"The mamas don't dare trust us with their daughters, Dick. It's wicked what we could do in the course of a schottische. To turn us loose among all those curls and flounces would be like running two Juggernauts through a field of daisies."

Although Richard hardly tried to conceal his humiliation, Paul's mood continued amused and derisive as the plans for the ball advanced. But unaccountably, on the very Eve of New Year's, it changed. Suddenly, he was sunk in melancholy. The change had nothing to do with the ball. When Richard suggested that chance, Paul made a puzzled denial. He admitted his melancholy, but for his life, he declared, he could not explain it. He even felt a little sick.

"It's like nothing I ever felt before. I'm not actually ill. But feel, my face is burning! Something seems to be hanging over me—waiting to close in on me and choke me. In short, I feel like the devil."

He stretched out upon his bed, his eyes closed, his figure spiritless, and when Richard made ready to leave for the evening's duty at the Kentish Arms, he protested with an unnatural vehemence.

"Don't go, Dick! Stay around!"

"But I told Joe he might have the night off."

"He would work if you asked him."

"I'll be back early," Richard replied. "You drink a hot toddy and get under your blankets."

"You can't make it early! Not on New Year's Eve!"

"You watch me," Richard promised.

He had meant to close up early in any event. Trade would be thin, with so many at the ball. Few of the colonists would visit his bar, and he was reluctant to face even those few.

Unlike Paul, he was deeply hurt by his omission from the list of hosts.

No previous slight had had the force of this one. None had so wounded him. The responsible critics on this occasion were not the women of the colony. They were his cronies: Hook, Earle, Trevenen, the Nevilles, with whom he had so often fished and hunted. Moreover the ball was not exclusive, as were those held in the homes. Even some Americans were invited.

Yet he knew that if it had been possible to do so, his friends would have included him. That admission put the blame squarely upon himself—and on the Kentish Arms.

His mood as he sat alone in the saloon had an almost visible blackness. It seemed to cling like a fog to the bent flaxen head, to the fine vigorous body. He was not drinking. He said to convivial visitors that Bevan was sick, and he wanted a clear head. The truth of the matter was that he wanted a clear head to survey the odious old year and the ominous new one.

He was doing this with corroding self-hatred, when a customer entered. He looked up to see Charley Halliday.

This was too much, Richard thought. He certainly did not propose to have it on his conscience that he had served Cathy's brother, who had never—he felt sure—bought a drink in a saloon in his life.

Charley said in a forced tone: " 'Lo, Dick. Give me a whiskey and soda."

Richard did not stand up. He merely raised impatient eyes. "The marshal would have me in the lock-up if I did. Clear out."

Charley flushed. "That's ridiculous," he said. "I'm not a minor."

"Trot along! Out with you," Richard said wearily.

"Dick, I really want a drink. I think I need one."

"Nobody needs a drink, ever," Richard said bitterly.

"But I want one. I'd like to have one and sit around and talk."

That prospect was more than Richard could endure. He wanted to talk to no one; least of all, to Cathy's brother.

"Go home where you belong!" he said violently.

The boy turned on his heel; the doors swung furiously behind him.

Richard closed the ledger, but he did not so easily drown the echo of his encounter with Cathy's brother. He still sat at the table, and he felt his angry temper yielding to other emotions. Why, he wondered, had Charley come into the saloon? A boy on the night of the big dance of the season should be happily calling for his sweetheart. Charley, Richard realized, had not even been in evening clothes. Evidently he was not going to the ball. What was wrong, Richard wondered tardily. He wished that he had not been so beastly rude. He wished he could call the lad back.

Presently he rose and began preparations for closing. A stray customer or two delayed him, but even earlier than he had hoped, he locked the door and set out for home.

Slowly he moved down the wintry street. Snow crunched under his tread. A bleak wind blew out of the night's invisible caverns, and he dropped his face protectingly into the collar of his coat. But he could not shut out the lights of the Balmoral, streaming across the snow. He could not shut out the sound of music. It danced into the icy air like a line of silvery elves, tripping, skipping, and curveting in fantastic steps.

Richard thought of Cathy inside. She would be dancing with Slabs Neville! But she would not, he thought, waltz with Neville as she had once waltzed with him. Whether or not he ever made Cathy his own, something of her being was his, just as something of him was hers. Each one would own a part of the other forever.

At the Log House, the fat Oarlock dozed in a wooden armchair beside the big base-burner stove. He was fatter than ever. He overflowed his collar and his capacious clothes. His great paunch swelled from the chair, his hands hung down like hams. Strange, Richard thought, that he should be kin to tiny neat Aunt Kibbie, who was now Meta's companion.

Without disturbing his host, Richard crossed the office to his own ground-floor quarters. The room was dimly lighted by a single lamp in which the wick had been turned low. The dogs, whining, met him at the door. Paul, still fully dressed, was tossing on the bed.

He was talking, and his English speech was oddly mixed with the German which had been the familiar speech of his happy boyhood.

"*Mutter, Mutter!*" Richard heard him say. And then, "I see you, Mother."

Richard leaned over the bed and put his hand upon Paul's head. It was feverish. Paul quieted under the touch; his words lapsed into gibberish. Richard sat down on the bed, at a loss.

Suddenly Paul sprang to a sitting posture. His long black hair was tossed into wild disarray. His gray-green eyes gleamed. He fastened his hand on Richard's arm.

"*Ja,*" he said. "I see you, my mother. But why do you come?"

In the shadowy room, the final unexpected question sounded eerily. Richard knew that no one stood behind him, on the spot to which Paul's gaze turned, but he was more than half minded to look around.

"Paul," he said, "no one is here but me. Don't you know where you are?"

Paul gazed at him with a troubled expression, brushed his hand across his eyes.

"Of course," he said. "Of course, old chap. But my mother—she comes through that door." He made a distracted effort to explain. "She is dressed in white. She is very pale— There, look!" He gripped Richard's arm again.

Richard turned to look and saw, as he had known he would see, an empty room. Nevertheless a chill ran down his spine. This was an experience he had never had before, yet it was somehow fearfully familiar. In the next instant he knew why. It created, he realized, the frozen dread he had felt as a boy on listening to tales of supernatural visitations.

"*Mutter, Mutter!*" cried Paul. "*Ja*, I see you, Mother. But why do you come?"

It was more than Richard could bear. He ran out to the office, shook the fat Oarlock.

"Get Dr. Shaw for me! Bevan is ill."

Oarlock rubbed confusedly at his eyes.

"Dr. Shaw? He's at the ball. I'll go for him, sure. But you'll have to wait—"

"I can't wait," said Richard. "You keep an eye on Bevan." He ran out the door.

"Here! Take an overcoat!" Oarlock yelled. But Richard was already running down the street.

As he ran, a conviction grew. The doorway that had been empty to him had not been empty to Paul. Paul had looked with the eyes of the spirit and had seen all that he said. Paul had truly seen his mother; she had come, for all that she had been visible to no one save her son. She had crossed half a world, and Richard knew why. Paul's mother was dead!

He ran into the lobby of the Balmoral.

It was brightly lighted, and the sliding doors which led into the dining room were open. From that room came a hum of conversation; ladies in evening toilettes, gentlemen in tail coats could be seen. As Richard entered, the music began and couples appeared on the floor.

The office itself was deserted except for Aunt Kibbie. Small and neat, her dress of black bombazine covered with a snowy apron, she awaited Lady Meta, her Bible on her lap. She was bent low over the fine type, pencil in hand. Alongside the Book lay the small blank book in which she recorded her resolute progress over familiar ground. She glanced up abstractedly as Richard's shadow fell across her page; but her glance changed to sharp scrutiny as she took in his disturbed face.

Richard seized the precious blank book and pencil and wrote:

"Mr. Bevan is ill. Where is Dr. Shaw?"

Aunt Kibbie nodded and hurried away.

When she returned she was accompanied not only by Dr. Shaw but by Lady Meta. Meta looked glowingly lovely as she always did at balls. White roses were caught in her dark curls. Her gown of white satin curved away from her shoulders to emphasize the round perfection of her bosom. Her eyes under their bird-wing brows were anxious.

"Richard! What is it?"

"Aunt Kibbie shouldn't have disturbed you," Richard answered. "I asked only for the doctor. My roommate, Bevan, is ill."

"The violinist?"

"Yes."

"What is the matter?" Dr. Shaw asked.

Richard hesitated.

"He is feverish," he said. "And he has an hallucination that he is seeing his mother. It sounds absurd, I know, but I believe—I believe that his mother has just died, and that he has been told, somehow."

"In England," Meta said. Her voice was awed.

There was a moment's silence; then the American said briskly, "Well, I'll go over, certainly."

"And I," said Lady Meta. She signaled to Aunt Kibbie.

Richard turned to Meta in distress.

"That's quite unnecessary, really," he said.

She flashed a reproachful look.

"Unwise? Perhaps. Unnecessary? No. If he is ill, as you say, and his mother has died, one woman will help more than a dozen doctors. Am I not right, Dr. Shaw?"

"You might be, ma'am," said Dr. Shaw.

Aunt Kibbie brought two cloaks, one for herself, and followed determinedly after Lady Meta.

In the great bare room at the Log House, the lamp was still turned low. Oarlock greeted them with obvious relief.

"He seems bad. I can't make out what he says," he whispered noisily.

Dr. Shaw and Richard, the corpulent Oarlock, and his tiny aged aunt surrounded the bed where Paul lay.

Lady Meta sat down beside him.

She took off her long white gloves and put her cool fingers on his head. Then she took his hand in hers.

"*Mutter, Mutter, Mutter,*" he whispered.

"*Ja, ja,*" she said, falling into the language that seemed closest to her always. "*Schlaf wohl, schlaf gut.*"

Paul opened his eyes. He stared, intent and puzzled. This was not his mother, certainly; but it was a lovely vision, dressed in white, speaking the tongue of his childhood . . .

With a long shuddering sigh, he moved his head to put his cheek upon her hand.

Lady Meta with her free hand stroked his hair.

"Ja. Das ist gut. Schlaf nun, Liebchen, schlaf wohl."

Richard was struck by the understanding pity, the calm devotion of her face.

CHAPTER SIX

AT CLOSING time, after the last customer had gulped the last potent nightcap, Richard picked over the firewood for a solid oaken knot. On first try the piece would not slide into the fat-bellied stove. But by twisting it with a shrewdness learned from much practice, he finally tumbled it down upon the bed of scorching embers. He got his own glass then and sat down, with the stove guarding his shins from the frosty draft which seeped over the threshold. He would have gone home, but Paul would still be awake, and he did not want to hear music tonight—nor praise of Meta.

His mood was thoughtful. The English, that day, had buried Major Scatchett; and standing by the open grave, Richard had had a startling realization of what aliens most of his companions were, of how completely they had failed—after one, two, three years in Minnesota—to make themselves Americans.

He had known what they were thinking, as they stood in the icy air in the unfenced cemetery and watched the Major put away. Not that it was sad to die, but that it was sad to die here. Not that it was sad to be buried, but that it was sad to be buried in the earth of Minnesota. It was all very well to come to this land, they were thinking, to hunt and fish, to look around, and to make a fortune if one could. Naturally, however, one would return to England. Yes, but what if one were not to return?

Richard pondered sitting beside his fire. His countrymen were not really adopting the new home. They had laid their dead in the soil of Minnesota—the Major was not the first. They had married and borne children here. But still they had put down no roots. How almost quaintly this was shown in the paid notices which recorded these events in the *Gazette!*

"Died, Mr. Ian Scatchett, late Major of Her Britannic Majesty's Fifty-eighth Regiment of Foot . . . London papers please copy."

The marriage and birth notices had the same foreign turn. They did not fail to mention, for example, that Miss Barrowcliff, who had recently married the senior Neville, was niece to the Very Reverend Peter Barrowcliff, Archbishop of Fold. When the infant Throop arrived, his pedigree was in type almost before he got his breath.

None of the old values was surrendered. At least none of the false ones. Some of the younger men had vainly tried to exchange sturdy British business practices for Yankee sharpness. But none of the colonists (except Halliday, perhaps) had made any real effort to assimilate new-world democracy. There had not been, Richard reflected, a single marriage between English and American. Very few friendships, even, had been formed; his with Bob Whipp was an exception.

The Americans had liked the English at first. But did they not like them less, today? Richard remembered that first summer, how he and a group of others had run a hurdle race to help Rainbow celebrate Independence Day. There had been a friendlier spirit then. He remembered the early references in the *Gazette* to "our jolly liberal-hearted English friends," to "the noble sons of Albion." Now there were satiric or disapproving flings. "A young English ex-farmer paid $10 into the Crockett County School Fund for the privilege of blackening a certain party's nose." Or, "There have been too many scenes of disgraceful rowdyism and bacchanalian revelry upon our streets of late. The Americans are not to blame." The *Gazette* was full of squibs, aimed to annoy the English. "Each one of Queen Victoria's journeys to Balmoral costs the English nation ten thousand dollars." Was this retaliation for an unjustified snobbery, Richard wondered?

Yet even while he blamed his fellow colonists, he took their part. Certainly they had spent their money freely, were spending it still, to Crockett County's profit. Certainly also they had been cheated and gulled. And which one of them had realized the high hopes with which he had come?

Richard decided, puzzling beside his fire, that every Englishman in Rainbow was in a thoroughly unsatisfactory situation. Well, perhaps not everyone. Halliday had his store, markedly successful in spite of Oates. He had his farm too, and that was doing well. But, after Halliday, who was secure, truly prosperous? No one!

It was not entirely reasonable, Richard realized, to hold this opinion, for almost every colonist was committed, energetically and enthusiastically, to one or a dozen projects. Of projects, this winter, there was no end.

In spite of the cold, Rainbow kept on growing. Its citizens, in fact, hardly felt the cold. The glow of their hopes kept them warm while the bitter wind swept across lakes and prairies to harry the little town. The old year had gone without bringing the railroad, true; but the new year, all believed, would be more generous. The railroad was more than ever on every man's tongue. It was in the very air.

It was this conviction of the railroad's coming which buoyed every man's hope. It was belief in "the cars" and

their power to haul in prosperity which had induced Englishmen all over the county to sell or mortgage their farms and
seek quicker profits than could be found in crops or sheep.
Hook and Trevenen had mortgaged the Eyrie; their money
had built the Balmoral. Barrowcliff had put up a lumber
mill. The Throops had backed a creamery. Lovell was
behind a grain elevator and the bank.

Beyond everything else, however, to quicken British interest, there were building lots.

Richard paused to marvel at the unanimity with which the
Englishmen were gambling on building lots. He doubted
that there was a single colonist, save himself and Bevan, who
had not bought at least one.

He was thankful that his own farm was still unencumbered. There was some advantage in owning a saloon which
burdened him so heavily that he had no desire for other
burdens. He had had to sell a ninth of his holdings to meet
his payments to Devlin; but he had sold outright, resisting
Oates's confidential advice to mortgage the whole.

Bevan was not sinking his scanty remittances into real
estate because he knew that he was leaving Rainbow. The
news which he believed his mother had come to tell him had
been confirmed by cable. She was dead. A legacy from his
father's estate would shortly rescue Paul from Rainbow.
But except for Paul all the ex-apprentice farmers were putting up every dollar they received, selling their horses and
everything else they could lay their hands on, to buy town
lots. They were pinning their hopes, almost deliriously, upon
the railroad.

Richard shivered out of a brown study. The oaken knot
was now itself embers. The seeping draft which had been
barely perceptible at the threshold was a cold presence
throughout the room. Midnight was close at hand, and the

fat stove was losing, as it always lost, its diurnal fight with February weather. Richard stood up to go for his coat and cap. As he set his glass down on the bar he saw that the drink he had poured was untouched. He would have given more thought to this irregular circumstance, if he had not already been concerned with another. This was that, during his brown study, his thoughts had dealt so little with himself and his own affairs.

The admission that this was a novelty startled him. It gave him a sudden grim realization of how much time, over the past year, he had devoted to self-pity.

Well, at least, he had not indulged in it tonight, he thought with satisfaction. If he had felt pity, it had been directed not toward himself but toward his compatriots.

And perhaps, he admitted, blowing out the lamp and letting himself out into the cold, perhaps they would soon have no need of it. Perhaps the railroad really was coming, and perhaps it would do all that his friends hoped and expected.

He was strengthened in this view the next day. Leaving the Log House for the saloon, he discovered that elation was abroad in Rainbow. Crockett was back. He had returned the night before, going directly and somewhat secretly to Anglo-American Acres. He had seen no one, but the town put one interpretation upon his unexpected appearance. He must have come to maneuver for the completion of the railroad.

There could, Richard conceded, be only one outcome of such an effort. Crockett was expert in string-pulling. The railroad would be in Rainbow in next to no time. He did not wonder that the streets were noisy with optimistic greetings.

Later, however, in the Kentish Arms, he discovered a different reaction to Crockett's return.

Joe was washing glasses behind the bar. Bannister was emptying them in unsocial solitude. Long since, Kit had formed the habit of dropping into the Kentish Arms. He and Richard were not intimate, but they no longer felt constraint in each other's presence. Except for these three, the room was empty when the door was driven back upon its hinges and a score of the younger sons whom Crockett had put out to service at a hundred pounds a head swept into the barroom.

The center of the pack was young Redding. Skates were slung over his shoulders, and at first Richard assumed that the crowd was a skating party. A closer inspection, however, revealed an exuberance which could not be explained by the stale amusement of skating on Lake Rainbow.

"Jack's come into a title!" some one cried.

Richard remembered previous mention of an uncle who was a baronet. Indeed, he recalled, it was the uncle who had put up the hundred pounds. Unwillingly! Jack referred to him always as the Curmudgeon. He explained the situation by shouting now.

"The Curmudgeon's croaked! And both his curmudgeous sons, by God! Carriage accident. It's Sir John Redding, baronet, now!" He waved his arms at Joe. "Pour out a round for everyone."

Joe frowned as the newcomers leaned up against the bar. Joe had learned to see the color of his customers' money before pouring out good liquor. Richard, however, nodded. Whether the new baronet could pay for his treat or not, he ought to have it.

Young Redding lifted his glass high. The others crowded around to clink theirs.

"A long, noble life!"

"And no forty-below weather!"

"And no pitchforks!"

"Give London our best!"

"Tell everyone you meet to 'ware Crockett."

"I'll drink to that last; glad to," Redding cried. He had another drink and sang an impromptu line of doggerel.

" 'Ware Crockett! 'Ware Crockett! Damn his eyes and damn his ears."

The others shouted their approval.

" 'Ware Crockett! 'Ware Crockett! Damn his eyes and damn his ears!" The uproarious condemnation filled the room and flooded thunderously into the street.

Jack held up a hand.

"Here's something still better," he cried. "Let's go out and tell the fat rascal what we think of him. He'll never be looking for that kind of a welcome home."

"Let's tell him with a few rotten eggs," some one amended.

"And a few rocks for his windows."

"Why not some tar and feathers for his thieving skin?"

The spirit of the crowd had changed. It was no longer exuberant. It was ugly. It was savage.

"Tar and feathers."

Bannister got up from his corner table and moved into the center of the noisy group.

"Gentlemen!" he said. His military bearing, his dark, bitter face forced attention.

"Gentlemen," he repeated. "Why bother with tar and feathers. Why not follow the custom of the country. Why not lynch Mr. Crockett?"

Some one laughed.

"Is that the custom of the country?"

"America's very own," Bannister assured them. "It was invented by a gentleman named Lynch back in the time of the Rebellion. In 1782 or '3, I believe. He used it to get rid of certain unneeded individuals in, as I recall it, Virginia."

"I say," cried some one. "That's just what Crockett needs."

"Who owns a rope?"

"Who'll bring some feathers?"

"Where can we find some tar?"

"Tallyho!" shouted Sir John Redding, baronet, and before Richard realized that they were in earnest they were off. The lot of them was racing down Main Street to the stables where their horses were kept.

Bannister walked back to his table.

Joe gazed thoughtfully at the Captain's retreating back.

"Sometimes I think that codger is half crazy," he said to Richard in a confidential tone. He looked with a troubled face at the litter of empty glasses. "And Crockett's in for trouble."

Richard shrugged.

"He deserves it," he said. Crockett had, he thought, a few rotten eggs coming.

"That lot of young buckaroos might work themselves into a bad hole," Joe said. "Hanging's bad business. Even trying's bad business."

Richard turned sharply.

"You don't really believe they'll do anything more than push Crockett around, do you?"

"They had three, four drinks apiece in here, and they'd had plenty before."

Richard snatched up his coat and cap.

Saddling Kentish Beauty, he heard a disorganized cavalcade race down the snowy street. He ran to the stable door in time to see Redding's band pass. It had grown since leaving his saloon. He glimpsed Charley Halliday, Vivian Lovell, other sons of respectable English families. The riders were nearing a bend in the road and when Richard got to his mount the last of them had disappeared.

He was confident, however, that he could reach Anglo-American Acres ahead of them. The others had made a confused and laggard start. They would ride hard enough, but not steadily. He counted, too, upon the likelihood that they would accept the deceptive invitation of a short cut which angled off the highway about two miles out of Rainbow. In summer and autumn it was a true time and distance saver, and these youngsters all had used it while hunting. They did not know that in winter its victims had to flounder through a succession of snow-filled draws.

About the entrance to the short cut the snow was trampled. The hoof marks of a score of horses outlined the path for as far as Richard could see. He urged Kentish Beauty forward, sure now that he would be in time. He needed, he reckoned, only ten minutes' headway. In that time he could warn Crockett, and Crockett could saddle a mount and get clear.

The Union Jack and the Stars and Stripes, waving at opposite ends of Crockett's big white house, came into view.

Kentish Beauty made the last half-mile at a hard run. As Richard swung off her back, he found himself under a big cottonwood tree that grew against Crockett's porch. One branch stretched out straight like a crossbar. It was, Richard realized, exactly the sort of branch Bannister must have had in mind.

Crockett himself opened the front door, responding to the muffled but audible thud of hooves along the snowy driveway.

"Chalmers!" he cried and hurried forward. "You are Dick Chalmers, aren't you?"

Richard was surprised. After three years he had had no expectation that the promoter would recognize him.

"Yes," he said, "I am Chalmers, right enough."

Crockett shook hands heartily. He was, as always, immaculately dressed. His big round body filled a frock coat which was fashionable to the last, minute seam. His linen was spotless, beyond the powers of any Rainbow laundress. His cravat had a perfection that Richard had not seen since London. The gloss on his boots must have cost Ole an hour.

His broad smile had the ease which such apparel inspires.

"I take it kindly of you," Crockett said, "to hurry out and welcome me home."

"I'm here to save your neck," Richard answered bluntly, and hurried through the riotously conceived project of the lynching. "You've got to clear out."

Crockett grew red, but from choler only. Richard could see no trace of fear in the big man.

"I clear out? Not Adam B. Crockett! If I can't handle a handful of boys, I deserve to have my neck stretched."

"They'll be here any minute," Richard warned, "and drunk!"

"You give me an idea," Crockett cried. "Quick. Into the house." Once there he roared commandingly. "Ole! Jackson!"

Both men came hastily in from the kitchen. Ole's heavy jaws still worked over a vast mouthful of food. The more polite Jackson was unobtrusively wiping his thin lips.

"You'll find three cases of champagne in the root house," Crockett cried. "Get them! Step! And stick every bottle into that bank of snow alongside the front porch. Stick them in so the corks show."

"Can I help?" Richard asked. Unexpectedly he felt a degree of amused admiration.

They got the last bottle into the primitive cooler as the first horseman of Redding's band came into sight. The rest appeared quickly, riding hard.

Crockett took a quick breath and stationed himself on the porch. Plainly, he meant to disarm his foes with the hearty greeting that he had extended to Richard. Ole and Jackson disappeared indoors. Richard followed Crockett, halting just out of sight.

The lynching party, if it still was that, came on at a gallop. Pouring through the wide gateway which marked the entrance to the grounds of Crockett's house, the riders discovered the big figure on the porch and set up a shout. They swung off their horses and gathered for a concerted rush.

In that instant, Richard stepped into view and took a place alongside Crockett. The attack swayed back, wavered. Hands. holding eggs and rocks, were lowered in surprise.

It was the instant Crockett needed. The moment of indecision was brief, but it gave him time to single out the leader.

"Redding!" he cried. The convincing friendliness of his voice rolled out over the disconcerted band, and he followed boldly after it, though not before he had said out of one corner of his mouth to Richard: "Thanks, young man. I needed that help!"

"Redding! By George, I'm glad to see you."

He grasped Jack's hand while the young man hesitated. "You're all just in time to celebrate with me."

"Celebrate?" Young Redding found his voice at last.

Crockett manifested a vast surprise at the interrogatory note. Winking exuberantly across Redding's shoulders to his companions, he conveyed that a revelation was coming, and that the knowledge was theirs in advance of their leader. By so much he won them to his side.

"Don't tell me," he cried to Redding, "that you haven't heard!"

"Heard what?"

"About the railroad!" And again he winked over Redding's shoulder.

"What about it?"

Crockett let go the hand he had held all along and, slapping his big girth, laughed loudly. A ripple of answering mirth ran over the crowd.

"This about it," Crockett cried. "It's coming to Rainbow." He sobered and faced his audience with the compelling formality of a trained speaker.

"Gentlemen!" he said. "I have the honor to tell you that dirt on our railroad begins to fly as soon as the frost is out of the ground. In ninety days the steam engine and cars will reach Rainbow. And if that event doesn't make profits for every man of us, then Adam B. Crockett is no prophet."

Out of a jumble of incredulity and delight, one sceptic put a question.

"Are you sure?"

"Sure! I am positive. I have just concluded the final arrangements. I have spent the past fortnight in St. Paul. I have seen every last man who needed to be seen. I convinced the ones who needed to be convinced . . ."

He had won them. They stood relaxed, elated at the good news they had heard. If violence had been in their minds as they galloped up to the porch, it was there no longer. Crockett had them. And he knew it perfectly. He wheeled to the house.

"Jackson! Ole! Glasses for my friends."

He wheeled back.

"Gentlemen! The champagne has been cooling this long

time. Drink with me, I beg of you." His great arm swung toward the rows of corks popping incredibly out of the bank of snow.

The quondam lynchers shouted with mirth. Champagne cooled in a snowdrift!

Crockett seized a bottle, and his fingers began to work the bloated cork.

"Careful," Redding cried.

The others drew closer, ready to try a rescue if disaster threatened.

Jackson appeared with a wide tray filled with glasses. Ole followed with another. Mrs. Jackson followed with a third. Richard walked down from the porch to stand at Crockett's side.

Crockett's nimble fingers were performing their task with the finesse of a maître d'hôtel.

"Easy!" cried young Redding.

"Don't you worry, my lad," Crockett assured him. "This is a situation I've got well in hand." He turned his head toward Richard. "With your help," he added in a grateful whisper. "Without you I might have been in a most embarrassing situation."

The cork popped high into the air and the assembled company cheered.

Richard slipped away and remounted his horse. He rode off with mingled relief and amusement. It was good to know that all threat of trouble had been put down, but it was laughable—indeed, it was a joke on himself—that Crockett should pretend that the threat had been so slight. Embarrassment! Embarrassment, indeed! Not Crockett's dignity but his hide, his very neck, had been within an ace of treatment that would have gone leagues beyond embarrassment. He laughed again, then he grew serious. He would not have had Crockett tarred and feathered, much less hanged. He would not even have had him stoned. But certainly the future of twenty-odd Englishmen was far from promising when they could be swayed so easily. How could any of them make headway against the manifold difficulties of this new environment if they could be hauled this way and that, like marionettes on strings!

He reached the main road and had gone a quarter of a mile, perhaps, toward Rainbow when he saw two riders approaching. Wide skirts flowing backward as they rode told him that they were women. One sat her horse with a feathery grace. Richard's heart galloped as it had not galloped when Redding's cavalcade charged into Crockett's grounds.

Cathy came up swiftly. It was Dora who accompanied her, and they both drew rein across Richard's path. Richard brought Kentish Beauty to a halt. Cathy spoke first.

"Have you seen Charley?"

"We heard in town," Dora explained, "that he and Jack Redding were riding out with a whole crew to make trouble for Mr. Crockett."

"There'll be no trouble, ma'am," Richard said, looking at Cathy. "I've just come from Crockett's. Everything is all right."

He could not take his gaze from her. The word he had found on their meeting at the church came back. She was still flawless.

"Do you mean that nothing happened at all?" Cathy asked.

"Nothing," Richard said. "When they rode up, Crockett was all ready and waiting; he told them that the railroad was coming, and in two minutes had them drinking his champagne to celebrate the good news."

"Ready and waiting!" Cathy repeated. "Was he warned?"

Richard wanted to claim the credit so legitimately due him, but he could not find words that seemed unboastful.

"The last I saw of Charley," he said, "he was shaking Crockett's hand and promising to bring his father out."

"It was you who warned Mr. Crockett!" Cathy cried.

A third hardly urged horse pounded up and saved Richard from making a reply. The rider was the senior Lovell, whose mutton-chop whiskers flared on either side of an anxious face.

"Have you seen Vivian?" he demanded. "Have you come from Crockett's?"

Richard grinned. It must have been a wild rumor, indeed, the one going about Rainbow, to have set the sober senior Lovell racing to a rescue.

"Richard has just come from there, Mr. Lovell," Cathy answered. "There is nothing to worry about, because he warned Mr. Crockett in time."

"You did!" Lovell exclaimed, and eyed Richard sharply. Words could not have revealed more plainly than that glance his surprise that Richard had not been in the raiding party. "Then Crockett got clear?"

"Clear?" Richard smiled. "Why, no! The situation wasn't dangerous enough for that. He stayed and opened champagne."

Cathy's whip beat an exasperated stroke upon the pommel of her saddle.

"Not dangerous!" she cried. "Don't you believe any such thing, Mr. Lovell. That silly crew meant danger aplenty when it left Rainbow. But Richard got to Anglo-American Acres ahead of them and helped Mr. Crockett to change their minds."

Mr. Lovell said "Ha-a-r-r-rumph!" He looked down the road toward Crockett's homestead, shifted a seat unaccustomed to hard riding, and frowned judiciously. "Well," he decided. "I take it that I could improve the situation in no way by going on, so I suppose I might as well return." He glanced toward Cathy and Dora, then cautiously toward Richard. "Shall we ride back together?"

It might have been a concession. Indeed it undoubtedly was a concession; but it was also a precaution. The manner in which he ranged his horse firmly beside Richard and waved the girls on ahead was evidence of that. This unexpectedly law-abiding young man might have staved off trouble at Anglo-American Acres, but he was still a black, an almost black sheep, and quite unsuitable for close association with the daughters of James Halliday.

By no maneuvering could Richard bring Kentish Beauty next to Cathy's mount. He got what consolation he could out of looking his fill as she moved in front of him. It was exciting, just to do that. He had not realized that her waist was so small. He had not thought that a neck could rise so sweetly as hers rose from her beautifully erect back. The lobe of one ear, below one smooth wing of her brown hair, became rosily transparent for an instant as it caught the sunlight.

That was when she turned to look back rebelliously at the shepherding Mr. Lovell. Her glance crossed Richard's, and he smiled. She whirled about sharply; Richard saw the ear redden.

"Eh, sir? I beg your pardon? You were saying?" said Richard, aware of words from Banker Lovell thrice repeated.

CHAPTER SEVEN

In early May an invitation came from the Eyrie urging Richard to join in a wolf hunt. Paul was both indignant and amused. He recalled how cautiously the masters of the Eyrie had withheld an invitation to the Bachelors' Ball.

"They want you to pull a chestnut out of the fire. But what thanks will you get?"

Richard inspected his riding boots and decided in favor of a polishing.

"They'll thank me when I bring the scalp home."

"About as much as anyone thanked you for keeping that lot of young hot-heads from overhauling Crockett!"

"Crockett was thankful," Richard argued cheerfully. "He told me I'd helped him out of a most embarrassing situation."

"Embarrassing! Embarrassing! Good God! You saved him a tar-and-feathering at least."

Richard decided that his riding coat could do with a pressing.

He did not care to make any admission to Paul, but he had had hints that some of the people of Rainbow appreciated the incident at Anglo-American Acres. Else why did the senior Lovell now stop to chat whenever they met? And why had the Reverend Cyril Cathcart (shortly to be married to Dora Halliday) actually spoken?

The Reverend Cyril had stopped in broad daylight, and in the middle of Main Street.

"Mr. Chalmers! It is on my conscience to tell you that the Englishmen of Crockett County are in your debt."

Richard had pretended ignorance, but he had been pleased. He would not, however, admit his pleasure to Paul, nor reveal the thought that had risen on the foundation of the Reverend Cyril Cathcart's gratitude.

"Those clodhoppers and shopkeepers!" Paul would have derided. "Does it make any difference what they think of you?"

It would do no good to tell Paul that it made a difference, but it did; and because it did he was going on the wolf hunt. Now that almost every landowner had bought sheep the death of any wolf was important. Beyond that, Richard knew the identity of the wolf that he had been invited to hunt. It was Bob Whipp's solitary marauder running amok to the south of Rainbow.

She had made that region her own. Her den, deep in the timber bordering the Sisseton River, remained undiscovered, in spite of a hundred pursuits, and her forays were bloodily successful in spite of the closest watch. So great were her achievements that now she had a name. She was Three Toes, damned as such, particularly and especially, by farmers for twenty miles in every direction. Lately, as though she sensed this concentrated enmity, an unbridled malevolence had marked her raids. On the previous night she had killed forty-odd sheep before pausing to make her meal off the hind quarters of one.

Deciding that his breeches would do as they were, Richard reflected that the man who brought back the scalp of Three Toes should win considerable approval from a large section of the county.

"Whatever are you mulling about?" Paul demanded.

Richard flushed. Never before had he consciously sought favor. He bolstered his resolution stubbornly, however. Why should he not? His own deliberate acts had put him down where he stood. Why should not his own act help him up?

"I was just wondering how Kentish Beauty would take the fences," he said.

Paul seized his violin case and a sheaf of music.

"I'm off! Lady Meta promised to practise with me this evening."

Richard grew more sober as he watched the door close. Paul's association with Lady Meta showed how little he cared for Rainbow's clodhoppers and shopkeepers. More, it showed how little Meta cared. They were together daily, and for all that Aunt Kibbie never left her assigned rocking chair, Rainbow was talking. Paul played, Lady Meta accompanied and coached him. She was, Paul had announced within a month of the extraordinary night on which his mother's death had been so strangely made known, as fine a musician as he had ever found.

"I don't mean her playing. That is good enough. But her taste, her ear, her appreciation! All are flawless."

An equally vain but less gifted artist might have meant no more than that Lady Meta considered his playing good. Paul did not, although he admitted that she praised him lavishly on occasion.

Meta unerringly checked him when he missed or fell short of the effect to which his ambition aspired. Often she stopped his bow in mid-stroke.

"No, Paul! Take that phrase again. Try it this way."

"And she is always right," Paul cried. "She is amazing. Sometimes I quarrel with her. But when I am back home, playing for myself, I see that she was right."

Richard was all too sure where Meta's rightness would bring herself and Paul. Quarrels with Lady Meta must come sooner or later to passionate reconciliations.

He was sure, from Paul's frank reports of their encounters, that no word of love had passed. Meta, he knew, did not give herself casually, and now she had particular reasons for deliberation, not the least of which was Paul himself, dubious and mercurial. Moreover, Paul was only lately showing any recovery from the shock of his mother's death. But if Meta made up her mind, as she might any day, the full measure of her dark beauty would encompass Paul; and when that happened they would care no more for Rainbow's gossip than rivers care for the rocks over which they flow.

Kentish Beauty was, as Richard had anticipated, in splendid condition. Her equipment did not require any attention either. The bridle was fit to the last rivet and buckle, and its bit was burnished free of any rusty roughness which might chafe her tender mouth. The saddle, with a new surcingle and new stirrup straps, was ready for any demand.

Next morning at the Eyrie, however, he found himself wondering why he had been so sure on the previous evening that he could succeed. The competitors gathered around him on the hilltop between the lakes where Hook and Trevenen had built their sturdy house, were formidable indeed. Richard appraised them in the sharp light from the east.

Hook also would be after Three Toes. Hook, who rode loosely and boldly, who turned aside for nothing, who missed a kill only when luck ran dead against him. Hook, small and thin, a featherweight to dismay any rival, waited for the starting horn astride a deceptively chunky white mare.

Bannister waited near by, Bannister who rode like a burr, scarcely rising off his saddle at a fence, but lifting his animal with unsparing powerful knees. Bannister rode a bay gelding as finely made as Kentish Beauty. She was fretful now, with the dogs whining around, and a casual observer might have doubted her reliability, but Richard knew that in the hunt she would run as smoothly as hot butter.

Hook and Bannister and Trevenen, Richard decided, were the men to be beaten. Trevenen might ride a shade less skillfully than the other two, but only a shade; and his rangy dappled gray had bottom and hunting sense. Over rough country he would pick his way as wisely as any fox or wolf.

Besides Hook and Trevenen and the Captain, there were a score at the hunt, and not a bad rider in the lot. Not a poor horse, either! Some, perhaps, were lately off a plough; because, although the tradition was maintained that every gentleman kept his hunter as he would have kept one back home, some unostentatiously gave their animals a double duty. Nevertheless every one could be safely counted on for a good run. Harry Earle, slender and erect, a thought too daring but splendidly accomplished on a horse; the three irresponsible, irrepressible Nevilles; a pair of eager Lovells; Charley Halliday, excited and tense; Jim Halliday, surely determined; Barrowcliff who rode furiously, as though to prove that an archbishop's nephew could be as red-blooded as any. In addition there were a dozen young bachelors of Crockett's latest importation, and a sprinkling of Americans. These last were the least dangerous. They bestrode solid broad-backed animals unlikely to offer much competition after the first hour.

There were a dozen-odd hounds. Every one of these had proved its courage and staying qualities over and over. Courage and endurance were essential because a wolf hunt might last for six or seven hours, and extend over thirty miles, and at the finish the kill had to be made. Usually the wolf was rounded up only after it had been, in Harry Earle's phrase, "clean pumped"; but even then it was dangerous. Only a brave hound would go in against even a spent wolf.

In the porte-cochère before the ten-foot door, Hook jockeyed his mare alongside Kentish Beauty.

"What odds will you give me, Dick, that I don't take the three dollars?"

That was a standard joke at every wolf hunt. The bounty on a dead wolf was three dollars, paid by the county clerk on delivery of the scalp, but the colonists never collected it because the trophy was always kept to decorate some mantel-piece.

Bannister heard the question.

"Mayn't I have a third of that, gentlemen?" he asked with the habitual undercurrent of irony shading his courtesy.

"Of course," Richard agreed, and Hook nodded.

"Ten pounds apiece," Bannister suggested, "and winner take all."

"Ten pounds! The devil!" Hook protested. "All of us aren't lecturing."

Bannister's soft laughter showed pleasure at the compliment.

"Say ten dollars," Richard compromised.

"I can manage ten," Hook agreed, "though I shan't be able to much longer unless Crockett's railroad helps out."

That brought a burst of talk.

"It's crossed Chanyaska Creek . . ."

"We rode out Sunday to watch them grading."

"Has anyone heard where the station will be located?"

For a few moments even the wolf hunt was forgotten in jubilant discussion of the coming cars.

Then the blast of a horn rang out through the dawn. Its echoes drowned the lively talk of men as well as the sweet confusion of bird voices in the budding trees. The responding sound was a purposeful thud of hooves, as horses which had been scattered through stable yard and drive and across the wide dewy lawn, poured down the driveway beneath the avenue of beeches and out into the tinted world.

As he took his place in the cavalcade, Richard watched the magnificently riding line, and his thoughts went back to his reverie the night after the day when Major Scatchett was buried. He had thought then that his compatriots were misfits in America. But they were not misfits now. This, he thought, was what they were fitted for: for riding! for jumping! This they did well, and nothing else. If anyone ever happened to be willing to pay for that sort of thing, they might do fairly well.

As he rode, he set himself the task of recalling the physical characteristics of the country through which the wolf hunt would carry. It would be wise to freshen up on these against the time when he would be too rushed to recall them.

While he strove for a complete picture, Kentish Beauty ambled gently. Hook was setting a leisurely pace. They had a ride of a good hour before reaching Three Toes' range, because they must travel slowly. Their quarry would be in small danger if the horses were not fresh at the start.

At the outset, Dick recalled, they would trail the wolf over open prairie. Open, but not easy. To the eye it might seem as innocently level as a calm lake, but the ploughed stretches concealed gopher holes. Grass masked ditches. Gullies were frequent; and fences challenged all too often.

This open prairie extended for miles. If the hounds found the wolf anywhere within its limits the hunt might end quickly. Beyond, however, was the sparse but wide belt of timber masking the Sisseton River. It was in this timber that the bitch had her den. She would, also, have innumerable hide-aways. If she reached the timber, she would gain a considerable advantage over the pursuit. The hunt there might be long and difficult.

Beyond the timber was the river, swift now and deep with the last of the spring flood waters. Cold, too, Richard reflected, and he hoped that the chase would end before it reached that chilling barrier.

Beyond the river was more prairie; but it did little good to consider that because the hunt would not in all likelihood extend into it. By the time they reached the river the horses and hounds would be worn out. Even if they had strength to swim the swift river they would not be able to go beyond.

"The river," Richard thought to himself, "is our last chance. If one of us doesn't make the kill at the river, none of us will make it."

Up forward the huntsmen had stopped. Trevenen and Hook were consulting an American farmer. A little way to the left the cobblestone chimney of a sod shanty rose above a small hill. Near by a ramshackle fence enclosed an acre of ground.

"Here is where the wolf made her last kill," Hook explained as Richard rode up.

The hounds began to rove about, whining through noses close to the ground.

"Ten dollars apiece, right?" Bannister asked.

Richard nodded inattentively, his gaze and thoughts upon the hounds. Hook laughed, shifting nervously. The other score of huntsmen spread out, working their animals carefully behind the roving hounds, each hoping he held a point of vantage. A hound gave tongue, and was off like a streak. The pack caught the scent and followed pell-mell.

"That's it," Hook cried, and sent his stocky white mare into a run. Trevenen, caught lucklessly on a flank, urged his horse in. Bannister, sitting his bay gelding like a burr, was well forward with Earle, Jim Halliday, and young Lovell. Richard found himself neither in front nor trailing and was satisfied with his middle position.

For a man of his weight, Richard rode lightly. Because of this, his mount lasted while the mounts of men of less poundage wearied under their riders' listless weight. He rode, too, with a close, tight, attentive rein. He let Kentish Beauty pick her own way but was instantly helpful if she faltered. He brought her carefully up to every fence, and when she got there he let her take her time.

The first fence was a risky barrier, made of split rails piled high and crazily. Kentish Beauty worked into a canter, then the tremendous springs in her hindquarters recoiled, and she was up and over. On the far side Richard put her smartly again into stride.

"Tallyho!" he shouted from sheer, heart-lifting joy at the perfect jump.

Off to the right he heard a crash. He risked a quick glance back. Vivian Lovell's black thoroughbred had refused the fence, had charged it and gone down, catapulting his rider head over heels. Richard risked another glance. The black was up, but limping. It was the first casualty.

At the end of an hour the hounds were singing no less confidently. The sprinkling of Americans had dropped behind. Several of the hundred-pound youngsters were out, too, their mounts exhausted less by their own efforts than by their bouncing masters. Of the wolf no hide or hair had been found, but the scent continued richly aggravating.

In the second hour Slabs Neville lifted his brown mare too quickly at an easy fence. Three of the youngsters, following close, made a high, kicking pile. Slabs got a broken collar bone out of the mêlée.

"Bring that bitch's scalp back," he roared profanely, "or don't any of you show up at the Eyrie."

The few within hearing waved derisive arms.

The trail led to a slough, and the hounds lost the scent. Richard had time to look about. He was well satisfied when he had compared the other horses with Kentish Beauty. Only Bannister's bay gelding and Hook's stocky white mare were as fresh.

The slough proved to be an obstacle known to the bitch and wisely used. She knew a way into it, but when a bold hound tried to follow the trail he sank suddenly out of sight fifty yards from solid ground. Rescue was impossible. Trevenen swore. Given his choice he would have kept the hound and lost the trail.

"We'll try the far side," he said in a furious voice, his smile, for once, absent. "I'll get that brute now if I stay out all night."

They trotted around, but picked up no scent. Trevenen spread the hounds out, urged them far back from the slough's margin. Still their noses caught nothing. The hunters settled wearily in their saddles.

Distantly, on the far side of the slough, a single hound gave tongue. Everyone stared. Bannister got away first. The rest rode hard after him. When they picked up the lone hound he was following a line at right angles to the previous trail.

"That wolf's smart," Trevenen conceded to Richard. "She never crossed the slough at all. She trotted in, looped back, and came out farther from her original scent than the hounds would ordinarily range. Then she angled away, on a detour."

The new trail seemed fresh, and the hounds crowded along, tails up, noses low, voices clamorous. Earle was close behind when his horse failed to clear a fence by the width of the two front feet. It crashed. Earle pitched forward in a long arc, arms outstretched. Inevitably, one arm was broken. "Keep going," he shouted as Richard and Trevenen cantered up.

A lucky fall nevertheless, Richard reflected. With his horse striking that way, Earle might as well have broken his neck. He was glad Earle would recover to ride again. A grand, reckless horseman!

The bitch's scent led now straight toward the Sisseton timber, spreading darkly along a distant horizon. But before the timber was reached the trail was lost again in a ploughed field. The hounds cast about widely under Trevenen's wise direction. A farmer was ploughing, but he said he had just come back from his nooning and had seen nothing.

Trevenen had an inspiration. Dismounting, he hurried to the last turned furrow. It ran straight toward the Sisseton timber. He lifted a piece of it, and called the hounds. They sniffed once and broke into a clamor. The farmer was amazed.

"Old Three Toes is lucky as well as smart," Trevenen said. "She ran along the furrow because it went her way and made easier going than the stubble. She didn't, of course, know that some one was going to plough fresh earth over her scent, but that is what happened."

At the far edge of the ploughing Trevenen turned the furrow over again and the scent was there.

The horses were strung out now, each taking its place according to its own strength and its master's skill. Bannister, Hook, Trevenen, Richard, Barrowcliff, and Jim Halliday led. Close behind came the two remaining Nevilles. The rest of the hunt trailed, almost in Indian file.

The hounds had been running with no more than an occasional yelp. Now they gave tongue furiously.

"We're closing in," Hook said. "She must have stopped to rest."

Nevertheless they rode until the Sisseton was little more than a mile away with no sight of the quarry. Anticipating a last hard run, Dick spared Kentish Beauty as much as he dared.

The she-wolf showed herself briefly. Far forward, on a little knoll, she stood in profile, her open jaws gaping at her pursuers while she took a long, unhurried glance. She vanished as instantaneously as she had appeared.

The hounds surged forward.

"With luck," Hook shouted, "we'll catch up with her at the edge of the timber."

He got his chunky white mare up to a faster gallop. Bannister whipped the bay gelding. Kentish Beauty let her stride out. Barrowcliff tried hard to keep up, and roared his despair as the other three outdistanced him in the wake of the triumphant pack. Halliday too, and at last Trevenen fell behind.

Where the first willow trees spread a blur of green, the bitch turned to slash at the lead hound. She laid its breast wide open, as neatly as a sharp blade could have done it. The pack checked and gave her time to slip into the undergrowth, but from that moment she was never wholly clear. The hounds swept around either flank. Occasionally one got in front. But none remained there long. The wolf charged each such adversary, ran him down, and tore him savagely as she fled on. She fled, but not swiftly. The three horsemen were able to keep close behind in spite of the impeding trees and clutching brush.

"We'll be at the river next," Bannister cried. "We've got to make the kill on this side."

He whipped hard, and for the first time in memory Richard saw Hook use a whip. Richard tightened his rein and lifted Kentish Beauty into a gait that might have been a breath faster. It was, at least, her best. Her obedience matched his determination. That burned fiercely. He would, he would, be the one to take the scalp!

The timber thinned out. The three horsemen emerged as one onto the strip of shore that bound the forest to the water's edge. As one, they took in the spectacle of frustration upon the river's bank.

There, reluctant in the face of the swift flood, the whole pack yelped. Just beyond their reach the bitch swam hardily. She was making little headway, and she drifted downstream fast, but she swam, and once she looked back with open, laughing jaws. She was on her way to freedom and to the death of numberless more sheep, and there was nothing that her pursuers could do about it. The muddy waters boiled over her head, but she fought to the surface.

Hook shouted and urged his stocky mare forward. Bannister whipped harder. Kentish Beauty matched their pace but could do no better. The three horses crossed the strip of sand, neck and neck. At the edge of the river their masters would have sent them in, but all three refused. Hook laughed helplessly. Bannister lifted his whip. But Richard knew that his mare was done.

"Good girl!" he cried, and swung off.

He put his riding crop between his teeth, twisted out of his coat, and dived.

When he came to the surface the bitch was halfway across. The turbulent flood held the man, but he gained. The wolf must have known this, but she did not look back. Her nose, just enough out of water for breathing, pointed constantly at the shore. Her paws paddled without ceasing.

She made the shore when Richard was still twenty yards

away. Free of the reluctant water, she crawled slowly up the bank and shook herself. Richard, in despair, expected to see her trot away, but instead she faced around. While the man struggled through those last yards she waited. He never was sure whether the beast was too tired to go on, or whether she thought to settle this single adversary at a disadvantage. At any rate she waited.

"You devil!" Richard thought. "You devil!"

The water shallowed. His feet grazed bottom. His knees sank into the soft mud. The water here was less than waist-deep. He grasped his crop and rose.

The wolf timed her lunge shrewdly for the moment when the man stumbled up the bank. His first blow only clipped a shoulder. The animal's aim was better. Her fangs slashed a forearm. Richard was off balance, and the shock sent him to his knees. The wolf had carried past and now charged back. Richard was still on his knees but this time he got his blow home. The wolf staggered. He finished her with one blow more.

Across the river Hook shouted.

"Bring that scalp!"

Richard stood up wearily, his torn arm warm with his own blood.

By now the survivors of the hunt had all gathered across the river. They made a rope of bridle reins and ferried Richard over on a log. He was almost too tired to enjoy their jubilant uproar as they made their way to the nearest farmhouse to rest and refresh themselves and their horses.

Leaving the farmhouse, they were three hours returning to the Eyrie, although their road was far more direct than the trail Three Toes had shown them. The afternoon was waning. As they gained the avenue of beeches, the sun dropped behind the hill like a billiard ball into a pocket.

The house was lighted. Miss Tabby Joy would see to that. Lights and the promise of food and drink streamed from the windows. Neville and Earle were waiting in the towering entrance door.

At sight of them talk rallied again. Richard's achievement was excitedly described. A shout went up about the great door, and then Richard saw that Hook had dismounted and was holding it open.

"Ride in, Dick," he said.

Richard reined in sharply.

"It's your honor," Trevenen cried. "Yours and Kentish Beauty's. We made it big for just such a day."

In the flaring entrance light, Richard colored warmly. He glowed with such pride that he was puzzled. Getting Three Toes was not such a great thing to have done! Then he realized that his pleasure welled up out of a hundred hurts, humiliations, and defeats which made sweeter the triumph of the moment.

"Kentish Beauty," he said, "deserves most of your laurel leaves."

"She didn't swim the Sisseton in flood," Hook said. "And she didn't tackle a wolf on the far shore. Ride along."

Richard's glance crossed with Jim Halliday's. Charley's excited face too was somewhere in the crowd.

As he guided Kentish Beauty up the steps and through the giant door into the hall with ice-blue walls where Three Toes' scalp would hang, he thought:

"They'll know about this at Green Lawn!"

CHAPTER EIGHT

Bob Whipp stood in the doorway of his own house and looked in upon the kitchen. It was time, he knew, that he got started. The team was all hitched, waiting. Lonabelle and her man, Bridey and the kids would all be waiting too, dressed in their Sunday clothes and nervous as colts. Old Sal and Al would have to step lively to get the lot of them in to Rainbow in time for the start of the show, and none of them wanted to miss a moment of the railroad celebration. This was a big day in Rainbow. The first train was coming; there would be speeches, a parade; they were firing off a cannon. Bob Whipp knew that he ought to be clattering along the road to Lonabelle's this moment, and yet he delayed, looking at his kitchen.

He was looking, to be exact, at the kitchen floor. Bridey's floor was laid at last. Clean white pine boards, factory-made, straight as columns of soldiery, ran the full length of the kitchen.

"A carpenter couldn't have laid it neater," said Captain Whipp, gazing with admiration upon his own handiwork.

"Just what her ma wanted," he continued, inspecting it. "Bridey's got 'em all now. Glass windows, an elevated oven stove, and an honest-to-god floor. No more stubbing her little toes on stones! No more mud puddling underfoot to mess up everything every time a little water spills. Warm, dry, tony-looking! Gosh, won't Bridey be tickled?"

He tried thus to whip up his pleasure in the floor, for although he had wanted it so long (for Bridey's sake), and had worked so hard to get it for her, and although it lay here now so clean and flawless, he was not happy. Where was the excess of pleasure which he had expected to feel?

He had known last autumn when he and Dick got a bumper crop, that he could afford the floor. But since he and Bridey were living at Dick's place, it had seemed foolish to put one in. This spring, however, although they were still at Little Goodlands, he had been impelled to do it. It was all he could think of to please Bridey. And he had been so distressed about Bridey! She acted so strange and unhappy—not like herself. Besides, Dick Chalmers was acting a lot more like *himself*. Bob had a notion that Dick might be coming back to his farm one of these days. So he had got the lumber from Barrowcliff's new mill, and brought it out here on a Sunday, and every Sunday since he had been riding over to the Three Sisters and working on the floor. In secret!

Now it was done, all ready to give Bridey the surprise of her life, but Bob derived puzzlingly little comfort from it.

"Good as a carpenter could do it," he said again. "Better!" He stepped inside cautiously and righted a chair. He was bringing Bridey home after the railroad celebration. She was to see the surprise at which he'd been hinting darkly for so long. (Not, he admitted, that she had seemed much interested in it.) He latched the door carefully behind him and went out to the team.

The time was June; and the day was perfect for the railroad celebration. He tried to cheer himself with that reflection as he sent Sal and Al briskly along the familiar road to Lonabelle's. Folks couldn't have had a nicer day for the affair; no, sir, not if they'd ordered it.

This was the kind of day you got only in Minnesota. Sky just couldn't be measured; lots of sky—plenty of sky. See the room that bobolink took, chasing his own shadow over the grass? And the grass all mixed with flowers; the prairie was one big bouquet. Lord! Those prairie roses smelled sweet in the sun!

Crops were looking right thrifty too. Bob Whipp shifted his thought to crops, for the beauty of the morning had given him no comfort. He was a persistent seeker after the bright side. He did not believe in feeling blue. But today he could not seem to help it.

He was oppressed by a queer feeling down in the pit of his stomach, a feeling he always had when he was worried about Bridey. He had felt it first the morning she was born. He had looked at the little squirming red mass, so ineffably precious for all that it was so ugly, and he had felt, with a forlorn emptiness at the pit of his stomach, that it could not be right for her to cry like that. He remembered how he had turned to Lonabelle. Big, cheerful, rough-and-ready Lonabelle who, with Grandma Ives had brought the baby. He had asked her if she was sure it was all right for the little tike to cry so.

"What do you think I spanked her for?" Lonabelle had asked with her big laugh. He remembered that big laugh now, and it made him feel better.

The forlorn emptiness had come again when Bridey had whooping cough. She was two years old or thereabouts, just learning to put words together. And she put "Pa" on to the front end of almost every sentence. "Pa tell," when she meant, "I'll tell it to Pa." "Pa show." "Pa give." She had whooped, he remembered, until she'd nearly strangled, and her mother had held her, looking scared and helpless, and

Bob had got on his old horse, Charger, the only horse they'd had, then. And had he sent that brute across country to Dr. Shaw's? He still remembered the wild ride!

Later when Bridey started to school she had been shy. The children had teased her—little brats!—and she had cried on his neck. The oppressive painful feeling had been worse then, for there was nothing he could do.

And it had been worse still after Bridey's mother died. He had been so anxious to do right by the child, to do just as her mother would have done. He had worried, he remembered, about her staying so close to home, going only to Lonabelle's. And then for a time she had seemed so well and happy, so spirited and gay, that he had not worried at all. But this spring she was different.

That was why he had sent her to Lonabelle's. It had been a wrench to let her go. They had never been separated before; and Dick's house wasn't the same without her. But he had felt that she needed a woman to talk to. Maybe a woman could make out what was wrong. Lonabelle was rough, but she was kind. And Bridey loved her.

What was the matter, what could be the matter with Bridey? Bob forgot to slap the reins, to tell Sal and Al to hurry. He went along slower and slower, and at last his head dropped to his chest. He held it there low while he listened to the question his mind whispered: Could some boy have gotten Bridey into trouble?

It seemed impossible because, in the first place, Bridey didn't go out with boys, she didn't see any boys, she didn't know any boys. In the second place, if she knew ever so many, Bridey would never take up with a bad boy. Never. Bridey held herself kind of proud, like her mother had done.

And anyway, what boy wouldn't want to marry Bridey? "Bridey's pretty," Bob thought. "She's a top-notch housekeeper. We're not poor. We've got a good name, always have had.

"Pshaw! It's all foolishness! How can I even be thinking such a thing!" He threw up his head, clicked to Sal and Al, slapped the reins over their laggard flanks. He even started to whistle. But the whistle sounded so thin, so worried, that he stopped it before it was half begun.

Bridey hadn't been well. She hadn't looked nor acted well. And that was a fact!

He was entering Lonabelle's land now. The road ran straight as a string over the vast flat prairie to the grove of cottonwood trees which rose beside Lona's house. The landscape today was strangely empty. Usually one could see a farmer or two at the plough and somewhere in the distance a prairie schooner pulling toward the west. But today the farmers were all in town, even the most greedy for labor. And the prairie schooners had halted in Rainbow to rest the oxen and watch the fun.

The road was quite empty except far down near Lonabelle's. There a small boy was running.

It would be Bobbie, the ten-year-old ginger-haired one, Bob decided.

"Come out to look for me," he thought. "They all got tired waiting." But in spite of this casual explanation, he felt his throat grow dry. Bobbie was running so furiously, not stopping to throw a stone, not stopping to grab a handful of the tempting wild strawberries growing beside the road, not stopping for anything! And as he drew nearer, Bob saw that Bobbie wasn't dressed for town. He was barefoot beneath torn pantaloons.

Bob reined in his horses.

"Jump in, Bobbie. What's wrong?"

The boy was crying.

"It's Bridey, Uncle Bob. She's took awful bad."

Bob snatched him to the wagon seat, laid the whip heavily across Sal's back. His voice when he spoke had a forced dry calm.

"What's the matter with Bridey?"

"I don't know. Ma sent Pa for the doctor, and the children over to Beaseleys, all of them but me, and she told me to run for you, hell-bent; and that's what I was doing when you came."

Bob lashed Sal again. Young Bobbie clung to his arm as the wagon rolled and racketed down the road. It rolled into Lonabelle's big untidy barnyard, which was empty of children for the first time in Bob Whipp's experience. Ordinarily it swarmed with them.

He said, "Hold the team!" and set off at a run for the house.

Lonabelle met him in the doorway. Her face was wet with tears. That was a bad sign. Lonabelle was never one for crying, not when there was anything else to do.

"Has the doctor come?" Bob asked in a hoarse voice.

Lonabelle shook her head.

"It doesn't matter," she said. "The baby's come. Before its time. It's dead."

Bob Whipp blanched; he swallowed; he said nothing.

"And Bridey—" Lonabelle's eyes filled again. "You can see for yourself. Bridey's bad."

Bob started to push through the doorway, but she stopped him.

"Bob," she said, "I don't know how you feel about this. But you don't blame—you wouldn't—"

"God, Lona!" said Bob. "What do you take me for? Don't I know that Bridey's an angel from heaven?" He swung into the room.

The kitchen was disordered. Bedding was piled in the chairs. Kettles of water sat about on the floor. A small white-wrapped bundle lay on the kitchen table. When loaves of bread came fresh from the oven Bridey often wrapped them just that way to preserve their sweetness and moisture.

Bob pushed through the doorway to the bedroom where Bridey lay.

The soft red curls were rough and tangled; Bridey never would have them so. Her small face was harshly pale; shrunken, pinched. The closed eyes seemed sunk into her head.

Bob stood looking down at her; then he dropped to his knees beside the bed. He took one small icy hand.

"Honey lamb!" he said. "Look at your pa."

Bridey's pale lids flickered open slowly. But the gaze from her brown eyes was steady and deep.

"Honey lamb," said Bob, "you've got to get well fast. Do you know the surprise I've got for you?" (Not the floor! Oh, not the floor!) "We're going out to Californy, you and me. We're going out to where there ain't no winter. Just flowers and sunshine, all year long."

"Pa!" said Bridey. The word was urgent. She brought it out laboriously, breathing hard.

"What is it, Pet?"

Bob Whipp leaned over her. He saw a small gold locket on her neck. It wasn't her mother's. He had never seen it before.

"Pa!" The tone was fainter. Sweat beaded her lip. He bent his head to hear. "I love you, Pa."

"Oh, Bridey! Bridey!" Bob Whipp could hold back his tears no longer. But still he was resolved that Bridey should not see them. He buried his face in the bedclothes, pretending that he only wanted to be near her.

He would not have to hide his feeling long. He knew. He had seen her mother die. Only then he had had Bridey. And now his world was empty. One arm holding Bridey close, his face hidden, he waited.

Waves of agony, weirdly familiar, rolled over his head. Then it had been Nora. Now it was Bridey . . .

He set his mind on waiting. He willed the tears not to run, although they brimmed his eyes and blinded him.

Lonabelle's voice came at last as though from a great distance.

"Come away, Bob. It's all over. Come away."

He yielded to the kindly hand pulling at his arm.

His cramped legs told him how long he had been kneeling. Lonabelle went with him into the kitchen, but he left her there and walked out to the woodshed to exhaust himself with weeping. When he returned, he had no tears. His dry eyes burned. He could see.

He could see with his mind, too, and as he approached the room where Bridey lay, he forced the confusion of grief from his brain. He did not enter nor did he turn his ravaged face toward the sheeted form upon the bed.

"Lona," he called.

Lona came out slowly.

"Lona, fetch that locket's on Bridey's neck."

"There's no locket there."

"You've taken it off then. Give it to me!"

She did not move.

Bob Whipp's fingers came down cruelly on her arm. "Give it to me!"

Lonabelle reached reluctantly into the pocket of her dress. "Bob—" she said. "Bridey loved him."

"Never mind about that."

"He's only a boy, remember."

"I'll remember my girl," cried Bob. "My little girl!"

His voice snapped. He opened the locket, looked at the picture it held, closed it again.

Out in the sunshine Bobbie held Sal and Al.

"Is she better, Uncle Bob?" he called.

Bob Whipp did not answer. He jumped to the wagon seat, seized the reins, and bore down with his whip. The frightened horses leaped ahead. They carried the wagon, rattling and swaying, out of the barnyard and down the Rainbow road.

CHAPTER NINE

A RUMOR spread through the crowd that had gathered in Rainbow for the greatest event in Rainbow's history. It flowed under cover, circled, seeped like water through a well. It might have been an invisible lariat drawing whispering lips to harkening ears—in the saloons which were crammed to their ceaselessly swinging doors, under the thronging Balmoral's imposing mortgaged portico, on the narrow sidewalk before Halliday's solidly founded store and Lovell's far from solid bank, at the hitching posts and in the livery stables. Mothers, hearing the rumor, caught their breath and looked down at their daughters standing safely by. Fathers heard it, and their faces grew bleak. Some others who heard it put tongue in cheek, pulled down the corners of their mouths, and winked as they drawled, sotto voce, "Bob Whipp is looking for Charley Halliday."

"Bob Whipp is looking for Charley Halliday."

Even the very young, boys in their teens and girls with their hair put up for the first time, thought they knew what that meant. Disturbing memories filled their minds—a face shamed and averted, a name spoken with harsh emphasis or never spoken at all because its owner had vanished. For young and old the sentence was a shadow that left a trail of darkness behind, while sunshine sprayed from a cloudless sky over the little town which sparkled in its gala dress.

Every store had put out bunting in honor of the coming

of the train. Bunting draped the new crackerbox depot rising at the end of Main Street. Bunting made gay the scaffolding beside the tracks where the Rainbow Cornet Band displayed its uniforms and offered promissory blasts. Bunting swayed from the yellow-painted omnibus which bore the sign "Balmoral House" and, below it, the inclusive commitment "We Meet All Trains." Dignitaries of the town wore flags in their high silk hats. So did the lightning-rod peddlers.

"You'd think those guys had brought the railroad on their tin sticks," indignant citizens declared.

Beatty, whose stage was superseded; Beatty, who would no longer crack his whip nor sound his horn nor miss fence posts by a hair to the shivering excitement of travelers— Beatty flaunted a flag in his buttonhole to show that he put the general good above his own.

The town was squeezed full of people: farmers, dressed as though it were Sunday with heavy woolen suits and paper collars; boys, who felt their feet strange and stiff in boots; women, whose dresses flowed out over copies of the *Gazette*, hoarded for weeks to make a proper bustle; little girls delighting in their sashes, their white dresses, their crimped hair, their flower-laden straw hats; country people; townspeople, visitors from Sisseton City who would ride back on the train. And here, there and everywhere, the English— "Crockett County's British": Englishmen with beards and whiskers as blond as harvest fields; Englishmen with monocles; Englishmen with canes; gentle Englishwomen seated in victorias; Lady Meta, under a small lace parasol, smiling, with Bevan on one side, and Aunt Kibbie on the other.

And through that holiday crowd, sobering it, ran the whisper:

"Bob Whipp is looking for Charley Halliday."

People are sometimes so terribly perceptive. They put two

and two together when the persons concerned would give their lives not to have the simple addition made. They do so when their minds seem to be engrossed with utterly unrelated concerns. This was true now in Rainbow.

It was a momentous day for the town. The community had suffered from successive plagues of locusts; money was scarce; farms and homes had been mortgaged; but now the railroad was coming to make everything right. The hopes and happiness of the entire county were riding into Rainbow on the cars that had already left Sisseton City and were— some miles away—rolling along the freshly laid tracks. Yet, although everyone had come to watch those cars make their triumphant arrival, although everyone thronged about the Mayor and the Council and the Committee of Distinguished Citizens—Mr. Halliday, Mr. Oates, Mr. Lovell, Mr. Jackson (the last acting, of course, for Mr. Crockett); although the Cornet Band had burst into jubilant music signifying the crisis of the day's activities, the grand event was suddenly obscured. On all sides people were giving their central interest to a whisper.

"*Bob Whipp is looking for Charley Halliday.*"

No one had known of Bridey's trouble. No one had suspected it. Yet now her neighbors put two and two together with pitiless exactitude.

Bridey was always with her father on gala days like this. She was not with him today. Bob Whipp was always cheerful, friendly, talkative. Today he was none of these. His eyes were bloodshot; his face was racked with grief. He was plainly a man overwhelmed by disaster. One thing and one thing only could do that to Bob Whipp!

"*Bob Whipp is looking for Charley Halliday!*"

The whisper ran into every corner. It reached Charley Halliday at last, on a far edge of the town. He heard it, and understood, and denied his understanding, in the same frightened surge of guilty thought.

"It's a lie!" he stammered. "It's a lie!" His mind filled with a familiar vision, a small, buoyant, rounded figure on tiptoes in the half-concealment of a giant cottonwood's trunk. "It's a lie!"

He started running toward his own horse at Green Lawn. He realized, however, that at Green Lawn a questioner might confront him, so he turned aside toward a livery stable. He would ride to the cottonwood . . . Oh, she wouldn't be there! But she would, she would—he would find out for himself. By skirting the town he could get away across pasture lands without being caught. He ran.

Hardly less accusing of himself, Richard pursued an end, forcing his way slowly but surely through the crowd to where the Committee waited upon the station platform.

"If only I had let myself see, that night of the ball," he thought. "He wanted to talk. He came to talk. If I had let him talk, I might have helped him. But no, I was too much concerned with protecting Richard Chalmers. I wanted to be able to say to Cathy, 'I never sold your brother a drink. Not me!' So I pushed him out and felt as righteous as hell.

"I should have known that he wasn't hunting a drink just to prove he was grown-up. I should have wondered why he was in my place instead of at the ball. If I had asked him just one question, he would have talked. But I didn't have time to ask a question. All I had time for was myself.

"I could have made a friend of Charley Halliday, that night. He likes me. He admires me. Always has. I could have found out what was on his mind, but I was too busy being sorry for Dick Chalmers. I was too much interested in the son of the Squire of Great Goodlands who has made himself the next thing to a sot! I let Charley walk out. And because I was weak and contemptible and wrapped up in self-pity, see what tragedy has fallen on Bob Whipp and must fall now on Cathy!"

Shouldering along where the crowd was thickest he came to the station platform. He passed Cathy as her name came into his mind. She and some of her brothers and sisters were standing in the front rank of the throng which hemmed the committee in. They were standing as close as they could to their father in his hour of glory. They were, at least, going to hear his speech.

Mr. Halliday was easily discernible. In the all-important group he was the very tallest. His silk hat was the highest of all the high silk hats. His broadcloth coat was the glossiest of all the broadcloth coats. He wore the most perfectly ironed shirt. Cathy herself had seen to that, inching a hot, waxed iron with minute care over the tucks. Cathy's eyes were fixed on the white shirt front, even while Richard shoved past. She did not see him. Richard reached Jackson.

"I've got to speak to Mr. Halliday."

He put his demand with a feeling of relief, for he could see from the bright undimmed excitement that here was one corner into which the rumor had not yet reached.

As he confronted Jackson, Cathy saw him.

"I must speak to Mr. Halliday, at once."

"But that is impossible," Jackson answered. He looked up imploringly, wetted his front teeth. "I'm sorry, Mr. Chalmers, but the train will be here any moment. Mr. Halliday is our chairman. He is introducing the Mayor—"

Richard brushed Jackson aside.

"Something has come over Richard," thought Cathy, watching his advance. He was moving resolutely toward her father. There was a new commanding force in his stride.

Her rush of pleasure was drowned in a rush of fear. Why was Richard thus urgent about speaking to her father? What was wrong?

Her eyes went swiftly around the surrounding group. There was her mother with Mrs. Lovell. Jim with Sally. Dora and Reg were with Cyril, Victoria, and Albert. She and Bess had Maggie and the twins. Everyone was here—everyone but Charley!

Richard was speaking to her father now, but she could not hear his words. Her father seemed to protest at first. Then he turned to Oates, and he and Richard moved away. They were well out of earshot of everyone. Down at the platform's edge.

Charley, Charley! Cathy thought of Charley's chart. She thought of his American girl. He had never consented to talk of her again after Christmas Eve. Cathy squeezed Maggie's hand and looked anxiously about.

Richard, meanwhile, was talking to her father, speaking in a low quick tone.

"Captain Whipp is looking for Charley."

"*My* Charley?"

"His daughter, Bridey, died today in childbirth."

It was out! The wretched message was given. Richard had hurried to bring it, hoping to interpose the senior Halliday's strong figure between Bob Whipp and a senseless revenge. He meant to interpose his own figure, too, but more than his own intervention was needed.

In pity, after he spoke, he turned away his head. He looked out over the close-packed crowd, but he did not see the citizens of Rainbow. He saw a cavalcade of Hallidays, astride their horses, crowded into their wagon on the day of their arrival in Rainbow. He heard Mrs. Halliday's tender laughing voice:

"It's a long task for me to introduce the children. But it goes quickly when they do it for themselves."

And three tall horsemen straightened up, smiling as they thumped their chests.

"Jim!" "Reg!" "Charley!"

"*My* Charley?" Mr. Halliday was saying that again. After a moment he added in a dazed voice, "But they don't know each other."

"But they did," Richard said. "And you and I must hurry. We've got to find Bob. He would be sorry later . . . He's out of his head now."

Cathy's father stood for an instant silent.

Before his eyes were the words of a scriptural motto. Ever since his marriage, it had hung over his bedroom chest: "As for me and my house, we will serve the Lord." He had tried to serve the Lord. He had tried to train his sons to that service. And now his Charley had done this dreadful thing!

Anger against Charley swelled in his breast and throat. No, he would not protect his son against that other father's righteous vengeance. Captain Bob Whipp! He had always respected Captain Whipp. And now a son of his had brought Whipp's daughter to death!

But anger was succeeded by a crushing humility. When he tried to blame Charley he found himself wondering where he, himself, had failed. He found himself wishing that he could submit to Whipp's vengeance.

His despairing gaze fell upon his wife. She was placidly waving her fan, her cheeks girlishly pink beneath graying hair. He forced himself to speak.

"Thank you for coming, Mr. Chalmers. I must do something, but God help me! I don't know where to start."

Far down the track a hoarse whistle sounded. A cloud of acrid smoke widened above the prairie. The first engine ever to haul a train of coaches along these shining virgin rails raised its black snout a mile to the east.

The surging crowd engulfed Cathy's father and Richard on the forward end of the platform. A roar arose to deafen every ear. The band burst forth. The cannon exploded. The crowd yielded to the great event. At last it forgot Bob Whipp.

Richard, holding Cathy's father by one arm, struggled to get free.

Out of the east the train was coming: diminutive engine, four small wooden cars—for mail, for baggage, for ladies, for smokers. Rainbow in a minute by the clock would be a railroad town.

Out of the east came the train; and from the south, across the pastures there, a boy rode headlong on a gaunt black horse. Bob Whipp still hunted Charley Halliday, but a vision had found the boy and possessed him, and he rode to keep a tryst with the vision's dear reality. He rode by the shortest path. Earlier he had been afraid of what might happen if he met Bridey's father, but he felt no such fear now. He was afraid only that when he came to the great cottonwood Bridey would not be waiting, tiptoe with love. But even if she were not there he knew that he could find her, by riding farther. Soon or late he would see again the sweet face, flooding with color. He would ride until he did.

He whipped his mount northward as the train pounded into the west. His cross-country trail ran a good three hundred yards east of the waiting throng, so that none could say surely what words he cried as he sent his horse up to the tracks. He may have shouted in horror, or he may have welcomed the fulfillment of his tryst when the engine's black snout struck, just as his horse bestrode the shining tracks.

BOOK FOUR

CHAPTER ONE

GREAT glistening clouds were piled in the blue sky. They rose as billowy hills around the prairie's calm horizon. They floated in the upper heavens, islands in a sea of azure. Radiantly white. Fleecily soft. Hot.

Yet the sky was not crowded. Its spaces held the clouds as the sea holds little boats. Vast airy regions, untenanted pinnacles, heights upon heights of empty blue, surmounted the vaporous forms. Its infinitude encompassed the prairie world with peace, as the sun—a bold blur in the west—flooded it with heat.

Beneath the sun, and the clouds, and the sky, August lay ripe.

The corn was tasseled out; its silken hair matched its drooping leaves for beauty. The wheat was golden. The oats, rye, and barley would soon be in the shock. Gulls followed the farmers in their labors. Over the meadows, where hardy bright flowers bloomed in the tall grass, red-winged blackbirds were gathering into flocks—harbingers of autumn in the savage August heat.

Lakes lay in frames of thick olive-green leafage. Hardly a harvester but could refresh his eyes with a glimpse of near or distant waters. Richard, shocking rye, could see Bird Lake. He promised himself a swim after the day's work was done.

A swim would be good, for he was drenched with sweat.

Shocking rye with the temperature at one hundred degrees in the shade was hot work. He hadn't known how hot, in the days when he rode Kentish Beauty to inspect another man's labor. In those days, which seemed now as remote as though they had been lived upon another planet, he had thought he could conjugate the verb, "to swelter." He remembered torrid chicken-shooting expeditions, how he had boasted of not having a dry stitch to his back, "—while I lay on that back in the shade and waited for the champagne to cool." Richard grinned as he pulled off his straw hat and passed a wet sleeve over his brow. "Hook and Trev are doing that this moment, I dare say."

But were they? he wondered.

From what he heard, things were not going well in Rainbow. The railroad had not done what people had expected of it. Business was slack, very slack; and that would affect Trevenen and Hook, for they had mortgaged the Eyrie—up to the hilt, Trevenen had said—and flung their easy dollars into half a dozen ventures. Including the yawning Balmoral.

"They may be worrying," Richard acknowledged. "Most of Rainbow is."

It had been a good summer in which to be away from Rainbow. Richard had hardly put foot in the town since the day when Charley Halliday had been killed—a suicide, some said; a victim, according to others, of his own blind horror.

Richard had only confused memories of that day's tragic culmination. He remembered that he had thrown what protection he could about Cathy's father, and then had looked for Cathy to find her enveloping her mother with passionately pitying arms. Then the Lovells and Barrowcliffs had quickly taken the Hallidays in charge. He remembered fighting his way through the crowd to the teeming uproarious Kentish Arms. He had emptied the saloon, turned the crush of people into the street. Then he had locked the door, put the key in a big yellow envelope, sealed the envelope, and addressed it with a thick black pencil. "To Cathy Halliday from Richard Chalmers." He had given it to Joe to take to Cathy, and he himself had set out to find Bob Whipp.

There had been little enough that anyone could do for Bob. What had helped had been born in Bob's bones, or in the sturdy heart of him. He was a man of strong passions, and Richard had thought at first that he would go mad with the fury of his grief. But madness was not in him. He was too strong and steady for that.

He had not returned to Little Goodlands. He had asked Richard for release from their agreement, and he had fought his fight—was fighting it still—in the log house which had Bridey's glass windows, her stove, and the floor which she had never seen. Bridey was buried under the Three Sisters.

"Rainbow is too far away," Bob had said. "Bridey was always such a one for staying home."

Meta had telegraphed to St. Paul for roses. Dozens and dozens of white roses had lain about Bridey Whipp in death. The little plot was fenced now. Bob had fenced it, aided by Lonabelle's Bobbie, who was his favored companion.

Richard had been puzzled, at first, by Bob's lack of resentment toward Lonabelle. Lonabelle had known all along about Bridey and Charley. If only she had told Bob Whipp, thought Richard, how much tragic sorrow might have been avoided! Bob, he found later, took a different view.

"I'd have interfered," said Bob, "and that might have turned Bridey against me, and everything might have turned out just the same."

He bore no animus either toward the Hallidays.

"That father's paid," he said. "I don't know that he was

in any way to blame, but anyhow he's paid—with the same coin I used. We've both paid."

Bob liked to talk to Richard, and Richard frequently rode out to the Three Sisters. But he did not go through Rainbow, although the best road ran that way. He avoided Rainbow. He was not ready for the town—not yet. The town meant Cathy.

He wanted to win back his respect for himself. The first step toward that had been taken when he closed the saloon; the second had followed when he wrote to his father, making a clean breast of his sins, mistakes, and failures. He had opened his heart to his father and posted the letter almost before the ink was dry. Then he had gone back to his land.

Bevan had stayed on at the Log House. But his residence there would not be of long duration. His legacy would be delivered soon, and he planned when that arrived to embark on his career as violinist. Richard had invited him to wait at Little Goodlands, but Bevan had refused with casual thanks.

"I think I won't go to the trouble of tearing up twice. I'll stay on here . . ."

"Near Meta," Richard thought. It was clear that Meta and Bevan were passionately in love. But their attachment held something more than passion. It was based on a strong common interest. Moreover Paul had transferred to Meta his adoration for his mother, while Meta, who had not known maternity, poured out on Paul the devotion of a rich and generous nature. They deserved something better, Richard thought, than stolen meetings. These were becoming more frequent, less well concealed. Gossip concerning the pair grew more furious daily. Of course, Richard reasoned, they were making the most of the short time remaining before Bevan's departure.

That explained too the infrequency of Bevan's visits to

Little Goodlands. He came almost never, and Richard was surprised, lifting his head today in response to a halloo, to see his friend sitting on the east fence.

"Come on out," called Richard, "and see how it's done."

"It's too hot. Come over here."

Richard looked up at the sun, descending the western sky. It was not quitting time, by two hours; Joe and the other two men would be busy until sunset. But a visit from Paul was a rare and welcome occasion.

A field of late corn stood to the right of the planting of rye, and Richard waved toward it.

"How about corn on the cob?" he shouted. "Fresh-picked!" All the English had grown fond of this American delicacy, although at first they had not known how to eat it.

"All right," called Paul. "But hurry!"

It was evident that he had news.

Richard hurried.

"Gad, I'm glad to see you!" he said, clasping Paul's hand. "You may scorn my corn, but wait until you eat it. I've turned into a cook, and as soon as I've had a swim—"

"Damn the swim!" said Bevan. "The bank has failed."

"The bank!"

"Yesterday! And today the town's folding up like a house of cards. Oates has mortgages on even more English estates than we thought. He virtually owns the Eyrie, and Pinewood, and the Lovells' place, among a dozen smaller ones."

"Green Lawn?" Richard asked.

"No. Not Green Lawn. Halliday's store seems to be solvent too. He is the only Englishman in the county with any sense." After a pause Paul said abruptly, "Oates has no mortgage on your place, has he?"

"I sold forty acres outright," Richard answered, "to settle with Devlin. But the rest is all mine."

"Then there are two Englishmen in Minnesota with sense," Paul decided.

Richard sat on the fence pondering the sober news. It had not been unexpected, but he was disturbed nevertheless.

"It's too bad," he said, "and hard on everyone we know. Ever so many of them own bank stock—Earle, Trev, the Nevilles—and we all had money on deposit."

"Probably every Englishman in Crockett County," Paul agreed. "All the hundred-pounders too."

Richard nodded.

"I've some news about myself," Paul said presently. "Some of my money's come, just a little, but enough to start me off, and I am leaving."

Richard found a new, sharp regret in this announcement. He laid his arm affectionately across Paul's shoulders.

"I am sorry. Where are you going?"

"Chicago, at first," Paul said. "I'm not ready yet for New York. But I believe that in Chicago I shall be able to arrange a concert tour."

Richard approved the plan with his slow, pleasant smile.

"Good luck," he told Paul. "Some day, when things are going well with me, I'll come to hear you play."

"You may have to travel," Paul warned. "My engagements may take me all the way across the continent." He hesitated, then looked at Richard directly.

"I am not going to Chicago immediately," he said. "I —I'm waiting for a few days in La Crosse."

That, from Paul, meant as much as any other man's complete confession.

Richard thought: "He is telling me that Meta is to join him."

"Let's have that swim," Paul said, leaping up. "And then you can cook the corn—if you really can cook corn."

The next two hours ran out briskly. They put the bank out of their minds. The lake was refreshing, and the corn tender. Joe and the two other hired men continued to work in the field, and Richard was glad to have his friend alone.

Paul started back to Rainbow as the sun shot the western clouds with color. A few tender stars had come out when Richard parted from him at the crossroads.

Paul gone! Meta as good as gone! Soon, Richard thought, the English colony in Crockett County would have vanished! There could be little doubt that the collapse of the bank and all the associated losses would turn the colonists homeward, or toward easier fields of endeavor. The men he had come to know and like would all go. . . .

Loneliness crowded in upon him, but he forgot that feeling in concern for his friends. They had not, as he had, good broad acres free of debt. They had spent their money with a free hand. They had helped to build up the county. And now they were leaving it. They had helped the Americans—how their prodigal spending had helped!—through the grasshopper plagues; and now such Americans as Oates owned most of their homes, or would soon. With the bank closed Hook and Trevenen and the rest very well might not have money enough to pay their passage back to England.

Richard remembered a thought he had had at the Eyrie, the day of the hunt for Three Toes. His hard-riding, hard-hunting, hard-drinking friends might have failed in their attempt to colonize on the Minnesota prairie, but there was one thing they could do.

He remembered their hurdle race at their first American Fourth of July. He called up the offer he had had to ride at the Blue Earth county fair. They all could do that. And the year's round of county fairs was about to begin. The state fairs, too. A man only needed to do a little organizing, form a troupe of hurdle riders and write letters to the managers of the fairs. There would be money enough in such a venture decently to line the pockets of half a score. More, because there was no reason why only one company could perform. There was room for two, perhaps three or four. And even more important than the money would be the reviving influence of such a venture.

"I'll take a shot at it," Richard said aloud, "I've been around. I know the people to be approached."

Some good was to come at last from the idle days he had spent at race tracks around the state.

He rode more slowly. Just above the horizon in the humid dusk he could see Joe and his two helpers walking slowly across the fields. It came to him that he would rather stay here than take the shot that he had resolved on so impulsively. But if there was to be such an expedition he must organize it. He was the only one who could, and beyond his own need for money, he felt an obligation.

He made up his mind, and quickened Kentish Beauty's gait. He had her in her stall, nose-deep in oats by the time Joe arrived.

"How would you like to be the master here?" he asked.

Joe scorned the alien word.

"You mean boss?"

Richard nodded.

"Are you leaving again?" Joe cried indignantly.

"Not to stay," Richard assured him. "I'll be back about the time you have finished all the hard work."

"What's up?" Joe demanded.

Richard explained first about the bank. Joe and his two hands grew grave.

"But why does that make you go away?" Joe wanted to know.

Richard explained that, too. As he explained, he grew confident, and later that evening he made his plans with assurance and satisfaction. He would telegraph Shober at Mankato, Jepson at Winona, Bruce at Owatonna, Prince at St. Paul, Grant at Minneapolis. But he would not stop with that. No! That would be only a beginning. Through Prince and Grant, he was sure, he could make other connections. If he routed his troupe swiftly enough he could get down into Iowa, perhaps even into Wisconsin.

"Eight riders!" he decided. "Eight ought to put on a good exhibit. Eight over lots of hurdles. We'll set up fences, hedges, bars on the race track at every fair. We'll show the Americans things they've never seen in all their lives. We'll take some foxhounds, too."

He would, of course, invite Hook and Trevenen and Earle. With himself that made four. One of the Nevilles had married, but the other two would be glad to come. That made six. Young Bromwell made a likely seventh. For the eighth he had, he knew, no alternative. Bannister was the certain eighth.

He added Bannister slowly. Kit was a magnificent rider. He rode better when drunk than most men rode when sober. But Kit would be difficult. He grew more difficult every day. He would take constant looking after. Nevertheless he had to come.

"He'll need the tin as much as any of us," Richard thought. "The lectures and articles he is forever talking about don't amount to tobacco money."

Taking Bannister would, moreover, be one way of evening up old scores.

CHAPTER TWO

WHEN Lady Meta learned that Bannister was to be one of Richard's band of hurdle-jumping horsemen, she took her embroidery frame every morning to a chair beside the Main Street window. She said the light was better there. She suspected that Aunt Kibbie saw through the small deception, and was more than half minded to confess her difficulty and ask Aunt Kibbie's aid. If Paul had not been involved she would have confessed. His necessity, however, made the risk too great, so she sat at the window and kept a lookout as she plied her needles.

On the third morning, Captain Bannister rode in from Exile Hall. Lady Meta had almost despaired of his coming, even while she reminded herself how desperate he grew after even twenty-four hours of solitude in the gloomy house above the marsh. He had scarcely passed out of sight down the street before she was mounted on her own horse riding back along the trail he had followed into Rainbow.

A little way beyond the town she met Bob Whipp. He checked his horse when he saw her, and waited while she rode down upon him. His brown face, formerly so bright and spirited, was grim and tired, but tired, Lady Meta knew, from sleepless nights. The death of his daughter was scarcely two months behind them.

"Good morning, ma'am," he said, and held out his hand.

Lady Meta took it with a brief sense of loss. She would, she realized, never again shake the hand of this valiant, gentle friend. That would be true whether her morning's expedition failed or succeeded.

"Is this a pleasure ride?" Captain Bob asked.

Subterfuge might be needful with Aunt Kibbie, but Lady Meta knew she had nothing to conceal now.

"I am riding out to Exile Hall," she said.

"Bannister just came to town," Bob Whipp advised her. "He passed me like a house afire three miles back."

"I know," said Lady Meta frankly.

The Captain wheeled his horse. "Mind if I ride a piece with you?"

"To be truthful," Lady Meta admitted, "I shall be grateful if you do." She understood as fully as if he had told her that his "piece" meant the whole way, and the whole way back, too.

The morning was hot. The weather had been hot for days. Even at night the smothering blanket did not lift, and each morning the sun came up with unrelenting brightness. Today there was not a ripple of wind. Like mirrors the lakes reflected the swollen white clouds. The birds did not sing. Out on the gold and purple prairie the picket-pin gophers hid from the sun's attack.

Bob Whipp cleared his throat.

"I have a notion that you're planning to go away," he said.

"Yes," answered Lady Meta. "I am going away."

"You can't figure out any way at all to stay?"

"No way at all, Captain Whipp."

"I'm sorry," Bob Whipp said. "I'll miss you, ma'am."

Again Lady Meta was invaded by that brief sense of loss. She would, she foresaw, miss him, too. She would miss little enough out of this environment in which she had been so unhappy, but along with Richard Chalmers and Kibbie Oarlock and her own lost Hanni she would miss Bob Whipp.

"Do you mind dropping a line to Aunt Kibbie now and then?" he asked. "I'd like to know where you land."

"But I will write to you, yourself, if you like," she cried. "I shall be happy to, as soon as I know where I—where we —are settled."

She was sure, from his swift side glance, that he had caught and correctly interpreted the "we." But he gave no other indication except silence. While their horses trotted a long mile he said nothing. When he did speak she perceived that he had been silent in order to shape a sentence carefully.

"Probably," he said, "you're going to have the best luck in the world. But if you don't, I wish you'd keep in mind that I'd be glad to help, any time you need help."

"Ah, Captain Bob!" Lady Meta cried, "I do not deserve so much. You honor me." Her eyes filled with tears. "Look!" she faced him honestly. "Do you know that I am going to run away, and with whom?"

"I know," he admitted. "At least I figured as much. And Bevan is the fellow, isn't he?"

"I am getting a divorce as soon as I can. We are going to be married."

All through the rest of her life, whenever she remembered that admission, Lady Meta was glad that she had made it. She would not have explained so much to anyone else. What others thought, she did not care. But she owed that much explanation to Captain Bob Whipp.

This courageous, forthright American loved her. Lady Meta was, of a sudden, as sure of it as she was sure that she loved Paul. She was equally sure that Bob Whipp had no idea of his own state of mind. How oddly potent, she thought, a title can be! He never would know that he loved her.

"That's fine," he said; "but, just the same, I want you to remember what I've told you. If things don't go as well as you expect, and you want a hand, I'll be right here in Rainbow."

"Captain Whipp," she said, "you make me more proud than I know how to say. I do not like to be helped, but I make you this promise. If ever I need help you will be the first on whom I shall call."

"That's fine," he repeated.

While they rode the swollen heavy clouds had moved to cover the sun. The world was suddenly darkened, and the two riders felt the urging of a sultry wind. For a mile or more they rode into deepening shadow and the wind strengthened. The horses grew fretful.

"Looks like we're in for an August blow," Bob Whipp said. "I guess we ought to hustle along."

"It won't be long until we need shelter," Lady Meta agreed, but she said nothing about a second reason which made haste advisable. Bannister reveled in such weather. If a storm came up he was more than likely to ride into it, and in such an event he would probably end up at home sooner than she had counted upon.

"You are quite right," she added. "We ought to hurry."

When they reached Exile Hall, Lady Meta found another dog, hardly less savage than the one she had killed to end her night of fear. He stormed out, a black, red-mouthed beast, his bark rising heavily, and with an odd, hollow reverberation, through the weird light.

Lady Meta was dismayed, but Bob Whipp leaned down from his saddle.

"Don't make a nuisance of yourself, pup," he drawled.

The dog's raucous assault diminished. His tail rose, then wagged a little.

"That's better," Bob Whipp murmured. "Now go take a rest for yourself."

Incredibly, the dog walked in the direction of his pointing finger. Without another sound he curled down alongside the sheltered side of the barn; and he lay there, motionless, when Lady Meta dismounted and opened the door of the house.

"Mighty few dogs I can't handle," said Captain Whipp with satisfaction.

Exile Hall had no housekeeper now. A hired man looked after the stables and brought in firewood, but Bannister lived alone; and the huge drawing room testified on every hand to the influence of his erratic personality. Everywhere his impulsive and uncompleted efforts at order were plain. Here was a broken chair with a glue pot beside it. A coat hung on a wall-peg, but below it a hat and a pair of gloves had been heedlessly dropped. The dusty accumulation of a week powdered the floor, but alongside the door that led into the kitchen a broom stood ready. One wall was streaked by water that had leaked down from the roof, but a scarf had been hung to conceal most of the stain.

One article of the room's furnishings, however, was painstakingly neat, meticulously neat. No housekeeper, not a dozen housekeepers, could have achieved a greater triumph of cleanliness and precise arrangement than Bannister had achieved upon the table at which, obviously, he wrote those articles that an admiring Rainbow discovered now and then between the cultured covers of eastern magazines. It was a massive table, long and wide. At its middle an armchair of equally magnificent proportions awaited the flood tide of the artistic mood. Just to the right of the chair on the broad plane surface stood a transparent inkwell in the shape of an elephant. Ink of a handsome green hue filled the glass creature's belly. Alongside the inkwell stood a tray containing at least a dozen penholders, each fitted with a bright new nib. Beside the tray lay a knife for the occasion when a false word had to be scratched out. Above the ordered inkwell and tray and knife stood a pile of clean white paper half a foot high. In a neat row, at the far edge of the table and extending along it from one end to the other, were folders of brown paper. An exact black border was inked around the uppermost face of each folder, and inside each such frame Bannister had printed in bold, exaggerated script, the title of the composition contained within the folder.

Lady Meta was eager to complete her errand and get away but she delayed to look at the folders and their contents. The titles covered a wide field; indeed they all but covered the entire world:

More Days in the Punjab
A British Clipper in an Indian Typhoon
An Iceberg in the Atlantic
Wives and Maidens of the Frontier
The Malay Kris
The Lone Wolf of the Sisseton

Impressed by evidence of so much energy, and thoroughly glad, too, of her discovery, Lady Meta opened one folder. Disturbed by its contents, she opened the next, and then all the others. When she had finished her pleasure was gone. She was filled with pity. The contents of each folder made plain how little weight should be attached to the proud imposing cover. The contents of each were no more than a thin sheaf of sheets unsullied save for the bold, exaggerated repetition of the title. Lady Meta closed the last folder with a harrowing picture of Bannister inscribing each title, then sinking into despair as no sentences came to make the narrative which the title had so exuberantly announced.

Outdoors the clouds had grown into a black mask that covered the whole sky. Twilight, misplaced by hours, darkened the room. The wind rushed upon the house with violent, racking blows. Just outside the drawing-room window a tall pine tree that Lady Meta had had transplanted gave before the wind with a thick, drawn-out sigh, and then split deafeningly above its first branches. The explosion of the rent fibers filled the room. Stray drops of rain struck distinctly upon the window panes, a warning vanguard. The deluge followed, a torrent of water from heavens burst wide open by an incessant cannonade of thunder.

Bob Whipp looked anxiously out at the horses, but they continued to stand obediently in the lee of the barn, their heads turned patiently from the blast, their tails blown between their legs flat along their bellies.

Lady Meta set about the purpose which had brought her, although she had less heart for it now that she had seen the folders with their mute declaration of frustration. She did not attempt any concealment.

Bannister, she recalled, had devised four hiding places, and unless he had made others after she had left, the jewels would be in one of the four. The first was behind the hewn beam extending along the top of the drawing room's western wall. The second was in the third-floor oratory. Because both of these were less accessible she decided to leave them until she had looked into the third and fourth repositories. The third was under one of the stones which paved the fireplace. It made a poor hiding place for jewels, but she looked. They were not there. The fourth was the one of which Bannister had been most proud. It was, simply, the concealing litter of chips and wood dust piled deep on the bottom of the wood-box standing alongside the fireplace. Here the jewel box was hidden.

Lady Meta opened it upon the splendid writing table. She poured the entire contents into her purse, but then with her gaze on the boldly written titles she spilled her purse back onto the table and thoughtfully sorted the jewels into two piles. As well as she could judge, one pile was worth as much as the other. One she put into the jewel box, and that she put back under the chips and wood dust. The other she returned to her purse. Then she sat down; and, taking a sheet of paper from the high pile flanking the green ink, the bright pen points, and the sharp knife, she began a note.

The brief violence of the August storm was abating. The roaring wind had died away to a mild susurration. The rain, lately a deafening torrent, was now only a thin patter. In the waxing stillness the pen scratched loudly upon the paper.

"Dear Kit," she wrote. "Since you saw fit to refuse me any money I have taken some of the jewels . . ."

She started over again.

"Dear Kit: I have divided the jewels as fairly as I could judge their value."

She did not like that, either, and tried once more. This time she left off the salutation.

"I have gone away to Paul Bevan."

She liked that least of the three, and in the end she wrote nothing for the box which she put back among the chips. She did, however, explain to Bob Whipp.

"Mr. Bevan has a small inheritance coming," she said, "but it won't reach us for several months. And in the meantime we must live. It is for that reason that I am taking my share of the jewels."

"They're all yours, aren't they?" Bob Whipp inquired. She nodded.

"Why not take them all?"

"Because, when I am gone, my brother will stop the remittances, and I would rather that Kit had his share of what we own."

The ground about the house was drenched. Captain Whipp told her to wait at the kitchen doorway while he brought the horses. They had continued to wait patiently against the barn, and when he approached they turned to greet him eagerly. In the quiet aftermath of the storm a brittle green light filtered up from the horizon and spread over the sky. Returning with the horses through this thin, funereal glow Bob Whipp seemed a little unreal. Far back along their trail, however, pure sunlight fell upon a prairie shining wetly, and mounting they rode rapidly toward it.

As they started away the black dog leaped out from the dry den he had found under the barn and loped anxiously after them. Bob Whipp ordered him back but he continued to follow.

"He has adopted you," Lady Meta said, smiling.

"Let's run for it," Bob Whipp answered. "If we go fast enough he certainly will get the idea that we don't want him."

He settled into his stirrups and gathered his bridle reins, but he did not set off. Instead, looking up the road, he exclaimed, "Thunderation!"

Bannister had rounded a curve and was trotting toward them.

"I guess we might as well sit still and wait for him," Bob said calmly.

Lady Meta nodded.

Bannister came on at an easy trot. He had, it was plain, ridden through the storm. As he drew near, his drenched state became apparent. He might have come through a river. The bay gelding was in a similar state. Her mane dripped water, and a wild pony's hair could not have been more bedraggled.

In manner, Bannister was unexpectedly calm. Lady Meta was nonplused. Even if he had not reasoned out her purpose in going to Exile Hall, he ought to be angry. That she went in his absence should have been enough to upset him. His greeting, however, was easy, and oddly enough somewhat bemused.

"Good morning, Kit," she said.

"Have you been to the Hall, Meta?" he asked, and when she nodded he made a regretful sound in his throat. "I am sorry I was not there to welcome you."

"I went to get some of my things, Kit."

"I hope you found them."

"I needed them," she went on, "because I am going away."

"I have thought for some time that you might be," he told her. "I am sorry. One of my articles is being printed in the next *Atlantic Monthly,* and I had hoped to read it to you."

She stared at him, wondering at his curious air of abstraction, of indifference. Could it be possible that the vocation which he pursued at his broad table in Exile Hall filled his mind to the exclusion of all else—of vanity, of pride, of jealousy? Yes, jealousy, too. For long after he had ceased to love her, he had been furiously jealous at the bare suggestion that another lover had taken his place.

"Where are you going?" he asked, but the question did

not indicate any active concern. He would have asked it in the same way of a casual acquaintance.

"To Chicago at first."

"I may see you," he said, brightening. "My agent is negotiating for a lecture there."

To her amazement his next move was one that clearly indicated an intention to go on. He reined his horse to the side of the road, but as he did so he saw the dog following Bob Whipp's horse.

"Pluto!" he said reproachfully. The black dog whined and backed down the road. "Go home!" The dog cowered. Urged by Bannister's knee the bay gelding moved along until it stood beside the dog. Bannister leaned over and whipped the dog's shrinking flank. He put all his strength into the blow, but the dog did not cry, it only sank lower on the muddy road. "Go home!" Bannister said again. The dog obeyed the second command. He rose under the threatening whip and slid down the road, his head turned apprehensively backward.

Bannister prepared again to move on. He gathered his reins and turned the bay gelding's head in the direction of Exile Hall. He was not bemused now. His smile was full of characteristic irony.

"I trust you will forgive me that little scene," he said, and smiled apologetically. "All my dogs, however, need correction occasionally. The truth is, they don't like me very well." As he started off his voice became regretful. "They are like my women," he said over a shoulder. "They seem to prefer another master."

Lady Meta grew hot with anger. Bob Whipp, she saw, was enraged, and her first impulse was to let him make the reply she could see rising to his mouth. Almost at once, however, she put a hand upon his arm.

"Don't," she said. "It doesn't matter. I shall never see him again."

Bob Whipp looked down at her hand. The anger went from his face as suddenly as it had appeared there.

"That's right," he said. "You are going away."

CHAPTER THREE

THE six men had been waiting for more than an hour. Earle sat far over, his elbows on his knees, his eyes scarcely seeing the floor, his fingers pulling absently at the long, soft ears of the hound that crouched listlessly between his feet. Young Bromwell sat at a table pretending to play solitaire. Percy Neville sat at the opposite side of the table with an opened book of newspaper clippings. These related the exploits, at county fairs in Minnesota, Iowa, and Wisconsin, of Mr. Richard Chalmers' Rainbow Riders. Neville pretended to read the accounts, but he looked often toward his brother, Slabs, who leaned in the open doorway of the hotel room. There was no pretence about the sober watch which Slabs kept to his left down the corridor. It was constant and determined. Hook sat propped against the head of the room's double bed, playing moodily with his watch chain. Trevenen braced himself, wide-legged and frowning, before one of the two wide windows. The busy clatter of a horse car drifted up from the street, but Trevenen, lost in thought, did not hear this any more than he saw the distant Mississippi shimmering below St. Paul's white cliffs in the warm, blue haze of late October.

Across the room Slabs Neville straightened in the doorway. Hook sat bolt upright. The other four came to sharp attention.

"Sorry!" Slabs reassured them quietly. "That was a blank covert. He is still as quiet as can be."

"Still sleeping," Trevenen surmised.

"And he ought to be," Bromwell said, returning to his cards. "After this morning's explosion he ought to sleep the clock around."

Slabs took up his sober watch. The other five relaxed slowly.

"Dick ought to be back any moment now," Trevenen said.

Slabs Neville looked to his right, down the other reach of the corridor.

"Here he comes now," he said, and stepped a pace back into the room.

The waiting men heard a half-dozen light, quick strides, and then Richard filled the doorway and entered. Behind him came a solid, assured man carrying a black, professional leather bag. Richard gestured toward the bed.

"You know Hook, Dr. Wightman."

The solid assured man nodded as he sat down at the table. Richard introduced the others. The doctor looked at each briefly, sharply.

"Well!" Trevenen said at last, and turned to Richard.

Richard spread his hands, palms down. The gesture was one of somber finality.

"You people have only put yourselves to needless trouble over the past two weeks," the doctor said sympathetically. "It would have been better if you had left him with me then."

Neville closed his book of clippings loudly.

"There ought to be some other way out of this."

"I say so, too," Hook put in. "How can you be so sure the case is hopeless, Dr. Wightman?"

"My dear man," the doctor answered patiently, "I never

said I was sure. I have merely given you my diagnosis, which has been, I may add, corroborated by my colleagues."

"I don't like even to think of it," Trevenen muttered.

"It would be more to the point," the Doctor said bluntly, "if you thought of him continuing at liberty. Suppose he had done to a man—or to a child—what he did to his horse this morning."

"But locking him up for all the rest of his life!" Trevenen protested.

"He may improve," Dr. Wightman said guardedly. "So little is known about insanity that I would not say for a certainty that he will not."

Hook drew out a handkerchief and wiped his hands. They were wet, and his forehead was wet and hot.

"What could have brought it on?" he blurted.

Dr. Wightman shook his head to confess honestly the limitations of his knowledge.

"Any severe mental stress might be the cause," he said deliberately, "at least where a predisposition exists. I have no information as to a predisposition, naturally. But certainly the stress was evident. Financial worries, nervous exhaustion, domestic trouble—his failure in Crockett County—all these on top of the catastrophe which ended his army career—"

He stood up.

"Accept my assurance," he said, "that the course you have taken is inevitable. You need have no qualms. The state would have been forced to step in if you hadn't. Don't be misled by his present quiet and rational mood. He will have many such. But violence will always be lurking underneath." He gestured to Hook. "You had him at your throat not a week ago, Mr. Hook. And only day before yesterday Mr. Chalmers was within an ace of being shot. You are his friends and may risk such assaults, but the public must be protected."

Richard walked slowly over to a desk and took out a dispatch case.

"Here is the cable that I told you about, Doctor," he said. "It makes plain that the brother-in-law will be responsible for a monthly allowance covering all charges."

Dr. Wightman took the paper, but he hesitated.

"As for any immediate expense," Richard said quickly, "and the charges that have already built up, I shall settle them."

"We'll all settle them," said Hook.

Dr. Wightman bowed. Richard moved toward the door.

"I'll fetch him," he said.

"Let me go with you," Dr. Wightman urged. He waved the others back. "The fewer he sees, the better."

A step short of the doorway Richard turned and, taking a letter from his pocket, handed it to Hook.

"This is for you and Trev."

He walked reluctantly into the corridor. The doctor followed. The door closed.

The six men heard a key turn in the lock of the adjacent room; they heard Richard and the doctor enter.

"Kit! Wake up, Kit."

Faintly, through the substantial wall, a bed creaked, a voice replied, bemused but calm.

"Ah, good afternoon, Dick."

"I thought we might go for a ride, Kit. I've—I've a new horse for you to try out."

"She won't beat my gelding, Dick."

"I just want you to look her over."

"Of course, Dick. But don't think you can make me trade the gelding."

There was a pause.

"I don't remember riding this morning, Dick. Was I? How did I come to be dressed for riding?"

"Lucky that you are, Kit. We won't lose any time."

"That's right, Dick."

"Come along, Kit."

"Coming, Dick!"

The six men heard the three in the next room walk out, heard six confused feet go down the corridor, the sounds growing more and more faint until silence was complete. Silence also closed in upon the room, like a hard hand.

Earle sat down, his elbows on his knees, his eyes seeing the floor only dimly, his fingers pulling at the long soft ears of the hound that crouched, shivering, between his feet. Percy Neville took up the deck of cards and slowly laid out a pattern for solitaire. Slabs and Bruce Bromwell watched. Hook played moodily with his watch chain. Trevenen braced himself, wide-legged and frowning; he faced into the room this time.

The silence pressed down. Under its intolerable weight Trevenen's thick shoulders sagged, Hook's fingers fell from his watch chain, and Neville's hands dropped upon the table.

"And that," Trevenen pronounced, braced and solemn, "might well be a sign of the failure of all of us."

His "all" meant the British colony in Crockett County. The five listening men understood this. Their own minds had been shaping the same defeated summary, and now they sat not moving, puzzling each for himself over the unpredictable, the incredible; the unforeseen disaster which had fallen upon them and their compatriots.

That the colony was ended, there could be little doubt. A few members, true enough, survived here and there. The

Hallidays were safe, even prosperous, with the store and unencumbered land. The Lovells might salvage considerable, too. But all the others had been caught in the collapse of the boom. Their lands had gone to Oates and his kind. Their resources were too exhausted to permit a fresh start.

The six men looked at one another wondering how they could have become so engulfed in ruin.

"We are paying high for our play," Slabs Neville said.

That was it! They had played too much and too long. In a frontier which demanded the utmost of arduous work they had done little save hunt foxes and play billiards. They had played billiards to kill the long winters, and with every summer they had donned red coats and killed foxes, or wolves when the foxes gave out. When their drawing accounts back home had been closed they had gone to Oates in order that their billiards and their hunting might not be interrupted.

What a curious page they had written in the history of their time and place! Long after the last of them had ceased to be important, they would be recalled as the men whose money had gone to provide play for themselves, and working capital for others.

"By God! We played and paid high," Earle said. "But do you realize that the money we spent, and nothing else, made Crockett County? Our dollars got nothing much for ourselves. But what else fed the Americans through the grasshopper plagues, and what else paid for the good houses and barns, and for breaking up the virgin prairie? Where else did the money come from that bought the cattle, the sheep, and the plough-horses? The cash we paid out has made a backlog that will last longer than we have."

The Neville brothers looked at each other and smiled wryly. So they had helped save the county! Even though they had frittered away their own opportunity for a place in the new, pleasant land, they had helped make the land secure and pleasant for others. Such consolation as they could glean from that act of rescue was theirs for the taking. Precious little comfort!

"Three cheers for the great adventure in beans," Slabs said.

"And for the great Adam B. Crockett," said his brother.

"Crockett wasn't so far wrong, at that," Hook remarked thoughtfully.

When they thought about it, he hadn't been. Of course, he had charged them five prices for their land. But it had been good land, for the most part. Properly worked, it would have brought a fair return in spite of its high price. Moreover, Crockett had had an additional justification. He never could have sold the land at all if he had not jumped the price. No Englishman, familiar with values at home, would have believed that land at five dollars an acre could be good land. No! Crockett had not been so far wrong. He had not been half as wrong as they had been themselves. And Crockett had lost, too. Oates owned more than a little of Crockett's land. The conservative Hallidays had come off better than the promoter who had brought them to Rainbow.

"A lucky thing," Slabs said, "that Dick thought up this tour. That, at least, saves our faces. We can get home without writing for funds. And I suppose all of us are going home."

Visioning the homeward march that must already have begun from Crockett County in their absence, they felt a common chagrin. It would not be pleasant to be a part of that defeated procession back across the Atlantic.

"It won't be so hard for me," Earle said thankfully. "My father never wanted me to leave in the first place."

"All three of us have an offer of berths in South Africa," Slabs said.

Hook had opened the letter that Richard had given him and now was turning it over and over.

"Perhaps this is the way out for Trev and me and Dick," he said. "Who knows anything about San Francisco?"

"Why?" Earle asked.

"This letter comes from there," Hook explained; "and, of all persons, it comes from Paul Bevan."

"The chap who ran away with Bannister's wife?"

Hook nodded.

"Listen!" He read:

"Dear Dick:

"This is to tell you first, that Meta joined me in La Crosse; second, that between us we arranged a splendid concert tour which has now brought us to this city; and third, that here I believe may be just the opening you would like, along perhaps with your friends Trevenen and Hook.

"This is one of the finest cities imaginable, but it is curiously lacking in certain directions. Particularly it lacks a riding school of character and distinction. You ought to bring your friends and open one. You wouldn't lose caste. As three Englishmen of good family you would be received everywhere. And you would, for certain, make a good deal of money. These San Franciscans have unlimited money and they are willing to pay it out freely.

"Several copies of the *Crockett County Gazette* that Meta has had from Captain Whipp make it plain that you and almost all of the English around Rainbow must consider something in short order. Meta and I would be happy to see you settle here. We shall return to San Francisco often. She asks to be remembered to you. We are doing very well. I enclose some newspaper accounts that will tell you how well.

"Affectionately,
"PAUL."

The clippings unanimously applauded the virtuosity of the visiting artist, Paul Bevan, and praised the charm of his accompanist and manager, Lady Meta Bannister. Usually, too, they noted social functions following the concerts.

"A title goes a long way," Trevenen said cynically.

"Bevan is a fine musician," Earle argued.

"Bannister's wife would make him out one, even if he weren't," Slabs Neville said admiringly. "She is clever. She has strength, too. She doesn't care a snap of her fingers what people say."

"They'll say enough when they hear about Bannister," the other Neville predicted.

"They shouldn't," Hook said firmly. "Bannister lived off her from the day they were married. Toward the last he talked about his lectures and his writings; but I doubt if they earned him two hundred pounds in all. If it hadn't been for Lady Meta he would have been in hock years back. And all she got in return was treatment that you wouldn't give your hound."

The Nevilles murmured agreement.

"I wonder just how far her affair with Dick went?" Trevenen persisted.

"I wonder if that is any of our business," Hook said sharply. "It seems to me that we are in a pretty poor business, picking Dick to pieces."

"Evidently Bevan didn't think it went very far," Earle offered in conciliation.

"Bevan wouldn't care how far it had gone," Hook said with reluctant admiration. "That fellow had his own odd code. He could ignore everything that happened in her life before they met. I doubt if he so much as thinks of it now."

"They can't ever marry, with Bannister insane," Slabs reflected.

"They are a lot more married now than most couples who stand up in church," Hook declared with conviction, "and I'll wager they keep together longer than most, too."

"I wonder if Dick will take Bevan's cue and go out to San Francisco," Earle pursued.

"Of course he will," Hook cried. "Why else did he give the letter to us?"

"He might have meant it for you alone."

"Not he!"

"Why shouldn't he go home?" Earle persisted.

"Third son," Trevenen pointed out succinctly.

"But he could find something to do. He is a good man now. He has changed."

They all knew how Richard had changed. In the clear-headed, determined leader of their expedition they saw little of the uncertain immigrant of four years back, nothing at all of the impulsive, defiant failure who had opened the Kentish Arms.

"You talk about Dick going home, or to San Francisco," Slabs Neville drawled; "but isn't there a strong likelihood that he will go back to Rainbow? He still owns that farm, free of any mortgage."

"Dick, a farmer!" Hook laughed. "Dick isn't cut out for that any more than we are. He failed at it, just as we all did."

"The old Dick failed, not the new one."

Trevenen was reflective.

"There's a reason," he said, "why he might want to go back—"

"Do you mean Cathy Halliday?" Hook demanded.

Trevenen nodded.

Hook laughed again.

"You're not serious!"

"Of course I'm serious," Trevenen said. He liked to gossip, especially about women, and he would have explained his conviction in detail if he had not caught sight of Neville's frozen mouth. Neville, his face stiff and quite without expression, sat gazing at the empty floor between his feet. Trevenen remembered how hard Neville had been hit by the Halliday girl whom he was now handing so freely over to Dick.

They all remembered.

"You don't know what you are talking about," Hook said loudly. "If she is all you have to offer, Dick is as good as in San Francisco this minute."

Trevenen looked away from Neville.

"You may be right," he agreed. "At least it ought to take more than a girl to make a Crockett County farmer out of Dick."

CHAPTER FOUR

On a late November afternoon, Richard stepped off the train at Rainbow.

It had seemed odd not to disembark as usual at Sisseton City. It had seemed odd to look through the window of the train and see Si Joslin, holding his whip like a staff, standing beside his team—and not to jump from the steps for his hearty greeting. It had seemed odd to fly by railroad over a land one had traversed so often on horseback and by stage. The journey that at one time had taken half a day was completed in less than half an hour. The train went as the crow flew. Not following Chanyaska Creek and its blur of bare purple trees. Not turning south where the lakes began. The rails ran west like twin silvery arrows, and they did not stop in Rainbow. They ran on, carrying, Richard realized now, not the quick prosperity the English colonists had hoped for, but something steadier, more important.

He stepped off the train at the tiny crackerbox station which held such tragic memories. A clicking sound came from the interior of the building. "Rainbow," the *Gazette* had proudly asserted, "now has the dot and dash."

Beatty hailed him, a Beatty as red-faced and jovial as ever.

"I'm driving a hack now. All the stylish folks pass up the bus to ride with me. Two bits to either hotel. And I'll mark it in the book if you're short."

"If I were going to a hotel you'd have a passenger,"

353

Richard laughed. "But I'm not. And besides, Kentish Beauty is in the baggage car."

Joe rode up, shaking his own hands in the air.

"Hi, General!"

Together, while the train paused, Richard and Joe unloaded Kentish Beauty. She submitted like a seasoned traveler.

"She's blaz*ay*, that mare is!" said Joe admiringly as they saddled and bridled her. "That gives me an idea, General. You'd better stay home for a piece."

Richard smiled.

"Have you seen Bob Whipp?" he asked.

Joe nodded.

"I looked in on him like you asked me to. Spent a couple of hours there."

"How is he feeling?"

"Pretty fair. That kid Bobbie is living with him. Bob spent half the time I was there bragging on Bobbie. Bob's going to send him to college, he says. To the State University at Minneapolis. He does seem a right smart kid."

The train, tolling its bell and belching thick black smoke, rolled off across the prairie. As its clatter died away, Joe asked:

"Is it true, General, what we hear about Cap'n Bannister?"

Richard nodded.

"Well, he always was twisted," Joe returned, heavily reflective.

Beatty, Richard was glad to see, had induced the single other passenger to ride in style for two bits. The Balmoral bus rattled away empty. The station platform was deserted except for Richard and Joe. Richard mounted Kentish Beauty. Joe swung onto the back of his own horse.

"You'll find the house as clean as a whistle, General. And

what I've got in these saddle bags will smell it up the right way. Steak and onions! A real cow steak! I cut it off the critter myself."

"Fine. I'll see you later," Richard assured him.

"You won't fail me, General?" Joe asked anxiously. "I'm all set to hear about those high jumps you took."

"I may be late, but I'll be there," Richard promised.

The day was gray, but the sky was opalescent. Behind veil-like clouds, the sun was trying to shine. The weather was warm, and the first thin snow which a day or two before had spread Crockett County with white was melting rapidly.

The smell of the melting snow, as Richard cantered out of Rainbow, had something springlike about it. The Flower Lake road was spongy, and the bare treetops, meeting overhead, looked like spring twigs, just ready to bud.

High in a distant tree, Richard saw a bluejay. The bird was so far away that its color did not carry. But the bold jaunty crested head was unmistakable. Richard smiled at this token of a Minnesota winter. The weather might feel springlike today, but he knew what lay ahead.

He sent Kentish Beauty forward briskly and soon came in sight of the palings of Green Lawn.

He passed through the gate. The grounds were deserted. In the garden a freshly made snow man was melting rapidly. It would not melt much longer, for the afternoon was growing late. The glow in the west had sunk almost to the horizon.

The house was gray and still. The lamps were not yet lighted.

Richard jumped from Kentish Beauty's back. He threw her bridle over the hitching post, paused briefly to pat her flank.

There was no further pause. Firmly, although lightly, he

ran up the steps of the Halliday mansion and put his finger on the bell.

The Hallidays were having tea.

They had been in America for over two years now, but they still observed the English custom of tea in the afternoon. Mr. Halliday quitted his store at four. The people of Rainbow declared that they set their watches by him. Driving himself, sitting straight as a dart in his spruce top-buggy, he went directly from the store to Green Lawn, and tea was always ready.

The brew itself was ready in the silver pot which—flanked by milk jug, sugar basin, and slop basin—sat on the great silver tray. Thin slices of buttered bread were piled in a plate alongside. The slices were very thin, so thin that one could double them in eating and still find them very thin. Cathy buttered the bread on the loaf; then she set the loaf on end and sliced it toward herself across the top. She had learned to cut it so the first year in Minnesota. Her finger still bore the scar of her earliest attempt.

In summer the tea tray was carried out to the lawn. It was pleasant to eat and drink beneath the embroidery of branches, watching the sunlight sparkle on the lake, watching the butterflies circle over the flower beds, and the birds fly in to the plant shelves on the porch, deceived by the fruitlike begonia blossoms.

In winter the tray went into the library, and that was pleasant too.

It was unusually pleasant today, for Dora was at home. She came out from the rectory as often as she could. One missed Charley less when Dora and Cyril were there, and when Jim brought in his Sally.

"Not less, but differently," Cathy had explained to Dora. "We don't want to miss him less."

"Of course we don't. We want to think about him and talk about him always. Father and Mother like it best that way."

Dora was at home today, but Cathy would not let her help with bringing in the tea. All of them were guarding Dora carefully these days. She sat now in the patent rocker (brought from England), but she was not idle. Both she and her mother were busy with dresses of sheer white lawn. They would be hand-sewn, every stitch, these dresses. Some of them were to be exquisitely embroidered. They were a full yard long but the head holes and sleeves were tiny.

"Funny-looking doll dresses!" said Vickie from her father's knee.

The twins and Albert and Maggie were building London Bridge with blocks. Cathy and Bess had just brought in the tea. Reg was staring out the window, trying to decide whether a cigarette was worth the climb to the glacial third floor.

The door bell pealed.

"I'll get it," said Reg. He might, he thought, sneak a whiff on the doorstep.

The family was unconcerned about the summons to the door. There were many visitors to Green Lawn, and there was always tea enough for an extra two or three. Only Mrs. Halliday mentioned the ring.

"I hope it's Jim and Sally," she said.

Reg's face was poked suddenly in at the door. His expression made it abundantly clear that the newcomer was not Jim or Sally.

"Father," he said. "We've a visitor."

He said "Father" and not "Mother." He remembered,

did Reg, the words which his father had spoken on the night of the Spring Ball. "If Mr. Chalmers should call, you will not receive him." Reg knew that, to his mother, his father's word was law. But his father, if he chose, could change the law.

He drew back, and Richard walked into the room.

Mr. Halliday put Vickie down and rose. His gaze rested for an appraising instant on Richard's face, while Richard's gaze went openly across the room to where Cathy sat, hands locked in her lap. Cathy's father held out his hand.

"Good afternoon, Mr. Chalmers."

"Good afternoon, sir!"

"We've been hearing some flattering things about you, Mr. Chalmers."

Richard's slow, pleasant smile appeared. He had either to smile or to shout his relief.

Cathy turned white. She turned as white as the white lawn dress into which Dora was putting meticulous tucks. The others, one and all, hurried to greet Richard. Cathy did not speak or even give him her hand. But when all of them were seated, her eyes met his.

She made no move to help Bess pass the cups. Cathy, sitting still while tea was being served! She did not drink her tea, and her eyes, two shining stars, moved to Richard's face and away again.

She thought she must be dreaming. It could not be true that Richard was sitting there, so big, so browned, so handsome!

He was speaking to her mother.

"I hope you'll excuse my dusty clothes, Mrs. Halliday. I came straight from the train."

He had come straight from the train! Cathy put down

her cup, and it clashed in her saucer. She bit her lips, trying to stop their trembling.

Richard was as calm, as poised, as though he called at Green Lawn every day. He was telling her father about the Rainbow Riders.

"And Mr. Hook and Mr. Trevenen are gone for good?"

"Yes, sir. The *Gazette* has the story right. Miss Tabby will be going to San Francisco, too."

"And the Nevilles are returning to England?"

"Yes. But they'll be back to Rainbow, I believe, before they go."

"And—" Mr. Halliday cleared his throat. "And you?"

"I'm staying," said Richard. "On my farm."

Mr. Halliday cleared his throat again, and half rose from his chair. He exchanged a glance with his wife and then he rose completely. He put out his hand abruptly, even nervously.

"Well—Richard," he said. "We are glad to see you. You must come again. And now, if you will excuse me—"

He turned and walked with dignity toward the door.

Mrs. Halliday followed dexterously, calling "James, my dear, will you show me . . ."

Cathy saw through the stratagem. She looked at Richard. He had stood up courteously for the senior Halliday's departure. Fire filled Cathy's breast.

Bess excused herself next, her dimples flashing, her grasp firm upon Vickie and Albert.

"But I haven't finished my *bridge*," Albert shouted.

"I told both of you, a half-hour ago, to wash your hands," said Bess.

"Oh-h-h-h! You never did," cried Vickie, aghast at such a barefaced falsehood.

Gerald and Geraldine stole a backward look from the door, but they too disappeared, in advance of Dora's gentle prodding.

Reg went out last.

Cathy watched him go. Her locked hands trembled in her lap, but they grew still when Richard walked over in Reg's wake and closed the door.

Richard, who had been calm and poised, was calm and poised no longer. He found it difficult even to speak. He reached down to Cathy's locked hands, drew them apart and held them in his own.

He said abruptly:

"I'm tearing down my house."

"Are you? But I thought you said—"

"That I was staying on? I am. But I want the house on the lake shore. Wouldn't you like it there? overlooking the water?"

"Why, yes," said Cathy. "Anybody would."

"But I'm not talking about anybody," Richard said. "I'm asking *you.*"

Sudden color burned in Cathy's cheeks, and her eyes, so wide and starlike, turned away—to the door, to the fire . . .

Richard dropped to his knees. He put his arms about her waist and his head into her lap.

Cathy began to cry. She drew him upward to her breast. Salt-sweet, her lips met his. Her arms held him close, close. They could not hold him close enough. But Richard's arms were stronger.

"Oh, Cathy!" said Richard. "I've been a fool."

"You are my love!" said Cathy.

"And you are mine. Isn't it strange? We only saw each other four times, really."

"No," said Cathy. "It isn't strange. It was written in the stars . . ."

There was a stir in the adjoining room, but Richard and Cathy did not hear it. Reg for the third time had forcefully put out the twins. On tiptoe now he approached the sitting-room piano and seated himself there.

Reg, when he chose to, could play waltzes as few could. He chose to now. He thought about Cathy and Richard; he thought about Charley; he thought about the sweetness and cruelty of life. He put his heart into his fingers as he played "Tales from the Vienna Woods."